STAY WILD

Annaliese Morgan

Black Daisy Press

blackdaisypress.com

First published in the UK by Black Daisy Press
49 Greek Street, Soho, London W1D 4EG

www.blackdaisypress.com

A catalogue record for this book is available from the British Library

Book ISBN: 978-1-8384163-7-9
Epub ISBN: 978-1-8384163-6-2

Black Daisy Press

About the Author

Annaliese Morgan is an English author for young and new adults. Originally from Yorkshire but based in London, she lives with her two sons, a Basset hound called Pineapple and too many books. Her writing career began way back in the late nineties and includes both non-fiction and fiction. Annaliese primarily writes in the genres of supernatural, urban fantasy and contemporary and she has been featured on BBC Radio, Stage 32, Woman Magazine, Woman's Own Magazine, Stylist and many others. Annaliese and her two boys (The M's or the three musketeers as they are referred too) are also avid travellers and a creative family doing life their own way.

Contents

Chapter One *The Beginning of Strange* 1

Chapter Two *The Talking Spot* 14

Chapter Three *Life Changes* 27

Chapter Four *Mystical Cartel* 41

Chapter Five *Not Knowing* 52

Chapter Six *A Road Test* 58

Chapter Seven *Irony* 69

Chapter Eight *Power-up* 80

Chapter Nine *Beyond the Junk* 93

Chapter Ten *New York* 105

Chapter Eleven *Trust is Tricky* 117

Chapter Twelve *A Lone Straw* 126

Chapter Thirteen *Tick Tock* 134

Chapter Fourteen *Raven Return* 147

Chapter Fifteen *Picture Talk* 157

Chapter Sixteen *Trip, Don't Fall* 165

Chapter Seventeen *Don't Look* 172

Chapter Eighteen *Rocky* 185

Chapter Nineteen *27* 192

Chapter Twenty *Clarity Follows Confusion* 206

Chapter Twenty-One *Interlude* 217

Chapter Twenty-Two *Ask the Beer* 219

Chapter Twenty-Three *Only a Name*...................................230

Chapter Twenty-Four *Black Coffee*...................................240

Chapter Twenty-Five *Switching the Steering*...........................250

Chapter Twenty-Six *My Seven*......................................260

Chapter Twenty-Seven *Next Sunday*.................................269

Chapter Twenty-Eight *Double Eye*...................................277

Chapter Twenty-Nine *Stay Wild*....................................285

Chapter Thirty *Casting*..292

Chapter Thirty-One *Shaking Shells*..................................297

Chapter Thirty-Two *Dear Diary*.....................................302

Chapter Thirty-Three *Knock-knock*..................................309

Chapter Thirty-Four *Through the Window*............................317

Chapter Thirty-Five *The End is the Beginning*........................325

Chapter Thirty-Six *Strategy is Dead*.................................337

"To those who were made to feel unwanted.
I see you." – Vozareia.

Chapter One
The Beginning of Strange

Dear Curse (because that's what you feel like),

I want you to go away.

You tell me I am barren and superfluous to requirements, but I want to hold onto my Star, run into the night with the wild love of the sky.

I tried not to aggravate Dad, and I tried to be a great walker over eggshells so not to make Mum feel guilty, yet it never worked. He still drank and flung his fists and she still rallied around terrified, and my importance dropped further down a bruised list.

Dad is no more. The bottle finally moved him to earth in a graveyard, and Mum reinvented herself with her own law firm and red lipstick. Why is it then, that I still feel like the teddy bear left on the platform whilst everyone boarded the train not noticing?

It's exhausting to have a mind telling me I'm not wanted because I'm wonky. To always look for and stay ahead of problems, in whatever way I can, in order to survive life. It shatters me to think I can't be a proper artist or have a dope boyfriend or a normal family with a normal upbringing. For these things are only for chosen people, which you say is not me, yet somewhere deep within my Star disagrees.

What will become of me? Who will win the tug of war between you and my Star? This scares me the most as I fear it will be you, and I don't know what to do or how to find a solution.

So, dear Star, please send help.

Love, Seven Madison (aged 16).

I tear out the letter I wrote in my notebook weeks and weeks ago. I don't know if I'm mad, upset, scared, or all three that nothing has changed, and no sign has appeared indicating my life ever will. So, I burn it down the alley and watch with intensity as the paper turns to ash. When it's finally in ruins, I walk away and head down the silent alley to meet Yasmina – Yas, as we all call her – to catch the bus to school. Near the end where the alley opens out into the main street, a gust of wind whooshes pieces of grey confetti past me, and I try to ignore the irony of my burnt unanswered hopes having the last word. As the dismal remnants of grey confetti disappear into the atmosphere, the sound of Yas' voice zips me back towards the bus stop awaiting me.

"Hey, over here," she says, waving excessively, followed by her casting a disapproving glare to the boy stood next to her who mimicked her actions because her elbow nearly hit him in the face.

The early morning bus crawls the main road to school, the whooshing air brakes almost rhythmic with the bus stopping every few minutes to let more students and workers pile in. The bus begins to fill with clutter and a muggy vibe, yet outside the world is spring bright as I scroll through old texts and photographs on my phone; photos of Nate and me, places Nate and I visited, Nate being funny…

"It should be me with him at the game on Friday, not

Lizzie," I say to Yas as she unties her hair with a long swish.

"It's his loss. There will be someone else, someone way better than Nate, but first, you need to delete those," she says, waggling her finger over the pictures on my phone. I snap my head up and stare at her in shock.

"What?"

"You need to make space for Mr Magical to swoop in," Yas replies, moving her arms outwards as though she was sweeping back an ocean full of junk. Except it's the only time I felt like I fitted together properly.

"I can't delete those. And…" I say, widening my eyes at Yas, "…look what happened the last time I followed your, and I quote, 'most fantastic idea'."

"So, my best friend advice was a little off back then… but do you want Mr Magical or not?"

I think for a beat.

"More than being an artist. Well, maybe not *more* than, because that's kind of a biggy, but it's right up there near it."

"Babe. Start deleting," she instructs, remaining unnervingly steadfast.

I click on a photo and my thumb hovers over the bin icon. Even though Nate and I are no longer together, and he's all buzzed up about dating – *ugh* – Lizzie, I can't delete our happy memories and the hope of their return. My phone takes flight out of my hands; Yas holds it up in the air, her thumb dangerously close to deleting as she swipes through the photos.

"Hey, give it back." I grapple, annoying the girls sat behind us. "Give it back."

We scuffle a little longer until Yas abruptly halts, absorbed in a photo.

"When did you take this picture? I don't remember being there?" she asks.

I had forgotten about the picture Yas is questioning – a snap I took of Felix and Leo at Wavies, the Smoothie Bar in Silversedge where everyone hangs out. Felix was kissing a random girl on the cheek and Leo's beach hair and suntan looked catchy compared to the backdrop of Londoners in winter, especially because he was wearing his silly Santa hat from Miami, but that's not why I took it.

I'd called into Wavies on my way home from central London, and Felix and Leo happened to be there already. It wasn't too long after twins Leo and Lizzie Joseph had moved over from Miami, and the bromance between Felix and Leo was apparent from the start.

"Leo had something weird above his head, like tiny lights dancing in mid-air. I was trying to show them both on a picture, but I missed them, or they vanished."

"Dancing lights?" Yas replies. "Had you been drinking?"

"Funny – not. Actually, Felix and Leo said the same, that was before Felix turned into a ten-year-old because he wanted dancing lights above his head too."

I spend the next five minutes explaining to Yas we hadn't arranged to meet up without her and she didn't miss out. There wasn't time to message her and, if I recall, she was out with her parents anyway.

"Probably," Yas says. "No doubt forced to go to a family event or equally hoorah bore."

"Your family is great! You have brothers to talk to and you can call cool places like Dubai home," I say, taking my phone back.

"Dubai is not cool. It's like living in an oven," Yas replies. She stares vacantly out of the window until the bus pulls up at the South Street stop, our stop, and I'm relieved my photos survived the ordeal.

We meet Leo and Lizzie at the zebra crossing by the bus stop. I can understand why Nate started dating Lizzie, she's on point: happy, sporty – a surfer for pity's sake – and bolder than most British girls with legs taller than the entirety of me. Whilst mine and Nate's break up was my fault, I didn't expect a hot American surfer to wander in from across the pond to take my place. I try to be pleasant to Lizzie but I'm sure she feels the block I placed around her. Felix says it's 'bitchy' of me, and I don't like that thought either because it's far away from the truth: it's the dislike of myself that prevents me from liking her and letting the situation go.

We make our way across the road as traffic impatiently waits for us to reach the other side of the crossing. As is the case most mornings these days, it's only the four of us from our group, the MGs, arriving together at school. We've given up waiting for Felix in the mornings, Nate is already at basketball practice and RV is still MIA.

We turn the corner; the familiar red brick building and its rows of tall arched windows and the 'Welcome to Silversedge High School' sign above the main doors are all as spotless as the streets of Silversedge. Drawing closer, I note how pretty the yellow flowers look blossoming amongst the bushes. I was about to mention this but thought better of it as we merged in with the crowd of black uniforms and black shoes migrating into the grounds.

We are all but robots.

Me, Yas, Leo and Lizzie drift through the iron gates that loom, open wide like the arms of a devil welcoming everyone in, until – slam – they lock tight, imprisoning innocent beings for another day.

***

I hear Mrs Price in the distance. The desks and the back of classmates' heads in front of me coming back into clear focus. Mrs Prices' voice grows like a volume dial being turned up in one swift movement, booming words from behind me as I emerge from a mini sleep or a daydream or— come to think of it, where the hell was I?

"GCSE exams are in less than three months. You all should know this by now. Seven! What answer do you have?"

She's done this deliberately; she spotted my mind leaving the heat battered classroom. God, I hate teachers sometimes.

I glance down at my French book praying to find the answer to a question I didn't hear. Except the only thing I've written – well, drawn – is a strange symbol. I can feel Mrs Price boring down at my book from over my shoulder as I wrestle with this odd creation and the answer to give her.

"Erm, erm," I reply to Mrs Price, looking to my classmate next to me for assistance, but she shrugs her shoulder and looks as blank as me. "*Err*," I repeat again. Mrs Price blows out her dismay.

"Seven thinks the translation is a triangle with a bird in it," she says, scrutinising the biro drawing more, "a raven, maybe. With a blue eye." The class begins sniggering and I close my book with embarrassment, silently wondering if her commentary falls under soft bullying. Mrs Price adds the translation to my pressure cooker of homework and directs her question to someone else.

"Michael, can you help Seven and her raven out?"

Unless obsessed footballer Michael can explain why I drew the symbol and what it means, then no, Mrs Price, Michael cannot help me and my raven out.

Soon enough the class are packing up and ready to leave. I sit impatiently, checking the clock and waiting for the bell to ring rather than listening to Mrs Prices' end of class spiel. When it strikes, chairs scrape in unison and a herd of people rattle out of the classroom into the corridor. Unfortunately, no one else in the MGs takes French. Whimsical thoughts of drawing in Paris and eating crepes down romantic cobbled streets were the reasons I opted for it, but I question my choice now. I could just go to Paris and learn with real French people.

Stuck in the lunchtime river of students in the corridor, I make a left at the end into the wide alcove leading to the girl's toilets – a key spot within the sprawling school, free from eyes of lurking teachers – and open The MG group chat. We decided the MGs sounded more original than 'The Main Group', so we kept it and the group grew over time until the MGs became us.

> *Seven is typing*
> Will be late to lunch. Going to art.
> *Yas is typing*
> Ok babe. We'll be in the canteen.
> *Leo is typing*
> That's rad, have fun.

Felix is typing

How the fuck is that rad?

Seven is typing

Shut up Felix, you melon

Felix is typing

I'm hurt

Nate is typing

Grab us a grilled chicken sandwich someone before
they all go

Lizzie is typing

I'm starving, see you all in there

Leo is typing

When are you not?

RV

Message status - Seen.

No reply, as usual.

I'm on a mini mission, because if I can persuade Mum that I am an important art genius destined for my own exhibits and gallery, she might – might – let me continue to study art next year at college instead of something academic. That's my plan, my only plan, because I'd rather chew tin foil on my fillings than study more academic subjects. What would I do with a string of academic qualifications, anyway? Be like her: become like the rest of the town?

Silversedge, West London. The la-di-da town of sunglasses and men in blue suits with tan shoes, where prams clog up coffee shops and young dreams are clipped to fit. It is muddling to me, because how I see it is, dreams are the true assignments and work of life; our deep desires, at first a mere smoulder, soon catch fire, and before long you feel like you might just die if you don't get to live them. That's how to tell if it's a true dream.

I glance through the small square window on the upper half of the door to the art classroom. No lights are on and nerves fizzle in my stomach as I push the handle down. Perhaps I should have asked if I could use the classroom at lunchtime, not just break in.

Classrooms are strange when you're the only one in them, they appear more grown up, and I feel twenty-five instead of sixteen-years-old. The desks are all tidy, the light grey surfaces shimmering slightly with their partnering chairs all neatly positioned around them. I press the plastic light switch and the strip lighting fires up like a sudden wake up call to the eyes. I retrieve my pile of drawings from the cabinet and begin to pick them apart, thinking perhaps a complete do over might be better.

I open and shut drawers and cupboards looking for inspiration, marinating in how art, even the materials like pencils, make me feel at home yet aimlessly lost and small at the same time. The work of the previous year's top students and success stories are displayed on the back wall. Celebrated by a mad shrine created by our art teacher Mr Henry. He does it every year, but it just assaults me – perhaps it shouldn't, but it does. Envy is not proud but vicious.

I fan through my art pad by the shrine and close my eyes. Drifting off into a random space, I search for how I can make my drawings better and try to discover the key to upping my game. I think of the stupid raven and its blue eye. *Is it a message or clue I can use?* The image becomes sharper and brighter, and I can almost touch the silver edge of the triangle. I reach out my hand, but the symbol zip zaps away, and I realise – I have nothing.

'*Seven.*' I hear my name spoken softly behind me; I'm unsure if that's what was said, and I freeze. '*Seven. Follow Seven.*'

There it is again.

I open my eyes, poised like a stone statue except for tiny goose bumps spreading upwards across my back like the rush of a cold, tight wind.

"Who said that?" I demand, turning around to find Mr Henry standing there.

"Who said what?" he asks with a scrunched face, looking round at the empty classroom.

My eyes dart all around the room and behind Mr Henry as I 'um' and 'ah' in total confusion.

What the fuck? I totally heard someone. That was weird.

"Oh, nothing. Sorry," I reply.

"*Okayyyy,*" Mr Henry says, raising his eyebrows and striding his octopus legs towards his desk. I dutifully do the same and stand next to it still scanning the room.

"Mr Henry, seeing as you are here," I ask, changing the subject, "I wanted to ask if you can speak to my mum? To explain to her there is future in art. Do you think I can have a career in art, that my work is good enough?"

"A big question for lunchtime… you're talented with great potential. Most of your work sits at an A grade, with hard work and determination I don't see why not."

"Most. Not all," I interject.

Mr Henry sits down on the red swivel chair and runs his

hand through his blonde curls. The delighted smile he had a second ago disappears into a closed sigh, and I sense disappointment.

"I'm happy to speak with your mum about the choices you have, and your talent, but who are you trying to convince here, really? Her or you?"

I'm uncomfortable. Like he's poked a sleeping lion I don't want disturbing. I fiddle with my hands twisting my fingers until I feel they might ping off. Mr Henry tilts his head; his curiosity searches my face as he pulls a large breath inward.

"Everyone wants to be the next Banksy, the next 'one to watch'," he says with air quotation marks as he continues, "most fade out as quickly as they fade in. The ones who 'make it', as you would say, possess *a je ne sais quoi* and an enchanting obsession with their craft. I get the feeling, however, that your obsession is about self-validation and proving you're an artist?"

The lion is up and prowling. I feel scratchy on the inside, and I wish I'd gone straight to lunch instead of coming here.

"Why do you like drawing cities so much?" He probes further.

I fluster, stuttering my attempt to find words amongst the emotional shrapnel he's just embedded in my chest, and I'm breathing like hunted prey. All I wanted was confirmation about my work and a 'yes, tell your mum to come and see me.'

"I fall in love with all of them," I reply, after what feels like forever. "The buildings, the people, the traffic… all these bring stories and make the city unique. Cities are saturated with data and dreams, and you can sense them – hear them sometimes. I like to translate it into a picture."

Mr Henry sits happier with my response which found its own rhythm after I blurted out the first few words.

"I agree," he replies. "Don't forget your dream has a purpose in this city too."

He swivels round in his non-ironed jeans and t-shirt, standard for Mr H, and begins clicking the mouse and scrolling on his computer screen.

"Let me know if your mum wants to speak to me, but don't let trying to prove yourself ruin what you love to do, because it can." He swivels back again to face me. "Now go and get something rank from the cafeteria for lunch," he says.

Unsure of how to react, I dither a thank you and leave the art classroom in a hurry. Desperate to flee both my uncomfortable self and the uncomfortable vibe of the voice – of which I momentarily forgot about – I rush to find safety in the only way I know: the MGs.

I speed walk to the canteen, and its warm cloud of school dinner smell surrounds me as I grab what's left of lunch. It only takes thirty seconds of wandering with my tray before I see the MGs; well, nearly all of them – Yas, Felix, Nate, Leo and Lizzie; bantering at a table near the door to the outside diner. Leo spies me first and points repeatedly with his arm in the air to the seat he saved for me next to him, and the warmth of my friends moves me like a setting sun.

"Oh, now you join us?" Felix yells from the other end of the table.

I throw a chip at his head and avoid eye contact with Nate and Lizzie sat together opposite me.

"Still no word from RV? Has he got in touch with anyone yet?" I ask, diverting my mind. Apart from odd sightings around school, empty answers sweep the table.

We still don't know what's happened to our friend – the conflicted East End boy trying to reform in a West End world – and it's worrying more than frustrating as to why he's cut us all off.

"Maybe he doesn't like us anymore," I say.

"That's totally something you would think. How can he not like us?" Yas replies, rotating her hand in the air, beaming sass.

"We need to do something," I say, but Nate and Felix are resistant to the idea in case it would run him out of town.

"Let him come back to us in his own time, in his own way," Felix says.

"I get that, but what if he's in real trouble again? We can't turn a blind eye," I reply.

"And we can't interfere with someone else's life either," Nate snaps. I clock the harsh look he throws at Yas, which she misses due to a make-up check using her phone. I look at Nate puzzled and move on.

"I get that too, but…" I say, moving chips around with my fork whilst I think on the spot, "…let's all meet at Wavies on Friday night and we can discuss it?"

Nate holds his hand up and opens his mouth.

"After your game, Nate, does that work?" I add.

Finally, we all agree.

Chapter Two
The Talking Spot

Three years have passed since Mum and me moved to Silversedge. We both wanted to leave our old house of haunting memories in a neighbouring town, and we bickered plenty over areas to move to as I didn't want to change schools. After two helpful estate agents brought the white house on the hill to Mum's attention, moving to Silversedge High School is exactly what happened.

"Silversedge is *the* place to live, and the estate agents have negotiated a deal I can't say no to. It's perfect for both of us: a great school for you, closer to work, the right sort of people and pastries to die for," Mum cooed at the time.

When did pastries become a reason to move life, town and house? I question her remarkable intelligent mind at times.

Our home, the white house on the hill, has a giant black front door with a shiny brass doorknob in the middle; white pillars stand either side and the original sash windows are all as pristine as the white building itself. Technically, the house sits on top of the hill distinctly separate from the neighbours' standard London homes. It looks over Silversedge town from the front, and from behind it looks out over the River Thames and a tree stocked park with a woodland café straight out of a fairy tale. It's majestic in many ways – I will give Mum that one.

I faceplant my bed, relieved to be home after school. Only two more days to go until the weekend, although weekends have been quite dead lately too. With revision for final exams taking priority, parties are thin on the ground. Even Felix, my other best friend slash adopted brother, doesn't know of any kicking off. He, like Nate, are rare natives of Silversedge and know everybody and every nook in town. Most people here are transplants from a plethora of places and countries; parties, Wavies and hanging at the park are what bring us all together.

I stretch out on my bed and push my shoes off at the heel using my toes and fling them from my feet to the floor. The last time *all* the MGs hung out was at the park with Friday night beers and a speaker. Nate was hammered and stood motionless with a beer bottle hanging from his hand, gawping up at the moon. He thought it was talking to him when it was, in fact, Lizzie and Yaz sat behind him.

'What an idiot,' RV had said, laughing as he lay down next to me, while Leo and Felix rolled around the grass trying to gain two girl's attentions sat in the café.

That night, RV and I found common ground of homegrown trauma and a love of cola bottle sweets whilst we lay on the grass looking up at the cosmos. I think a part of my inner freak healed or flew with a sense a pride that night.

I roll over and hug my duvet, my intention to have a quick nap. The tiredness of the final year of school pounds at my chest like our survival as a species depends on these exams. I begin arguing with the feeling, telling it exams aren't a reflection of true knowledge and talent. This only comes from study of your craft, from study of life, from study of interests. Exams test memory, I continue telling the feeling, and I am failing to see why we are whipped by society for having a poor memory when I know parents who forget to pick up their children from school or pay for school trips. Irritation floods my body, and I can't lie still; my legs keep flicking and my spine feels like an ant is crawling through it. I throw off the duvet and decide to strike the art debacle whilst my determination is flowing like water through a burst pipe.

I march downstairs and pause in the large square hallway which sits between the kitchen and sitting room; I push my shoulders back and lift my neck to alleviate my eyes from a floor focus to a straight-ahead focus. The chandelier dangles grandly above my head and the tiling of the black and white floor feels welcomingly cold against the soles of my feet. I can see Mum in the sitting room through the double glass doors she's left open, and I make my move.

"Mum," I say, tapping gently on the glass.

Perched on the sofa, she switches her attention from papers on her lap, to documents on the sofa, to files piled up on the floor and then finally to me, as though I am her assistant interrupting Gabby Madison's most complicated case.

The television is on but muted, and the teatime sun glares through the windows spotlighting a few of the many pictures hung on the walls throughout the house.

"I realise you're in the middle of something, but can we talk?"

Mum tucks her blonde hair behind her ears and places the

papers and her pen down. She holds her arm out and pats the sofa.

"Of course, what's the matter darling? Are you okay?"

I wiggle in beside her and the papers and hurl the words out as fast as I can.

"I know you're not happy for me to pursue art as a career, but it's the only thing I want to do and the only thing I'm good at, and just today Mr H – sorry, Mr Henry – said my grades are excellent and I have talent. He's a professional too. Would you at least listen to him? He said he's happy to talk with you?"

Mum leans back slightly crossing her arms as her firmer lawyer look returns; she knows I hate a lawyer face.

"I know it isn't what you want to hear, and it isn't because I don't think you are talented, you are. It's that art is no foundation to build your whole life upon. I do have this case to finish but—"

"That's your opinion," I cut in.

"It's not an opinion, Seven. It's reality. Do it as hobby, I'm more than happy to help out with that."

A hobby?

"But you buy art? You have it hung all over the house! How do you think it got there for you to buy? Can't you even listen to Mr Henry? To hear what he thinks? Please, Mum."

Then I don't understand what happened: the television unmutes itself and starts playing a documentary at high volume while Mum explodes like a dormant mine I stepped on by accident, yelling and flinging her arms like a crazy woman. I'm not exactly listening to her as I am distracted by the sight of the TV remote and Mum's phone on the armchair by the fireplace, nowhere near either of us or any falling documents. I don't get how the sound turned back on and so loud too.

"The art in this house has nothing to do with this. Nothing," she yells, as she rummages around with the TV remote trying to turn it off. "I suggest you put your aspirations into something else. There are plenty of more viable careers than art… and I have to prepare for this case in the morning." She picks up a few of the fallen papers and ruffles them straight before trying to iron out the agitation in her legs with her hands.

I stand up feeling creaky, my body battered by her wrath. "Whoa. Thanks. Thanks for the belief in me," I turn and leave. Ignoring her pleas and apologies to sit back down as I slam the glass doors shut and shoot up the stairs to my bedroom, only to remember I left my phone in the kitchen.

Bloody hell. Please don't let me bump into her.

I rush back down the stairs into the hall and through the other set of glass doors opposite the sitting room leading into the kitchen. I snatch my phone from the kitchen island ready to hurtle back upstairs, but as I pass back through the hall, I see Mum through the sitting room doors wiping her face, her shoulders juddering. *Is she… crying?* I tip toe to the bottom of the stairs and peek out from behind the side of the wall through the doors to spectate longer. She's definitely crying, then she screws up a handful of papers into an angry ball and throws it at one of the pictures before hanging her head in her hands. I turn away, slowly retreating up the stairs to my bedroom.

Pick up, Felix. Pick up.

It goes to voicemail. I ring again.

Pick up. Pick up.

"It's Wednesday evening, what do you want?" he says.

"Oh yeah, sorry. Forgot it's Wednesday night: bubble bath night."

"Make it quick. My time is valuable, and I have my beauty rituals to do," he replies.

"Sorry, King Felix. It's kinda long. Mum says I'm not allowed to do art as a career then she exploded after a ghost unmuted the tele, now she's crying and throwing things and my life is over."

"Perfect. A simple chat then," he replies. A drawn-out groan follows and then he pauses. "The great Felix will meet you at the talking spot in an hour. Does that work?" he asks. I swear I can hear him blowing the foam in the bath, and if I wasn't all knotted up, I would be taking the rip.

"Sure, thank *youuuu* Felix."

He mutters and hangs up with his usual, 'B-b-b-bye. Bye'.

For a second, I squirm at the vision of Felix in his candlelit bathroom and bubble bath and wonder what beauty rituals he does. I bet he's got cucumbers on his eyes and everything.

***

The evening will cool soon, and I decide one of Mum's cashmere scarves will be ideal to take with me. I figure I'll leave now and wait at the Talking Spot, rather than waiting here, with her. I roll myself off my bed and into Mum's dressing room, a room of magazine glamour sandwiched between both our bedrooms.

We often chat, try on outfits and twirl in front of the giant pewter framed mirror, which elegantly stands on the wooden floor. This dressing room is to be my future art studio, apparently. The inviting space of natural light and exposed brickwork will be mine once Mum eventually moves her clothes, shoes, boxes of old treasures, boxes of old crap and jewellery somewhere else. I don't know why she doesn't move it all upstairs into the converted – and very empty – attic room on the third floor, currently only used as a through way to the small roof terrace.

Stretching up and with quick hands I grasp the burgundy velvet hatbox filled with scarves from the shelf. Simultaneously, a smaller box on the shelf above tumbles to the polished, dark floorboards. I tell myself I must have caught it when pulling the scarf box down, but that strange sense of *knowing* something else is going on returns and fills my chest like floating clouds in a vast sky – I know damn well I didn't touch it or bang the upper shelf to make it fall.

Letters, mementos and odd things such as the stubs of old flight tickets spill out from the smaller box and scatter across the floor. I chase the contents around the room like peas on a plate, collecting them and placing them back in the box, hoping they weren't in any special order, but one escapee postcard catches my attention. Too nosey not to read it, I pick it up. It's addressed to Mum, posted from Sicily not long before I was born.

Baffled, I keep flicking the postcard over and back again. There's a message written in what I think is Italian, or maybe it's Spanish…

> *Ti stavo pensando, vorrei tanto che tutto fosse diverso, e potrei stare con voi entrambi. Ma sarebbe stato troppo pericoloso.*
>
> *Il mio cuore batterà sempre per te.*

It's definitely not French – *see, I have been paying some attention in French class* – and it's signed with a short, swirly and totally unreadable signature.

Since when does Mum speak a different language? Why would she keep this?

Checking the time, I take a picture of the message on my phone and throw a black scarf around my neck. I neatly place both boxes back on the shelf and race down the stairs into the hall and open the giant front door.

"I'm meeting Felix; won't be long," I shout to Mum and close the door with little regard of its signature boom.

The Talking Spot is halfway between my house and Felix's swanky penthouse apartment. At the entrance to the park, long before you reach the woodland café down the park's incline, stands an old building patrolling the grounds. Its pale red bricks and cream stone etched with ancient patterns and designs scream old London strength. Derelict for years, its windows and doors are boarded up with weather beaten wood panels, but its flat rooftop is ideal for those looking to escape. Known only to a few, it is accessed through a mini forest of trees off the side of the main path. There's a wrought iron gate at the end of the mini forest, its black paint old and peeling off in most places. The handle is wrapped in a meaty chain and padlock, but the gate is only waist high and easily clambered over to get straight onto the rooftop.

Me and Felix come here to sit amongst the vista of the treetops in the park and the River Thames, where dainty boats in the distance flap on water which looks like steel. The presence of sparse twinkling lights make it look the complete opposite to Silversedge town behind us. At the Talking Spot, we dissect our worlds to make sense of the past, the now and the yet to be future. People at school used to think me and Felix were going out together which is laughable. We don't look at each other that way, we never have, never will. Our chance meeting at the woodland café led us to find solace at first, and then a friendship few discover in a world jammed with people, buildings, and pollution.

I sit solo for a while on the dirt and crushed pebbles of the rooftop watching the boats, careful to stay away from the edge because it makes me feel funny if I go too close. A raven lands directly in front of me on the ledge of the building. Watching wildlife and the sky from here has always been one of the nicest things about it, and I watch as the brave bird totters around the rooftop, edging slightly closer to my tattered trainers. It isn't until the third raven arrives, and then another, and then another, that I began to think of it as odd. They continue arriving until a line of the deepest black, shiny feathered ravens balance perfectly still, watching me from the ledge of the building.

I try not to look at them or move, yet with a calm insistence the ravens stay.

"Are you lot trying to tell me something, or is this your place to chill too?" I ask the ravens. "Do you want me to leave?"

Why am I talking to birds?

I hear feet land behind me in the distance and dusty gravel crunching to the sound of footsteps, and the birds swoop away in one elegant display of flight and disappear.

"Oi," Felix says and plonks himself down next to me.

He smacks at his black skateboarding trainers to bang the

dust off, which he regrets wearing as they are new, and he was saving them for the weekend, he tells me.

"Should have worn old trainers like me," I say, "but I appreciate the effort to impress me," I joke, he shakes his head at me.

"Shoot the problem then," he replies.

I launch into a monologue of the events of the evening and fire questions like an AK-47 – how did the TV unmute itself and why? Who am I to think people will invest in my art and success? Why did Mum react so dramatically?

Felix's advice, albeit direct and simple, is often correct yet finding enough nerve within me to follow through on his equally direct suggested course of action always seems impossible. How he does this in his own pursuit of self and goal to becoming an actor, whilst remaining so steadfastly certain and confident, remains a mystery to me. I seem to stay stuck in spinning my wheels of why, who and how.

"Sounds like you pissed your mum off. Can you think of any reason why?"

"Because it's me and I'm a disappointment."

"Damn, woman. Leave the pity party would ya," he responds.

To the point.

"You can try and find out why she was so triggered, but what she said is bollocks. You can totally make a career out of it. You tell her what you want to do. Not want she wants. It's her problem, let her deal with it. Sign up for whatever course you want to do and tell your mum with confidence. You gotta live life how you want to."

I love the idea of this, but I daren't.

The implications could be devasting. Felix is blessed, his parents at least understand his dream and its pursuit.

"If it tanks, there's always a spare bedroom at my place," he adds with a 'it's not that deep' look.

"Maybe. Your place is sick. I'd happily live there," I burst into laughter. "Can you imagine your mum and dad's faces if I show up with all my stuff."

"It would likely take a week for them to notice. They're cool and all, but you know what they're like: always on set, in production meetings, or or or."

His answers about the TV and the falling box being the antics of a poltergeist, and how these entities love to mess with teenagers, were not as helpful. I won't be able to sleep tonight, and I spin off into thinking how I can persuade Mum to move to another house or whether I need to find a vicar to eradicate the ghost that I fully believe in now.

"Sorry. Didn't mean to freak you out," he says, pulling me in sideways for a hug. "Use your intuition. Your gut feeling… when it happened did it feel bad or scary?"

I replay the TV and box incident, the only weirdness I've mentioned to Felix. I kept the voice in the classroom, the symbol, the ravens just now, and the peculiar sense of *knowing* I get (like an invisible teacher fed me the information) to myself, but I mull them all over along with the dancing lights above Leo that Yas reminded me of earlier.

"No. It doesn't. It's intriguing, cosy almost."

"That sounds like something different then. Not a poltergeist."

I'm not sure I feel any better, because if Felix is thinking like this it makes it truer and not a result of my daft imagination.

The big orange sun begins to sink behind the trees, so we stand up and dust the back of our jeans off to make a move back home, when Felix casually drops that he has an appointment to discuss his tattoo design.

"What the hell!" I reply with a thump to his arm. "You have to be eighteen not sixteen to get inked. What about your mum and dad? And your acting… are tattoos allowed?"

He rolls his dark eyes at me like I've asked dumb questions when these are probably the least dumb questions I've asked all evening.

"One," he states, holding his thumb up, clearly about to bullet point with fingers each of his dumb responses. "I have fake ID; how do you think I go out in central? Two, plenty of actors have tattoos, either in places easily hidden or make up covers them up, which means I'll have to be shit hot to warrant the extra cost and time of doing so – and I will be. And three, Mum and Dad will never know." He ends with a shoulder shrug like he won the hand, but the lone wolf roaming in his eyes is all too real to me at times.

"Let me come with you," I say.

Felix eyeballs me, comically moving his mouth side to side, assessing my trustworthiness.

"Okay. But no nervy talk or being stupid."

"Done," I reply, and we seal it with our wiggle handshake – touching fingertips only and wiggling them rapidly against each other.

"I'm glad we have each other through our struggles of life," I jest as we walk back to the gate. A chunky raven flies past me again as I climb over the peeling gate, and we emerge back on the path and out of the park. Felix breathes in deeply and hangs his arm from my shoulder.

"Life is not our struggle, my dear Seven, self-belief is," he says. The words smack and we turn in silence to go our separate ways home.

"Two o'clock. Saturday at Jamming minds. It opened a few months ago on the road behind Wavies," he yells back.

"I know. I've always wanted to go in to look at the paintings they sell. It doesn't look like a tattoo place."

"That's because it's all customised and owned by a proper artist—"

"Gusti." I finish the sentence for him. "I've seen him around."

"He's a G, originally from Bali. Think you'll get on with him. Catch ya at school tomorrow."

And there's that invisible teacher again, telling me I *know* I will too.

Chapter Three
Life Changes

By Friday, Mum is still being overly nice in a bid to make up for our fight and smooth things over; I can agree to the shopping trip on Sunday she offered as summer is coming up, and according to the soon to be fashion stylist to the stars Yas, I need to rethink my look to accentuate my "artistic flair", but I can't find the place to agree to let all this go with her. It feels deeper and as though I'm being punished unjustly. I nearly told her no until it struck me the shopping trip could be a savvy move and the ideal opportunity to reinvent myself. This thought of reinvention is lifting, and I decide, by looking forward to our MGs meet up at Wavies tonight to discuss RV and focusing on my new style, I can begin to steer this in a different direction. No more strange happenings have occurred either, unless the coincidence of literally banging into Gusti yesterday on a packed bus counts… When the bus came to a holt at one of the stops, those standing, like me and Gusti, were forced forward and I knocked into him causing his coffee to plop out of his takeout cup and spill onto his shirt. Thankfully he didn't seem to mind and waved my apologies off with his ring laden hand and a warm smile. The sleeves of his white shirt were rolled up to his elbow, his amber arms exposed a watch and a silver bangle with a turquoise stone. He intrigues me, and I've noticed him about town more recently. Come to think of it, a few weeks ago I saw Gusti and Leo talking in Wavies as I walked past, and I rapped on the window to wave hi. I thought I had disturbed them, but Leo said he was only explaining American Football to Gusti after Richard, who owns Wavies and isn't American but British, got him hooked on it.

"Hey, Richard," I say, walking into Wavies to meet the MGs as tunes pulse and blare around the place, "thanks for holding the door."

"No problem. The others are over there," he says turning his baseball cap round backwards and pointing to the long table at the back. Hung on the wall behind our regular table is a large chalkboard, chalked with a 'saying of the day', as written by Richard each morning. Instead of going straight over I stay by the door with Richard, moving my head side to side to view the jungle of tall, leafy plants Richard loves so much – I like them too, they match the tropical décor and photographs of Richard's extensive travels perfectly. Everyone is sitting around the table, and it appears I am the last to arrive. Felix is slurping from a navy and orange mug, 'the finest Cappuccino in town' he claims. It's the froth and chocolate sprinkles he likes really, so Richard always gives him extra. Basically, it's a cup of foam with chocolate powder. They all seem preoccupied listening to Yas or slurping foam and haven't noticed I've arrived, which is ideal.

Richard lets the door sweep shut and tries to give a thumbs up to a passer-by, but I pull him to the side behind a plant, making him stumble into the foliage. Batting a leaf away from his face, he looks at me slightly bewildered.

"You speak different languages, right?" I ask.

"Random question?" he replies, confused as to why I'm harbouring him by a plant.

"Not really; you've travelled half the world."

He scoffs at his language skills before admitting to knowing a decent amount of Spanish and enough to find the loo, a bar and the train station in Italian and French.

"Can you translate this? I don't trust Google," I say, handing my phone to him with the picture of the message, "is it Italian?"

He stares at my phone screen and reads the message a few times rubbing the back of his head and then looks to me with a more serious tone.

"Is this message to you?" he asks, wrinkling his forehead.

"Sort of. What does it mean?"

He pauses and holds the back of his neck, his eyebrows puckering, and his lips mouthed some of the words in silence. Aside an odd word he says, it's beyond his vocabulary, but he takes a picture of it and said he'll ask a friend who will know.

"You're absolutely sure you want to know what it says?" he asks.

"I am."

"It could be like opening Pandora's box?" Richard checks again.

"I want to know. It's important," I reply.

"If you're sure then," he says, sliding his phone back into his pocket and returning to his counter.

I think he understood more of the message than he let on which only makes me want to dig into it further. I sneak back out from behind the plant unnoticed and casually join the rest of the MGs.

"Yo guys. How we doing?" I ask, shuffling onto a seat and moving around to find a comfy angle. Lizzie nods at the board chalked with the message, 'The purest desire wins'.

"That's bull," Lizzie states, "I really wanted to win the surf championship, but bitchy Tara won. I was depressed for a month."

"Only a month?" Leo says. "Try a year."

"Oh sorry, brother dearest, that I'm gutted for screwing up my career. Jeopardised further because of having to be in London."

"You'll be back in town before long. Quit your whining,' Leo replies.

"Who's Tara?" Nate asks.

"Leo's ex," Lizzie answers.

"Oooo, do tell, Lizzie. You kept that quiet, Leo," pipes Yas.

Leo ignores Lizzie and Yas and turns to me disinterested in being the topic of gossip and offers to get me a drink. I reach in my pocket to find the note I stuffed in it.

I'm sure I put it in here, where is it? I fumble and tug inside my pockets when I feel Leo touch my arm.

"I don't want your money, just your order."

A normal person, Yas for example, would have just accepted his kind offer and answered the question. But not me: I knock his gesture insisting, whilst I continue fumbling around, I have the money somewhere. He repeats himself again, and now I feel unorganised and bad. If I can't even believe someone would want to buy me a drink just because they would like to, how the fuck am I going to believe anyone would want to buy my art or love my heart? I want to hit my stupid head but given I'm in public…

"I'll have a Racy Raspberry. Thanks."

Leo disappears off to the counter. I disengage from the group's chatter and slyly lean back on my chair to spy. A group of girls from the year below are at another table ogling Leo who is oblivious to his fan club as he talks to Richard.

"Oi. Seven. What do you reckon? Hello?" I hear Felix say.

"What?" I say, turning back to the group. "Erm. I don't think you should be down on yourself Lizzie because of one competition. Leo's right, a few more months and you'll back in Miami and on the waves. You're a top surfer from what I hear."

Everyone is staring at me, have I missed something? And why was I all supportive and lovely to Lizzie – I dislike her.

Nate rolls his eyes, shaking his head. "Always in your own world," he adds with a half-smile.

"What do you think about a pre-exam party?" Felix says, speaking the sentence in slow mo. "It's the last summer we'll all be together as well?"

"Oh. I see. Yeah, we need a decent party," I muster back.

Lizzie is as surprised as I am at what I said, and for a fleeting moment there's a sense of relief as if the usual cold wall of ice is melting between us. It touched me, as much as I don't want to admit, even as Nate hugs himself into her shoulder with his sullen face.

"Don't talk about you and Leo moving back to Miami at Christmas. Your year here is going too fast, it's depressing," Nate groans.

Lizzie leans back into him, smoothing her hand over his hair. "December is ages away yet," she replies.

"*Awww*, look at the love birds," Yas squeals from the other end of the table, snapping a picture on her phone.

"Sorry to interrupt but has everyone forgotten we're meant to be sorting a party?" says Felix.

Leo strolls back and takes the seat next to me, not the one on the back bench where he was sat opposite Lizzie. I'm undecided whether it was because he doesn't want to sit next to his sister anymore or because he wants to sit next to me.

He hands me my drink and places a bowl of crisps onto the table: a Friday treat from Richard. We're surely his favourite people who come here, he's always giving us little freebies.

"These, by the way," Leo says, sliding the bowl into the middle of the table, "are chips."

"No, they're not. Chips, you eat with a burger," replies Nate.

"*Noooo*. They're called fries, and you have cookies or jello after," Leo says.

"Jelly not jello. And cookies, my friend, are flat with chocolate chips, everything else is a biscuit. Don't start on the biscuits, bro," Nate says pointing a jokey finger.

"Don't you call aubergine, eggplant? Why? I mean it's never seen egg in its life?" I ask Leo, unable to resist the *you say we say* debate.

"I hate eggplant," Leo replies.

"Aubergine," Nate corrects.

Leo rambles on about his hatred of eggplant.

"My Aunt Violet back home broils it – grill I think you say here – it's gross."

"Broil? Broil?!" Nate yells, leaning forward across the table in disbelief. "How is that a word? It sounds like a Victorian peasant soup. Stop it. I'm never going out to eat with you. Fuck knows what we'll end up with." Nates swipes his hand back and forth in the air and we all heave over the table in hysterics.

"I'll be sure to tell Mom and Dad," Leo says, cracking a smile.

"Mum," Nate corrects again.

"Don't worry," Lizzie says to Nate. "We're not allowed friends over at the moment, therefore, no chance of eating anything dodgy and *funny sounding*."

In Miami, Leo and Lizzie would still have another two years of high school, but here in the UK they find themselves dumped at the critical high school end point with all the exams. Understandably, they are both struggling with the new format. It must be impossible for them; it would be like me trying to graduate American high school in the last few months.

"Apparently extra study will help, they said. I don't even understand what grade I'm in," Leo adds.

"Year," Nate corrects again, "you're in Year 11."

"What grade is that?" Leo returns.

"Fuck knows," Nate replies.

"Exactly!" says Leo.

The whole group is roaring; people's heads turn to look at what the noise is all for, and Leo's fan club look disjointed at their non-involvement.

"Haha. Oh. Haha. You're all hilarious. Has everyone forgotten about the party to organise?" Felix bellows with arms out wide over the table, but we are all more occupied with Brits versus Americans.

"What was that, Felix?" Yas asks, wiping a laughter tear away.

"I give up," Felix says, throwing his arms up. "So, Seven. What's your plan about the big RV then?"

The plan turns out to be what Felix and Nate had suggested the other day. It was eventually agreed by all to let RV come back to us if and when he wanted to. We have already said to RV in the group chat, private messages and voicemails he never returns, if he needs us, we're here. He must still have interest in staying friends with us as he's remained in the MG group chat, and he reads all the messages – he's still around at school too. We've noticed, from a distance, he walks around less sluggishly, holding his head a smidge higher than he used to. His honey brown hair is still long on top but cut shorter and groomed into a neater style.

"If he is back with 27evens he wouldn't still be here and looking better?" Lizzie suggested, convincing me in the end to stop clucking over him.

RV grew up in a dodgy part of East London and stumbled into gang life. In a moment of drunken vulnerability, he told us gang life was natural and often a logical route to take in his town. He saw it as it way to survive and have an OK life, to be able to protect his home, his mum and dad and his hope of a future.

RV and his mum and dad moved to Silversedge when the allure of the illusion, which RV thought was his ticket, turned dark: a rival gang We$t Yard Estate stabbed RV in the leg. Street politics exploded and RV's mum and dad refused to be part of it anymore. They found a way through grants, friends and an ultimatum to RV to move to West London into a teeny flat on the outskirts of Silversedge. An opportunity they took.

While others at school judge him and don't bother to look beyond his fiery guard, we admire him; the risk he's taken running from 27evens is a serious one. It haunts him every day, I know it does. He's become a solid friend, and in the exchange of friendship and support we found a young guy who gives a damn. Whether it's right or wrong for me to say, I always feel safe when we're out with RV; he's street wise, quick and far smarter than any of us, and something about that sets me at ease.

****

I wake up, eat breakfast, arrange with Mum the time for our shopping trip tomorrow and put off doing homework until after I've met Felix. I once heard the day your life changes starts off as any other ordinary day – and this was an ordinary morning.

I leave home and walk down the road towards Silversedge town centre. At the bottom by the junction, I step into the road to cross over it when a shiny black luxury car hurtles past towards the top of hill where the park and my house are; it must have jumped a red light at the junction. Its beeping horn carries the luxury car and its fancy private number plate over the hump of the hill and disappears.

"Dickhead," I yell. An ordinary day.

On the way through the centre of Silversedge, I sidestep beetling tourists who stop in the middle of pavements with their pull-along travel bags to check maps or gaze at scenery who are causing mini piles up of people, a sure thing to annoy Londoners.

I pass Wavies. Richard was busy and didn't see me trotting by as I turned up the side street to the road behind. I meet Felix outside Jamming Minds, a cute charcoal painted building with fairy lights draped around the window and door. A brown wooden sign embossed with Jamming Minds in glittery silver lettering swings on a metal arm above the window. An ordinary day.

Leaning in towards the window of Jamming Minds, I place a hand above my forehead. In the back corner a pair of high back wooden chairs with deep purple cushions sit tall either side a low wooden coffee table with what looks like photograph albums on it. Delicate batik fabrics covering wooden tables with fat legs display jewellery and a few odd books. No one else is in the shop apart from Gusti who sits quietly on one of the chairs writing in a thick journal.

"I wonder if the colour of those cushions is aubergine or eggplant," I say to Felix, still staring through the window.

"They're frickin purple. Come on," Felix says, flicking his head at the door, indicating impatiently for us to get a move on. He pushes on the brass hand panel of the door, and it opens with a bell dinging and tinkling.

"After you," Felix says, holding his arm out.

I move myself inside and instantly fixate on a wrought iron spiral staircase in the corner. Like a fireman's pole it pierces from the floor above, and through this one to the one below. More fairy lights threaded through a twisted spear banister add to the sheer delight of this odd shop, and I smile as a stone water feature gurgles next to a whistling kettle.

I feel like I'm levitating and take a quick look at my feet to make sure they are on the ground as Gusti looks up, placing his journal down on the coffee table.

"Felix, young sir," Gusti says, walking over to us to shake Felix's hand. "Good to see you again."

"This is my friend, Seven."

"Nice to meet you, officially," Gusti says, reaching out to shake my hand also. Felix looks at me with crumpled eyebrows.

"I'll explain later," I say, wafting one hand around whilst taking Gusti's hand with my other to shake it. As I do, a faint zing fizzes through my hand and up my arm, and I must look like an idiot; I can't help but stare sat my arm, then up at Gusti and then my arm again. Felix, oblivious, drifts off into pulling pictures up on his phone. I snap my hand back and try to ignore the *knowing* I can feel in my stomach that tells me Gusti knew that would happen. I can see it in his eyes, like the silence of old wisdom.

I flex my hand back and forth, rubbing my wrist with the other and move past Gusti, deflecting my confusion towards the art and jewellery. With a brush of my finger, I gently touch each piece of silver, some with gemstones, some not. Bracelets, bangles, pendants, rings, charms; it's impossible to not want to touch their beauty. The paintings and drawings for sale feel like finding new friends, which oddly does not elicit one strand of envy within me, unlike Mr H's shrine. One in particular hung above the shop's old, black, iron fireplace is a fascinating picture of tiny drawings connected by patterns that surround a prominent triquetra in the centre, and I stare at it, wondering what the artist was trying to communicate. Lost in thought, I jump at the sound of Gusti's voice.

"Have a seat if you wish, Seven, while I speak to Felix. There's more artwork and flash in the look books if it interests you," Gusti says, pointing at the albums on the coffee table.

I don't reply, just nod and sit down on the aubergine-eggplant-purple cushions, taking in this unfamiliar yet comforting energy I find myself sat in.

"Did you paint that one?' I ask, glancing back over at the painting above the fireplace, bamboo filling its grate.

"Me? No," Gusti replies, smiling to himself as Felix keeps clicking his phone's camera roll. "My artistic talents are purely in tattooing and jewellery design. The paintings I sell are on behalf of others, others more talented than me, I might add." He looks to the floor and then takes an iPad from his desk to show Felix the design he's drawn for him.

"It's sick," Felix says, his face dazzles the room with joy as he holds the iPad up to admire whatever it is Gusti has drawn, but their conversation begins to diminish into the background as I notice the journal Gusti was writing in, and I do a double take.

I don't touch the journal, rather circle my head around it with eyes feeling twice their normal size. The large leather journal is old and well used with hundreds of cream pages edged with fading silver. A page marker of thin blue ribbon with a metal symbol attached at the end dangles off the edge of the table. I hunker down and close in on the symbol.

I don't believe it.

It's a silver triangle encasing a black raven with a bright blue eye, exactly as I had drawn. My breath reaches for a sharp intake of air, and I look over to Gusti to ask about it.

"That makes me happy, Felix. I just need to see your ID and we can get going?" Gusti asks Felix.

Not the time for nervy or stupid things, Seven, Felix will strangle you. Wait. Wait a minute.

I march back over to the fireplace, Gusti and Felix still deep in conversation as it dawns on me: the signature of the artist – the style of the writing – I have it seen before. Nerves break out their flutter and my stomach flip flops.

It can't be.

I slide my phone out of my back pocket and find the picture of the postcard with the Italian message, feeling quivery as I compare the two.

"It's the same. It's the same fucking signature," I whisper out loud to myself.

"Is it? Nah it's not fake," I overhear Felix saying to Gusti, and I look over to the commotion. "It can't be, are you sure?" Felix says taking back his driving licence from Gusti's hand, flipping it around as though he's somehow mystified as to why the DVLA sent him a fake one.

"Sorry to interrupt, but who is the artist of this picture. What's the name?" I ask, pointing behind me to the fireplace.

Felix looks like he wants to kill me, but I don't care. Gusti tells me he doesn't know the artist, it's a painting he found in the room downstairs, the room he transformed into the tattoo studio part of Jamming Minds when he first took on the shop.

"Thought I'd frame it and display, it's an interesting piece," he says. Felix is glaring daggers at me as I return to sit back down wondering what the hell all this means.

"A readable version of the artists' name is on the back on

the canvas, 'Palm', if that helps," Gusti slots in, before offering apologies and a discounted jewellery piece instead of a tattoo to Felix.

I want to leave; the day is no longer ordinary.

Chapter Four
Mystical Cartel

"It's not that funny," Felix says, refusing to take his sunglasses off, even though we've been sat in Wavies for the last ten minutes.

"It is," I reply, pulling a stray piece of paper straw from my mouth. "'It can't be, are you sure?'" I mock in my best Felix voice, and his face is deadpan. "Sorry. I'll stop now. What are you doing the rest of the day?" I ask instead, stifling sniggers.

Felix, glad to move swiftly on from the tattoo disaster, is distinctly chirpier as he tells me about an audition he has on Monday evening, for a play at a theatre near central. Not the lead, but still a decent role and one, more importantly, his parents have not had a hand in swindling. I respect Felix for wanting to make it as an actor on his merit and not because of who is parents are. I assumed they would be helpful connections for him, but he hates it. He hates the way others in his circle think he has it easier than they do, which isn't true. He hates how they think it's his parents which get him roles rather than his talent, which is not true either. He's talented alright but feels he has to prove it twice as much. The last role Felix had was a lead in a Christmas play last year. The vine works quickly, and his fellow cast members made his life hell because 'Charlie should have got the lead'. It messed with him, lovable annoying Felix was short fused and depressive for a while, quite unnatural. None of the MGs or even a party could lift his spirit. I told him to quit if it was making him feel this bad, but he was determined to see it through. After the play had finished its run, he threatened to change his surname and insisted to his parents he is dealing with his career alone for now on, making it harder on himself than he needs to, in my opinion. I know Mr and Mrs Rose, and they adore their son; they know how tricky the industry can be and question what exactly is wrong with a helping hand. I'm sure Charlie and many others would have no issue accepting helping hands if the situation were reversed.

Not to mention Charlie properly sucks.

"With that, King Felix needs to go and prepare for Monday. Don't tell the others about it," he says, finishing his drink, stretching up and out of his seat.

"Maybe it was meant to be that you didn't get the tattoo today, could have jeopardised your chances," I say, standing up to join him. He knows I'm right and mutters the comment away as we do our wiggle handshake.

"You walking up home?" he asks.

"No. I'm staying a bit longer, have some thinking of my own to do. By the way, how well do you know Gusti?"

"Not that well, but enough to know he's legit despite him refusing to ink me. Why?"

"No reason," I dismiss, shaking my head like a vibrating ball.

I trust Felix's judgement of people; he's well-tuned in that way. He puts this super skill down to being brought up in an intuitive led environment, all I know is he's good at seeing through people's fluff and is usually spot on. I feel comforted by his answer as I sit back down and watch Felix high five Richard as he leaves the building. I lean my head a little to the left to carry on watching Felix through the window, and when I'm sure he's gone, I down the rest of my juice, pick up my bag and the empty glasses. I leave the empties on the counter causing a loud clatter and dash forward to rush out of the door.

"Seven, hold up," I turn around and Richard is scooting out from the counter asking his waiting customer to bear with him a minute. Wiping his hands on his navy and orange apron slated with mashed bits of fruit, vegetables and latte stains, he slides his phone out from his back pocket and flits over to me by the door, and I take my hand off the handle.

"Glad I caught you, can't stop, but I have the translation. A friend of mine is Italian."

My heart sinks to my feet, Richard glances back over to his counter and the other customers adding to the queue. It feels like an exam result I want to know but at the same time don't want to know. He passes me his phone open on the message with the translated paragraph almost pulsating out at me.

"Take a picture of it," he says, "haven't time for you to write it down." Richard signals to the customers he's on his way, and I take a picture of the text message whilst forcing myself not to read any of it.

"I don't know what it's all about, nothing to do with me," he says, holding his hands up. "But if you need anything, let me know, okay?"

He takes his phone back from my flimsy arm and he does his silly skipping walk back to his counter as I let the information land, that this message is as important as I was hoping it wouldn't be.

"Yes ladies, thank you for waiting. What can I get you?" Richard hollas, holding an arm up to me as I mouth thank you. I leave wondering whether to read the message now or when I get home, but as soon as I'm outside, I open the camera roll and stand in the middle of the pavement like an annoying tourist and read the translation:

> *I was thinking about you, I wish so much that everything was different, and I could stay with you both, but it would be too dangerous.*
>
> *My heart beats always for you.*

"What the fuck? Seriously, what the— Who is this dude?"

Returning to my original plan, pre-Richard, I walk with such determination not an inch of space is available for doubt or questions. I power past Wavies, back up the side street and straight to Jamming Minds practically bursting through the door, the bell flinging madly as I do.

"I think we need to have a conversation," I bellow to Gusti who is sat back in the same chair he was earlier, writing in the same journal with the same triquetra picture; it seems to fills the whole chimney breast wall above the fireplace – it doesn't, of course, but it feels that much in my face it's impossible for me not to be distracted by it. I don't have a plan for what to say next, and it's only this second it crosses my mind I could be wrong and how incredibly stupid I might look right now if that's the case. Still, I said it and I'm proud of myself for coming through on a suspicion. Something strange is going on, and he knows something about it – I'm sure of it.

I thought he would be startled or confused at my entrance; instead, he sits in a mist of Gusti mystique, places his journal back on the table and swoops himself across to me. His still dons the same bangle with the turquoise stone he had on when I saw him on the bus, and it twinkles under the blare of the shop's spotlights as he extends his arm to shake my hand.

"I've been expecting you, for some time actually. Wondered how Vozareia would have us meet," Gusti says.

The situation has me feeling oddly content, and I reach out earnestly to accept his gesture, then I remember the handshake from earlier and snatch my hand back, and the momentary foreign bliss diverges and is lost to a distant inaccessible space.

"What do you mean you've been expecting me? I don't want a tattoo, although they are excellent."

Shut up, Seven – don't compliment the guy at a time like this.

The cogs in my mind take over and churn rapidly as I try to figure this guy out: is he legit? A magician wanting a gig, or the local looney?

Oh god, oh god! What do I do? what do I say?

"Vozareia?" I exclaim. "What are you on? Are you causing all this paranormal stuff? The-the-the ravens, drawing symbols, voices, turning the tele up, I mean… how?!" I pull my phone out of my pocket, holding a locked screen up to him. "And this Italian message," I say, pointing frantically at a dark screen, "it's by the same guy who painted that." I stab my hand behind him towards the fireplace. "Palm! What's that about?" I'm yelling at the man now and throwing my arm around. "And why is your handshake zingy?" I can hear my heart pounding in my ears, and I only stop because I've run out of puff and, frankly, words too.

Gusti only smiles at my incredulous self and nods, seemingly unphased by my questions, before he begins sympathising about how unusual, if not far out, it all must seem. How he at first, many years ago, thought the same but promises he can explain. I delight for a moment that I was right; he does know something; and it feels empowering I was so without evidence or adult conformation. *I was right.* He returns to the coffee table and picks up his journal – though, I'm starting to question if it's a journal at all.

Oh wow, what if it's Grimoire? That means he's a—

"Please, sit," he asks, offering me one of the tall chairs and a glass of water, and although he appears all wise, oracle like and friendly, with glossy black hair and perfect skin, I decline and defiantly stay where I am. I keep the distance between us as I daringly ask him if he is a witch, or a warlock, which I think is the correct term for a male witch, but he assures me he's neither.

"I'm what is known as a Zeffo," he says, with such joy it pops my mood.

"A Zeffo?"

"Zeffos are 'Mystical Gangsters', chosen and appointed by Vozareia." He circles his hand around between himself and me, "we are humans with added magic. Skilful masters of energy… as outlined in the Book of Lights," he says tapping his journal with two fingers. "The Zeffo's abilities are powerful and different for each of us." Gusti pauses giving me chance to catch up with what sounds like genuine hocus pocus. "Although as a Dex, I have most of the skills and we—"

"We?" I say, "you keep saying we?"

"Yes. I know it's unexpected and confusing now, but you, Seven, are a Zeffo."

I refuse to remain in the building with him, I've no idea what he is babbling about, and I inform Gusti, who's decorum is impeccable, that I will listen to what he has to say, but out in the street where plenty of people can witness it. Of course he obliges without question, and he stands, gesturing politely to the door. I think of RV on my way out; if ever there were a time I wanted RV to show up or text me, it's now.

Standing on the cobbled street in front of Jamming Minds' window, I wait for Gusti; he excused himself to retrieve something he needs to show me, giving my mind a minute to slow down. My thoughts slow enough to allow intrigue to creep in, and I feel the burn of need, to know more. I can't deny all the recent strange happenings or his zingy arm, and I decide to hear him out. Tourists pass me by like it's a totally normal day, they 'ooo' and 'aaa' at the quaint street and the dinky row of houses next to Jamming Minds with their stamp sized gardens and tiny white fences. Locals don't notice anymore as they rush down the street, which has by default become a shortcut to the tube station.

"It's closed for half an hour," I say as two women, all hyper over the jewellery in the window, approach the door. Thankfully they listen and walk off when the brass bells tinkles behind me. Gusti appears a second later holding his journal, I can't recall what he called it, and a second identical journal with the same blue-ribbon page marker and the raven symbol dangling from the end. He hands me the second one and I gently take it from him as if it is a new-born baby. I'm taken in by the weightiness of both its pages and mystery, and it stuns me into a befuddled silence.

"The Book of Lights. For you," he says.

I run my hand over the dark leather cover, the words 'Book of Lights' are stamped in the same glittery silver lettering as the Jamming Minds sign above my head.

"Every Zeffo has one. It is both the identity and mirror of you," Gusti says.

I pick up the corner to turn the cover, but Gusti places his hand on mine, the familiar zing up my arm reminding me this all has to be real.

"Later. This isn't the time or place," he says. For the first time today, I agree with him.

People keep meandering over to the window and our conversation becomes fragmented in hurried spurts. Gusti continues the best he can in his enchantingly wise manner, but his words are zooming over my head as I try to catch them. The hub bub of the street continues to distract me as I sneak glances at people walking by in case they suspect we are having a weird conversation, but nobody notices. They just keep on a-walking and a-talking.

I grasp onto one of his rushed explanations about Vozareia. Vozareia, apparently, is the Originating Spiritus of the World and rules with good magic, love and peace. *It* is both immortal and invisible and is carried upon the winds and in the voice of the people. Except most humans don't know because they are unknowingly ruled by the Boras. Vozareia, for reasons I yet don't understand, gives those *It* chooses to be Zeffos supernatural and magical powers, and communicates symbolically, mystically and through paranormal incidences only Zeffos can decode.

"Why? What's the purpose of Vozareia?" I ask.

"More life for all. The true nature and dreams of every human are both the foundation and the future of the world," he replies, "there's more about it from the Empress of Vozareia in her message in the Book of Lights," he adds.

I have a zillion questions, and as Saturday afternoon would have it, we are interrupted by a man and his wife. The man keen to tell Gusti about a tattoo from his first marriage he wants covering up with a map and a compass. Five minutes later the man is booked in, and he and his new wife smile touchingly at each other as they totter off down the cobbles. Gusti checks no one else is in eavesdropping distance and rolls a falling shirt sleeve back up, revealing the beginning or end of a tattoo that must cover the top of his arm. I want to ask what it is, but I don't think it's the right time.

"The problem is, two-hundred years ago the Boras cast a deep and wicked curse on all our ancestors," he says, drawing me in with tales of ancient times. "The Boras were a sinister group of people who wanted to rule earth and all its inhabitants, but they could not overpower Vozareia and lost their battle. Their numbers dwindled, until the last one standing made a dark wish for their work to continue after their deaths. In order for them to advance, without form, they cursed all the people who lived at that time – our ancestors."

"A curse? What curse?" I interrupt.

"A curse of darkness, bad luck and adversity encrypted into their minds and passed on to each mind of each generation. The same situations repeat over and over. People believe their minds are broken by nature, their circumstances due to chance, and it keeps them unknowingly bound to the Boras. The Empress of Vozareia details this more as well in her inspiring message," he says, lovingly glancing at the Book of Lights. "The Empress is a wonderful, erm, wome –"

"The letter," I reply in more of a penny dropping whisper than voice. "I wrote a letter." I can't add anymore as the enormity of this situation is whooshing through me at speed.

"You were chosen as a Zeffo by Vozareia some time ago, but your letter caused the initiation. Vozareia has been getting your attention of late, no? And well, here we are. The answer to your request for help," Gusti says with ta-da arms.

This is so not what I meant, and I am deeply regretting writing the letter at all. It's not what I thought would happen and it's making me dizzy and nauseous.

"And these Zeffos, what do they do?" I ask, handing the Book of Lights back to him.

"Break the curse of the Boras," he says like it's obvious. "Humans blindly accept their cursed minds thinking they have been dealt a bad hand in life. This enables the Boras to syphon the power of an individuals' true prosperous life and use it to grow in influence and power. They are now a large malevolent underworld of great concern, Seven. They want to rule over Vozareia, and we need to stop them."

Holy. Fuck.

A young woman in an oversized top hanging off one shoulder rocks up, her jeans are overly ripped, and I think she may as well just wear shorts. The woman smiles at Gusti but scans me head to toe, and I decide she doesn't like me.

"Can I help?" Gusti asks her, as she reaches for the door.

"I'm booked in at four. I know I'm early, but can I wait?" she asks.

The woman wanders in and takes a seat but keeps fluttering around like a bug and she hovers by the window, tinkering with various jewellery pieces as me and Gusti call time out.

"Wait here," he says.

Gusti disappears with the Book of Lights back inside the shop, the shop hiding a mystical cartel, and returns a few minutes later holding a Jamming Minds paper carrier. Inside the bag is my personal book wrapped in a white, drawstring bag made of silk.

"Keep the Book of Lights in the bag when you are not using it. When you are ready, open it and read all the information it contains. Come back and see me on Monday after school; the shop is closed on Mondays so we can't be interrupted."

I nod in disbelief. I've still so many questions. I take the bag anyway whilst utterly convinced they have the wrong person for the job. Yas would be a far better choice for this carry on.

"What if I don't want to do any of this?"

"Then your life of struggle will worsen. You remain under the control of the Boras, as will your mum and all your future generations. Look back at your family history and tell me if I am wrong. You're the key to breaking it, for you and your family at least."

Brilliant. Fucking brilliant.

Chapter Five
Not Knowing

From within my wardrobe, the lure of the Book of Lights tucked in its white bag calls to me like dessert: it's tempting… but is it worth it? I keep looking at my wardrobe then flicking back to watching a reality show on TV, and I twiddle my hair a little more each time.

I feel a fierce need to open it, and I want to know what it says. I'm almost certain I will open it, how can I not? But am I ready for what it says, for whatever it contains? If I open it, like tonight, will I seal my fate at being a Zeffo by default? Huffing, I pick my phone up from the bedside table and open the MG chat.

> *Seven is typing*
>
> How do you make a decision, the right one?
>
> *Felix is typing*
>
> That's a big question for a Saturday night.
>
> *Nate is typing*
>
> I always list the pros and cons.
>
> *Yas is typing*
>
> Logical but how does it help you decide?
>
> *Nate is typing*

Can be easier to figure stuff out when you see it written in front of you.

Felix is typing

That's dead Nate. Go with the one you want.

Lizzie is typing

But what if that is the wrong one?

Felix is typing

Why would it be wrong, for who?

Seven is typing

But what if you don't know what you want Felix?

Felix is typing

Bullshit, you always know. Not knowing is an excuse because you daren't make the choice you want.

Leo is typing

Go with the belly.

Leo is typing

And… what Felix said.

Yas is typing

It's not always that simple. You two are harsh, with an angry face emoji.

Felix is typing

No. We just don't dance around the obvious Yas.

RV

Message status – Seen.

No reply.

The chat escalates into a fracas of voice notes about how maybe it's easier for males to make clearer decisions than females, at which point Yas nearly exploded. I rang her to give her the opportunity to verbalise her fury, as rows of angry face emojis at the boys' lack of understanding and thought only seemed to wind her up more.

"Maybe guys are more confident," I say down the phone, admiring my newly painted toes.

"Confident at the expense of everyone else. They're dinosaurs: outdated and insensitive."

I laugh at her excessive put down of Felix and Leo, although some dinosaurs do still roam. Look at my dad who, though dead, still stomps around my mind squashing any hope of self-worth, and if I admit it – at the risk of being morally skewed – my mother inflicts her own stomping on my soul too. Her fears and behaviours from those earlier years are undeniably justified and understandable, yet I'm bitter. Bitter she inflicted her fears onto me too, making me scared not to disrupt life. She, rather than dad, is probably the reason I can't make any decisions or trust myself, all she did was teach me I'm not worth making a stand for, and for a mother to do that hurts far more than any punch dad threw my way – but I digress. I sense a different, deeper point within Yas' outburst on the chat.

"I take it the conversation about becoming a stylist to the stars instead of a doctor marrying a good Muslim boy bared its teeth again."

"I hate my family," she says.

I console my sobbing friend, who has little to no chance of becoming a fashion stylist. Her family's desires for her are rooted in good intentions and power which I'm not sure Yas can overrule. I feel for her, and my heart cracks at the sound of her tears. At least I don't have to prove myself to three brothers and two parents, just one lawyer mother who happens to be triggered by discussions over art with an honesty I am beginning to question.

I bet RV would know how to make a decision. He chose to flee his gang for fuck's sake. I mean he's literally hiding from death, yet he did it. Suddenly my career and personal issues feel stupidly small.

Exhausted by the whirlwind of asking a simple question I drop my phone onto my bed, tie my hair back and open the wardrobe door.

Leo's answer plays over in my mind: 'go with the belly', the only reply that made me sit up straighter.

Go with the belly.

I think he means how it feels, not what my head thinks.

"This is ridiculous," I call out, yanking the bag out from behind a pile of clothes I was supposed to have hung up but stuffed in the bottom of the wardrobe instead.

I sit cross legged on the bed with the bag in front of me, its drawstring pulled tight. Like the Book of Light's page marker, the drawstring is made of blue ribbon with a symbol attached at the end. I flip the metal symbol repeatedly in my hand taking longer each time to examine it. The silver triangle, I discover, has the letter V engraved on its top point, the letter E on its left point and the letter H on its right point. The triangle encases a black, brushed metal raven with its blue eye represented by a stone, similarly to the one on Gusti's bangle. It's exquisite and captivating, and I take the Book of Lights out of the bag, and along with it falls a handwritten envelope addressed to 'Seven', underlined with a swishy line.

I open it with one ripping swipe of my finger and unfold

the cream paper bearing sea-blue inked writing.

Seven,

Sorry our first meeting was a little frenzied; they usually happen at inopportune times so it was no surprise to me, although I know it was to you. I hope your disbelief is subsiding. It must be if you are reading this.

The Book of Lights contains all the secret information of Zeffos; the mystical powers gifted to you, a message from the Empress of Vozareia, details about our Zeffo Academy, our laws, the Zeffo Ode, history of our talisman and space for you to document your journey against the Boras.

I'll see you on Monday to choose your talisman and complete the accession to officially become a Zeffo and commence your quest against the Boras. In the meantime, my mobile number is on the back if you need anything.

Dex Gusti

He's speaking like my agreement is a done deal. I'm struggling to decide whether to open a dusty old book, never mind officially becoming a Zeffo and all it entails… are he and Vozareia aware I have final exams coming up? It's not exactly the ideal time to go galivanting on mystical missions. Placing that aside, the more I think about all this, the more enticing and cool it is becoming. I have Zeffo powers! I wonder if I can move things, shoot fire from my fingers or jump super high? That would be awesome, and flying too… *God, I hope I've got flying skills.*

I decide on a sensible road test first, to prove to myself the words of Dex Gusti are true. Before I open the Book of Lights I figure, from what I know so far, Vozareia led me to find the Italian message through to its sender – Palm. As I join the dots backwards, I can see how I decoded this paranormal incident of the box falling off the shelf. All I need to do is ask Mum if she knows someone called Palm. If she does, and if Palm or something to do with him is significant to me in some way, then yep, call me a Zeffo.

Chapter Six
A Road Test

Over and over, I practise asking Mum the question in my head, followed by pre-emptively guessing her excuses and answers in an attempt to have any response I might need to hand. I'm hungry to ask and find out this minute when Mum shouts upstairs, informing me we are leaving for the shopping mall at 10am and to hurry up. I sneak a final glance at the bag now safely returned to its place behind the clothes pile in the wardrobe and close my bedroom door.

Midway down the stairs I can hear Mum talking to someone on the phone, and I hover, listening with such hard concentration my toes curl into the fluffy carpet.

"It's no problem, Rio, but I've got to go. Seven will be down any second, and I shouldn't be talking to you from home. I'll see you then. Bye."

Mum ends the call. I suck in air, my eyes feeling they are open an inch wider than physically possible and fly into the kitchen like a crazed woman.

"Were you talking to RV, is he in trouble?" I ask.

"Morning to you too. You know I can't disclose anything, even to you," Mum replies.

"So, it was RV, and about work?"

"*Severrrn.*" She hands me a mug of tea.

"How can you not tell me anything? You know I'm concerned about him. I, we, have been cut out of his life like a… like a doctor slices off warts," I jabber while chasing her around the kitchen.

"There is no need for such dramatics," she replies, "drink your tea, we're leaving shortly. Do you know what you want to get today?"

"How can you think about shopping? I can't believe you won't even tell me if he is okay. He must be in trouble if you're involved."

"Look," she states, bored with my questioning. "I know you care about him and if it helps – RV is fine. There is no need to fret." She kisses me on the head and rattles about in her handbag for the car key.

"Let's go," she says, bright with happiness in anticipation of our escapade, and trots off out of the front door to the car. She leaves the door ajar, and I growl in my throat at her resistance. I slide my mug on the island and close the door behind me as I follow.

We drive down Silversedge Hill and through the town in silence, except for the radio playing old hits, and I twiddle my hair as we drive out of Silversedge towards central. We cruise by a gallery on the end of the long road before it joins the packed dual carriageway, the type of gallery where men stroke their manly beards and women adjust their hair and handbags deciding if the piece is for them. I always spot galleries, and each time I see one I hope with all my might that my drawings, one day, will be exhibited in one, not that the beard and handbag brigade would pay for my type of art. Then again, I was told yesterday I'm a Zeffo, able to banish curses with mystical powers, which makes me pretty much open to any possibility now.

I can hear the pendulum of time swinging between continued silence and bubbles of excitement Mum keeps throwing out about our day together; shopping and lunch out is a luxury we don't get to do a lot, so I appreciate asking Mum *the question* whilst driving amongst London madness as we join queues for the shopping mall might not be the best time, but it just sort of fell out.

"Mum, can I ask you something?"

"Absolutely."

My stomach feels like a kaleidoscope being turned at speed, and I lean my elbow on the car door to hold the side of my head, looking straight ahead.

"Do you know someone called Palm?"

The car jolts to a stop. It was all Mum could do to stop us running into the car in front as she whips her head around to me, her jaw somewhere back towards Silversedge.

"What? Where did you hear that name? Sorry, are you okay? That jerk just braked suddenly." She's scratching her face, then her neck and checking herself in the rear-view mirror. "I meet lots of people in my world, it's possible. I'll have a think whilst we get parked up," she says. Mum fiddles with car buttons and finally rolls her window down a smidge and wheels the Beamer around the corner, up the ramp and into the multi-storey car park. She's relentlessly chuntering about nonsense, anything, to prevent the conversation returning to my question, which answers the question in itself: she does know this Palm dude.

"Where shall we go for lunch, Reds? What do you say, we haven't been for ages?" Mum asks as we walk spritely to the lift. It deposits us onto the main floor of shops in the enormous mall filled with hundreds of shoppers.

"Cool," I reply eventually, as my question disappears into the crowds.

***

The atmosphere is past weird and has morphed into an unknown place. It's an atmosphere I'm milking, however, as Mum is happily buying anything I clap my eyes on; two new pairs of jeans, two tops and a pair of sandals.

"Thank you for all these. I love them," I say to Mum.

"It's a pleasure, darling. You deserve it, and because I love you THIS much," she says grinning and holding her arms out as wide as she can, with shopping bags dangling from both wrists.

"Table for two?" The waiter asks, stood welcomingly in a blue shirt and cream apron hanging from his waist to his ankles. We stand at the entrance to Reds, a restaurant on the top floor of the mall, where the waiter strains his neck around the lunch time clatter to locate a free table and, with a speedy flick, he retrieves two sets of menus out of the wooden box bolted on the wall. 'Dominique' signals with a dutiful wave to follow him to a side booth halfway down the restaurant.

"Is this okay, madam?" he says, placing the menus squarely on the smooth navy tablecloth.

"Perfect," Mum replies.

Dominique flitters off to find water, and my phone is pinging and beeping with messages; one from Felix asking if it will be cold on Monday after school, five from Yas about everything, and a surprise one from Lizzie asking if I can meet her tomorrow. Lizzie never asks to meet up, something is wrong, and so naturally I default to – *I've* done something wrong. I start typing quickly under the table.

> *Message to Yas*
>
> Can't wait to hear! I'll call later. Out with Mum xx
>
> *Message to Felix*
>
> I'm not even answering that x
>
> *Message to Lizzie*
>
> Hey, I d

"Seven, put it away. No phones at the table," Mum instructs.

Damn it. I cancel the message to Lizzie and shove it back in my pocket.

Mum is moving cutlery and glasses around on our table to make room for plates the size of the moon swiftly delivered to us on the arms of a buff waiter.

"So," I say, winding pasta ribbons around my fork, "I take it you do know someone called Palm."

The colour drains from her face like the central heating plummeted, and she plays with her food in a sad and slow motion which makes me feel sad myself, and then guilty that I've selfishly focused on my feelings without a thought about what it may mean to her. She barely lifts her eyes up from her plate of food.

"How have you heard the name?" she asks.

"It's funny you mention that…" I reply, and in an attempt to ease the answer in, I go for a vague explanation. "It's a long story. More of a puzzle which has led me to asking you the question." Mum fixes her stern eyes on me, seemingly unaccepting of my vague attempt to elaborate, and I plea silently by leaning forward with my arms stretched out across the table to her.

"You're not in any trouble. It's important for me to know how you found out about Palm."

"Do you believe in omens... signs?" I say, jutting my hand and index finger up and down in the air. Mum's glacier eyes stare down into my dark ones, dismissing my jumping hand indicating higher powers. We're so opposite at times.

"I like to think there are certain coincidences," Mum replies in a non-committal fashion.

I'm about to vomit everything out. All the coded messages, Gusti, the Book of Lights, curses and Zeffos, I'm bursting to talk to someone about it, but...

"It was a total accident," I blurt out, "I wasn't snooping, I promise. One of your boxes fell off the shelf when I was searching for a scarf, and a postcard landed by the mirror with a message written in Italian." I swear her heart leapt out of her chest and across the table, but I keep on trucking. "I translated it," Mum remains silent, giving nothing away, and I'm unsure if this is good or bad. Not once I have seen my mum this uncomfortable or short of an answer.

"A few days later, I was talking to the guy from Jamming Minds," I continue. "He has a painting there; it's signed by Palm. I recognised the signature, Mum. It matched that on the postcard."

"Wow, and I reckon I'M the lawyer," she half laughs while looking at her full plate with despondency. "Yes. I knew a man called Palm; he sadly died years ago. He was an incredible man, and I miss him a lot." She raises her head and peers off into the distance, doing that weird biting on the inside of her cheek thing which she does when she's trying not to cry, or yawn – apparently it works for that too. "I'm sorry Seven, you've completely knocked me off my perch. In fact, I still find it surreal we are having this conversation." She waves her hand up and down in front of her eyes, as if asking the pain to cease and places her napkin back on the table. "There is more I need to say, more we need to talk about, not here though. Let's wait until we get home."

"How did he know about me, the postcard was dated before I was born?" I ask.

"I'll explain at home," she replies, pushing her full plate aside, the sparkle of the day's expedition dulled, and I sense the Palm story is a dormant volcano ready to erupt.

***

Sunday afternoon in my sitting room with Mum and a volcano – my days are getting more glamorous by the second.

"I wasn't expecting to have this conversation, not today anyway." Mum casts her eyes downwards at the sofa before meeting my gaze and slowing her voice as she takes my hand, imploring me to listen to her without interruption or judgement. My mind begins jumping around for explanations, but for once I tell it shut up and listen to what she has to say.

"Go ahead. It's fine, Mum. Really."

"Palm was an artist. It wasn't what he was known for, he would have been ecstatic to know one of his paintings is on show. Although how it is there at the shop is mysterious." She pauses for a second, rubbing the top of my hand. "Palm's real name is Vincenzo Petralia. Palm was a nickname. He was Sicilian, Italian."

"Yes, I know where Sicily is, Mum."

She stops talking for few seconds and I can't take me eyes off her. I'm taken aback by how quickly her face has become sucked in and worn looking.

"I met Vincenzo in London twenty-odd years ago. I was rushing, on a break from court, and charged into a bistro for lunch – and there he was, sitting on one of their high back wicker chairs with huge puffy floral cushions, sipping coffee and smoking a cigarette, watching the hustle of London's streets. He was unaware I had dissolved completely the moment I saw him. Or so I thought."

I smile at her but keep silent, marinating in the warmth of how two people meet, how she reminisces with such grace and how love must exist. I always love to hear stories of how lovers meet.

"It was like we had both been on the opposite ends of a convoluted path, connected with an invisible rope. Inch by inch we had pulled ourselves to one another, finally reaching the middle and meeting on that day on September 7th."

"We became inseparable, jetting back and forth between here, Sicily and Italy. We made it work. He was a gentleman of strong force, yet easy to be with. Passionate, adventurous, witty and talented. So romantic too – what Italian man isn't?"

"Why did you two split up then? It sounds like a love story written by the Holy Ghost?"

"We were together for years, had plans to marry. He was

a well-respected man and well known. Not so much for his talent or heart, but because, he was…"

I lurch forward, holding my hand out asking her to carry on. To spit it out.

"…because he was in the Mafia."

"Mafia? Bloody hell, Mum. You bad ass!"

"Thank you," she says with a touch of female prowess. "Not really. It became complicated as he became a target. Palm thought about leaving the Mafia, Italy, the lot. He adored me and the life we had, but leaving the Mafia isn't something you can hand your notice into, and legal advice isn't really the ticket to save the day in that world, nor is it welcome.

"Threats were being made and he was increasingly concerned; tense over my safety, over safety for you; and as hairy moments escalated, so was I. There is little mercy shown, you know."

"To keep you and me safe, you split up?" My rose-tinted glasses are murkier. Love finds love, right? I always wanted to believe that, but now I'm saddened at my view of destiny that the right love trumps all. How could Palm and Mum be wrong?

Just a minute, why would he worry about my safety, I wasn't even born?

"Then I met Simon, your dad. He seemed a safer option, and so I settled for him thinking it was the best thing to do at the time. I let Palm go, trading love and purpose for security… just like my mother did."

High pitched ringing screeches in through my left ear and leaves just as quickly. Although brief, I twitch my head to the right in reaction as it caught me off guard. Gusti's words are literally ringing true.

"We kept in touch periodically, not that Simon knew," Mum continues, thankfully missing my random twitching head. "Then a few years ago, I received word Palm had been killed in a shoot-out gone wrong. It felt like the bullet had hit me too, and there's been a gaping hole there ever since," Mum sighs, blowing her lungs across the room and shaking her head with dismay. "Trust Palm to appear again from oblivion. I don't know what to do with it all."

She tries doing the biting cheek thing again, but it fails. Tears roll from the mountains of love and pain behind her eyes, and I hug her. It's as though our roles have reversed, and she is the lost child. I'm stumped for something to say, I feel gutted for her.

"I'm so sorry, Mum," I say, trying to be supportive. I know what Mum and Palm had is the kind of love I want, and I at least know it can exist, but I left this bit out as I didn't think she would find it helpful or healing. Mum nods and rips a tissue out of the box on the coffee table, and pulls her emotions back in.

"There is something else you need to know," she adds.

I'm all in.

"Sure, but can I ask something first? You said he was concerned over your safety and *mine.* The postcard mentioned me, even though it was dated before I was born. How did he know about me when you were with Dad and why would he be concerned about me; I was nothing to do with it?" I enquire.

She places a hand over her eyes, and I honestly do not

know what to do or say, so I sit and dither. Her sad tears place me on the verge of crying myself. My throat aches holding it back, and I keep gulping to try and relieve the aching lump. After a minute or two, she glances up and grabs my hand.

"This is where I need your understanding, Seven. Please promise me that. You are my entire world. Know I only ever did what I have out of love and what I thought was right for both of us."

I'm full-on crying with her, nodding my promise and squeezing her hand tighter than she is mine. Both of us adding to a mess over something I don't even know about. It's like the worst goodbye in the world. She continues…

"Simon is not your dad. Vincenzo – Palm – is your real dad."

Chapter Seven
Irony

I swear only a couple hours have passed when I hear the fun tune that is my alarm play rowdily on my phone. With eyes barely open, I reach across to my bedside table and tap around the phone screen to find the exact spot so I can silence the thing. I also discover a new message from Felix, sent three hours ago. I doubt he is up for a run along with the fitness freaks who jog around Silversedge at stupid hours. He can't be ill, he would have woken his mum up, which leaves the obvious scenario. I click the message with a strong tap of my finger.

> Went out tonight. Bit of a blur. Cover for me at
> school. X

I want to kill him; I don't have the patience for this after yesterday's grenade and text him back.

> No. I said last time I wouldn't cover for you again.
> What about your audition? Get your shit together.

Message sent.

I slide my phone back onto the bedside table and stare down at the floor and the Book of Lights sat back in its bag. When I opened it last night to read it, I was too tired to walk the short distance to the wardrobe to return it to its hidey place, and so I left it on the floor next to my bed. I hear the floorboards creak on the landing and realise Mum is heading to my bedroom, and I quickly shove the Book of Lights under my duvet in the nick of time.

Mum bobs her head into my bedroom briefly before she leaves for work to see if I am still okay and rattles on about how we can talk more tonight if I want to. I told her I'm fine and glad I know. I tell myself the betrayal eating my stomach is me being oversensitive.

I am glad I know, but I would rather have known years ago instead of living a lie. Instead of losing out – twice – at the chance of happy families, and the chance of finding my lost piece of self. If Mum had told me before Palm was killed, I would have said to her, 'Go for it. Go get him'. I would have supported love; I would have backed her and him all the way. Life could have been entirely different. Happy! Instead, I'm frustrated at her for choosing a scumbag and choosing misery in her career, never recognised by her old law firm for her talents and passion for justice. The curse of the Boras succeeded, a curse I cannot let myself fall victim to as well.

***

"Felix Rose?" our form tutor asks as he peers around the classroom with his register book hoping to see Felix jump out and announce his presence. I'm also hoping Felix will throw the door open and appear at the last minute.

"Anyone seen Felix Rose?" Mr Tammus inquires further. A weighty blanket of silence lies above everyone in the class, and I squirm in my seat.

This is the last time, Rose.

"He's at the dentist, sir," I reply, poker faced. I sense Yas glaring over at me with a baffled look. She knows I'm lying, and I'm pretty sure the entire class and sir knows I'm lying as well.

"Really, Seven?" He begins to sink his *I call bullshit* hooks into me. "Wasn't he at the dentist not too long ago? You seem to know Mr Rose's whereabouts extremely well."

"He mentioned it at the weekend. A filling, sir." My deadpan face and response don't falter, and I almost believe in the lie myself…

"Send him to me when he comes in."

"Oh, I will, sir. I will," I reply, wholly grateful the bell sounds.

Shooting out of the form room, I beetle down the corridor towards the career advisor's office for my career meeting with a man called Mr Stone, who wears overly tight, camel-coloured sweaters and believes good exam grades are the answer to everything.

I'm dreading it.

"Not so fast, girly. Has Felix asked you to cover for him again?" Yas asks, running to catch up with me.

"Yes, but I'm not doing it anymore," I reply. I carry on walking, but Yas stops me mid-stride with a hand to my shoulder.

"You don't want to get dragged into his drama too," she says.

The teachers low key dig Felix but dislike his, some might say, lackadaisical attitude; what teacher doesn't get annoyed with students who refuse to comply with their demands? Felix will say he is focused on a life that's right for him. And his teenage cunning does make them laugh, on occasion.

"You shouldn't keep doing it, babe. I know you are good friends and all—"

"Okay, Yas. I get it," I say, raising my eyes and voice a notch. Yas tilts backwards with a slight touch of her hand to her chest and crumples her eyebrows, and I can feel my chest grow heavy as though someone has sat on it. "I'm sorry. Didn't mean to be gnarly. I've got a lot on at the moment."

The sun is yet to burn its way through the arched windows into the corridor, and we walk the rest of the dimly lit, grey feeling passageway with linked arms and comfortable silence. We reach the junction leading to more corridors and the main stairs, and we go our separate ways.

"I'll call you after school," Yas shouts back, speeding up to make her class in time. I hold my hand up to pause the situation, but she's vanished down the main stairs and into the science block.

I can't speak later, Yas.

Fifteen minutes later, I'm tapping my fingers on the plastic chair outside Mr Stone's office and curling my hair around my index finger. I let out an impatient sigh which changes into a sharp intake of breath; the door opens with force as RV walks out of the office. I haven't seen RV close up in a while, and he's definitely different; he's smiling, and his face is more voluminous than bony white. I jump up like a cat and something beautiful sat in his hazel eyes vanishes when he sees me, and my heart plummets.

"RV. Hey."

"Hey, Seven. What's up?"

"What's up? We're all wondering where you've been, that's what's up."

"I know. Life has been different lately, it's complicated," he says.

I drop my intensity, quieting my voice in the eerily silent corridor, except for impatient noises of coughs and shuffling papers leaking out of Mr Stone's office.

"I know you've been speaking with my mum. Don't block us out, we're your friends. I'M your friend." I search his eyes to try and find the sereneness that was there seconds earlier, but I can't.

"Your mum shouldn't have said anything."

"She didn't. I overheard her on the phone with you."

"It's not what you think, I've—"

"Seven Madison, your turn," Mr Stone says, stood in the doorway. Adults really know how to mess stuff up at critical moments. We share a closing look, and RV lifts his arm as though looking to touch mine before retracting it at the last second.

"Good luck in there." He nods towards the room as Mr Stone turns and goes back inside, and I watch RV walk away as he rounds the corridor and disappears once more.

***

"Where's your sidekick then?" Nate asks, sliding his lunch tray onto the table and banging the chair legs against the floor to knock chips off the seat, ever so kindly left from its previous guest. "Scruffy gits," he adds.

He drops his bag onto the floor and sits in the now free from food seat. I look up at him feeling less than perky and wait to swallow the mouth of food I'm chewing before answering.

"If you mean Yasmina, she's talking to the career advisor. If you mean Felix, he's in detention for chewing gum when he eventually rocked up this morning."

"I meant the first. Unlucky for Felix," he says, poking around his food, scraping the batter off his fish. "The food is rank here. It's a good school, why is the food so bad?"

"I don't know, Nate. I'll ask it." A piece of greasy fish escapes my fork and smacks onto my plate. For the first time since last year, we both smile and share a giggle at the falling fish.

"How's things with you then? Good?" Nate asks, pulling a face at the food he's eating as though it's toxic.

We pass chit chat back and forth across our touching lunch trays, mainly about basketball of course. How much both Nate's school basketball team and his London team take up his time. How they won the last game, which means his team made the championship final and am I coming to watch it. I can hardly say no, although it's tempting.

"I'm pleased for you. You've worked hard for it," I say.

I move my plate and cutlery to fill the gap of quiet between us despite the noise of the canteen clattering in the background. Nate unexpectedly turns the conversation from basketball into our breakup, commenting how he'd heard Yas and sixth former Danny had finished following Danny's two timing with another sixth former. Nate smiles to himself, which turns into strong laughter whilst shaking his head. He shovels a fork full of food into his mouth before meeting my fixed glare at him.

"What?" he replies with his mouth half full. He swigs from

his can of pop to wash it away. "You gotta admit, now you've both been served karma. Forgive me while I revel in that for a minute."

"I made a mistake," I say, "I apologised and tried to explain to you a thousand times. Not that it matters."

I'm half disgusted with my begging self until I realise, somehow in this moment, this thing between us that I have been clutching and holding onto for months diffuses to a different place or into something else, and I'm done. I give it up. I give up, finally, trying to get Nate to understand and come back to me, because he never will. I feel free in an instant and clap my hands onto my tray, pick it up and begin standing ready to leave.

"Hang on a minute," Nate reaches forward, and I debate over whether to leave the table or not. "Yas starts dating a fancy Year 12 and thinks it would be neat if you date his best friend; the guy with a surname for a first name."

"Carter," I interrupt, releasing my tray and staying put.

"*Whatev*. That way you can all hang out together and be cool and shit. You drop me and then surname boy immediately dumps you because – surprise – he's a dick. Then you want me back? It's messed up," he says, swigging his can again.

"Maybe it is, but I never cheated on you."

"Oh, that's okay then," he says, shovelling more food at the rate of knots down his neck. He softens his tone and leans in.

"We could have been good together," he continues. "Do you know how hurt I was when you did that? You didn't even tell me the truth. You said you wanted to break up to have more time for study. Gah." He pushes his can down the table and it stops just shy of falling off the edge.

I don't know what to say. Everything he is heaving out is completely true. I am a witch, the worst wickedest witch of the west. I thought Nate wasn't all that bothered about me when we were together. He has his pick of girls for sure, and I'd convinced myself I wasn't that special person to Nate. The special person I so badly want to be with. My dumb brain told me I was just another high school girl to him, and how wrong it seems I got it. Goddamn it, my dream was literally in my hand, and I didn't believe it.

"The biggest pisser of all, Seven, is you didn't do that because it was how you felt. You did it because Miss Queen of Arabia talked you into it. I was certain about you; it was clear you weren't about me." He looks away from me and out of the window, and I want to cry. The wound filling the space between us is stinging. The irony of it makes me dislike myself and detest – hate – the Boras Curse infecting my mind. I'm so mad I could punch a wall.

I pick up a white, paper napkin from the centre of the table and gently wave it in the raw air, signalling my surrender to the mess. Nate nods, hanging his head. We'll never return to the golden couple we were before despite flickers still twinkling, but it's time to halt the struggle. It's time to let our embers die of natural causes.

Suddenly a hand slaps down on the table, and Nate and I jump backwards in our chairs, startled by the noise, dragging us out from under a dying fire.

"Why do you two look deathly?" Felix is standing to the side grinning, proud of himself.

"I don't want to know what you're grinning about," I say, holding my palm up to him, "and you owe me one."

"Thought you were in DT," Nate adds.

"I was. Waste of time. Get this though Gs: I managed to get the DT teacher to smile. It's never been achieved before."

"What did you do?" Nate asks, giving Felix a fist bump.

"Without thinking, 'cos Felix only thinks about important shit, I turned up to the chewing gum DT, chewing gum."

"You didn't…" Nate and I ask in sync, laughing like we had done in better days.

Felix bows to his audience. "Apparently, I'm ironic," Felix adds.

"Ironic or moronic?" Nate adds.

"Aren't we all," I mutter out of ear shot. Today is turning into a bit of a beast and I can't wait for it to be over.

After school, I call in at home and collect the white bag from my wardrobe before I walk down into Silversedge Town and straight to the cobbled side street. The Jamming Minds sign is glittering even brighter as it swings in the breeze of a spring afternoon. The shop is in darkness, and I half hope Gusti isn't there, but when I try the door, it opens with its welcoming tinkle.

"Gusti," I yell out. "Are you here?" It's as quiet as the moon; there's no water trickling from the stone feature or whistling kettle in the background as I look around the empty room.

I see the tips of his shiny, burgundy brogues above me on the spiral staircase, then the soles and then all of him. He stops and holds onto the banister. I don't wait for him to answer me.

"I didn't get flying, or high jumping, which is massively unfair. You need to have a word about that." I beam.

He mirrors my grin and trots down the remaining steps to the ground level so smoothly it almost looked like he floated.

"Those are not Zeffo powers. We're not vampires… though they would be cool bonus powers," he says.

We shake hands, and the zing is as immediate as it was before. It's not painful like a bee sting, more like a gentle buzzy sensation, and it feels like gold, somehow.

"That's how you know you've met another Zeffo," Gusti remarks, sweeping off to lock the door.

"There's more of us? Even in Silversedge?" I ask.

"Yes. To both. And no, I can't tell you who they are. They show up as and when you need them, but our work is primarily solo and done in secret," he replies, "for now anyway. As you likely know by now from the Empress's message, there are plans to scale our presence and work. Exciting times, Seven!"

Silversedge, I learn, is not only the place to live because of pastries and sunglasses, it's also a hub for Zeffos. Who knew?

"Can't you feel the mysterious magic in the air?" Gusti asks.

I hadn't thought about it until now. What a sheltered life I have led.

"Shall we?" he says, holding his arm up to the staircase. "First order of business is fitting you with your talisman."

Ah, the talisman. A magical piece of jewellery or tattoo charged with the force of Vozareia, connecting me to my specific set of Zeffo powers. I read the Book of Lights from start to finish last night and learning which powers I have been gifted made riveting reading and gave me a glimpse into feeling special. The symbol, the raven with a blue eye set in a triangle, is on the reverse of the talisman, although try as I might, I can't remember what the letters on the triangle mean. Nor can I commit to memory all the Zeffo meanings and laws, there's so much information in the book I'm convinced I'm going to forget something important.

"So how do I use my powers to get rid of the curse?" I ask, wanting to cut straight to the fun and bone.

"Slow down my young Zeffo. Take a seat upstairs and open your Book of Lights. Tea?"

Chapter Eight
Power-up

I step off the top of the spiral staircase. A white, gothic archway stands between me and a square room with round corners, and I stop, leaning against it, as I take in the room on front of me. An old-fashioned writing bureau and classic chair, in the same purple velvet cushioning as downstairs, sits snug in the corner against a wall covered in symbols and words drawn in turquoise and black. Gusti, I presume. The other walls are plain and snow white with two windows on the left. A large wooden table stands poised in the centre with four matching chairs, and chunky white candles flicker cosy light randomly around the room.

I decide it's safe to proceed and flinch at the unexpected return of the zing in my arm as I pass through the archway. I glance back, examining the archway's frame over my shoulder and the atmosphere surrounding me. I've entered air holding a different vibe to that of the everyday; it's a vibe of home. It floods me with a sense of accomplishment, confidence and freedom, and it feels nothing short of grand. I've wished for years to be this way. Right this minute, I feel I could walk the pavements of London with the swagger of a celebrity. I slowly draw myself closer to the table and realise the carving on the top is a large Zeffo symbol. I trace my finger around the triangle, around the letters H, E and V and over the raven and the turquoise gemstone eye. I switch my gaze steeped in awe to the window and view skimming over Silversedge Town; cute top floor windows popping out from grey slated rooftops remind me of Paris, and I recall my vision of queuing for crepes in a Parisian street with a pencil in one hand and a dope boyfriend holding the other. Gingerly, I pull out a chair and sit to open the Book of Lights, smoothing over the first page with thoughtful respect.

The pages may smell of new paper, but they are filled with elaborate writings of old in black ink and detailed drawings of talismans and our symbol. Written in the same black ink below the symbol, is my name and date of birth. The book reminds me of olden day poets and mythical texts as I cram in last minute revision hoping some of it sticks. I scan over the meanings of the Zeffo language…

Meanings

Vozareia – The originating Spiritus of the world.
Zeffo – Human Mystical Gangster. One per family lineage.
The Boras – A dark, evil energy operating in the minds and lives of people across the earth.
Book of Lights – The identity and mirror of each Zeffo.
Zeffo symbol– A silver triangle, in its centre a raven with a turquoise eye. The letter V for Vozareia is engraved on the top point; the letter H for house is engraved on the right point and refers to a Zeffo's soul; and the letter E for energy is engraved on the right point.

Zeffo talisman – A charm or tattoo containing the magical coding of a Zeffo's set of unique powers and connection to Vozareia.
Bippers – Humans under the Boras Curse.
Remmies – Humans free from the Boras Curse.
Dex – Master Mystical Gangster, the highest form of Zeffo.
The Hoci – A large, solid triangle of pure silver engraved with the Zeffo symbol which is given to a Zeffo when they reach prestigious Dex status. It's power and magic are so strong they can only be used by a Dex for certain circumstances.
Zeffo Room – The magical room and nerve centre for Zeffos and their culture. They are most often designed in white and turquoise, filled with dark wooden furniture and flooring and adorned with a white, gothic archway filled with an invisible curtain of Vozareia energy that allows only Zeffos passage in and out. Meetings, storage of talisman equipment, making of the talismans, accession for new Zeffos and Smoke Outs are all carried out in the Zeffo room. Located in various parts of the world at the place where the Dex lives and works.
Zeffo powers – There are thirteen different psychic and magical energy powers. A unique set of these Zeffo powers are granted to each Zeffo. More can be accrued over time, as experience and service to Vozareia and other Zeffos is gained.
Smoke Out – A procedure carried out by a Dex to recharge a Zeffo and their powers after heavy or extended use.

Next, I flick to the page worrying me the most – Zeffo Law, because what if I break a law and don't realise? I sit and whisper each one to myself.

Zeffo Law

- Dex and other Zeffos may assist and offer guidance, but they must not work out and decipher the translations, clues and coded messages received on a Zeffo's quest.
- The talisman needs to be worn at all times as it connects a Zeffo to Vozareia and their powers.
- Do not use the powers and information translated from Bippers or Remmies to interfere with their own natural course of life.
- In the event multiple Zeffos need to emit a Zeffo power surge, it must be agreed by, and led by, a Dex.
- Powers provided to a Zeffo or a Dex by Vozareia can only be used directly on Bippers or Remmies if their life depends on it.
- Accession from Bipper to Zeffo must be carried out by a Dex in the designated Zeffo Room.
- Accession from Zeffo to Dex must be carried out by the Empress of Vozareia at the Zeffo Academy.
- When either accession is complete, a Zeffo or Dex cannot leave or renounce their status.
- Breaking any of these rules will result in suspension of Zeffo or Dex status, accrued powers and, in certain cases, eviction. Both return you to the control of the Boras and the curse.

I expect Gusti will be here any minute with the tea he's been making and time to read more is scarce if not futile. I give up trying to remember anymore and instead begin to re-read the message from the Empress of Vozareia, as it makes all the apprehension of what's about to happen seem worthwhile.

A Message from the Empress of Vozareia

A most warm and high welcome to one and all,

You have been specifically selected by our beloved Vozareia to be a Zeffo. In truth, you were chosen as the special one in your family line before you came to earth. Have no doubt of your importance; do not distrust that you are the ideal person to fight the Boras Curse placed upon you and your entire family lineage.

Those chosen to be Zeffos are some of the most prominent and significant humans on earth, and your acceptance will alter history for the better, not only for you but for many others and the world at large. We work in secret, but one day we will be the most recognised and influential beings known to the world.

Following your accession to officially become a Zeffo, Vozareia will send you on a personal quest. During this quest you must fight the Boras with your Zeffo powers, and do so with complete willingness at all times, both in your mind and body, in both your spiritual reality and physical one. If you are successful and the end is reached as planned, your curse will be broken for you and all your present and future family.

This journey can be fun yet dark and comes with great magic and responsibility. You will meet other Zeffos for support, help and friendship when appropriate, and you need not be concerned with how. What should concern you is knowing that eventually, together, we can destroy the Boras permanently. Presently we have no choice but to break the curse one family at a time via your individual and very personal quests, but as our force and numbers grow, we will be able to take the Boras head on – as one – to eradicate it completely.

> As the originating Spiritus of the world, Vozareia rules
> diligently with good magic, love and peace, so all
> humankind may expand life beyond their individual
> edges and be free from chains and fear. Its silent voice,
> carried upon the winds and in the voice of the people,
> is unseen, but it is the brightest power and will lead
> you to the destinies you seek and dream of. The
> desires, talents and passions you feel and recognise
> were given to you, by Vozareia, before you came to
> earth and are the illuminating lanterns you need to
> guide and expand yourself through what has been your
> dark life. Your dreams are so much more than you
> think… they are the future and foundation of the
> world.

Gusti enters through the gothic archway, disturbing my reading and I am unable to finish reading the remainder of the Empress's message, my favourite part of the Book of Lights, well that, and the part about my Zeffo powers. He holds two small cups of pale brown liquid and places them on a shelf before lowering the blinds on the two windows.

"Do you miss Bali?" I ask.

"London is great, but I miss home every day," Gusti answers, pulling out a chair next to me. "Your weather here is lousy, the food is yuck and I miss my wife, Ni Luh." He looks over at a double photograph on the shelf, one is of a Ni Luh surrounded by tropical greenery, the other is of them both with their families the day after their wedding ceremony.

"She's pretty," I say. "I'd love to go to Bali."

Gusti drifts off into his wife's eyes, it must be a culture shock moving from an exotic haven to chaotic London. By his sinking face, also heart-breaking to leave your wife and family.

"She's coming over in the summer," he says still staring at his wife, "Ni Luh is a Remmie and understands my duty as a Zeffo, and that for the time being, I am needed in London."

"That's tough." I try to sympathise. He handles it well, or he appears to. I would be a wreck if I found the love of my life and then had to be separated by thousands of miles for who knows how long. "How did you know you needed to come to London? Doesn't the distance worry you?"

"I follow my instructions and guidance just like you are about to. Distance is no barrier to true love, unless it's part of the Boras Curse on you, then it messes with you, but true love always survives."

I can see he believes this to his core. It makes me feel better about the whole love game, how hope must exist for love to be in my future, and for Mum too. Although her true love is dead so, slight problem there. We sip our tea; I prefer normal tea with milk and a spoonful of sugar, but I don't think he drinks that kind, and I drink the pale brown, lavender tasting liquid offered.

We move on from reminiscent talk of Bali and Ni Luh onto the choice of talisman for me. School proves to be a spoke in the wheel as I'm not allowed to wear pendants, rings or bangles. Mum and the MGs would also question what it is if I have it on show. Some Zeffos have a tattoo of the symbol, a modern-day talisman; magical properties are charged in special ink, all mixed and prepared on land owned by Gusti's family and sent over.

"That's sick. Why can't we do that? A tiny dot of a tattoo on my hip, no one would see it. Yeah, let's do it Gusti!"

"You're only sixteen and it violates the law," he reminds me.

In the end we decide on a belly button ring, loads of girls have them at school and it's easy enough to hide. I would rather a pendent or tattoo, the thought of a belly button piercing turns my stomach – I don't even like drying it with a towel as it makes me feel queasy.

"How come strange things were already happening to me? I didn't have the talisman then?" I ask, turning the page of the Book of Lights to the list of Zeffo powers.

"A slight taster. Vozareia will always get your attention by means you will understand and notice. *It's* clever that way," he smiles his sweet Balinese smile and rises to unlock the writing bureau with an old-fashioned silver key he pulls out of his shirt pocket. I am, in fairness, quite excited about these powers now, and with reflection Gusti is right, I have always had an edge with the ones identified as mine, which, I discover, have been dormant within me from birth. It is only now Vozareia deems me ready for my accession proper.

He opens the writing bureau to reveal boxed sets of pure silver bangles, pendants, rings, inks and a tattoo instrument wrapped in cling film. From my seat at the table, they look exquisite; I want to take one of each, but a belly button ring it must be. I can change my talisman later he informs me whilst holding up two different choices of silver belly button piercings before placing them down on a velvet cloth.

"I need to check which powers are yours again," he says, sashaying back to the table. He stands quietly behind me and focuses on the page titled Zeffo Powers.

"Don't fret, you'll learn how to use them as you go, and I am here to guide," he says, placing a reassuring hand on my raised shoulder, picking up on my fears about wielding these powers and getting it wrong – I'm bound to get it wrong. There are no instructions under each power only a description about what each one is. The missing vital information of how and when to use them, Gusti divulges as he faffs by the bureau and pulls out more candles from the cupboard underneath, is only passed on verbally by Zeffos to Zeffos.

"You know more than think… tell me names of all the powers. No peeking," he says, closing the book shut with a curly flick of his hand across it.

Whoa. He didn't even touch it, how?

"Is this meant to make me feel more confident?" I ask.

"Just do it."

I blow out a deep long breath, which sinks me deeper into the chair.

"Clairvoyance, clairaudience, clairsentience, claircognizance, mediumship, zevitating, z artist, healing, ability to move energy, telepathy, ability to read objects' history and er, the last one is, er… the mystic shield."

"Excellent work. Confirm *your* set of powers to me," he continues.

"Clairaudience, clairsentience, claircognizance, z artist, ability to move energy and mystic shield."

"See, you totally know what you're doing. Come on."

"Oh, you're a mystical comedian too I see."

Moments later, I stand like a cardboard cut-out by the table, clenching my fingers and toes. I hold my breath, waiting for pain and nausea from the piercing cutting through my belly button. And I wait. And wait. Nothing. I open an eye, more to check Gusti's still there and not done a runner, but he is there magically passing the piercing through with only his fingers; no needle or punch gun, no cutting or waves of sickness, only the sensation of a feather touching a crystal glass.

"All done," he says, standing with empty hands displayed out in front of him.

I'm about to comment on how cool it looks when I feel a movement within me. A sense of strong yet meek air floats down like a waterfall from the top of my head, through my chest and abdomen and down my legs. I recoil a little at the sensation.

"It's only your energy connecting and calibrating with Vozareia's. Relax," Gusti says.

Relax. Think blankness. I am safe.

Gusti is moving both his and my Book of Lights from the table to the shelf and placing three lit, white candles speckled turquoise in the middle of each side of the carved triangle. My body begins to sway side to side, only marginally, until I feel fluffy and spacey inside. I query I might float away.

"Stand by the base of the triangle. Place one hand over the E and one over the H."

I do as I am told. Gusti places both his hands over the V, and he closes his eyes briefly as I look on in amazement. Our hands are smoking a swirling bright blue light, and the fluffy energy within me strengthens to the point I feel so good I reckon I might explode with the lightness. The flames on the candles are dancing about their wicks, and Gusti looks me straight in the eye and begins speaking, his voice deeper and stronger than normal, the pace of his words slower and more considered.

"We welcome Seven Madison who has accepted and committed to be a Zeffo. I hereby connect V – Vozareia, the originating spiritus – with H, the house, and Seven's body with E, Seven's energy."

The flames dance higher, and the blue swirling smoke widens until it encircles my hands, the triangle and Gusti's hands as one. The eye of the raven begins to glow bright turquoise; the room feels electric. I feel electric. I say nothing, I daren't. Gusti closes his eyes again and instructs me to close mine too. We stand for a few minutes, cocooned in electric blue. I want to feel like this forever, and I breathe down to my hips.

Gusti breaks the silence and tells me to open my eyes, his stare remains completely fixed on me. He begins to hum and recites from memory the Zeffo ode from the Book of Lights:

> *"Our mystery is just a sky,*
> *we need no gas, we run on fly,*
> *with Vozareia, House and Energy,*
> *unite us with the eye."*

He nods at me for me to say the same, turning to the Wall of Words. The words of the Zeffo ode are highlighted on the wall, all mixed up and in different places.

I don't panic about not remembering the order or not being able to do it, and it's refreshing not to as I speak with the most confidence I've ever heard in my voice or felt in my heart:

> *"Our mystery is just a sky,*
> *we need no gas, we run on fly,*
> *with Vozareia, House and Energy,*
> *unite us with the eye."*

The raven's eye shines a beam of turquoise light and then returns to its normal unlit gemstone in the centre of the table; the blue smoking light retreats, and the electric vibe buzzing everywhere dies down. The flames stop dancing atop the candles before going out completely, and the room returns to normal – as normal as can be considered.

"All over. Well done!" Gusti says with immense pride.

He checks if I am feeling okay both in my mind and my body. I feel the best I've felt in my entire life and for the next hour we talk Zeffo powers; he guides me through my specific powers, how to use them and when. A short practice session shows me them in action – he can levitate! Gusti has all the powers except healing.

"I never jived with that one," he says, as he places the candles back in the cupboard and tidies the jewellery pieces back into their original slots in the bureau.

"I want to zevitate," I say. "I jive with it a lot."

Gusti laughs as he twists the key in the bureau to lock it once more. I'll take his laughing as a no then.

"You can accrue more powers as the years go on," he replies.

"Why? If I have completed my personal quest…"

"To continue it. There's always more, and one day we hope to have enough Zeffos to clear towns, countries even, of the Boras… helping those who will never become Zeffos or missed their chance."

He's such a dedicated, caring, family man. It's unnatural yet endearing for me to witness.

"Thank you." He smiles.

Damn it. I forget he can translate energy and thought like a mofo.

It has been an unbelievably empowering couple of hours, but before I leave, the admin side of being a Zeffo needs to be completed, which basically consists of documenting everything in the Book of Lights. I turn the pages towards the second half of the book – Your mirror. It's filled with blank pages for our personal writings about Zeffo life. I always think blank pages are hopeful of profound writings or drawings being cast upon them… I hope I serve these pages well.

"Each day you must write in the Book of Lights: any guidance you receive, any out of the ordinary situations that happen, development and use of your powers. Your Mirror is meant to be a mirror reflection of a Mystical Gangster."

"Why?" I ask.

"Reference, for future Zeffos and for you. You won't remember everything, and it's good to refer to it. Sometimes answers are in what you've already written. The white bag keeps Bippers from interfering with it, should it be found."

I want to stay longer but time has ticked on, and I must return home before Mum starts ringing and instigating panic over my whereabouts.

"Thank you, Gusti," I say again, shaking his hand at the main door, and I hold in a giggle at the zing in my hand and arm. "That was unbelievable!"

"Practice. Trust. Go forth with confidence. My phone is always on and my door always open. Ring me tomorrow to check in," he says.

"I will," I reply.

The bell tinkles and the door shuts. I stand in the cobbled street and look to the sky with bigger eyes and a bigger understanding, before joining the rush of commuters to walk home.

Chapter Nine
Beyond the Junk

Half asleep, I roll over disorientated, drifting out of deep sleep and into awareness of a disturbance.

"What the hell is that noise?" I say, sitting bolt upright, hazy from the unexpected awakening from a pleasant slumber.

I tap my hand around to find my phone on my bedside table and groan at the time – 2.46am. My entire bedroom illuminates in repeated flashes and my house feels like a base guitar being strummed. Raucous long rolls of thunder follow. My bedroom curtains swing back and forth, the bottom of them wet from the rain hammering in from the semi open window. I rise from bed, shove the sash window down and turn the lock on the top, muffling the noise.

"A frickin storm. I thought it was Armageddon."

My mind is slow with night fog and hampered by confusion about the window. I never sleep with the window open – it invites creepy crawlies in, and I'd rather not have those join me in my bedroom. I carry on talking out loud with only the moon to listen as I try to reason how my window magically opened.

"Maybe I forgot I left it open, maybe Mum opened it. No,

she wouldn't, she knows my rule about it. It was definitely shut."

It's peculiar, not haunting like it ought it to be, just like the falling box incident was peculiar, but not haunting. I pace around; I can't leave the thought alone.

"Hang on," I say, lifting my hand up, still walking the carpet up and down. It dawns on me I'm no longer a standard human: I'm a Zeffo, a Mystical Gangster – *duh* – which means more awaits me below the surface appearance of a window that opened itself during the night.

"It was you, wasn't it, Vozareia? You wanted me to wake up?"

It is now that I remember Gusti explaining how my power of clairaudience – supernatural hearing – works. Not that I hear things louder than they are, rather I hear Vozareia speaking to me, when in a calm state of stillness. Sometimes I will hear actual words, like I have before, more often and likely though, chunks of thought will be downloaded to me which I will translate into speech, leading me to clues or information, and so I do as Gusti taught me and riff on the contents of my thoughts. It's the only way for me to make sense of why Vozareia wanted me awake.

"You woke me up, huh, in the middle of the night? The window was a neat trick to make the storm louder and my room colder. Cheers. Why did you want to wake me? To do something? See something?"

I part the curtains and look out, but nothing is there other than hard rain and amber lights. I stay silent and control my breathing to allow Vozareia's energy to flow, and I continue to ramble words and sentences aloud; some make no sense, some hurt, some are moth eaten lines from my past. I ignore these like Gusti told me to and plough through, although it's harder on my own, without him. It's a method to cut through the junk, the Boras junk in my mind, which prevents me finding the real message I need to translate. I'm assured this gets easier and faster the more skilled I become. I carry on hoping Mum doesn't hear me.

"I need to do something. Upstairs." I begin to move my hands around in front of me like a student of martial arts and return once more to riff the information unfolding. "Karate Kid, what does Karate Kid have to do with this?"

I'm waving my hands and arms in mad patterns in front of me just like Karate Kid does in the movie, except I look nothing like him. I'm hoping I'm going to nail this message soon as I look utterly ridiculous. Stood at the end of my bed facing the window, I sweep my left arm out once more, and the curtain moves to the left.

Whoa. I'm moving the energy.

"He practises. Outside." Bingo. This is the fitting answer. To practise outside in the dark when no one is around.

I stuff my feet into my slippers and go out onto the landing. I peak my head round the door of Mum's bedroom – she's fast asleep – and I tip toe my way up to the third floor, avoiding the squeaky step.

The top floor, a converted attic, has a short corridor leading to a large room with a sloping ceiling and skylight that amplifies the noise of the rain.

On the far wall of the room is a glass door with wooden grids; bits of old, white paint have flaked away from it over time and can nick your hands if it catches the skin.

I turn the key kept in the lock and open the door out onto the roof terrace. Another ball of thunder lets rip and I'm about to close the door, too much of a wuss to stand out in a storm.

Why couldn't you have done this when it was dry?

I stay, watching the storm for a minute from the open doorway. Three wooden steps like those found at beach houses lead down onto the terrace. I dig these steps and often sit on them, imagining and drawing. Pots of all sizes and rattan seats mask the decking in need of re-staining. My favourite bamboo wind chime we placed above the steps has been caught by the winds and is frantically banging out a tune as it twists and turns itself into an undoable knot. The pounding rain bounces off the ground like tiny basketballs and runs down the leaves of spindly plants whilst flower petals bow under the weight of the water, yet they don't cave. The seat cushions are saturated – Mum will be annoyed she didn't take them off – and the metal hat on top of the patio heater has temporarily turned into a symbol, clanging away freely. The storm has silenced London and emptied its streets, all except for me as I breathe in the cool revitalising air of a spring storm and begin what I'm here to do.

"Shush," I say, moving my hands back and forth in front of me; they shake, but the rain moves back and forth with my hands regardless. "Shush." I keep moving my hands, calming my shaky nerves, and the rain follows the pattern as I walk down the steps slowly, one at a time. I move my arms more, then faster, swirling them with confidence in a large circle until I create a dry space around me. I'm smiling, laughing joyously, laughing as hard as the rain.

"This is so cool!" I yell, walking further into the middle of the terrace. I'm so pleased with myself. "I'm doing it!" I yell again, swirling my hands and arms in front, behind, and above my head, moving energy and all in its path with it.

A fork of lightening cuts the sky in two and jolts me from my fun. Distracted, I turn to the left looking at the church, its spire lit up and kissing the sky. The wind gains momentum. Below, the garden attire in the neighbour's gardens are rattling and jumping, as though mystical creatures have been brought to life, and are now on the move. Forgetting to keep my arms moving, I lose my connection and I'm soaked to the skin in seconds. Sopping, cold pyjamas cling to my body and icy wet hair grips my head. It's uncomfortable and I rush back up the wooden steps and throw myself inside. With chattering teeth, I lock the door behind me, slightly bothered I became too confident too soon, but note the lesson to not be distracted by other events when mid-power.

I head back down the stairs like a dainty drenched fairy trying not to squelch and narrowly missing the squeaky step. My trail of wet footprints on the carpet should be dry by morning. I check in on Mum again, nope, no stirring from her. I dump the wet pyjamas in the laundry basket and pull out my best toasty warm fleecy ones. I rough dry my hair with a towel and wrap the towel around my head and as I slide back under my duvet, I notice my phone is lit up on the bedside table with message notifications.

Message from Felix, Yasmina and Lizzie, eight minutes ago.

Message from Felix

Yo anyone up?? It's mad outside.

Message from Yasmina.

I am now, thanks for waking me up Felix.

Message from Lizzie.

This is nothing guys, you should try being in a hurricane!

I open the group chat to reply and find the conversation continuing.

Nate is typing

Knock it off you lot. Man's trying to get his beauty sleep.

Seven is typing

I've just been up to the terrace; it's like a monsoon. This is karma for your antics this morning Felix.

Felix is typing

I had an appointment. Nate, you're growing old mate. Leo you're quiet - Where you at?

Lizzie is typing

He won't hear it, sleeps through everything. Always has.

Yasmina is typing

I'm with Nate on this one. It's a storm, not a Prince rolling up. Go back to sleep.

RV is typing

Wait. What? RV is typing?

Connected only by a mobile phone signal, our group's paralysis is breath holding. I'm sure everyone can feel it; Nate even quits typing his no doubt sarcastic reply to Felix as we await RV's message.

Alright G's, scared of a little rain?

Synchronistic messages saying, 'Hey RV' and various other joyful exclamations make the rounds, and I can't believe Leo is missing this. Another ball of thunder rolls on by, but the storm has become insignificant.

> *RV is typing*
>
> You can all calm down, I'm sound. I owe you all a conversation. What about Wavies, Friday 7pm?
>
> *Seven is typing*
>
> Definitely. We all need a proper meet up.
>
> *Nate is typing*
>
> A proper meet up? What are you on? We meet up all the time.
>
> *RV is typing*
>
> Nate back off. She's right.

I ignore Nate's comment and pinch his sarcastic spin on humour can have at times. The dreamy and clever basketball star I'd placed on a pedestal, who was mine for a time, is pivoting further away. I feel mean about secretly talking smack about Lizzie, smack I further dissect with Felix and find that, as usual, he is right: she did nothing wrong. Lizzie wasn't or isn't the damned mistress, and she didn't tease him away. I dumped him before she even arrived in London.

I'm brought back to the chat by a pinging stream of 'see you there, bro'.

> *RV is typing*
>
> Safe. See you then.

The group chat finishes, everyone disappears as quickly as they all arrived and Leo missed it all. I send a private message to RV to say hi and thanks for the Nate response and to ask if he really is okay.

Message from RV

You care too much. I'm cool. <3

A sinking wave of disappointment hits the bottom of my stomach, and I wonder if I do worry too much.

***

"Hello, hello, hello." Yas trots up to the lunch table and places her tray on it, wearing a smile the size on the Grand Canyon. "Sorry I'm late," she continues, flicking her long dark hair over her shoulder. "Today is just sparkly, don't you think?"

Nate, Felix, Leo and Lizzie all look blankly at each other, and I'm not quite sure what to say.

"You been smoking weed?" asks Felix.

Yas throws an empty plastic cup at Felix's head.

"What did I do?" he says.

"There's obviously news. Do tell," Nate says, polishing off his food like a starving animal. Yas carries on grinning to herself.

"Has that Danny guy made up with you?" Lizzie asks.

"Pah. Not. A. Chance. His name is banned by the way," Yas replies, neatly arranging her lunch on the tray.

"You've met someone else, haven't you? I can tell. Come on. Spill the deets," I say, wondering how the bloody hell she does it.

"Seeing as you're asking…" Yas says, leaning in across the table.

The boys, not interested in Yas' love life, return to their

conversation about the national school basketball championship final. Silversedge High are through to the final and Nate has talked about it non-stop. Nate carries the team with his enthusiasm and diligent standards, but since my chat with Mr H, who saw straight through me, I question at times the same of Nate, whether his fanfare is for the love of his team and sport, or to convince himself basketball really is his destiny in life.

I'm becoming so goddamn wise.

"He's called Andrew, and he goes to the private school. You know the one with the logo of a kitten holding a glass. It's on the school building and their bags," Yas boasts.

"It's a lion holding a chalice," I say.

"That one, yes. Andrew is a proper gentleman. He's taking me out on Friday." She taps my arm. "Would you believe he lives at the bottom of my street! How have I not noticed?!"

"They always say the answer is right in front of us," Lizzie adds.

I can't deny my intrigue as I look over at Nate sat opposite, still talking shop with Leo and Felix; now it's about American football and how American schools big their teams up way more than British schools do. Nate glances up from their boy talk briefly, mid wide smile, joking around, and accidently catches my eyes for a second too long. I wish he wasn't full of mixed messages. I wish I could let it go. I think I have and then wham – emotion grips my heart again. Felix clocks the sneaky eye contact, and I know he'll question me on it. Nothing gets past that boy, far too wise at times.

"That's great," I say, hugging Yasmina, "didn't like you being all miserable."

"It's why I was late. He rang me just to see how I was."

How nice it must be to have a guy who cares enough to call just to see how your day is going. I'm lucky if they reply to a text.

"Yas, not to blow your news up," Felix says, "but we are meant to be meeting RV on Friday, and we can't let our boy down. Bros before hoes, love."

She begins to stutter, holding her hand up, and I can see her mind turning over as to how she can make it work when Mr Henry glides by our table and reverses when he notices he'd walked past me.

"Seven! Just the person. Thanks for handing in the extra drawing, it wasn't necessary – you have all the pieces you need – but it was an incredible drawing, well done!"

The MGs stop talking, and the group's gaze moves to my end of the table. The other night after finding out about Palm, a vision wouldn't leave me alone and I began to draw it. It didn't take me long at all, I must have been in pre-Zeffo mode – often it can be a drag to hit the point of flow where my pencil moves by inspiration, and this drawing came much easier. I don't understand what the picture is about, but Mr Henry likes it and I do too; it had friendly feels about it.

"Thank you, sir," I say.

"Truly, you've created excellent work. I like how you went beyond what was required of you also, therefore," he pauses to drum roll his fingers on the table, "I am thrilled to tell you, you are our new Artist of the Year."

"Oh, wow. Thank you, sir, I don't believe it," I say, averting my eyes from Mr H to the table. My stomach tightens with tension, and I exaggerate a smile. I shouldn't feel nervous and shy when I've just achieved something I've wanted since I first laid eyes on the Artist of the Year shrine. It's a mother noteworthy achievement too. This is a good thing to happen – why don't I feel ready for the achievement I've claimed I've been ready for since birth?

"Once the examiners have marked all the work, a display featuring you and your art will be in the main entrance until the end of the year as well," Mr Henry adds.

"Oh gosh, it gets better!" I say, feigning excitement "Can't it just be in the classroom rather than the main entrance, like normal?" I reply, feeling a fraud. It's like I want people to notice me but only from behind a brick wall I insist on sitting behind.

"Absolutely not! You deserve this, and let your mum know," he says with a confident nod indicating he thinks the award will help my case.

Beaming Mr Henry bids farewell, and the MGs burst into a round of applause.

"Don't know why you fret over it," Nate says, "you're a sick artist."

"Totally," Leo chips in, "you need to come to the art scene in Miami."

"Didn't realise Miami had one? Thought it was all beaches and drinking shots?" I reply.

"You're kidding me, right? It's epic. And, yeah, our parties are legendary too."

"Don't involve me in your party life," Lizzie interrupts.

"Ignore her. She's boring," Leo replies, laughing and dishevelling his sister's hair, winding Lizzie's dial.

I can't work out whether he is serious or not, but Miami does sound better than Paris – I won't have to learn French.

"TP," Felix coughs, provoking laughter. "Teachers pet right here, everyone." Felix booms louder, pointing in my direction for all in the canteen to see.

I grab another plastic cup from amongst the debris of lunch and lob it at Felix's annoying head.

Chapter Ten
New York

I fiddle with the remote, pause my after-school TV show and hit play on the voice note notification:

> "Hey, it's Lizzie. You didn't open my message the other day? Can we meet at Wavies at the weekend, just me and you?"

Shit. Totally forgot about her message the other day.

I spin through a roller index in my mind of ways I might have upset or irritated her, apart from the obvious of course, and begin calculating what I can say back to her. What can I say though? I took a dislike to you because you have what I want? I'm such a cow. I'm tempted to tune in to see if I can hear – translate – her energy to prepare myself, but I'm pretty sure using my powers in this way violates the rules.

'The purpose of your powers is to break the Boras Curse upon you, not to barricade yourself from it,' I hear a voice from behind me say. It's the same voice I heard in the classroom.

I've grown closer to the Book of Lights and have moved it from the wardrobe to the drawer under my bed stuffed with old artwork. Before the message fades, like dreams do on waking, I quickly write it in the Book of Lights along with describing an awareness that followed. Maybe the thing between Nate and me, and the thing between Lizzie and me, is my personalised Boras Curse intent on keeping me in a painful place. What if Nate is not actually good for me? What if Lizzie is actually a good friend? It figures really, a classic trick of the Boras – I'm left with the shit end as the Boras syphons the happiness that I would otherwise have with my true boyfriend and new, cool American friend. It's an embryonic version of Mum's story, and I'm dazed by whether I'm right or not. I had always thought Nate Johnson was my destiny, or at least my high school destiny.

Deep. Back to Lizzie.

I note down a few responses I can give to Lizzie in my normal notebook and send a voice note back in my pretend happy voice to apologise; I say how I've had a mad few days and all is okay with her. I'm deeply hoping we can resolve whatever this is via voice notes rather than face to face.

Sorry Vozareia. One uncomfortable hurdle at a time hey.

A return voice note lands a minute later and I'm not enjoying this one bit.

I press play poised with anxiety:

> "I thought we could sort out the weirdness between
> us. I get you and Nate have history, but we're
> friends too, or I hope we are. I think you're cool
> and we would get along great if we try."

This is where Americans are different to British people. Americans are bolder and have no problem addressing the elephant in the room. The British mutter annoyance under their breath or to friends and don't go back or voice their grievances directly. I play the message again.

She thinks I'm cool. Ha! SHE thinks I'M cool.

I don't have a response for this. My roller index is empty. I thought she was about to start bitching down the phone at me. I sit in silence for a moment and try to turn the page of my written responses in the notebook by moving the energy with my hands. The corner of the page flitters up but falls back down. I turn it myself, thinking of right answers and decide, uncharacteristically, to not write anything down but to reply spontaneously with my truth – the thought of it is both liberating and freaking me out. I place two fingers on my talisman to sooth myself and begin speaking. Before long, it turns into a twenty-minute phone conversation; I tell her my version of Nate and I and the disappointment I've held at myself over it, and how I wanted to be friends with her beyond the block I made, and how her iciness with me on numerous occasions only fuelled my justification of maintaining the block. Lizzie admits she felt whiplashed by me when she first arrived but has been trying to befriend me ever since. She convinced herself I didn't want to know her or want her in the group, it upset her – and so the beat goes on. By the end of our chat and plenty *OMG what a pair of idiots we are* type responses, we feel freshly detoxed with a foundation revealed for friendship. We arrange to meet at Wavies in a few days, just the two of us, because you know, Yas – as much as I love her – will bring interference, and Lizzie and I need bonding time.

I sit on my bed staring at the paused television show on the TV screen and then jump up and break out into thumping the air repeatedly.

"Take that Boras!" I shout, feeling like a champ.

The TV has become bored of waiting for me and turned

itself off, or maybe it was Vozareia so I would return to my Zeffo work. Taking the hint, I open the Book of Lights and document my updates: the turn up from Lizzie and the Artist of the Year award, two random, beautiful surprises. It feels alien to have a whiff of being wanted, to have things go well, and it switches my thoughts to Palm. It's from my father, my real father, I have my artistic interests from, and I stop to play around with ideas of him. What he looks like, and do I look like him? I'm guessing so as I have dark hair and more olive skin, whereas Mum is blue eyed and blonde. What were his favourite TV shows and what did he like to paint and how? I wish I'd known him, if only for a short time, as it would have been better than only a name from a tearful story I had to prize out of my mother. I've still so many questions for Mum.

I can sense Palm's energy via my claircognizance – the clear knowing power of Zeffos. The more I think of him and deeper I tap into the invisible, the larger this foreign energy becomes. It is clear to me it is not my energy I'm feeling, it's his. Internally I feel an emotion of being supported, like I'm floating and bopping on a waterbed filled with strength, love and proudness. I've never felt this before, and I want more of it. I want to know why I'm picking up on it. Is Palm trying to speak to me? Get my attention? This emotional cloud hovering about my person of proudness, love, joy and connection is reciprocal on my part, also. On paper he's classed as a baddie, a label I don't believe at all. I call his name out loud for the first time. It feels chancy to say the word Palm, but I do in case the energy I sense is his spirit coming to visit, and I don't want him to think I'm ignoring him. A minute later the feeling is gone, but I'm glad I called out his name on the off chance it was his spirit passing by.

On a roll with beating the Boras, I put the Book of Lights in the drawer under my bed; I slide it to towards the rear of the drawer and cover it with a pile of drawings before trotting out of my bedroom to go and find Mum downstairs. From the landing I can hear her on the phone to someone, probably a client. I slow down as I edge myself forward on the wide carpeted landing, standing in stillness at the top of the stairs, unable to make myself go down. It's hitting me, burning me in flames this whole Simon-Palm-Mum mess. It's all collapsing around suddenly. My throat aches as it tightens, and my breathing begins to judder. The trauma of childhood and the trauma of now grabs me by the throat from nowhere. The burn from my stuffed-down emotions and questions begins to spread, eradicating the joy and relief I felt moments ago. Tears drip off my chin and the ache in my throat stabs deeper as I grip the banister and sit on the top step feeling abandoned and confused. Lost. Again.

I don't have the huff or know-how to power through this one and sidestep the issue of socialising with Mum, so I head straight back to my bedroom to stare at the ceiling while my heart breaks open on my pillow.

I don't think I can do this. It's relentless.

I feel around on my duvet for my phone and make the call without even a blink at the ceiling.

"Gusti?" I say to his voicemail. "Can you ring me back?"

I end the call and let the phone fall from my hand onto the bed, only to pick it up again thirty seconds later unable to lay still. I make another call to the only MG I could face right now, and he answers the phone almost immediately.

"Can I come around to yours for a bit? Need to tell you something, and I want to hear all about your audition," I say to Felix.

***

"I'll be right down," Felix says. The sound of his voice is comforting through the metal speaker as soon as he answered the screeching buzzer.

The main door to Felix's building, painted dusky grey with two frosted glass panels and a smudge free chrome handle, swings wide open. Felix finds me standing at the top of the steps in a heap of puffy eyes, messy hair and a lasagne-stained hoodie, and I sink easily into the hug he envelopes around me.

"I would have come and met you," he says, releasing me to wipe wet spots from his shoulder. "Watch it, you're marking the goods," he jokes, flicking his hands over his matching, and snug looking grey T-shirt and shorts.

"Do I look like I care right now?" I reply, as we drift across the cream tiles of the large foyer towards the lift.

I hear Sam, the concierge man, chuckle to himself as he sorts papers and mail behind the reception desk. I like Sam; he always looks out for Felix – saved his arse a few times too. Like when he rang the school to say the building was in lockdown due to a false security incident, so Felix would be late, or how he keeps a spare key for him, or how they have weekly discussions on life's pressing topics like cologne.

"Good evening, young Felix, and Miss Seven. How are you both?"

Sam stands with pride behind a large black desk on the

right of the foyer, giving him full vision of the grandiose entrance. To the side of the glossy reception desk are perfectly set silver mailboxes, each engraved with a flat number on the front in deep bronze. In the corner by a large arched window, winged, quilted chairs surround a glass coffee table with an exotic floral arrangement atop it. I can almost imagine Palm – or is it Vincenzo? or is it Dad? – sat there with his crew, hustling mafia style.

"We're sound, mate. Chill night tonight," Felix says, twisting round to give Sam a salute.

"Evening Sam!" I wave over the top of my head. Any eye contact or 'what on earth is the matter, Miss Seven?' will send me over the edge.

Felix presses for the lift, and the doors glide open immediately.

"It's very organised here, isn't it?" I say, glancing across at Felix as the lift takes us up to the top floor.

"It is. They've copied off the Americans; inspired by New York City, I should say."

"Don't you get lonely here, rattling about by yourself in… Hotel de Home?" I ask.

"Mum and Dad are producers, what do you expect? It's always been this way; I know no different. Sometimes I crave a traditional life," he expresses, "mostly, I think it's frickin sick."

The lift stops and pings.

"Eighth floor," a mechanical voice states.

The doors open, delivering us into a small square hallway with two further grey front doors.

"Hmm, your apartment is gorgeous," I say, "and there's a

pool! I'd love to live here, for a while anyway, or maybe as a second home after my beach house," I half joke but intend seriously.

There are only two penthouse flats; apartment 808 is on the right of the hallway, Felix's to the left. As we approach, he attempts to coast the ten second walk to his door by sliding forward with one foot but fails as the tiled floor squeaks with resistance against the rubber sole on his trainer.

"Damn it. One day I'll get that right," he says.

Standing in front of his front door, Felix pats around his pockets, first his shorts then his chest. He pauses for a couple of seconds baffled, then throws his hand up knocking his baseball cap off.

"Shit. Came out without the key." He promptly turns back round. "SAM!" he yells as he struts off back into the lift, fixing his cap back on his ruffled hair. I can't help but burst into hysteria.

This is why I come to Felix's.

His apartment is full of glass walls, gadgets and lights, and it does remind me of New York, not that I've been. If I were a singer, I would bellow Empire State of Mind to the silhouette of Silversedge from the wrap around balcony. It's not your average dinky, rectangular balcony. Would one expect anything less?

The kitchen is tiled white, scattered with expensive looking, silver appliances. A dining table is situated just beyond the long pine island bar, and five dangling lights hover above it, illuminating the space. Chalkboards are attached to the wall with to-do lists and random phrases written on them – I bet they nicked the idea from Richard at Wavies. Lilies and greenery in glass vases effuse the smell of a flower shop as I attempt to purge the Palm and mafia love story from my system, devastated by the unhappy ending of it.

"Don't you think Mum was wrong though, she should have been honest years ago?" I gripe.

"It's a shocker, but—" his voice is drowned out by the horrendously noisy blender contraption he is using to fix up one of his concoctions. Once done, Felix un-clicks the lid and dips a spoon in to taste test his pink creation. "Bit more ice," he says, before chucking more cubes in and pressing the button to instigate the pneumatic drill again. "Right enough she should have told you time ago and you're gonna be vexed, I would be for sure. On the flip, we don't know what it was like for her. And I know your mum, she wouldn't intentionally mess up or hurt you. It was probably fear of doing just that which caused her to do what she did. Here, taste this," he says, sliding a glass of his perfected drink across the island bar. "You don't know the full story yet," he says, wagging a spoon up and down in front of him.

Sighing, I run a finger around one of the low-lying silver lampshades. I want to paddy, and I want Felix to join my paddy and he isn't.

"I don't think you get it. You know how shit my life has been and now this. It's not fair. Why can't it just work out for once?"

"I do get it. I could say the same… how unfair and unjust it is I've spent my entire life as an accessory to my parent's lives. Spent year's feeling hard done by, but that malarkey will take you down every time. I'll always help you, but not as a co-victim."

Felix has whipped the rug out from under me. I sigh more. "I hate your wisdom."

I quietly survey the kitchen, my finger drumming the glass of mushed fruit and ice to the RnB tunes spilling out in surround sound.

"Do you think I should leave it alone now. Move on?"

"No! You need to ask your questions. It's called having a relationship with her. You can't avoid this one." He bounces his head up and down while faffing with buttons on the music's remote system, changing tunes to one that clearly pumps him up. "And bloody hell, Seven," he yells over the pounding beat of rap, "look at it this way. Your dad is a proper OG. That's fucking cool!"

He makes a good point, there is something about having a mafia dude, a top mafia dude, as my dad. It lifts me up although it shouldn't; I know the type of things they do. I wonder if this makes me Mafioso, like an heir to a (non-mystical) gangster throne?

We flop down on a sofa each in the sitting room, Felix's phone pinging with messages from girls he doesn't want to date – but they still try. The fact he isn't into dating, only acting, seems to attract more of them.

Apart from Sophie, because she went all stalker weird on him, he does reply to them; he only began responding at all after Yas and I explained ghosting girls, some of whom might have taken days to muster up the courage to send a message, is not good – it hurts and is, quite frankly, damn right disrespectful. A mobile begins ringing as I sit and stare at the skyline view of Silversedge, and Felix throws a cushion at me from the opposite sofa.

"That's yours ringing, not mine," he says.

"Oh." It's Gusti. I decline it and text him instead.

> Can't talk. Can I come by tomorrow? Also don't
> sell the painting above the fireplace
>
> *Message from Gusti*
>
> Sure. I've already taken it down. Had a feeling
> you'd want it

Speaking to Felix has quelled my desire to throw the Zeffo towel in for now, but I still don't know what I'm doing… and when will I know I've beaten the Boras Curse? As I drag myself up from the sofa to leave, I check in with Felix about how his audition he'd been buzzed to get by his own merits turned out. It's odd he hasn't told me anything about it. He slides his glass around in a circle on the coffee table, and I know it hasn't gone well. For all his bravado, he quickly turned into a sad boy.

"Did you not get it?' I ask, walking over to sit by him.

"Didn't go," he answers, still circling his glass and flopping the smoothie in it from side to side. "Turns out my wonderful parents put in a word after all."

I lay my head on his shoulder, gutted for him. He was looking forward to it and was super proud of himself.

"It's like they think my acting isn't good enough, not unless they've thrown their weight in."

They'll think they are helping, like parents do – like my mum probably did – when they actually are not helping, but I suppose their decent intention is there.

"You still should have gone for it. It was a big opportunity for you even if they did… help," I say.

"I'm not about that," he says.

I join him in circling my glass on the table, trying to pep him up like he did for me, but nothing I say makes him feel less flat. His mum and dad should be here with him. I offer for him to stay at mine, but then we hear the front door bang shut.

"Hi darling. Guess what? I'm home," shouts Alexi Rose.

"I'll leave you to it," I whisper to Felix.

"Hi Alexi. G'night Alexi," I say to her as we pass each other in the hallway.

Surprised at my leaving as soon as she arrived, Alexi tries to lull me into staying for a catch up on Mum and me.

"It's been ages since we had a chat. You look well!" she gusts, placing her shoes in the shoe cupboard and re-poofing her pixie haircut in the mirror.

I thank her, but with a move of my eyes and a sideway flick of my head I point, tapping the air towards the sitting room. With that, I leave.

Chapter Eleven
Trust is Tricky

During the last lesson of the day, I can hear talking, background talking, like a muffled conversation behind you in a restaurant you can't quite make out. The classroom is silent. I keep leaning my ear on my left hand to quieten it, I subtlety flex my neck and turn my head quickly a few times to shake it off, but it's still there: Vozareia downloading information, though I can't hear it clearly. Its sheer persistence is annoying and untimely, yet evidence of its importance.

The teacher vomits another manic attempt to instil how our futures hinge on passing GCSE exams. It's a message repeated so often it's had its way with some students who turn up every day with bullied, chaotic minds. Others have stopped listening as meaning has become impassionate and robotic. Panic is the road to destruction, but it's hard not to be swept up by its collective momentum running the school.

I shuffle about in my chair, and I can see Leo keeps glancing over at me, overtly unfazed by the pressure of disturbingly archaic British systems; Lizzie seems equally unperturbed as she fiddles with her fingernails and stares out the window. Leo said as they're only in London until Christmas, they'll do what they need to do, it will be when they return to Miami the screw will tighten.

"You okay?" Leo asks, as we and the rest of the class bump our way out of the door and the school day.

"Me? Yeah fine, why?"

"You looked on edge in there, or weirded out?"

"Oh, I was getting a headache. Sick of hearing about how my survival depends on the grades of ten exams. I'm good, thanks for asking," I lie. Not a complete lie, because I am sick of it, which makes me feel better about being dishonest to a friend.

"If you're sure," he says, swinging his backpack over his shoulder and holding the main door open for me.

It was a second, a split second of a look, like my mum gives me when she knows I blustered a line of BS to her. I'm stuck on a stuttering a word that's trying to escape to justify myself, my lie, when Felix rolls up, decidedly perkier than last night.

"Hey man," Leo says, with an obligatory fist bump.

"Leo, just the man. We have business to see too," he says, draping his arm across Leo's shoulders. "Alright Seven," he adds, looking across at me behind Leo's back as we walk out of the gates.

"Sounds like bromance talk. I'm off," I reply.

"You'll hear all about it at Wavies later on," Felix says.

"Sounds interesting," Leo says, keen to hear his news.

Leo and I exchange a smile veiled with an odd connection I can't place.

"Can't wait to see RV and have him back in the group," I say, diffusing the odd moment with Leo. We all agree as I separate off from their little rat pack and head into Silversedge

Town to see Gusti. Fortunately, Yas is meeting Andrew after school in order to make Wavies later, which means I don't need to catch the bus home with her and make up more lies as to why I'm not going straight home.

Walking down the main high street in Silversedge Town, just shy of the cobbled side street to Jamming Minds, I'm hit with the same oppressive darkness in my mind like before at the top of the stairs. The seething, rolling grey fog of despair and fear which has tormented me my whole life is now mightier than I've ever known it to be. This is all too complicated, too difficult and too ridiculous. I'm ridiculous… I managed to move rain – big fucking whoopee – but how is moving rain meant to help me? How do I banish an ancestral curse with that, rinse my head in raindrops? It feels like it's going to take a lifetime to change this, if indeed it's possible to change it. I know Gusti has done it, but he's different to me: more capable, older and wiser. My self-loathing reaches my chest, fluttering my heartbeat and burning the muscles in my shoulders. I take an alarmed respite on a bench outside the greengrocers to catch my shallow breath, and I can feel myself failing to escape the circumstances of my life; the part of me cloaked in shame and embarrassment rears its head, and an evil part of my mind laughs at my attempts to move forward. It doesn't stop.

In attempt to fight the damaging dialogue, I counteroffer back to myself.

I won Silversedge High School Artist of the Year, and my friends rate me, they like me! Including Lizzie. They wouldn't all stick around if they didn't.

But I'm strange, different to other people… the fog of the

Boras insists. *That's why no one really wants me, always kept at arm's length, and the Artist of The Year thing is just a little pat on the head to humour me. My own exhibit in a gallery? Now that would have been noteworthy – it's the dream after all. High school level is my limit.*

Amongst gaggles of people beetling around this elegant town, I feel lonely and isolated. The muffled conversation behind my left ear returns louder though not any clearer, and I can't stand it. I can't stand the pain of myself being tossed around as though I'm life's plaything, and I can't stand the so called Vozareia offering nothing but static, and I want to scream.

***

Inside the room upstairs in Jamming Minds, the room remains its same serene self, with a hint of a floral smell – rose, I think – but I can't be sure as I'm not clued-up on floral scents. My arm zinged as I walked through the arch, and I'm becoming more acquainted with this concealed identification. The oppressive darkness seems to inch away as though it's wary, and I begin to feel the glimmer of special pride. The Wall of Words is back to normal with no hint of the hidden Zeffo ode mixed in its alphabet soup. I begin to settle; my chest and shoulders lighten, and finally relief oozes out, deflating all remaining despair and fear.

"Vozareia is trying to correct energy disturbances in your body and mind from the Boras. It's those disturbances which make you believe – and behave – in the Boras' way. You must be stubborn." He half laughs to himself, sat opposite me at the table.

I'm glad he's finding this funny because I'm not. I stand up and reach over to the shelf for my glass of water, neatly placed next to Gusti's cup of pale brown tea. I told him the tea is rank and it makes my mouth all dry.

"Don't be disheartened, we're all stubborn at the beginning. The darkness poisoning you is the last thing to go… once you have broken the curse," he says. "It's imperative to ignore its influence and also to use your powers in any way you can to bypass it, or you'll miss your cues."

"I've no idea what I'm doing!" I yell, throwing my arm out open wide, water plops out from glass and splats onto the floor.

He sits, not flinching or visibly bothered at all by my outburst. He's fully engaged and interested in what I have to say as I ramble about oppressive darkness, despair, Lizzie, art and moving rain. Then there's Palm too.

"None of it makes any sense. How is finding out about a second dad, also dead, helpful?"

"Do you feel any closure? Like when you knew you hit the right answer to go and practise on your terrace?"

"No."

"Then it's not done," he replies with utmost certainty.

He can tell I'm not satisfied with his answers – I'm sure it's obvious – and he twiddles with his bangle talisman wrapped around his wrist as he explains in more detail about the quest I must endure and conquer. I will know when the curse is lifted because my mind will be free, it's unmistakable, and life will be the miracle it is meant to be, not scarred and mauled by bad choices and bad thinking. There are usually three areas of the quest set by Vozareia to complete, each situation correlates to a Zeffo's three biggest desires.

"From what you have told me so far, the art award is a sign you have broken into higher ground on the career topic." He flicks a finger about as though I need to pay attention to this matter. "The other two are likely to do with romance and family – those are your three deepest desires, correct? Career success, romance and a complete family… of some sort at least?"

I nod at his rapid assessment of me, he makes it all sound so simple. It seems so simple, that Vozareia will lead me to all three simultaneously knowing the Boras is out to get me, to stop me making it to any of them. I would much prefer to know what I must do and face rather than try to figure it out myself as I go, because it's scary not knowing. I have my powers along the way to foresee, battle and protect, and Gusti is in the background guiding, but there's only me to make executive decisions. I'm not used to being a decision maker; it's always Mum or teachers. Or Yas – she's a good decision maker.

"How can I receive the information Vozareia was trying to give me earlier?" I ask. "I'm worried I've missed something."

"It will repeat it, but here, let's try together. You're a Z artist, it can be prudent to draw messages sometimes, and you'll learn which skill to use when. This time, I'll translate for you. You draw."

It explains why my pictures of late have been enchanting, the last one in particular which catapulted me to school Artist of the Year.

Gusti opens the writing bureau and shuffles out a few blank pages of paper and a pencil from its cupboard and lays them on the table in front of me. He signals for stillness by moving his hand down in the air next to him, and I mentally note the technique.

"You could tell me anything," I say.

"I think we're past distrust, don't you?"

I simply nod in surrender. Gusti signals for stillness again and we both breathe all the way down to our feet and back up. He retakes his seat opposite me, forms his hands in the shape of a triangle and, with softly closed eyes, begins speaking out loud to Vozareia.

"I have Seven Madison here, what message do you have for her? What should she draw? What do you need her to know?"

He repeats it over and over and over then stops before opening his eyes again,

"There is a vehicle, a car possibly. It speeds past quickly and out of my vision. It's the only one," he says.

It tickles me how instantly he changes from someone so calm and collected into gesticulating like an excitable mad professor, as though random pointing and hand swishing will help me grasp what he can see. I'm glued with fascination and thoughts of fortune tellers. Gusti interrupts my curiosity with a sly hand and begins pointing and flicking his index finger up and down at the pencil and paper, and I'm jolted into remembering I'm meant to be drawing his translations and any other insights through my powers I might pick up on the way.

"Continue," I say, as though I had it under control all along. I start drawing on the paper and a car begins to form with trees and fields behind it. This isn't my best work, but

I'm scribbling at speed and keeping up with Gusti's translations and the odd extra bit I add which appears to automatically flow from the pencil, or my hand operating it; either way, it's working.

Within ten minutes, I've added two men walking, the code 'SOS' and a peculiar looking building; a school, a house, or piece of London's history somewhere, it's hard to know exactly what it is; apparently, that's my lot.

"Well, this makes sense," I say, rolling my eyes and holding up the paper in front of me to scrutinise it.

"It will in time. The story is for you to figure out and follow where it takes you," he replies as he begins tidying our materials away and spritzing the air with a clear mist in a chunky glass bottle. "Clears the channels," he adds, adding an extra puff of spritz over the top of my head, making me blink excessively.

I fold the paper with my drawing on into quarters and slide it in my blazer pocket. I'm eager to sit and study it in solitude. Obviously, it's a warning of some sort, I've concluded that much, but why, for who and what is the rest about?

We make our way down the spiral staircase; it's already past 5pm and Gusti has a neck tattoo due in on a chap who, apparently, is a complete baby.

"I may be here all night," he jokes.

"I would be a baby too." I laugh.

I open the tinkling door, switching into normal human, non-Zeffo mode, and make an immediate plan for the next segment of Friday: dart back home, eat, change, head to Wavies and be on time for RV (text Mum on the way to say

I'll get my own dinner after Wavies), come back home and tune my powers into understanding my drawing.

"Thank you. Again. I feel better: re-fuelled and not wanting to quit on everything, which is why I rang you last night," I say to him in the doorway.

I know I can't leave; I can't quit being a Zeffo, but last night I was sure as hell going to give it go. After this afternoon, my mojo has returned, my mind is fitter and I'm ready. I'm ready.

We wave each other out of the doorway, and I hang around on the cobbled street for a moment to readjust myself. About to start the walk home, Gusti calls out to me from the doorway holding a Jamming Minds paper carrier and hands it to me. Peeking inside I can see it's the picture Palm painted, from above the fireplace.

"It belongs to you," he says.

I fight back emotion of feeling the closest I've ever felt to Palm and knowing that the father I've craved for is reduced to a canvas painting in a paper bag. Gusti touches my arm, the zing streams silent sympathy and understanding, and I manage a half smile in return.

"Don't be passive," he adds, "as loving beings as we are, sometimes we have to fight."

Chapter Twelve
A Lone Straw

It reminds me of last summer: friends, laughter, hanging out at Wavies and tasting each other's drinks, one of us always stirring the pot of resentment convinced that somebody else's drink was better than our own.

Richard appears at the end of our table, proudly enthused about the plate he is carrying, bearing a selection of treats for us.

"New vegan cakes and cookies. I'm trying them out. Let me know what you think," he says, like a child presenting a picture they've drawn with pride, waiting for us all to tuck into his latest addition to the menu.

With wary eyes we all eyeball the cakes and cookies, which to be fair look like normal ones. Nate, always up for the latest fad to improve his fitness, is the first taker, followed by Leo.

"I think I prefer the free chips," Leo says, after chewing sponge and yellow looking cream.

"You mean crisps," Nate adds, smiling at the memory.

"Don't start that again," Leo returns.

Interest in the vegan freebies dwindles as we recall the conversation which had amused us a good deal not too long ago. It was a shame RV missed it, and I feel we ought to be moving the conversation on.

"Good to see you back, man," Richards says, slapping RV on his shoulder. "Have a cookie. All-natural and local ingredients," he boasts, pushing the plate towards RV. He stands with his hands on his hips, persistent in giving his on-trend, down-with-the-kids menu selection one last shot.

RV grimaces, shaking his head. "Nah, bro. I prefer other natural edibles."

Richard takes the plate back and flounces off to a different table. "These are better for you," Richard yells back, holding up the plate. RV answers him with a salute and a cheeky grin, and I am glad to see it back.

Weed isn't my game, and it isn't Nate's. I tried it once, felt dizzy and fell asleep. I don't see the attraction of it, really. Yas likes the occasional smoke – she is the most un-Muslim Muslim I know. If her parents or brothers found out about the weed, her dates, or the drinking, it would be the end, and the current career and vocation argument would become a minor one. RV, on the other hand, swears by his weed time, which doesn't bother me or anyone else; I think his alone time with a joint and earphones is precious to him. Given he's already recovered from a stabbing and is effectively on the run from 27evens, who can deny him his vice?

"Before we get into anything else, sorry RV won't be a min, I have an announcement to make," Felix says, not that RV seems concerned by his delayed airtime. "I've got a free house in about two weeks. Pre-exam party is on. If you want to bring plus ones, ask me first."

"Nice one, man. The final will be over by then too," Nate says.

Felix and Leo roll into the agenda: pre-drinks (MGs only of course), the times for everyone else to arrive, people invited, people not invited and house rules. Leo has written all this down, and Felix is setting up a group chat.

"Leo takes his partying just as seriously in Miami too," Lizzie mocks.

"I'll be bringing Andrew for *def*," Yas informs.

"It's gonna be the best night ever… end of an era," I pipe in.

My last comment deflates the atmosphere a touch, and a few groans follow from everyone. We quickly agree not to think about the end of the MGs; it's just too sad, and who knows, maybe we will always be the MGs, wherever we are. Our eyes begin to wander over to RV who's busy re-tying his trainer lace with his leg stuck out the side of his chair. As he resurfaces, it's Leo who steps up to ignite the conversation we are all here for.

"You okay, bro? What's been going on?" Leo asks RV.

Deep silence spreads like gossip across the MGs, perhaps intimidating but a sign of the intense interest we all have in what RV is about to tell us.

"I'm not back with 27evens. Haven't seen 'em. You can all stop fretting," RV says. An audible wave of relief floods the table as everyone exhales, releasing the tension we'd clearly been holding onto, and our chests all relax upon hearing the words. Yas breaks into a song and dance ramble of happiness about this until Felix kicks her leg under the table, cutting her off as she jumps back in her chair mid-sentence and glares at Felix for dampening her zeal.

RV shuffles about, rubbing the side of his thick set neck

and the top of his arm. He picks up a lone straw from the table, turning it around and around in his hand, and looks up from under his baseball cap.

"Cheers, Yas," he says, finally sitting taller and placing the straw back down. Yas flicks a *what the hell* look to Felix, but RV holds his palm up to let himself continue.

"It's a different world for me here: I've been rammed in a prison of my own mind since I came. It's harder than life with 27evens in some ways. I knew how to handle that life; it felt safer to me, even though it isn't. Fighting judgment from pretty much everyone except you guys and the paranoia of them coming for me, I'm surprised they haven't already, but it messes with ya. It's like being a double agent and whichever side you decide to stick with, you're as good as dead anyway."

His mind sounds so much like mine, and I want to tell him so badly how much I understand that prison, how the fear of violence – the fear of fear – squishes you until no one can see you at all, but I can't. Like he told me the other day: I care too much.

"Then I began to see a glimpse of a life I could have, one you all have, and a job I've wanted since being a kid. I want to work in crime investigation. It fascinates me, always has." He laughs to himself, shaking his head as though he just muttered the most embarrassing thing he could have. "No disrespect, but I needed space from you all, from everything, to figure out which side I'm on. If I'm staying in Silversedge I need a plan, to get my shit together. He's helped me a lot," RV says, nodding over at Richard. "I fessed up one day, when I was sat in here miserable, and he's been getting my thinking right, and..." RV pauses briefly and turns to look at me. "It's why you heard your mum on the phone to me, not because she was getting me out of more trouble. She's been helping too: speaking to my parents, highlighting career routes available and letting me shadow her work a bit."

A trigger is pulled within me, and I can feel fury building.

"What? My mum has been helping you?" I boom a bit too loud. I feel mad, not at RV but my damn mother. I plant my hands down on the table with force, forgetting about being a Zeffo. My channelled energy is charged and causes me to carelessly move a wave of energy ahead of me, and it knocks over my glass of Choc Rock shake, I downplay the incident with, 'I hit the table harder than I thought' as I erratically mop around with a batch of napkins I snatch from the centre of the table.

Why would Mum help RV with his career but not mine; why would she help someone else before her own daughter?

Yas picks up on my trip of shock and immediately distracts the MGs in her sparkly fanatic way.

"I'm so glad you chose us!" she screams with her arms in the air as though she's on a rollercoaster. "You did choose us… right?" she asks as an afterthought.

"Yes, Yas. I'm staying. Crime investigation and you guys it is. God fucking help me," he smiles, looking to the heavens and then inquisitively at me.

"What if 27evens come and find you?" Nate asks.

"I deal with it," RV says conclusively.

The table falls to silence again as it dawns on all of us, his old gang life will never leave him, and he'll be on the run forever. My claircognizance power informs me RV always rests with one eye open. It seems unfair for him, and it makes me think of Palm. He would have known how to handle this; Mafiosi would have known how to help. Isn't that what we all want – someone around who is stronger than we are, who knows what to do?

"That's hella sick," Leo says.

"I admire you, man," adds Felix.

The boys all fist bump one another, and Yas continues to dazzle the table with drama, giving me a wink as she does so. It's so comforting when friends get each other without saying a word; it's the warmest place on earth, being surrounded by people you love and experiencing that rare feeling of being truly understood. Lizzie and I run around the table to hug RV, and I can see Richard from the corner of my eye looking on from his counter, standing like a proud father with his daft, boyish smile with the plate still full of his vegan treats in hand.

We all leave Wavies. Like a display of jets in the sky, we each divert onto our individual routes home. Felix is meeting an acting buddy, so I walk most of the journey on my own.

The high-street is almost asleep, the dim lights in shop windows illuminating mannequins that wear forty-year-old women clothes; all different shades of the same extravagant design, all the same, same, same; while jovial drinkers stand inside by pub windows creating silhouettes of drunken behaviour. A waft from the Italian pizzeria leaks out across the end of the high street. It smells addictive and makes my mouth water for food as I hike the hill towards home. I'm fuming, going over what I will say to Mum when I get back. I no longer care what she says. I'm studying art next year and being an artist is what I am going to do with my life.

"Oi, Seven. Seven! Wait up," I hear.

I hear footsteps running towards me from behind and turn around to see RV standing there. He's a little out of breath as he's run all the way to find me.

"What's going on? You looked like you wanted to kill me in there."

"Oh my god, no. Not you. I'm so happy you are staying and not with 27evens. It's my mum."

His worry lifts and he walks me home whilst listening to my story about the ban on being an artist due to its instability but that it's more likely because my real father, who I've only just found out about, was an artist, and my mum is still broken over his death from eons ago. I left the mafia part out.

RV is raising his eyebrows, swearing, and seems to grasp the hurt I feel. Why would Mum help him with his career, which let's face it is a more secure choice, but not help me?

He suggests I talk to her again, not yell at her, and make her understand her personal pain cannot be used as a reason to block me from living out my uniquely wild purpose in life. Who knew RV was so philosophical?

"You know," he says as we reach my front door, "now that you know the truth about your dad – Palm did you say his name was?" I nod to him, and RV continues, "You'll stop feeling like you're dangling. He might not be here anymore, but it must have clicked inside."

"You're quite something, Rio Vanns, do you know that?" I say, feeling more whole than I did half an hour ago, more whole than have in my life, if I'm honest.

He turns, looking misplaced and guarded about the compliment, and looks at his restless feet. He digs his hands into his jean pockets as he mumbles a 'thanks', and I slide my key in the lock.

"You deserve people – someone – who sees your heart, Seven," he adds as he parts to go home himself.

Windswept by his words, I watch him slope off down the road. He has a long walk back to his house from mine, and I find myself still gazing at the road long after RV has disappeared. I return to my hand still on the key in the lock and think Zeffo mode for a beat. I release my hand from the cool metal and signal for stillness, just like Gusti had done. Replacing my hand a few inches from the key, I begin to sway my hand and move the energy like I did with the rain. I couldn't turn paper over earlier with only one hand let alone metal, but I'm determined, and slowly, gradually, the key begins to vibrate. It begins to turn until – click – the door opens.

Ha!

I strut in and let the door full-on swing shut so the noise reverberates around the house – Mum hates it when I do that at this time of the evening.

"Mum! I need to talk to you," I shout out in the hallway. "I'll be in kitchen."

Chapter Thirteen
Tick Tock

I'm in my bedroom," Mum yells back. "You'll have to come up here."

Of course! If you call for me, I have to come to you, but if I call you, I still have to come to you.

I debate whether to be all pompous and demand she meet me in the kitchen but think better of it. The light in the hallway shines brightly from the chandelier, and I reach across to the dimmer switch by the door. I twist it until I find the contentment of a soft glow better fitting for home. Since my accession, I don't like bright artificial light, it feels like it scrapes at my corneas and ambushes my Zeffo field, neither of which I can tolerate for long. As I make my way upstairs, I remember the picture Gusti gave me and retrieve it from the drawer under the bed. If only I had the ability to read objects – this painting could give me plenty of clues, I'm sure of it.

"Is this one of Palm's paintings?' I ask, barging into Mum's bedroom with the same lack of patience and tolerance I have around bright lights.

Her face chills as I thrust the painting in front of her, she leans forward from the grey bedhead she is resting against and places her book on the bed. Her mouth begins to open, and her lips subtly move as though she is about to speak, but she doesn't, or can't.

"I'll take that as yes then, and if you don't mind, I'm keeping this one – seeing as it's the only thing I appear to have from him."

"Darling, what's the matter? I mean, yes, absolutely you can have it, but I don't feel like it's the reason for this anger?"

"Do you not? Well, you are correct. I guess that's why you're a lawyer…"

I stand in the doorway, looking at her looking at me, looking utterly fucking bewildered. I stand my ground, waiting for her to catch on, waiting, waiting, until impatience overrules me.

"I've been talking with RV. He's told me everything, including how you've being helping him?"

I watch her for a hint of remorse, or guilt, but nothing – *nothing!* I lay into her with accidental venom, how all she's done by doing this is add to the weight of the unworthiness I already bear. I verbalise my aghast about how she is supporting RV with his career but not me, all because of Palm, and because she thinks being an artist is a dead end.

"I'm right, aren't I? I ask.

"Not quite," she says, lifting the duvet and swinging her legs over the edge of the bed.

"Have you any idea at all how my life thus far makes me feel?" I continue. "You kept this secret from me as well. What's wrong with me yet so right about everybody else?"

"Nothing is wrong with you!" she replies. "RV needed immediate help and guidance which I could give, and still will. He was the one who wanted it to be kept quiet whilst he sorted his head out. I would have done the same for any of your friends if they asked. It wasn't about you."

She picks up her open book on the bed, slides a bookmark between the pages and places it on her bedside next to the lit lamp. The jewel stones hanging off the end of the shade begin jostling about, creating dancing shadows on the wall and a touch of eeriness. Mum looks uncomfortable as she scans the room, claiming she didn't touch the lamp. She's right, she didn't. I know, however, it's a little wink from Vozareia letting me know I'm on the right track and it urges me to continue with full heart.

"I'll be honest," Mum says finally, "I find your career choice difficult because it reminds me of him." She stops and pulls her hair from her face and over her head, delaying the rest of the sentence, and it's irritating. "But I want the best for you. I'm mortified you think you're not worth it. I don't want you to struggle like I had to; like I still have to. It's not just about everything that happened with your dad— *err*, Simon —but with my career, Seven. The arts are insecure. Admittedly I come from a line of corporate people, so perhaps I need to understand your world more," she says, looking up at me, her face now stricken with the blow of my bite and the return of her old decisions biting at her.

The struggle you have, Mother, on all accounts, is because of the Boras Curse which I'm trying to rid us both of.

It's tempting to blurt it out, but I keep it as a thought. I think she'd have rung for the guys in white coats if I'd have told her. I appreciate her attempt to extend an olive branch, but like a hill destined to landslide in a monsoon, my pent-up emotion of late tumbles out.

"All I know is you could have told me the truth – you do it for a living! Yet you took away my choice and boxed it away like you do with yourself. Did you not think I'd feel the disconnect?"

She shakes her head, remarking she didn't and how she genuinely thought it was all less painful this way. How she wrongfully thought I was fine, bopping along finding my own path as I tend to scoff at any advice or help offered by her. My hands and body are shaking, almost shivering as though an ice-cold wind is weaving its way around my bones, as I begin divulging my deepest truths, turning a blind eye to the idea of pretending – an unknown and uncomfortable behaviour for me.

"I would have understood," I say, my words broken from the shivering.

My god. I familiarise myself with the ice-cold chill and sense it is the Boras trying to stop me doing what is right – normally, before all of this, I would have relented to it, but now I refuse. The cold penetrates my face and my jaw begins to chatter, and then I remember my powers.

Open shield.

The invisible shield runs over the outside of my body like a waterfall, and the iciness slowly diffuses.

"I'm gutted for you and Palm. You deserve a King, but to keep it – me – as a shameful secret… I don't get it."

"You are not a shameful secret. I love you. Palm loved you. I can't believe this," she says incredulously. "I made wrong decisions; don't you think I know? You are everything to me, but we need to talk about it."

Please, do enlighten me.

"The baseline is clear, Mum: I'm not wanted, by anyone! It's all making sense now."

"You have this so wrong," she pleads, her voice cracking with teary squeaks.

"Do I. DO I? Look at the facts, Mum – you'll like this – Vincenzo didn't want me, Simon didn't want me, you didn't have the balls to stick up for me and fight for us, which by default puts you in the same basket as them!" I'm nearly out of breath as I gasp my closing line, "Case closed, your honour."

I had to say it, expel what feels like clouds of toxic air from my chest as our eyes stay locked, neither knowing what to do next. Mum matches my sigh with a shaky one of her own, wipes her hands across her cheeks and sunken eyes and throws them up in surrender.

"You know what, Seven? You're right. I fucked up."

Mum never swears, not in front of me, and I fear I've crossed a line.

"I hear you, I do, and I am not discarding how you feel. You didn't ask for this, nor do you deserve it, but you certainly do not get to throw vile accusations around without knowing the full story." She shouts and parades around the bedroom telling me how hard all of this has been. How all she wanted was her, me and Palm to be together. How she dreamed of more success in her career, not to have a daily battle with it.

"I question at times if the struggle with the law firm, my law firm, is worth it," she adds, "it's not going anywhere."

Mum picks up a silver box from her dressing table and for a moment I think she is about to launch it across the room, but she places it carefully back on the dressing table, dusts her hand across it and looks through the air.

"Next week I'll go into school and speak to Mr Henry. We can organise a plan together," she says with a half-smile and wet eyes, "right now, will you listen to how all this happened?"

I nod my head, feeling rotten about what I've just garbled, because it seems she has felt as alone as I have all these years.

She told me during our talk that her and Palm had agreed to split not long after she found out she was pregnant with me. He had become more of a wanted man, which increased the attention on him and, therefore, her. Mum would raise me on her own, they decided. Palm would send money (lots by all accounts) each month and anything else we would need. Mum would send updates, school reports and photos of me eating my first banana, and Palm would be the doting father he wanted to be, just not physically present, so we all could live safely and freely.

It worked only in theory.

"The heart knows what it wants," Mum says, "anything less than – whatever that is for a person – simply won't be accepted by it. It's not sustainable, and it's debilitating."

For the sake of their sanity, communication was cut, but he insisted on sending money and the odd letter.

"I had an instinct you were going to be a girl," she happily coos, "Vincenzo and I made a pact: if we had a girl we would call you Seven, because we met on the seventh day of September." Her sweet smile turns saddened as she remembered their plans.

Enter Simon, a friend of a friend who knew of Mum's vulnerable, pregnant, single position and clawed his way closer. His greedy radar sensed her wealth and professional status – attractive to a circling vulture. When I was born, Simon suggested they make a go of it, and he would think of me as his own: we would be a family. It was a plausible, realistic and more normal life than Palm could offer.

The cracks widened as the years passed, and Simon grew to resent Mum and me. Blaming us, continually smacking our confidence and self-worth through the floor to mask the lack of his own and his crude ulterior motives.

When Palm was gunned down by an enemy, he left everything to Mum which enabled her to buy our house in Silversedge.

"Sorting out money and Vincenzo's life belongings between here and Sicily without letting Simon know was an experience I shan't forget," Mum mocked.

"The guys in Sicily are, yes, powerfully mean, but their hearts are made of putty. Had Simon not died of his own accord, they would have done it for him. They despised him. I haven't seen or spoken to them in years, but those Sicilian men will always have your back and mine. Never forget that."

For the first time, I feel special, like I'm the safest, most significant girl in the world. It's such a freeing feeling, like an animal that has been trapped in a basement its whole life and sees outside for the first time. I don't even know these Sicilian guys, yet I feel closer and more connected to them, and this man Vincenzo Petralia, than I ever did to life with Simon or life before this. Is that crazy, or real love?

Mum quickly dismisses my suggestion of going over to Sicily to visit them, but maybe we will one day.

"It would be sick," I say.

I cannot hold back unexpected tears in spite of my efforts

to do so, and I break down, wrung out and raw.

"Do you have a picture?' I ask, crying unconsolably, "I want to see what he looks like."

Mum takes the silver box from her dressing table, placing it on her bed and beetles off into the dressing room to locate more treasures of her sapped soul.

"Hundreds," she says, returning holding two of the beautiful boxes kept on the shelves where I received my first hint of this situation with the postcard.

We sit on the floor, our backs firmly against the foot of her bed and talk, laugh and weep our way through memories and photographs.

Close shield.

I don't need it anymore. I've done it, I've been honest, and I feel amazed at myself.

"You look hot, Mum." I giggle, quite surprised about how hot she and Palm did look together. Mum is sat on the bonnet of an open top car and Palm is stood next her all macho and proud. I can feel their connection through the photograph. I can feel the energy of Palm, the same energy and feeling as the other day, and a piece of me clicks into place. I can see myself in his face, and it's healing. We flip through pictures of their lives split between, Sicily, Italy and England until midnight strikes and she tucks me into bed like she used to when I was young.

Feeling steadier in the aftermath of the hurricane which swept through our house tonight, I dislike her a little less and love her a little more. Given where we are now, I'm glad I said what I did. Mum slips out of my bedroom and back into her bedroom, and the day feels like a surreal blur – how quickly an evening can change on a dime.

Message to RV

I yelled. A lot. But we've talked for ages. I feel less dangly now. Thank you for tonight (X

Message from RV

Good. Anytime x

Message to RV

Are you ok, after tonight and everything? I'm so proud of you!

Message from RV

Yup, and thanks.

He is a boy of few words, I think to myself, or meaningful words, like earlier when he managed to make me feel like I want to be wrapped in his arms.

Message to RV

Ok. Night. x

Message from RV

Night. See ya Monday x

***

The following morning, I wake early with an emotional hangover and a voice speaking as clear as if the person were stood to the left of me.

'He's here, he thinks of you.'

I sit bolt upright, overwhelmed with feelings. I signal for stillness and touch my talisman for support. I don't need to, but I find it helps. I close my eyes and whisper.

"Who? What do you mean?" The connection is filled with radio silence. I breathe long and deep down to my hips, back up and out and take another run at it. "I need more information. Please give more information."

A puff of new energy enters my space and grows in size until it feels like a giant sun is occupying my bedroom.

Oh my days. You are right, Vozareia, I got it. He is here.

It's Palm's energy – I know it is – and I'm so excited I can hardly contain myself. The energy I feel in my body is the same as I felt with the photograph the other day and, when I think about it, the same I feel from his painting. I try to dispel my emotion from hearing the words, 'he thinks of me', before the retched background interference begins again. I wish I could make out the words or thoughts, but I'm overrun with feeling alive and can't connect to it clearly; to hear him, to hear my dad, it's overwhelming. Instinctively I lean down the side of bed, reaching and pulling at the drawer under it. Straggling hair obscures my view, but eventually I feel around and find the bag housing the Book of Lights with the drawing also stuffed in it. I drag it, followed by myself, back onto the bed. I take a pen from my bedside table, make a note of the message in the Book of Lights and don't question the urge to draw and let the pen flow onto the page I'd already drawn on.

I add a pocket watch, with an arrow turning around the clockface, and a man's face; he is staring at a ceiling, lying down with his hands slid under the back of his head. I stare with intensity at what it's looking like, a collage or a weird mood board, and ask again, louder, for more information.

"It has to be a clue about Palm. The man's face I sketched must be you, Palm, because in my mind, a pocket watch is synonymous with mafia dress code. The two men I can sense are older guys, but what… what are you trying to tell me?"

The sunshine is all round me, and I must assume it's

Palm's energy I'm connected with after Vozareia performed Its little intro and spoke the thoughts in my head.

"Am I in danger? Is Mum in danger? My friends? 'SOS' and the arrow around the clockface must mean someone is, or the message is urgent."

Please tell me what it means. I don't understand.

I return to the talisman, placing fingers over it once more to disperse my cocktail of despair and excitement, and ask a final time for more information.

"Where is this building? The speeding car? Who needs help?" I continue to speak, searching for clarity. I'm struggling to find the bingo fit of this or the next step I need to take. It doesn't make sense.

"Palm, do you need help? Um… Palm?" I say, wrinkling half my face with confusion at the crazy suggestion. "I can feel you, but with all due respect you're behind schedule, because, you know, you're already dead. Why would you need help?"

Perhaps he needs help moving into the spirit realm; I've heard about ghosts or poltergeists who become stuck between worlds with unfinished business.

"Do you need me to go somewhere? Collect something? Deliver a message to someone?"

But the sunshine of his spirit I was sensing vanishes as quickly as it arrived.

Goddamn, I couldn't hold it long enough.

Holding my hands at a distance from each other, I push the energy closed, and upon my touching hands the Book of Lights claps shut. I slide it in the bag and pull at the blue-ribbon strings to tightly fasten the bag.

I need to call Gusti.

"Personally, if I were you, Palm, I'd just pay a ghostly visit to your mafia pals. I'm sure they could deal with the pressing matter better than I," I say, wiggling the juddering drawer forward. My bedroom door opens with force, and I jump backwards, closing the drawer under the bed with a bang as my heart beats twice its normal speed at the sight of Mum in the doorway.

"SEVEN. Breakfast is ready. I've been calling for ages, didn't you hear me? Are you alright, you look startled?"

Damn it, Mother. I was on the trail. Given a bit longer I might have solved the latest coded message… with a little Gusti assistance.

"I'm fine, I was just thinking."

I bet she hasn't been calling for ages, more like she shouted once and expected me to teleport downstairs immediately.

The two plates of an extra special breakfast are sat prepared with knives and forks on the end of the island in the kitchen: eggs, bacon, toast, mushroom, tomatoes and fresh orange. The kitchen smells of oil and cafes, but nothing beats an English breakfast to warn off hangovers of any kind. It's sweet Mum is trying to make up for the last sixteen years with eggs.

I lightly spring my fork up and down, casually asking Mum if Palm used to wear a pocket watch, or if there is one she has I can look at. I need to acquire his pocket watch; it could have something inscribed on it or stored in it, and for a moment I bliss out, marinating in the investigative trip of all this.

"He was always a well-dressed man, but he wasn't a gangster from the 1930s! He did have one though, his father's. Why do you ask?" Mum enquires while stabbing a mushroom.

"I just wondered if real gangsters look like the ones in films," I reply, covering up my intentions for questioning.

"Years ago, perhaps. The Mafia don't like to be noticed as a rule, they dress to blend in… think about it," she says as she drains the last of her orange juice and sips her tea.

"Any chance I can see it? I'm intrigued."

"I believe it's with family or colleagues in Sicily, sorry darling. I've other things you can look through if you want to choose something to keep?"

I can't trot off over to Sicily and turn up at random people's homes – not that they are random, they are family and family friends I long to meet – but, yeah, super awkward. Maybe the pocket watch idea I latched onto is the wrong avenue in the story the drawing is trying to tell.

"Great. Thanks," I say, exaggerating my smile.

Chapter Fourteen
Raven Return

Maths revision class. After school on a Monday.

This place does my head in.

What about art revision class or drama revision class? All the other subjects? The world is not fuelled and maintained on maths, English and science alone.

Maths is my most disliked subject, it's definitely Felix's and RV's attendance to it was previously variable. Therefore, we all slum it in the bottom set, and now even more so in a mandatory revision class to support us in the run up to exams. The teacher informed us of our fate the other day and I've wanted to run for the hills ever since.

The new RV has switched his lane; he doesn't enjoy maths at all, but his foot is on the metal knowing it's an exam he needs for his new life in Silversedge and crime investigation. Felix couldn't care, and I'm just all *I refuse to let this class muddy my waters* about it.

Yas and I walk with linked arms to the revision classroom; her, Leo and Lizzie are heading to Wavies whilst we sorry three revise for an hour. Nate's at basketball practice; the final is on Friday and any conversation from Nate is B-ball related and best avoided at present. Yas hasn't got anywhere with her parents agreeing to let her venture into being a fashion stylist and we are trying to think of alternative tactics.

"Can you set up as a side hustle?"

"I'm sixteen babes, not an influencer or twenty-five with adequate training," she replies.

"Some people our age have done it. Maybe not as a stylist, but you're talented and infectious. Don't not do it. Promise me?"

Yas tugs me into her, appreciating me as she gazes ahead, and I wish had a decent answer to give to her.

"What if I spoke to your mum and dad, would that help?" I suggest, leaning into her arm. "They like me," I say smugly, grinning.

"They do, and it won't work. They are convinced only they know what is best. But hey," she says, tapping my arm, "you did well with your mum, at least she is coming in and willing to sort a plan with Mr H. He'll seal it for you."

"To be honest, she hasn't got much of an option. I'm not going back on it."

"Wish I had your determination," Yas says. I feel her dismay, literally feel her dismay. My stomach drops like a fairground ride, she's a Bipper and I must have tapped into her energy.

Open shield.

This is interesting to me, because I am, for the first time since becoming a Zeffo, noticing where I end and somebody else starts. I'm not mistaking it as my own emotion and buying into another trick of the Boras to drag me down using Bippers. I continue to keep my shield open, charmed at my discovery.

"If I can have it, you certainly can. You also have Andrew, so we are at fifty percent each."

We laugh and spin around the corridor junction towards the classroom door. I'm happy for her, and for a moment I consider why I haven't told Yas about the dad not-dad saga, Palm and the Mafia. It seems of late, I speak more honestly and personally with Felix; me and Yas have always been friends in a different way, and in some ways it doesn't surprise me I haven't confided in her. Our girl chats and texts, once upon a time, saved both of us multiple times and we pinned them as the highlight of daily life. These days, they seem thinner on the ground, and I can't help but feel Yas and I are changing more into surface-level best friends as I grow into my own skin more, Zeffo power or not.

"Bye babe," Yas says, "talk to you later."

Close shield.

I turn and walk into the classroom; it smells of the usual end of day stuffiness, and it feels like it's sticking to my body. I study the grid of desks, all facing the smart board at the front, to make my selection. The desk I pick is by the row of long arched windows looking out onto the playing field, and I slouch in the plastic chair, balancing my heel on the toes of my other foot. I admire how vast and consistently matching the colours of nature are, and I note how every artist and designer of anything must surely choose colours and combinations from nature itself. The brown barks of trees always sync with the numerous shades of green leaves, while white clouds always appear beautiful or dramatic against blue or grey skies. Flowers with their limitless colour palettes are never awkward amongst that landscape.

Mr Tate churns out his next question about a calculation too complicated for me to even consider, as he scans across the heads of his students for the answer. He ignores Isabelle Riley with her hand up and jumps on Felix, who is leaning on his left hand, gawping over to the right.

"Felix, what's your answer?"

"Me?" He jolts upright, pointing at himself.

"Yes, Felix. You," replies Mr Tate.

"I didn't put my hand up."

"Just have a go anyway," Mr Tate insists, rattling Felix immediately.

"Listen, if I put my hand up, like this," he says as he sticks his hand up in the air, "then I know the answer. If I keep my hand *dowwnnn*…" Felix demonstrates by pushing his arm under his desk before he continues, "…it's because I don't know the answer."

"Well, it's always good to participate, Felix."

Mr Tate is all but stabbing pins in Felix. I can see Felix trying to maintain his cool, but Mr Tate has set him off and he's gonna roll in – five, four, three two, one.

"Sir. Isabelle put her hand up. Ask her," Felix states, turning back to the right to face Isabelle. Isabelle keeps her hands firmly in her lap, averting her eyes towards her desk and away from the drama. The poor girl is cringing with the spotlight she's under.

"Also," Felix twizzles back in his seat to face Mr Tate and continues in a respectfully blunt tone, one I'm not sure Mr Tate is seeing in the same way Felix is. I look on with amusement and the rest of the class are quietly revived.

"Why are we even learning this? When was the last time

you used—" he stutters and flips his hand around, "—why don't you teach math stuff we can use in life?"

Mr Tate opens his mouth, lifting his hand up but Felix nips in before Mr Tate can respond.

"I want to be an actor, sir. Entertain people and distract them from unhappy realities, probably caused by maths, and make them smile. I want to hone my craft – and I work hard in these areas before you say I'm lazy – so please tell me, sir, how this…" he says and whirls his hand around in circle to encompass the smart board in front, "will help me, or anyone else?"

"I agree," I say, butting in, "I said the other week about how the greats as we know them didn't become successful because they studied unrealistic curriculums. I understand some of it's useful, but schools are focusing on the wrong stuff."

"Exactly," Felix says, opening his arms like a conductor leading an orchestra.

"It's true," RV weighs in with his deep growly voice to the shock of the class. RV seldom speaks out in public. "I'm trying my best to pass this class, but *I* made the choice to do so, not because of you lot. If you teach us how to find what we want to do and WHY, you might get more kids paying attention and participating," RV adds with mock hand quotations. "Because it's driven by our desire, not yours."

Go RV!

Felix stands up and fist bumps RV sat at the next desk but one to him. RV glances my way, and I realise the size of the smile I give him verges on a beam and he returns to Felix as though his glance was mistake.

"*Yesss* bro," Felix adds.

"Right on, RV," I holla.

The rest of the class is stirring, like lids rattling on overboiling saucepans.

"The pressure put on us is a joke, except no one listens. No one does anything," James remarks.

"My friend is on tablets from the doc because of stress. It's ridiculous what's happening to teenagers," chirps Ella, and it escalates rapidly into a raucous classroom. Mr Tate points straight at the door.

"Felix. Get out," he declares, cutting the chatter to silence.

"What?" Felix's expression shifts from amused to bemused.

"Get. Out."

"For real?"

"Yes. For real. You and your tomfoolery are disrupting the class, again."

Felix pushes back his chair, sighs like a horse and casually winds himself between the rows of desks towards the door, shaking his head in disbelief as he walks out the classroom and closes the door behind him. The entire class hears his intentional-not-so-whispered comment.

"This is bullshit."

I investigate the shiny cream wall next to me to avoid the compelling urge to look over again at Felix, who is peering in through the square central window in the door with a baffled face. Like a goldfish he is swishing his head side to side viewing the room, attending to his audience. I try hard to keep my body tight as not to laugh, but my inner sniggers begin to transform me into a vibrating human ball, and I lose any attempt to keep myself quiet.

"Right, any more distractions and you'll all be joining Felix in detention after school tomorrow. Is that clear, Seven?" Mr Tate thunders. "Who wants to answer the question? Rio, let's hear from you seeing as you, too, are vocal this afternoon."

RV repositions himself in his seat, straightens his blazer and flips through a book on his desk.

"I don't know, sir," he says eventually. "I need to look over it again."

Mr Tate radiates disappointment over the classroom and peers around the class with a slow burn.

Please don't ask me. Please don't ask me.

"Isabelle. Why don't you inform the class of the answer?"

Thank the world for Isabelle.

***

There's an air of spring bounciness about Silversedge, hanging baskets and people sat outside drinking coffees without thick coats, the motivation of summer lifts the dull of earlier wintery months. I am beginning to feel lifted myself, despite the confusion over what my next move is, a question I have constantly running in my head. I wish Vozareia did email or Snapchat – it would be far easier.

I take a moment to inhale the sight of the town on my way home and signal for silence discreetly, deciding to translate the energy of the café goers across the street – for training purposes only, of course. Selecting a couple, a guy in a white T-shirt and a bonny woman in a linen blouse sat next to him, I purposefully dial into his energy from across the road. It's becoming easier and quicker to do and I'm pleased at my progress. Between thoughts and audible words being offered in my head, underpinned by foreign feelings I can sense, I detect the guy in the white T-shirt is disagreeing with the bonny lady over holidays or travel… *oh, I don't think the guy wants to go at all. Oh. Aw no. Wow.* He's going to break up with her. I stand and watch as his decision lands in her world, and I don't need to be a Zeffo to see that she's shattered.

I feel intrusive as it's nothing to do with me. The practise, too, is quite draining on my energy and I expel a yawn as I vote to slip out of Zeffo mode and back to my walk home.

Reaching the bottom of the hill, I gaze up to the hump and I pull my phone out of my bag to call Gusti. There's a message from Lizzie saying she is looking forward to meeting at Wavies on Thursday after school and I fire a message back saying how I am too. I press on the name Gusti to ring him and, drifting sloth-like up the hill, I wait for him to pick up to see if he can help me figure out my conundrum about Palm and my drawings. He answers and tells me he's sat with Richard in Wavies enjoying Silversedge's' calling card of drinking coffee with good people.

"Talking American football?" I ask and laugh, envisioning the two discussing a sport which makes no sense to me at all.

"American football? No! Can't stand the game," he replies, "I'll call back in a couple of hours, unless it's urgent?" he asks, careful not to use my name.

Hold on.

I'm sure Leo told me he was explaining the rules of the game as Richard had turned Gusti into a fan of it, that day I saw them through the window at Wavies. A pristine black raven flies across me and sits on the wall, and I pause in my drifting to look at him. I haven't noticed the ravens in a while, and it's a welcome sight, a friendly face.

"Leo did say that didn't he?" I say to the bird.

The raven twitches his head to the side, releases its wings to full span and soars across the road to perch on the low stone wall which encloses the park, only to continue staring at me.

He's trying to punctuate something...

I watch the raven through the gap of parked cars, all neatly positioned in front of the wall. I didn't misunderstand, did I? I think over and over, but our stare down continues. It was then I see the black fancy car with the private reg, the one that sped past me at the junction the day of Felix's tattoo. It's parked facing upwards, a couple of spaces up from where the raven is sat. With my phone still in my hand, I type the reg number in my notes and crawl further forward, leering my eyes sideways to spy inside without turning my head and it makes my eyes ache.

The rear windows are blacked out. Two men all suited are sat in the front talking, and I'm hit with an intuitive pang inside me, so unexpected and strong I outwardly gasp. The drawing of the car and the two men flash before me, and when I turn back, the raven has gone.

Shit.

My pace changes from sloth to panther and ten minutes later I'm safe in my house, in the comfort of my bedroom desperately looking into the picture for further clues. I feel Palm's energy, and the sunshine in my life returns almost as soon as I called out for it. But I'm frustrated and fuddled, and practically ignoring him. All mixed up, I try to receive another message from Vozareia and consider for a moment that the message could actually be from Palm; I wasn't scared, oddly enough, of the two men, more alarmed and shaken at the accuracy of the mystic messages I'm downloading and piecing together. This has shifted gears, and I'm not sure what to do.

Sat motionless with my pencil, I begin to add onto the sketch of the building: an archway at the front, a large one, and a grey, depressive sky. I'm compelled to draw a triquetra in a small window on the right of the building, then the flow ceases. This building has to refer Palm; it's the symbol on his picture I dotingly hung on my wall. I glance up to check it's the same and immediately I can see that it is – Palm must have something for me in this building.

"Could you not have given me the name of the place instead? You are not the best at communicating sometimes, Palm."

I think, think and overthink my way to inspiration: I decide the drawing of the car and the two men are to do with the black car I came across on the way home, and Palm… he needs me to get a message or something to them. Palm is in a graveyard somewhere, I bet, and I'm guessing the building, then, is a church. I need to go to his grave, whatever this message is, it must be there.

Chapter Fifteen
Picture Talk

After taking Palm's painting down from the wall in my bedroom, I hug it to my chest and beetle into the kitchen. Thanks to Mum's new purchase of a steamer, the turbo steam makes the kitchen feel like a sauna at a spa and it turns hair frizzy in an instant.

Mum is preoccupied cooking dinner and checking her emails on her phone.

"I think I would like to hang this in the sitting room," I say, breezily searching the junk drawer for a picture hook and a hammer.

It was the only idea I could think of to immediately bring Palm to the forefront of the conversation so I can delve deeper for information and insist she takes me to visit his grave. In spite of my ulterior motive, I hope by visiting his grave and hometown with me in tow – the two people Palm most utterly adored, as I'm told – Mum will be able to find the closure she desperately needs, closure I'm finding more of day by day but not enough for it to be done.

I leave no time for Mum to question me, and she finds me minutes later staring at the sitting room wall, admiring my handy work.

"I like it there," I say, "this picture feels different to all the others hung around the house. It feels like family." I smile at her and she comes over, placing her arm around me. I was embarrassed for a moment until she said she felt the same. We stand whimsically adoring the painting hung behind the sofa, lost in lightness, when the steamer pings and snaps the lightness in two.

"I love how well you are dealing with all this, darling," Mum says, speeding off into the kitchen. "I am very proud of you. I know Palm would have been too. I only wish he was here for real," she voices brightly from the kitchen.

"Me too," I yell back.

I smile with hearty eyes at the picture one last time and join Mum in the kitchen. Holding out the dinner plates for the salmon and vegetables she's prepared.

"The salmon looks pale. Is it alright?" I ask, dissecting the fish on the plate. My mother's law knowledge far outweighs her culinary skill. Odd-looking meals worry me, and her reassurances are hard to believe.

I'll just eat the vegetables.

I ramble on, explaining we need to visit Palm's final resting place for closure and for learning more about my heritage. I lay it on thickly, but Mum is zoning out, shutting down like she does and it instantly winds me up.

"You can't deny me seeing his grave surely?" I ask.

"We are not going. That's the end of it. Have you finished with that?" she deflects, pointing at my plate with the lonely pale piece of salmon untouched. I look at the plate and shake my head, more in disbelief at her than in answer to her question.

"We need to visit where Palm is buried. We need closure together. I have a right to see where I come from, you owe me that much at least." I speak louder – frankly I'm at the end of my rope with this constant battle of Mum's refusal to work with me on anything I try to sort out with her.

"We are not going to Sicily, Seven," Mum fires back, her patience notably gone as she clatters the steamer and plates into the dishwasher.

"Why not?" I ask loudly.

She takes off her sparkly dress ring, places it next to the sink and squirts hand cream into her hands. With a heaviness she returns to sit down on the bar stool opposite me, gathering her answer before she discloses the verdict, I've seen her do this with difficult clients refusing to accept her answer.

"You are making this far more dramatic than it needs to be." She pauses and slides off the chair to turn towards the window with folded arms. "Plus… I don't know where he is buried," she rattles off as though it's a petty detail.

How can she not know this? Seriously, how can she not?

"You went to the funeral; it will be at the same place?"

She inhales a large breath and returns to the island, rearranging the salt and pepper shakers and today's post stacked in the middle. It's incredulous. I watch her momentarily and then snatch the post out from under her hand. My face, I'm sure, wears the same perplexed expression that I'm feeling.

"I didn't attend his funeral, so I couldn't say," she says.

Oh, my fucking god. All I can do is stare at her, speechless.

Heated situations are an area of my life I need to gain control of and I must master my Zeffo powers to quickly ascertain truth in stressful moments – a tricky technique. With a deep breath, I lower a hand in my mind and dial into her energy and join it with my own. It feels frazzled, like a crackling fire in my chest; it's difficult for me to translate and I'm about to give up, but in that final second I gain a glimpse past her fire enough to translate that she is being honest. She has no idea where he is buried.

"No need to stare so hard," she retorts, "it was complicated; Simon was being difficult, and you were my priority. I decided with the guys in Sicily, it was better I stay here rather than ruffle feathers. I held my own farewell to him in private."

I'm still staring at her. Still speechless. Not only does this mess up the plan, but I'd quickly grown fond of the idea of visiting his town and grave. It would have been beautiful and healing, for both of us.

How can probably one of the most brilliant minds I know NOT go to the funeral, NOT know where Palm is buried and NOT think to ask?!

She offers instead to take me to 'their place' where they often met in London, where he would arrange lunch or cute surprises. Romance marked their lives, and 'their place' is where she held her own farewell for him. It wreaks of sadness whichever way I slice it, but I agree as it's better than nothing.

"I called in at Jamming Minds today, by the way," Mum adds out of nowhere. "Spoke to a chap... Gusti?"

I jerk back towards her just as I'm reaching the doors to leave the kitchen.

"What? Why?"

"I wanted to see where you found his painting, and what

the shop was before he had it," Mum replies. "I can't understand how it ended up at Jamming Minds, streets away from our house. Palm and I never visited Silversedge and he didn't know the area."

"What did Gusti say?" I ask, unsure if I'm coming across as casual or intense.

"It was a boutique art gallery many years ago. It closed down when the owners went bust. Since then, a few others have tried to make a go of an array of businesses there but haven't lasted the course. Gusti believes the painting is from the art gallery era and was left in the back room, forgotten. No one has bothered to move it or claim it."

"Do you reckon Palm had something to do with the gallery? He must have if his painting was there."

"No. He didn't deal with art business, only painted it. The painting must have been given to them, or Palm gave it to someone who passed it on, who passed it on… a thousand explanations could apply."

Something is going on here, I have hunch as big as London, but I don't know what exactly, and I need to speak to Gusti to help work this out, because I can't.

"How can you be certain? Isn't the Mafia secretive?" I ask. Mum smiles as though I need another sweet pat on the head and closes the white shutters inside the kitchen windows. She absentmindedly presses a button on the dishwasher sending it into a whirr.

"It's called coincidence, and yes, I'm sure Palm had nothing to do with a small boutique art gallery in Silversedge."

I look at Mum, she doesn't believe that any more than I do.

"We have his new picture now and I think we were meant to find it. That's what I think all this is," Mum concludes as my phone starts ringing in my pocket. She rolls her eyes as I look at the caller. Gusti.

"Go," she says, a smile forming as she wafts her arm forward. "We're done here, anyway."

We're not, but okay.

I take the stairs two at a time, making small talk with Gusti until I click my bedroom door shut. He plays along, knowing I need to reach a place where I can speak freely.

"I need help," I say. "There's a message, or an object, or a something I need to find and it's urgent, or on a time limit."

I tell him about the new additions to my drawing and how this story, or stream of cryptic messages, is to do with Palm and that this part is the only thing I am sure of. I explain Palm has visited me more than once. I met my dad, if only as sunshine, but I met him. I say it with a swell heart, and I sense the infusion of Gusti's happy glow at our union through the ethers. Energy doesn't understand distance – *it just is.*

"But I'm at a loss," I gush. "My idea about the pocket watch was good, but it's in Sicily. The visit to his grave is also a stellar one, but Mum doesn't know where he is buried. The two men hanging around Silversedge in the black car are involved but I don't know how, all I do know is that they aren't threats. When I call on Palm, he doesn't give me anything apart from the arrow around the pocket watch and a man lying down. What the fuck, Gusti? What the fuck?"

He's entertained by how much I can speak without breathing, but I can't say I share his feelings on the matter.

"Very good detective work. You're making it a little more

complicated than you need to," he replies. "Don't forget to ask Vozareia to send more clarity, more messages, and use your powers to lead you to things more. As you are seeing already, this is how it works."

"I get all that, but can't you help me out? What am I meant to do?"

We go through each scenario, drawing and clue again. All he says is a non-committal 'hmm' and 'okay' calmly to each, and only asks if I actually heard Palm – a different voice and thought process – or if it was just his energy which inspired the new drawings.

"I nearly heard him; I'm sure I could have gotten to that," I add, like I should have been able to.

When I consider his question, I must admit there was no indication of other communication from him. I couldn't sense his voice that I so long to hear at all.

Gusti runs through a few tips I can use, insisting again I need to be bolder and more trusting with myself as a Zeffo. 'The Boras is tricking you into a scatty and sprawling state' he says, 'I need to keep it more controlled and tighter' he says, but as the quest against the Boras is my own, he's not allowed to figure it out for me.

"You're doing well. I will add one thing, which I believe you will find exceptionally useful."

"Yes," I bite. "Anything."

"You missed the obvious," he says.

I have?

"I agree you found and connected with his energy and are translating it, but I am afraid it wasn't him coming to you in spirit form to converse with you."

"How is this exceptionally helpful? It makes me feel like shit," I cut in.

"Because, young Zeffo, with your powers you receive vital and direct information from Vozareia. Vozareia is the main Gangster, not me. You can also use your powers to dial into Bipper and Remmie energy to assist you, but only Zeffo's with the power *medium* can dial into and communicate with those who have died and passed to the other realm. A power you don't have. Check your Book of Lights. Therefore, the fact you are picking up his energy and translating it means—"

"—he can't be dead. He has to be alive."

Chapter Sixteen
Trip, Don't Fall

I can't say I've listened all that much in school today, apart from when Mr H announced to the class I had been chosen as Artist of the Year and my display will be in the main reception for all to view. It was nice, the stuff my secret thoughts are made of, but when it happens it's unsettling; a newfound layer of me not yet ripe enough for my own fruition. I mean, where do you look in these circumstances? who do you look at whilst someone gushes praise about you to a class of thirty others? The atmosphere was an amalgam of applause and green eyes and all I could concentrate on was: *he's alive.*

Palm is alive.

The home time shuffle about the school ensues, and the MGs surface from different classrooms and corridors all meeting in the main corridor junction. Talk is mainly from Nate about the basketball final happening on Friday whilst Leo and Felix play out an imaginary final and the winning hoop down the corridor as we near the main doors. A sheepish Yas interrupts play, saying she won't be able to make the game as she is trying to keep on the good side of her parents and wants to be home to prepare dinner and be a 'doting daughter'. I feel for Nate who slumps a little at her news; this game means a lot to him, and we mean a lot to him. We've always been there for as many games as we can, especially his bigger ones, and I know Nate was banking on all of us being there. I think it supports him more than any of us know, not that he would ever say.

"Part of a wicked plan to get them on board with you picking out clothes for a living?" Nate says, pushing the door open hard with his spindly arm.

"Moi? Wicked? Never," she says and smirks in return, "and it's not picking out clothes." She pushes at Nate's shoulder, oblivious to the hurt Nate has disguised as a stinging comment.

As I trot on behind, the last one through the doors, my unruly bag catches on the door handle, and I trip out of the door instead. Nate is the nearest and it's Nate's arm I grab. It's all I could latch onto to break my tumble and prevent myself ending up on the floor in a heap. Holding his wrist with my hand, the commotion of home time is instantly erased as memories pass back and forth between our eyes and motionless bodies, and it makes me wonder once more, what if, and for this brief second, I know Nate does too. Why, why is it every time I let it go, something happens to re-spark it?

"You okay?" he asks, breaking the moment. I only nod as he lifts me up with one swift movement of his arm.

Yasmina darts in, just as Lizzie and Leo turn back around to see what the delay is and Felix puts his arm in front of RV to stop him coming over to help, which seems excessive of RV given it was only a trip not a fall down a flight of stairs, and it's clearly in hand.

"Come on dinky." Yasmina giggles. "Hold onto me, I'll

walk you to the bus stop and make sure you stay upright," she says. A farce is averted as we all huddle, free of school, onto the main road.

"Have you said anything to your coaches or Mum yet?" RV asks Nate bluntly and out of nowhere, surprising us all.

"About what, bro?"

"The fact you don't want to go pro with basketball," RV replies, like a smart detective quietly figuring out the unspoken truths of Nate Johnson. "It's obvious, man. Your big talk doesn't fool me."

Nate is taken off guard, and by the look on his face RV's words are salt to a wound I had only suspected was there. The others have been clueless, it seems, that it was there at all, fully believing Nate's showmanship of how much he loves the pressure of being forecast as London's next Michael Jordan. What I think Nate hates more is RV calling him out on it in front of everyone.

"I'm great at basketball, and it will give me options. Take me to places I wouldn't be able to go to otherwise… and why wouldn't I want to go pro, man?" Nate replies, holding his arms out wide to RV like a bird flapping its wings as a territorial warning.

"What places? Places you don't want to go to anyway?" RV continues quizzing Nate and I'm confused as to where it's all come from.

"RV. Knock it off," Nate says with a heavy hand to RV's shoulder and a point-blank range stare. Nate then shoots across the road saying he'll see us all tomorrow. "Get your game faces on for Friday!" he shouts back over the traffic, as we all bob along the main road to our different bus stops home.

"I think it's him who needs to do that. Not us," quips RV.

"Didn't know you were a comedian, RV," Felix says.

"Shut it, Rose," RV replies.

"My twin bro here definitely needs help in finding his way in life. You can help him instead," Lizzie says to RV, imitating a panic-stricken toddler looking for its mother, amused at her own sarcasm.

"Screw you, Lizzie," Leo retorts, turning to get her in her face. "Think you and your surfboard have it all figured out don't ya?"

Lizzie slams Leo's chest with the palm of her hand. "Don't take your shit out on me." Lizzie's slams Leo's chest again, harder, causing him to bang into Yas, but he returns to remain in Lizzie's space.

"Think you're all hard?" Leo says.

"Get out of my face then," Lizzie replies, squaring up to him.

"Whoa, whoa. No fighting on my watch," Yasmina roars.

We stop walking along and come to a standstill in the middle of the pavement, other students making their way home split apart and walk either side of us forming an ellipse around us. Leo moves with fury to the other side of the group, away from Lizzie, and leans on the garden wall of one of the many rows of semi-detached houses further down the road from school. As they cool off, I point out to RV he was a bit harsh to Nate. Whilst what RV said may have some truth to it, approaching Nate in private would have been better, seeing as he feels so concerned about Nate's future. RV, looking like he's ready to flip, throws me a dark scowl and walks off, hands in his pockets, not saying a word to anybody to catch the bus to his after-school tutor. Lizzie, distracted by RV, suddenly finds Leo ragging her bag off her shoulder and he lobs it far into a garden and storms off, claiming he'll get his bus at the next stop.

"Real cool, Leo," Lizzie shouts, "see you at home. I'll have your milk and cookies ready,"

Leo yells back without looking, informing Lizzie he's not going straight home, but Lizzie continues firing jabs until Leo turns around and flips her the finger on both hands. Lizzie stomps off to retrieve her bag from the garden it landed in and marches off to her bus stop. Yas, Felix and I look on in silent confusion.

"What the hell happened? How did we all get to bickering because I fell out of the door?" I ask.

Sliding in between me and Yas, Felix wraps an arm around each of our shoulders as we make another attempt to make it all the way to the bus stop.

"Looks like it's just us three then." Felix grins, before sticking his arm up to flag the 391 into Silversedge Town.

Jumping out through the central doors of the red bus in Silversedge Town, we wheedle through the streets, waving at Richard who is taking a delivery at Wavies from a truck and getting beeped at by angry car drivers every two seconds. Richard doesn't seem stressed by the jam his delivery truck is causing, instead he looks extra dopey and smiley, talking to a lady in between signing something on a clipboard. I recognise her but can't place her, and after a couple more glances, I still can't shake off where I know her from.

"I bet he's finally scored a date," I say to Yas.

"'Bout time," Felix adds, "anyway, lovely ladies, I need to collect my ASOS parcel from the post office."

"See you," we both say and laugh. When he's gone, Yas and I begin drifting on the main street for a quiet five minutes we don't seem to have had for a while.

"How's things with Andrew?" I ask.

I look over my shoulder again at the woman Richard is talking to, when I remember it was the lady in ripped jeans who came for an appointment at Jamming Minds whilst I was talking to Gusti. Behind them both I catch the rear view of Leo, alone and turning with purpose up the cobbled street, up to where Jamming minds is.

"—then, Andrew said I was the most beautiful girl in the room, can you believe how fabulous he is?"

"Oh wow, how great it must be to hear that," I say, jumping back into our conservation, hiding my hiatus in hearing what she is talking about quite well.

I'm happy for Yas, she deserves someone who cares and will look out for her and support her. The closeness with a special person, the inside jokes between two people and the feeling of being safe is a luxury few seem to find, a future always an inch away from our grasping hands.

"He is ripped too." Yasmina continues with intermittent squeals, and I find myself squealing as well although I don't know why. I'm in shock; she's seen her Tarzan's chest! I fret over kissing – I can't enjoy the moment without asking myself if I'm doing it right, questioning whether I use tongue or not, and how I make that not disgusting – and who do you ask to check these things? I can't ask Nate, the only boy I have kissed, it would be weird. When does a chest situation happen and what does one do with a torso? So many questions with answers I can only think will be lurking on YouTube videos I need to find.

Sod it.

"So, what do you even do in that situation?" I ask. "When someone has their top off in front of you, what do you do, exactly?" I feel positively idiotic already.

"You just smooth your hand over it," Yas says. "Like you do on their head or back when you are kissing, but it's on their skin and feels so good… It makes your stomach fizz!" I'm positively tomato in colour and feel more inadequate and inexperienced than ever.

"Practice on yourself if you are nervous about it. Sounds silly, but it helps," she says.

We pass the plethora of coffee shops, the chairs where the couple sat as they broke up into new eras of their lives are empty, and two chefs at the Italian at the end of the main street stand by the side door talking with exaggerated arm movements, smoking cigarettes as they gear up for another evening of pizza and vino. I think about practising smoothing my hand over my chest and, nope – *nope!* – I can't do it, it feels ridiculous and embarrassing.

"I think Nate still likes you," Yas adds as we are about to go our separate ways home. My insides bubble over a statement I've longed to hear, but she warns me off because he's not in the best of places. "He's with our friend Lizzie, and he seems all mixed up. You need a boyfriend who is surer footed about himself than Nate is, and sure about you."

"Maybe I don't need a boyfriend at all."

"Maybe. It's just a feeling but watch out for it. It will only be trouble," she says.

We hug goodbye. "Mr Magical is out there, babe. On his way. You'll see," Yas says and turns to walk home.

Chapter Seventeen
Don't Look

Oh. Yes.

Felix created PARTY group chat, 20 people added

I scroll down the list of people in the group chat, flooded with some familiar Year 11 and Year 12 names mixed with a few I don't know from his drama class. This party might be just what I need.

Message from Felix

Yo. Party at mine next Friday. All yous are invited.

Message from Leo

Gonna be awesome

Message from Nate

I'm down, what about drinks though?

Message from Felix

I have fake ID and a few older mates. Let me know if you want me to get you anything.

Message from Bea

Looking forward to it xx

Message from Ben

I'll come. I'll bring a crate of beer.

Message from Lizzie

I'm in

Message from Amy

Hey Felix, thanks for inviting me. It's a yes from me and Emily. Is it ok if I bring my boyfriend?

Message from Ozzie

You know ya boy, need to ask the parents

Message from Lewis

Yeah buddy but I'll be late. Can you get me bottle of Vodka?

Message from Yasmina

Andrew and I will be there!

Message from Elliot

Damn, I'm out already. Soz

Message from Kaine

Sick. I've fake ID too, I'll bring shots

Message from Penny

I so need this party Felix! Kaine, can you sort some pear cider for me?

And the rampage of messages continues.

Message from Michael

I'll come. Not drinking though, football training Saturday morning

Message from Felix

Michael, just have a few beers man. Bea, I'll get your Malibu and I'll meet you before the party to give it to you

Message from me

Yeah, I'll come. Felix, can you sort me a bottle of white wine for spritzers?

Message from RV

Yeah, G. I'll sort myself out

Who Is Bea? Felix hasn't mentioned this.

Voice note to Felix.

"Who is Bea? Have you met someone and not told me? And how you allowed to have all these people round at yours?"

Voice note from Felix

"She's from the college near my drama class. Mum and Dad said I was allowed a gathering, their way of apologising over the acting issue!"

Voice note to Felix

"Is Felix dating an older woman? This isn't a gathering it's a party!"

Voice note from Felix

"Same thing, and Bea is friend. Stop being nosey!"

A tapping on my bedroom door halts our conservation, and I click my phone off as Mum slopes in holding a glossy brochure. Twilight has set in outside, and I'm sat in a room of darkening hues. I hadn't noticed the time moving on. Before the group chat, I was immersed in consulting the Book of Lights and discovered with no surprise that Gusti is right: I don't have the power of medium. All my notes referring to meeting Palm's energy indicate I had dialled into his energy like I can with other living people, rather than conversing with him as a person who has passed over into the other realm.

I turn my lamp on to rid my room of feeling like it does when you open the fridge and there's nothing in it except the light and a block of cheese, and the lamp brings cosiness at the flick of its switch. Mum hands me the brochure, a prospectus for an art college nearby.

"I spoke to Mr Henry today, at length," she says, sitting herself on the bed next to me, running her hand across the duvet, "there's no question of your talent, but he made me see the opportunities available… and the problems if I stop you pursuing this."

Thumbing through the prospectus I sit in an appreciation of Mum, I know this must have been difficult for her, putting aside her pain over my art interests, reminding her of Palm and her flawed judgments about a creative career. After all, creativity does not starve souls but saves them. Mr Henry has worked a miracle, and perhaps I have too as I begin to accept myself as an artist, and I feel the accomplishment of a slither of a breakthrough against the Boras Curse on this matter.

"While we're on the topic of art, I wanted to discuss Jamming Minds," Mum says.

Cross legged on the bed, I look away from the page I'm reading and up to her weighty forehead. I shouldn't be surprised that she has been burrowing around in the background, checking out the place to see if there is any connection between Jamming Minds and the Mafia. I tentatively continue the conversation, batting a bedevilling angst in my mind about what her enquiries have uncovered.

"I find it odd Palm's picture was there. It doesn't make sense."

"You needed to do checks on Gusti? He's not in the Mafia!" I exclaim.

I can assure you, he's not a mafia dude.

"Maybe not, but the building belongs to Palm's… colleagues. Have you noticed anything strange at all recently?"

Plenty.

I'm stunned, not only about my own life, but because Mum has not dismissed this Palm situation as I assumed she had. She likes facts, evidence, certainty, and it slipped my consciousness that she is not one to discuss or make decisions until she has all the information she feels she needs. How different we both are.

"I was around Palm's lifestyle long enough to trust myself when I sense something going on," she adds.

Mum is acutely aware when anyone, and definitely when it's me, is withholding information, and I need to give her something. I fess up about the car and how I've seen it twice, one time nearly knocking me over by accident – much to her concern – and how, like her, I got a feeling around it. I give her the reg number I noted in my phone, and she tootles back out of my room, returning half an hour later confused and rattled.

"The car is associated with them too," she says, squeezing her forehead between her fingers.

I can feel my cheeks drop into seriousness as the realisation of what the boys are back in town means. I begin to wonder if they are out to harm me and Mum, because someone is in danger, and maybe it's us? But then why the hell would it be us, and after all this time?

"Gusti is correct about the chap who used the building as a gallery: he went bust and lost the family home, car and savings to an art deal set to catapult him into big news and riches. Except the deal was a fraudulent one."

"Do you think the fraudulent deal was operated by Palm? I thought you said he didn't deal with art?"

"Perhaps I thought wrong, I was wrong about your art career." She swigs from her mug of tea and swirls it around as she looks out of the window, when a loud smack sounds from the corner of my room, causing both of us to jump back an inch. A towering pile of books teetering on the end of the shelf has toppled the top book, Love Quotes, onto the floor. I bought the book in anticipation of using some of the quotes in handwritten love letters to my guy, a sweet notion I fantasise of, but so far Love Quotes has been a waste of money. Mum, with a hand to her chest, sees the book on the floor and dismisses it as an inevitable incident, bound to have happened due to my untidiness, and tells me I need to sort the shelf out. She draws the curtains, shutting out the evening and the raven sat on the window ledge; of which I stop myself from waving at because I realise that's kind of weird; before moving to pick up the open book.

"No, I'll do it," I say, leaping off the bed and across the room.

It wasn't an accidental tumble: it's from Vozareia, and I need to read the page it's landed open on. I make a note of the page number, 211, and place the book back on the highly unstable pile of books, vowing to sort the shelf at the weekend.

"You said you were on good terms with the boys from Sicily. Can't you just call them up and ask them why they are here?"

"No," she replies, wheeling out the chair under my desk and sitting down. "They will know I've been delving. It took a long time for me to earn their trust and respect. Me being a lawyer compromises the code," she says.

With a new perspective on secret organisations, I am duly fascinated as Mum restlessly explains the Omertà. It's a code of honour, a code of silence, most mafia organisations have to abide by at all costs, or risk being killed – family and relatives are not spared in some cases either. Avoiding contact with authorities and the law is one of the Omertà's rules Mafiosi must swear to, as well as not ratting anyone out, of course. Mum babbles on, with no answer about what we are supposed to do, as I play over my drawing in my mind, tempted to whip it out of my draw and explain it to her.

"Leave it with me. I'll see what else I can find out. If you notice anything odd or strange – anything – you must tell me immediately," she instructs, standing up from the chair for the twentieth time.

I nod my head and watch her wrap her oversized cardigan around herself as she walks past me to leave my bedroom.

"Mum," I say, and she stops at the doorway to turn around and face me, hugging herself and the cardigan tightly. "You are sure Palm's dead, aren't you? Because your details are sketchy, and people survive gun shots all the time."

"Of course, I am. This isn't a fairy tale or a movie."

Later that evening, eavesdropping by my bedroom door to eavesdrop on talk coming from Mum's bedroom (under the false pretence I would hear something useful in my hunt to solve this quest) I am saddened. I hear Mum in her bedroom, crying softly, muttering to Vincenzo about how she wished he was here and misses him. Even after all this time, no one can take his place and what a fool she was to give up. Tip toeing away from the hallway, I click my bedroom door shut as lightly as I can and lean against my wardrobe. I feel bad and long for him too. My intent was to give her a ray of hope, suggesting Palm could be alive, not to inflict pain and activate feelings of grim regret. Sighing, I pick up Love Quotes, hover my hand above the first page and watch the following pages flip until it reaches page 211.

> You heard my call because I heard yours. Be equal in self to the romance you ask of life, for they are already here. Are you?

"Does everything have to be fucking cryptic?" I ask.

'It's how you learn,' I hear back.

"Oh, go away. Also, I'm clearly here, look!" I prod myself proudly in the chest a tad too hard. "Where is *he*, is the point?"

Why do I even have this dumb book full of love and romance quotes? I clap the book shut and place it back on the towering pile. With the power of Vozareia flowing through my hand, and more than a little bit of concentration, I move the books into a straighter pile by motioning the energy forward between me and the stack, the heaviest weight I've moved to date.

Sinking into bed, three things are clear: I need proof – proper proof – that Palm is alive, I need to find the car and the men in it and I need some serious lessons in romance.

***

Sat on the school bus, I text in the MG group chat not to wait for me and Yas at the bus stop as we are running late.

> *Nate is typing*
>
> No prob. Meet at the outdoor basketball court.

Yas is upset and deeply confused whether she is an Arab Yasmina or an English Yasmina and we need a little extra time to bring her back from the ledge she's on.

"I prefer London to Dubai, so why am I missing Dubai so much?" she asks between wails as we disembark and deliberately take our time arriving at the school grounds.

"It's okay to miss places and people, and you are the great Yasmina, not a nationality."

"Thank you," she says and sniffles, fiddling with her blazer cuff.

Dubai was Yas' home for thirteen years, and I guess she will miss it. Maybe in times of need we return to what or where feels familiar to feel safe, and it dawns on me that Nate is my Dubai.

Today is the Year 11 assembly in the main hall, a mandatory attendance event. Yas and I walk along the front of the school, past the playing field and onto the little path around the back, as I decide walking the long way around to the main hall would give Yas enough time to settle her emotions and allow her eyes to de-puff.

"It appears the gentlemen made it before us," Yas says, tipping her sunglasses, as we see Felix, Nate and RV playing basketball on the courts. A few other Year 11s are playing tennis on the court behind them – a lively morning.

"I don't think I've ever seen Felix be early for school," I reply, tipping my sunglasses down too.

"Hey, you two, catch!" Nate throws the ball full pelt at us; I squirm, holding my arms up in front of me not knowing what to do with the impending pain I anticipate from the ball hurtling towards me. As I feared, the large ball hits me right in the face, knocking my sunglasses off along with half my brain.

"Watch it, Nate, you moron. You alright, babe?" Yas says, collecting my glasses from the ground as I shake the daze off and readjust my hair.

"I'm fine." I slide my glasses back on as the three boys burst out laughing.

I do not find this funny at all as Nate runs over to the edge of the court where we are standing and splutters an apology.

"Sorry. Didn't mean for that happen," Nate says as the morning bell rings out across the school, raising everyone's attention.

The tennis players pack up and wander off. Felix and RV jog over from centre court to join us, and the three boys gather their bags up and slide on their blazers, readjusting their tie knots to the correct position, all the while distracted by their own banter about the game just played.

"Come on, you lot," Yas insists, "we'll be late."

Nate wipes his neck and face with a bright white towel, not responding to Yas' paranoia about receiving detentions for being late, and in his own time stuffs the towel back in his bag before declaring he's now ready to go.

"You all go to assembly. I'm gonna skip it," RV says, not joining us as we head off.

In unison we hold off walking any further and stare at him, knowing this is exactly the type of thing certain wolves at his door are waiting for him to do.

"We have the gang awareness talk in assembly today, right?" he continues, "Who do you think they'll all be pointing and looking at when they bang on about it… they know jack all. I don't want to hear about it, and I can't be arsed with it."

"Ignore them, RV. They don't know shit about you," Nate replies whilst rolling the lethal ball over in his hands.

"Easier said than done, man," RV fires back as he turns to walk back towards the playing field.

"Fuck them, RV. Not going will give them the ammo they want. YO – Leo, Lizzie – over here," Felix yells as the twins come into view at the other end of the court, "you go after RV, Nate. I'll be there in a sec."

Nate and Felix's chat with RV must have worked as all seven of us are in assembly sitting in a line in the second row waiting for the noise to hush. Mr Donnelley, the headmaster, stands behind the wooden podium anxious to begin.

Thick burgundy velvet curtains reserved for school performances, are drawn back, framing the long stage Mr Donnelly is now pacing. His bald head shines under the harsh lighting above, and he stands out in his truly awful, ill-fitting grey suit. The year group quietens, and Mr Donnelley returns to the podium to begin his address.

A surprise announcement of a new deputy head is made; I didn't know the last guy had gone, but Mr Donnelley proudly opens his right arm to welcome Miss Grace, who is uncharacteristically young with good fashion sense and a sick hairstyle.

"That's more like it," I whisper over to Lizzie, who is sitting towards the end of the line by the aisle, "as if someone as dope as her is the new deputy," I continue whispering to her. Yas pokes me in the ribs from the right with a fully extended arm, and speaking through unnervingly still lips she tells me to be quiet before they notice me talking

"Thank you, Miss Grace," Mr Donnelley says, nearly tripping over his own feet in excitement about the newest staff member. *Gross.* "Now, each year we honour the fatal stabbing of Thomas, an innocent fifteen-year-old London boy. We do this by discussing with you, Year 11, the dangers of London gangs and street culture. We will show you how not to get caught up in this world which leads to nothing but devastation and destruction." RV glares forward, his body turning rigid and his eyes to stone.

"I am holding this talk earlier than normal this year, as it has been reported that people, suspiciously from the aforementioned background, have been hanging about the school perimeter on various occasions. That will be dealt with accordingly, but—"

"Why are you looking at me?" RV shouts out to Mr Donnelley.

Nate nudges RV. "It's not worth the hassle, bro."

Mr Donnelly appears taken aback by RV's comment, but RV is right, he was looking at him a lot and in our direction.

"I am not looking at you in particular, Rio. I am looking at the entire year group, my gaze is falling upon various people," Mr Donnelly replies with a thoroughly unconvincing tone. I want to zap him; I could easily unnerve him by making the curtain waft or flapping the ends of his blazer.

The atmosphere in the hall turns uncomfortably thick and heads all swivel towards RV. Yas, Lizzie and I dutifully throw death stares back out at the crowd. I place my hand on RV's knee, who is sat to the left of me, trying to make him feel better. I don't think RV even notices I've done this as he doesn't flinch, he's too preoccupied and guarded, but I keep my hand there anyway and hope it helps.

"No. You've been focusing in on me. You think I've got something to do with whoever's hanging around. Is that it? Or am I just an example of what can happen?" RV, heavily agitated, stands up to walk out. A few gasps and tuts break out across the so-called fellow students which he cannot help but of heard.

"RIO VANNS, sit down!" Mr Donnelley booms, "I am implying nothing, and I will speak to you after assembly."

I'm no rule breaker, always scared of the consequence usually, but on reflection, I think RV was right about skipping this assembly. It would have been kinder. It's not like he needs to be made aware of gang life and its repercussions, nor be made a spectacle of when he has moved mountains to leave it behind.

I tug on his blazer arm sleeve to sit back down, and Leo, Nate and Felix all give him a nod to leave it.

"Don't rise to the bait," Leo mutters to RV.

RV begrudgingly sits back in the plastic chair, and I link my arm around his for the rest of the assembly. This he does notice, and he glances down at our joined arms and then up at me; it's a gentle exchange of care and I want to tuck my head into his shoulder – I'm sure I felt him want to do the same, but we don't. Instead, we both sit facing forward, not looking at each other again.

Chapter Eighteen
Rocky

The rest of the school day swings yin and yang. Leo tried to perk things up at lunch in the canteen, suggesting we all go to Wavies after school. Yas can't, Nate is training for the final tomorrow, me and Lizzie don't want to as we are meeting at Wavies later, and RV is in detention for his outburst this morning. He's been distant most of the day following the assembly, passing a blunt answer or comment here and there. Other than the detention, he has said little else about what Donnelley said to him afterwards.

After eating, we all sit out the rest of lunchtime on the field, tanning our arms in the sun with our heads laid on our bags. RV, lying on his puffa coat, is sandwiched in the middle of us, listening to music on his earphones and staring at the blue sky. We don't hassle him or make small talk and decide to leave him be as we all lie like a line of pencils.

"I'll come to Wavies for a bit," Felix pipes up from behind his sunglasses.

"Awesome," Leo says.

They reach over Nate and fist bump one another before we all carry on tanning in silence, drifting close to sleep until the bell sounds for the start of afternoon lessons.

***

"Gusti," I say over the tinkling bell of Jamming Minds as I walk in. He's sat in his usual chair contemplating an array of new tattoo drawings laid out in front of him across the coffee table. "Teach me how to fight," I say, stood like Superwoman.

I have a knowing, a tip off telling me to refine my skills and increase the use of the Zeffo powers allocated to me. I need to use them better, stronger and more confidently. I don't know why but nudges by Vozareia must be taken seriously. If someone is in danger, needs my assistance, or if I am in danger, I ought to be ready.

"I only have an hour, so we need to make it snappy," I say.

Gusti gathers up the scattered pieces of paper filled with drawings and pats them into a neat pile. He eyes his watch and winces at the time.

"Have you never watched Rocky?" he says, locking the door and flicking the kettle on.

"What's Rocky got to do with this?"

"Nothing. Other than he didn't learn in an hour."

"*He* wasn't a Zeffo, and *you* weren't his teacher," I say, folding my arms across my chest.

He laughs coyly, looking at the spotless floor shaking his head, and comments about how he's impressed with the progress I'm making and asks me to meet him upstairs in the Zeffo Room.

"Don't worry," he says as I climb the fairy tale staircase, "I know you don't like my tea, I got some of that juice in that you like."

I pause, resting my hand on the lit banister taking in the

thoughtful gesture. Someone took notice of small details about myself, I thought no one noticed.

"I appreciate the love but chopity chop, we've a lot to do in an hour and you need time for a Smoke Out afterwards."

I Didn't think a bit of practice would require a Smoke Out?

"Take this with you," he adds, nipping over to his main desk. He hovers his hand over a small ball wedged between sketchpads and his iPad. As he begins to raise his hand, the ball calmly follows until he holds it still in mid-air, before he taps it forward and directs it upwards straight to me. Thoughts of the basketball smacking me this morning return, but I refrain from throwing my arms around and catch the ball easily with one hand.

"Excellent," I say, feeling the most excited about being a Zeffo since I found out I was one.

My Zeffo powers of clairaudience, clairsentience, claircognizance and Z artist aren't used for action but for receiving information directly from Vozareia and for being able to dial into people's energy fields and translate their energy – helpful if I need to know their intentions, a truth, more clues, or if the Boras Curse is negatively affecting me via Bippers. The Zeffo powers I can use for action, movement, fighting or defending are my mystic shield and ability to move energy and objects, and these two beasts need levelling up.

"It doesn't seem like I can use them for a whole lot. If mafia are after me, I think I may need something more powerful," I say to Gusti, disheartened by how many Zeffo powers he has and how he is a master of them all. My progress seems so small by comparison.

"Want do you want, a Tommy Gun?" he says, eyebrow raised.

"Could be helpful?" I reply, feeling giddy.

"It would not." Gusti shakes his head as he often does when I'm around and being by all accounts quite daft.

"I disagree, but let's get on."

We commence with the easier of the two: my mystic shield. I practise reinforcing it so I can call upon a stronger version of it at will. I've used my shield to protect myself from being influenced by Bippers energy before, but now I am upping the game using my shield to block solid objects, not just energy infected with the Boras from Bippers.

Gusti throws the ball at me. At first it keeps hitting me, bouncing off my arm or my head – the head taps make me feel particularly stupid – but I persist in listening to Gusti, dropping my mind into my chest, and purposefully expand the six-inch invisible shield by radiating its strength out from my chest centre. Before long, I am stopping the ball from touching me and graduate to blocking Gusti's arm and, with slightly more difficulty, his foot. He was sweet, apologising in advance should he hit me if I fail to block the move, but as I radiate more of my power, heat floods my entire chest and I sense the shield growing stronger and brighter. I block or withstand his moves until I can hold back his whole body; I managed it only for a second, but I did it. Holding back the weight of a human or animal requires a considerable amount of concentrated power and I need more practice to cultivate the skill.

Short on time, we swap our training onto moving objects. Recent practice of this on rain, books and the door key have given me a head start. He teaches me a similar technique to the shield, but this time I don't use my chest, I direct the power and heat down my arm, out of my hand and wherever I want it to go. I find I keep touching my talisman for support when need be, that is until I move a chair and begin to feel like some sort of goddess. On a roll and eager to do more, I begin swiping items out of Gusti's hands. It's not about moving my physical arm but directing the heated Zeffo power. Finally, I manage to pelt a coaster off the shelf and across the room – I didn't think Gusti would appreciate me chucking his china teacup.

"Can I move a Bipper this way?"

"It's possible to knock any human over. Remember though, we are not here to injure, harm or kill others."

"I know that… out of interest though?"

Much like holding a human back with my shield, knocking a human over uses more power and I can't quite manage to knock Gusti over or out of the way.

"You will. That's enough for today," he says, collecting balls, coasters and papers scattered around the room as though tidying up after a small child. Gusti places his cup and my glass at the room's entrance to be taken back downstairs and ensures all is in its correct place as I realise I've been hit with a giant come down from our session.

Floppy, weak, feeling unwell and burning hot, I slump into one of the chairs at the table. Stricken with confusion and fear with no energy to walk, I'm surprised that Gusti doesn't seem phased or confused at all, murmuring something about the Smoke Out for recharging my empty mystical tanks.

Without a Zeffo room, a few hours are needed for a Smoke Out. The only shortcut is to activate the symbolic table in the

Zeffo Room, a procedure like the accession process but simpler, which is soothing to my battered mind and body. With my head laid on the table, I lay my flimsy arms out over the crow and mutter into the table whilst Gusti stands at the other side speaking as vibrantly as always.

> *"Our mystery is just a sky,*
> *we need no gas, we run on fly,*
> *with Vozareia, House and Energy,*
> *unite us with the eye."*

The crow's gemstone eye fires up bright turquoise, emitting it's beam upwards. It sprays outwards like a silent firework, showering the room with delicate pretty droplets of blue energy. I lay in this blue light shower, mesmerised and peaceful, until, as Gusti predicated, ten minutes later I feel perfectly fine.

When using Zeffo powers in stronger ways, it depletes our systems. The most intense use of Zeffo powers is a collective surge, I learn, and it's only to be used in urgent moments. It is performed by two or more Zeffos linked by arms, and uses the collective power provided by each member of the surge. It has to be precise, equally shared and direct; there's no room for error. If it's done wrong, a Zeffo can die from this process, drained beyond repair. Gusti has only performed a surge once, in Bali, and the most extreme state of depletion overcame him immediately after, taking him over two hours, instead of the standard ten minutes, of lying down in the Smoke Out to recover.

"Tonight," Gusti says, unlocking the door to let me out,

"I am planning Li Nuh's trip over here in the summer. I want to bring her to London sooner rather than later."

"Aw, I bet she misses you."

"We miss each other, we don't sleep well apart. Not to be rude, but unless it's dire, please don't disturb me. She's getting up at four in the morning to speak with me on Facetime."

Too cute and too sad at the same time.

"I know she probably hates you being here, but I'm glad you're here, Gusti," I say, stood on the cobbles.

"Zeffo power," we both say, knocking wrists together.

Chapter Nineteen
27

Walking down the alley towards Wavies in Silversedge Town, I recall the morning I burned my letter here on the way to school. Its ashes are long gone, but it feels like yesterday…

It's a long, narrow alley, stretching from the top of the hill down into the centre of Silversedge. It's a long time to be trapped in a narrow space by two high walls, and Mum would kill me if she knew I used it. It's not often I do, and I only when I'm rushing as it shaves a good ten minutes off the normal lengthier way into Silversedge town from my house; down the hill, right at the junction and round onto the high street.

The alley's walls are dark, damp and stand intimidatingly high. Even in summer it feels uninviting, as most of the alley is covered by a canopy of trees, overhanging from either side, and the floating smell of weed from people using the alley's quiet walk for a quick smoke often lingers in the air.

Not long after setting off down the alley I sense something bad, but I'm unable to place it. I open my shield, but the feeling is magnetically heavy around me and I'm relieved when Lizzie rings. I answer my phone pronto.

"Hey, running ten minutes late. You okay? You sound strange," Lizzie says.

Leo had news to tell her from when him and Felix had been at Wavies earlier, making her late, but I'm not in the mood to listen to gossip. I'm gripping my phone so hard it's squashing my ear and fingertips as I see a person in the far distance walking up. Nerves seesaw in my stomach as I try to quell what I'm feeling by treating it as an overreaction to calm me down, but I know it's not. By now I'm halfway down, and I can see a person, a man, heading towards me. I stop, lean against the wall, and tell Lizzie to stay on the phone with me until the man passes and I reach the end of the alley. She's uneasy about me walking it on my own and after giving me a safety lecture, Lizzie begins telling me a story to keep me company. Another attempt to strengthen my shield, as Gusti showed me only hours ago, doesn't seem to be working, I'm too distracted as the man draws closer. The bad feeling grows larger, and I fire off the only thing filling my mind.

"Lizzie. Get RV. Tell him to get here."

"Are you okay? Shit, what's happening? I'll have to put the phone down," she says.

"Just do as I say," I say before I hang up so she can ring RV.

My heart is racing as the man slows his pace and wears a thin smile as he walks towards me. I look down pretending to mess on my phone whilst my hips and face tighten as I dial into his field.

"Excuse me," he says, ceasing his stroll directly in front of me. His words are friendly and polite, but my translation of his energy field tells me different.

I ignore him and the smell of cheap cologne and step sideways to walk away.

"Excuse me," he says again, copying my movements and walking alongside me, "I'm new here, is the town centre this or that way?" He points up and down the alley.

He's lying, he knows which way it is, and then I see '27' tattooed on the inside of his wrist and realise the dreadful mistake I have made. I fumble with my phone, which feels alive in my hands trying to text Lizzie or RV, to tell him not to come. My fingers are shaking as I try to press my phone screen but the man spits grotesquely on to the floor by the of side of me, and it intimidates me enough to stop and look up at him.

"Why don't you put that away, pretty girl, and tell me where he is?" the guy asks, nodding at my phone and staring so hard at me I can't help but reply to him. My childhood training, the response ingrained in me to be meek and cooperative when the intimidating and threatening come to visit, is in full flight, and I can't seem to get past my own flaw.

'Who? I don't know what you are talking about," I say, moving away from him but whichever way I turn he pops right in front of me, blocking my way.

"Our good friend… Mr Rio Vanns." He smirks. "I need to talk to him; that's all," he says, continuing to smirk like a loose snake.

I feel nauseous, my stomach has plummeted fifty feet below ground, and I rapidly search my mind for what to do and question how this sicko knew I would be here. I ask Vozareia for help; I'm still too slow to prepare myself in the space of a few seconds and need to buy myself extra minutes. I don't reply and try to move on again, willing my shield to strengthen and I cultivate my inner heat to move energy with as much force as I can generate. This time he puts his arm out to stop me, but it stops a few inches short of touching my torso.

Oh my god. Thank you, Vozareia, thank you.

The guy is taken aback, thrown from his threatening stance, and I feel the Zeffo power kick in and my fear subside. I'm angry – angry he's doing this and angry they won't leave RV alone. He doesn't deserve this and nor do I.

"Leave. Him. Alone," I spit back. "And leave me alone," I say.

I move a leg forward, eager to leave the alley, and find RV before he gets here. The guy's manly ego delivers another block as he sticks his foot in front of my leg, and the same thing happens – it stops inches short of me, like I'm protected by a magnetic field intent on repelling him.

"What the fuck are you?" he asks, looking at me with disgust and… is that a touch of fear I sense?

He's fuming, his field is translating as danger and hatred. He's been outdone by a girl and it's not sitting well with him, nor has he got the information he wants.

"Tell me where he is, or I'm gonna fuckin' shank ya," he says, sliding his hand into his pocket and pulling a knife.

I hold my arm out, the heat rushing down my arm and outwards. The knife glimmers in a narrow sunbeam, striking through the overhanging branches as he laughs at the cupped hand I'm holding straight out at him.

Please be with me. I chant silently to Vozareia. *Please.*

I direct the energy, remain as focused as I can and swipe the blade from his white knuckled hand. It clatters to the ground; I hear him calling me a bitch and he vows to take me down, but I pay no mind and keep my stance.

Each time he leans down to pick up his knife, I move it along the path, causing him to chase his precious weapon like a thief desperate to catch a loose bank note in the wind. He misses it each time, until the guy looks ready to explode and takes a run at me. With everything I have, I muster my power and strengthen my shield and, using both arms, torso and legs and without touching him, I punch him in the chest, sending him backwards. Surprisingly, he stumbles, and I'm impressed with my efforts. I punch him again by moving the energy forward at high speed, and he stumbles a third time, banging into the wall. His head is snug against the mossy stone, and I watch the consequences of my skills unfold in slow motion. He sways the opposite way as he peels himself off the wall and falls. He smacks his head hard on the opposite wall and then again on the ground as he hits it with a terrifying thud. He doesn't get up.

I remained poised in my position and stare, tapping his leg with my foot before reality swoops in.

Fuck. I think I've killed him.

I start breathing increasingly harder and faster as I flip back into human mode and search for a rising and falling chest in his limp body, and I'm relieved to find one. Glancing up and down the alley to check for onlookers, I pull my phone from my back pocket to ring Gusti, or anyone, when a strong voice bellows from behind me.

"Seven. Are you okay? What's up?"

RV is running like a warrior towards me and stops like he applied an emergency break to himself when he sees the man on the ground, still out cold with a cut on the side of his head, oozing a trickle of a blood down his check.

RV looks at me in turmoil. The horror of seeing his gang friend – member, ex colleague; whoever the man is to him – is time freezing. The gravity of the situation settles into both of us as RV slowly turns away from the mess to look at me.

"What the hell have you done?" he asks.

I went from gangster to scared girl in a fraction of a second, throwing out my arms and explaining the guy was going to kill me. "I didn't know who he was until it was too late. He wanted you. He pulled a knife on me – a knife, RV! – I had to stop him. RV I'm scared." I begin to cry and shake from adrenaline pounding through my veins.

"How the fuck did you manage this?" RV is in utter shock as he examines Ashen – he tells me the man is called – and taps his cheek.

"He's gonna come after us again. What do we do?" I ask, on the verge of hysteria.

"Don't worry about that for now."

RV tries to comfort me, running his hands over me and checking I'm okay. He holds me close, tight to his chest, and it feels unbelievably good.

"I'm so sorry this happened to you," he whispers.

"I think we need to get out of here," I say.

"No. I need to sort this out," he replies, his voice confident but is face contorted in concern.

"RV," I say, tapping his back.

"What?" He releases me from our embrace and catches the sight of a group casually walking up the alley.

"That's them, isn't it?" I say.

He rubs his forehead, and I can feel the tension infect his

soul, turning his body to stone.

"Seven. Get out of here, now." RV is stern as he stares unwaveringly at 27evens.

"Well, well, well," someone says to us, walking closer and noticing their friend who is still knocked out on the path. "Think we need a chat, RV," the same guy says, puffing his chest out and rocking an inch forward with his hands stuffed in low hanging jeans.

One of them reaches down to Ashen, grabs his shirt by the shoulders and drags him out of the way before slapping his cheeks and repeatedly calling out his name. The rest of them glare at me and RV like we are their helpless sitting prey.

"I'm not leaving you," I say to RV. "I can help you."

"You've done enough," RV scoffs at me, "leave now, it's not safe. I deal with this," he replies in such a cold tone it's like the RV I know has evaporated.

"We'd listen to our boy," a smarmy older man says, flicking his joint out of his fingers onto the ground, hissing a cloud of smoke out between closed teeth, "and don't think about calling the pigs either."

I look at RV to plead with him, although to do what I don't know. Translating the group energy of 27evens is sickening; they are going to be horrible to RV. I need help, and I can't take on all these guys.

"GO. Seven, NOW." RV is shouting, barely able to make eye contact with me.

I hesitate before I run past 27evens and down the rest of the alley. The canopy of trees begins to break, letting more light in, and I know I'm near the end. I can't look back. I'm full of panic, fury and love, questioning if I will make it to Jamming Minds in time for Gusti to help. I reach the end of the alley, the side of my calves burn and my chest aches as I turn the corner into the wider main street and – WHAM – I run into someone and we each fall to the pavement in an exhausted heap. Gathering my disoriented thoughts, I look across at the girl laid on the pavement next to me. It's Lizzie, and Leo is with her, still upright, untouched by my hefty barging.

"Oh my god! What's happened, are you okay?" Lizzie is hugging me, and I'm sobbing, muttering and mumbling a string of incoherent words.

"They're going to kill RV," I say, switching between Lizzie's blank face and Leo's.

"Who are?" Leo asks.

"27evens."

"Shit. We were just on our way to warn you," he adds, running his hand through his blonde waves.

"What?" I say to Leo.

"They were in Wavies when me and Felix were there. Richard guessed who they were."

"I don't understand," I say.

"Never mind. I'll tell you later."

"We need to get him help!" I scream.

Leo reaches his arm to Lizzie to help her up. I push myself upright with the palms of my hands studded with grit, before I take Leo's hand, accepting his offer to help me up.

We freeze. I keep hold of his hand but we unable to remove our eyes from each other's as the tangible golden zing fires up both our arms.

"I knew it," Leo says. "I was right."

I can't speak. Lizzie is blank, glancing between her brother and me, as I remain seated on the pavement holding Leo's hand.

"She's a Zeffo," Leo says, smiling proudly at Lizzie.

Lizzie rolls her eyes, tossing her arms up and letting her hands land on her hips with a slap.

"Great, another one," she says. "Well then you two, what are we gonna do?"

Leo pulls me up and I insist we must get Gusti, saying that even though he is talking to Ni Luh I think he'll understand. Leo insists we don't, and we can handle this.

"He won't see it as urgent, neither of us two, as Zeffos, are in danger."

"Yet," I add.

People wander by, still returning home from work or walking their dogs in the evening light. A few try to go up the alley and Leo tells them it's closed due to a flood.

"Burst water pipe, ma'am, we're waiting for the water board to come," he says with his American charm.

I don't think the lady believed him, but she declined to walk up the alley all the same.

"Come on," Leo says taking my arm. "RV is getting beaten. I can see it. We need to go."

He moves me along with my arm, instructing Lizzie to wait at the alley's entrance and tell people the story about the burst pipe until we return. I'm mighty pleased someone else is here and seems to know more what to do than I do.

"What powers do you have?" I ask as we scuttle along.

"Seeing, feeling, healing, shield and telepathy," he replies, quietly zoning in on the alley as we stand at its entrance unable to see them with human eyesight.

"They're just below the halfway point," Leo replies, "what powers do you have?"

"Hearing, feeling, knowing, shield, moving energy and Z artist."

"Nice," he remarks. "Okay, this is what we are going to do."

I listen to his plan and seconds later we walk further up the alley, enough to make them out in the distance but not in detail. I can hear them talking and yelling, pushing RV against the wall and kicking him to the ground, and they don't stop. My heart feels like its lurching forward to him and I want to follow it, not stand here doing nothing.

"Don't listen to your emotions at this point," Leo cuts in, "if you ask me, he feels the same way about you too, but this isn't the time for it." He flicks a cheesy smile at me.

I stand ready to defend myself, but I stutter when I realise how much I like RV and there's no point in lying to a Zeffo. It appears Leo is more aware of the feelings between me and RV than we are, and I wonder if Leo is right about RV feeling the same. Leo clicks his fingers in front of my face, snapping me out of thought and into action.

I return to centring myself, heating the energy ball in my chest, filling my body as quickly and directly as possible whilst listening to Leo's directions who can see the situation in detail using his clairvoyance power. We both blast forward a wave of a powerful energy, sending out an intimidating feeling to unnerve 27evens. They don't understand where it has come from, and the group pause for a moment, scanning each other, but soon return to RV.

"Punch to the right," Leo says with closed eyes.

I hesitate, I can't see clearly what I'm doing.

"Just do it," he says again. I do and see a fuzzy body drop down to the ground.

"Straight forward. Punch straight forward," Leo says.

Another goes down.

By now, confusion is beginning to reign amongst the gang, and they are flummoxed as to what is happening. They step back from RV, picking up their fallen men and brushing them off. Me and Leo quietly teeter back to remain securely out of view; we wait for a minute and walk forward again.

"Send another a blast," I say.

With synchronicity, Leo and I lord another dose of Zeffo energy over them. Some gang members begin to back out, giving up, disturbed or disgruntled about the interruptions.

"Swipe to the left," Leo says.

I do, slapping another gang members' face with the power of my force. With that, they let up and run, scarpering up the alley.

We pelt up the alley to RV, and I take a sharp breath as I realise he's not moving. Laid out flat on the ground, his face is bruised and cut, his right eye shut with a purple swelling the size of a plum. His hands are cold to the touch, and I fall to my knees, gripping the front of his puffa coat with both hands. The sound of the black material scratching as I do.

"RV." Warm tears roll out down my face. "I'm so sorry, this is all my fault." I stroke his hair and look to Leo. "Is he going to be okay?"

Leo places his hand on my back as he hurries around to the other side of RV, kneeling on the ground.

"He'll be fine," Leo says with a cavalier attitude, "I have

healing power, remember?" He begins to raise his hands above RV's body and his demeanour changes to one more focused and serious. "Give me a few minutes with him."

"Won't we get into trouble for using our powers on Bippers?"

"No. It's clear a situation of RV's life dependent on us helping him," Leo replies with confidence.

I sit and watch as Leo wafts his hands around RV's body. He continues moving his hands and arms over and across RV, keeping his eyes shut as he works his magic. Every now and then, I can see small swirls of blue light hovering in the air above RV which seem to disappear into his wounds. I gawp in disbelief as the swelling, bruising and cuts diminish. RV's eye shrinks back to normal size, and eventually, we see his eyelids flutter before opening fully to see me and Leo looking back at him.

"What the fuck has gone on?" RV groans, lifting a weary arm to his face.

"They knocked you out, man, that's all. Or maybe you fainted," Leo says, slapping RV's shoulder in jest.

"I don't do no fainting, bro," RV says, giving a half smile to us both as he comes to. "Cheers, where did they go?" he adds, wiping his hand across his face. "Fuck, I'm so sorry about this."

Leo offers him a hand to pull him up. Now that it's done and I can see RV is okay, I'm stuck in silent shock about how quickly Leo healed him.

He's completely fine.

"Dunno, we can talk about it later when you've recovered properly," Leo says as we walk down to Lizzie.

"I'm fine," RV says sternly, and we leave the subject of embarrassing him alone.

As we reach the entrance and Lizzie sees the three of us approaching, she screeches in her relief at everyone being in one unbroken piece.

"Let's start again. Wavies anyone?" She laughs, and we head off down the road towards the main high street.

"Sure. Me and Seven will meet you two there. We need to call in at the shop first," Leo says.

"You can get drinks at Wavies?" RV says.

"Yeah," I say to Leo, tapping his arm.

"Not the kind we need," he says, smiling back at me.

Lizzie nods, understanding her brother's code talk and finally clicks on. Lizzie waffles over the bafflement coming from RV as to why me and Leo need to go to the shop – poor RV, he must be so confused.

Leo and I watch Lizzie and RV as they drift down the road and disappear left onto the high street, and we make our move the opposite way to Jamming Minds.

"I've sent Gusti a message to let him know we are on our way," Leo says.

"I wish I had telepathy," I reply.

We both begin to slow down, me more than Leo, as we propel ourselves through what feels like knee deep mud, down the cobbles and to the door of Jamming Minds. The light is on in the window upstairs, not the Zeffo Room but the small studio apartment next it where Gusti lives. We thud our fists on the door, our bodies slumped against it.

"Gusti," we groan faintly.

Although I'm leant on the glass door, I don't see Gusti

come down the stairs. I only notice him as he trots across the shop floor holding his laptop out, speaking to the screen as he fiddles one handed with the lock to open the door.

"We need two Smoke Outs," Leo says as we fall forward onto the shop floor. I can see Gusti looking at us in loving annoyance, and then back at his screen.

"Very sorry about this, Ni Luh," I mumble out the side of my mouth.

"Can I call you back, babe?' I hear Gusti sigh. "In about ten minutes?" he says, looking down at the pair of us slumped on the floor like the pair of Zeffo muppets we are.

Chapter Twenty
Clarity Follows Confusion

Revived from our Smoke Outs, Leo and I head up the cobbles and around onto the main high street towards Wavies. We talk as brightly as the setting sun, as though the past hour didn't happen or was totally normal. I guess, for the likes of me and Leo, it is totally normal. Leo broke his curse not long before they moved over to London, therefore, Lizzie and his family are all Remmies now. His parents don't know about the Zeffos, but Lizzie does. One hot Miami night after football training, it became too much and too weird for him, and after Lizzie caught him writing in the Book of Lights, he blabbed to her to ease his feeling of loneliness, out on the edge of life.

"Lack of support and financial problems have battered our family for generations. Lizzie and I always felt we were our parent's remorse as Mum and Dad took their turn and seats at reviving our family newspaper… the Josephs' legacy," he says casually, gazing down the main street.

"Now I know better," Leo continues, "every person in our family felt alone growing up, whilst the adults wrestled with the stress of trying to keep the paper running because money was constantly non-existent."

Bradley and Antonia, Leo's mum and dad, are both journalists and left their flashy jobs to take on the paper by its horns. Like those before them, despite the paper's audience, it was relentlessly marred with unsolvable problems. Mysteriously forcing anyone who attempted to make a go of it into financial and mental ruin.

"That's sick you have your own family newspaper! What's it called?" I ask in awe.

"The J," he boasts, looking all sun kissed again. "I want to run it one day. It covers entertainment, writing, music, art, theatre… Dear old Uncle Edward began it in the late 1800s, with a feather quill no doubt," Leo says, amused by his vision, "before he killed himself with wine and a dagger when he realised he'd lost everything. Same type of thing has happened to everyone who took it on since."

"Wow. You must have been worried your mum and dad would do the same?"

"Exactly, but alas. Leo the Zeffo did what he needed to do, and the curse is banished." He snaps his fingers in the cooling air. "Like magic, The J received interest from an investor wanting to combine the youth scene in Miami and the youth scene in London. We've expanded to include street dance, rap, photography, and the screen. It's old school, new cool and doing well – finally."

"That's why you moved to London," I say, looking up towards him. "How come I don't know about this paper?" I ask.

"You do now," he says whilst we dally about outside the door to Wavies. "Lizzie has no interest in journalism, unless it's to do with surfing or oceans, but I do, and I have an idea. Talk to you about it later."

"Sounds interesting." I tap my hand on his arm to stop him reaching for the door handle. "How did you break your curse; did it take long?" I ask.

"Looking back, not really, and Gusti is sound. Another conversation for another time," he replies.

Leo swings the door open and the hub bub of Wavies' music, the smell of fresh fruit and coffee overwhelms our senses. Lizzie is sat on her own at our table, and we pull out two chairs opposite her, sinking ourselves down into the seats with a high.

"RV left as soon as we got here," Lizzie sighs.

She had tried to keep him here until Leo and I returned, but he wasn't feeling social and wandered off home. Lizzie had offered to walk with him, which earned her the remark, 'I can look after myself.' She repeats it, mimicking RV, and we smile fondly at her impersonation because we all know how RV would have said it to her. He's in distress underneath it all, and it casts a hue of our helplessness – with this, he's pretty much on his own.

"I wanted to wait for you two because – what the fuck guys?" she says with inquisitive eyes.

Bringing Lizzie and Leo up to speed with my own Zeffo discovery and quest so far is liberating. The three of us find a mutual, deep trust with each other that intensifies as the conversation goes on, and it's freeing to have friends who get it – and are it – who are my age. Their eyes widen when I reach the part about Palm and the Mafia, how I need to find him because he's alive not dead, and that something is urgent about it.

"You're going to have an interesting showdown." Leo

laughs, mocking me like only a close friend can do.

"Is that what happens to finally break the Boras? Small tasks increasing with difficulty that lead to a full-on monster event, all of which I have to beat?" I ask, completely intrigued. I want to know everything.

"Pretty much," he replies. Unwilling to discuss it further in front of Lizzie, so we move onto the events preceding the alley drama, accepting a round of smoothies Richard brings over to us in an unusually sombre mood, and it's strange when his happy dopey vibe is his normal attire.

"I've a lot of time for RV," Richard says, "and I don't want those dickheads wrecking everything for him," he adds, popping the three glasses of smoothies on the table. "They'll fill you in," he says to my confused face, clearly oblivious to what else has gone down.

"Don't think any of us know how this can work out yet," Leo replies to Richard.

Richard raises his forehead with a deep breath and reaches into his apron pocket, pulling out his order notepad and a pencil. He leans forward on our table and scribbles a phone number down.

"Here, this is my mobile number. Give it to the others too. RV already has it. Call me if you need anything."

"Cheers," we all say as Richard moves on to another table collecting empties.

Leo slides the piece of the notepaper across the table, placing it in the middle of the three of us, and begins the story that explains how 27evens knew I'd be in the alley.

Turns out, Felix had text me earlier when I was at home getting ready. He and Leo didn't want me and Lizzie crashing their bro time, and they asked me what time I would be walking down so they could vacate Wavies well before me and Lizzie showed up. I had text Felix back to let him know I'd be walking down the alley around 6.30pm, thinking nothing of it – it was a mindless detail.

"27evens were sat in a huddle at the back," Leo says and nods over to the back tables near the toilets, "but we didn't know. I walked over to the restroom as Felix bellowed to me, as he does, that you'd texted back and would be at the alley around six-thirty to meet Lizzie, so we needed to leave at six forty-five.

"When I came back from the restroom, Richard came over and warned us 27evens were around, obviously looking for RV. Been in Wavies a few times recently, he said, and he clicked on who they were and was concerned about it. I bet it's the same people hanging round at school too… turns out they've been watching all of us," Leo says, despondent.

"That clears up that mystery then," I say, equally despondent.

"It also clears up the mystery as to why we are in London; it ain't only because of the poxy paper, you're here to assist Seven too," she says to her brother then looks at us both, waiting for a response.

"Zeffo's in love with a street gang boy and a missing mafia father… Epic," Leo says mockingly as we clink glasses.

"I am not in love with RV," I insist as they both splutter into laughter at me. "I'm not!" I push Lizzie's hand on the table. "After Nate – I'm off boys. I'm more concerned about my dad now. My real one."

Later that evening back home in my bed, I toy with feelings I can't deny have slowly emerged over the last few weeks.

Particularly potent, after I seem to have removed Nate from my hopes and dreams and have chipped away at the curse of feeling unworthy of good love. Nate felt noisy, crackly and all in my head. RV, or our friendship at least, feels like moonlight in Paris.

I wonder what RV thinks, if he feels any of this at all, for I can't be sure. Then again, he has bigger problems on his hands, like staying alive, that far outweigh romance for two. I ring him nonetheless to check in and to see if he's okay, and surprisingly he answers. He's not all that talkative and I don't push him to speak, but he appreciated the help that Leo and I gave him.

"Didn't like you seeing me like that," RV says. "I don't like they involved you. I'm so sorry Seven. I don't like any of this…" he trails off.

I gaze at the ceiling, wishing I could hug him and tell him it's all fine.

"What are you going to do?" I ask.

"Dunno yet," he says, and I mouth the words as he says them, knowing it's what he would say.

"I'm here for you," I reply. Knowing it's what Mum would have said to Palm back in their day.

"Me too. Ring me anytime you're worried. Okay?" he replies before ending the call.

***

It's Friday. Game day for Nate.

Yas and I dawdle along the main corridor when Nate shoots past us like a bullet.

"Good luck for the game later!" we both say in unison and it makes us chuckle.

Nate turns around to face us as he slows to a jog. "Nice one. See you there," he yells, holding his arm up while clutching a book in his hand, before turning back around and running on.

"Do you reckon Nate's okay?" Yas asks.

"Yeah! He'll be rushing off to the game," I reply as the corridor fills with students loosening their ties off ready for home.

"Hmm. I suppose. He always acts a little shut off, you know. Lately he's been worse; you must have noticed. My parents say that's a sign of hiding core feelings. You never know," Yas says, hitting my arm with a magazine, "RV could be right? Maybe I should talk to Nate at the party? I happen to know what controlling adults are like," she says as her energy widens like her eyes as revelations spark.

"He's not one for being gushy, for sure," I reply, looking down the corridor he ran down. "You need to chisel through his wall a little at times." I bring my voice down to a mutter, "I wouldn't go interfering though."

If Nate won't listen to RV, or himself, he definitely won't listen to you, Yas.

"He's heading for a train wreck. You watch," she says, hugging her magazine.

"We're not responsible for preventing other people's train wrecks, Yas. Concentrate on your own. See you at the game in twenty," I say, walking off and holding my fingers up above my head in the peace sign.

"*Errr.* Yeah… bye babe," I hear Yas reply from behind me, and I can't believe I just said that to her.

We're all sat uncomfortably on long wooden benches in

the sports hall waiting for the stars of the show to appear on the court. Leo and Lizzie, who are used to stadium type seating in their school in Miami, say the seating arrangement is backward and no cheerleading is 'boringly British'.

"The UK is always five years behind you guys," I say to the MGs.

"Only five?" Lizzie says, rolling her eyes.

Small crowds gather around the perimeter; those supporting the opponents are on the opposite side of the hall. Nate's sister, Claudine, waves at us from her little Year 9 posse by the main doors. Last year Claudine told me she wished for pins to be stuck in me like a Voodoo doll – so that was nice.

Claudine was too much; it wasn't her boyfriend that had dumped her for another someone. Nate grew tired of Claudine and her bitter nose and threatened to divulge to Felix her secret crush on him unless she quit making me pay for breaking her brother's heart.

Nate told on his sister and her secret to us all anyway one day at lunch. *Lol.*

'Can't you block her on Instagram or something, Felix, she's driving me nuts,' Nate said at the time.

Felix loves Instagram and would never block a devoted groupie, so Claudine continued to drive Nate crazy about Felix and practice her weird voodoo on me – I think she may be the wrath of the Boras personified.

I elbow Yas in the ribs. "Crazy witch is warming to me," I say, smirking.

"Well, I'M not warming to her," Yas replies with a catty glare back at Claudine. I return a wave along with the others, amused at Claudine's naivety of Yas' comment.

We take a group selfie of all our feet stretched out in front of us as a celebratory memento. The feet thing was RV's idea at being creative, and it would have worked had we all been wearing our own style of clothes and shoes, instead of black school shoes and uniforms. Still, I like it and decide I will print it out, write our initials on the shoes in metallic pen and pin it above my computer when I get home.

"Nate and the team should smash this one," shouts Felix quickly, before blowing a loud wolf whistle above the cheering and clapping as each team jogs onto the court. As he always does, Nate leads the way for Silversedge.

"He looks well proud," I say, leaning into Lizzie's ear as the clapping marathon continues.

"He does, doesn't he?" Her eyes sparkle with her reply.

"We should have bloody cheerleaders, you're right. Americans have all the perks," Felix says to Leo who grins over his reminiscence of cheerleaders at his football games. The teams jump up and down on the spot. Then, silence. Positions are taken. The ball is thrown up. The buzzer sounds, and the fight to win the championship is on.

The first half isn't much of a fight, more of a no brainer. The other team scrape together to score a few points, but Silversedge own the court and it's as though the ball is on their side. Nate looks so alive when he nods at Claudine with his winning face before spotting us and yelling, "Come on!" A roar from the MGs and the other Year 11s fills the room. Until…

"Nate is not happy," says Lizzie. "He needs to keep his head out of it."

"He told me at lunch they were going to take the win, but I'm not convinced. They haven't got long left," Leo adds.

I'm not convinced either and I'm beginning to feel riled up at the supporter's gloating over their unexpected (and quite frankly undeserving) lead.

"Come on, get back in the zone," Lizzie says, wincing as the other team score again.

The mood is flat, tense and restrictive, and the strip lighting running along the high ceiling makes me feel like my face must look pale green in colour. Not that Felix is aware, he's sitting on the other end of the bench preoccupied on his phone, texting people about the party next Friday. He peers up, watches the game for few minutes and says, "Nate's got it covered, don't doubt him." Almost as soon as the words leave his mouth, he's back immersed in his phone reality.

RV flicks his head back. "Sure, he will," he says.

With a sly hand and a quick foot, Nate scores, and the mood shifts from grey to pink. The tempo of the game changes completely, and it was like one good shot was all that was needed to move the mountain out of the way.

"Told you," Felix says smugly, as Silversedge High takes the win – but only just.

Nate's team jig around, revelling in the hype of success, all except Nate who is not as buzzed as I expected. I thought he'd be dishing out high fives and fist bumping everyone, but it's like he's faking joy to hide deflation. He traipses around the court clapping the audience and saluting his sister, before he darts to Lizzie and lifts her up. I barely notice their smiling, kissing mouths. For all his talk about this game, he doesn't seem all that bothered to have won it.

RV shuffles past me down the line of MGs standing in front of the wooden bench.

"Told ya," RV says, placing a hand on my shoulder, "doesn't wanna do it," he whispers in my ear and sneaks out from our row into the aisle.

"Hey, where are you going?" I ask as RV begins to wheedle himself to the double sports hall doors.

"Home. I'll text you later, and tell Nate I say congrats," he replies.

The door rocks shut, and RV is gone.

He's not going home.

Chapter Twenty-One
Interlude

The following week rolls by in a calm before the storm type of way, mixing me all up. Its eeriness has me on edge, waiting for the other shoe to drop, that or a mysterious miracle, but nothing: no backlash from 27evens, Vozareia is strangely dormant, no more sightings of the black car, ravens or any Palm information. I've been dialling into Bipper energy fields all over the place in the hope of gaining a scrap of information, a small tip off – something – to send this quest to the next level, but it's a never-ending ream of vapid, personal information which need not concern me. Gusti and Leo say I need to be more selective and discerning as wildly dialling into everyone's vibe juices will only exhaust me and send me nuts, apparently. 'Nosiness, forcing information or panicking brings nothing valuable,' Gusti says. Leo reckons it's a period, and I need to be okay with being uncomfortable. 'It will soon change,' he said, but it's like an itch you can't find the location of.

I complete any homework and practise all my Zeffo powers daily, spending all my spare time with the Book of Lights, re-hashing my journey so far by perusing all the notes I've made.

Tonight, I'd like to write more, but nothing is happening, so I draw myself holding a crystal ball. Hung over the crystal ball with ropey string is a wooden sign. I write on the sign out at sea, 'back soon', and think about drawing a duplicate and adding it to my own art collection.

This is what interludes in life are for I guess, reflection and mastering skills? That, and failing to convince mothers that dead dads are still alive, obsessing over friend crushes doing something reckless and practising caressing naked torsos on yourself.

Chapter Twenty-Two
Ask the Beer

Bea is already at Felix's when Yas and I arrive at his apartment, where music is flipping from tune to silence to tune as Felix fiddles with the sound system in the kitchen. Yas and I turn to each other with raised eyebrows as we watch Bea shake crisps into bowls and dot them around the kitchen and sitting room… pre drinks is meant for the MGs only.

"Cosy," we both say.

Bea, with her blonde bob and killer eyebrows and a thing for business, which she studies at college, is the opposite to what I thought she'd be like. Perhaps Bea's business head and Felix's creative head will prove to be a good balance; she's friendly and not intimidated by meeting us lot or abhorred by their age gap of thirteen months. If they were older no one would flinch about it. It makes sense Felix is with someone older, someone who matches his soul age not his numerical one. Do we all have two ages, I ponder?

"A well-stocked fridge, ahhhh. What a beautiful sight," Felix says as he admires his handiwork of neatly lined up alcoholic bottles. He flicks the top off a bottle of beer. "Spritzer? Or whatever your baby drink is called?" Felix offers to me.

"It's not a baby drink, it's white wine with lemonade, and it's classy," I reply while opening a bag of vegetarian crisps that taste eerily like real bacon.

I stand in the doorway between the kitchen and the sitting room cradling my spritzier and observe. Yas is gassing with Bea on the sofa which looks out over the astonishing view of Silversedge. Yas will either be approachable or quizzing, and I'm sure Yas will deliver her conclusion about Bea to me later in the evening. Nate and Lizzie are sprawled out on the opposite sofa talking sport as Lizzie chucks pretzels towards Nate's mouth. Lizzie seems calmer, more focused and solid about her sporting career when compared to Nate's hub of bold yet flighty talk. Leo is on his way; he didn't want to come with Nate and Lizzie. 'Only so much surf and basketball talk a third wheel can take,' he said earlier to me on Snap.

RV isn't here yet either. The thought he is with 27evens and not showing up tonight sends an emergency flutter across my chest, but I push it down. I'm confused about whether the flutter is my habit of over caring – projecting my agenda onto another because I never cared much about myself – or if it's because I'm scared about falling for someone who doesn't want me back. Scared of falling for someone who on paper is risky, a bad choice and a wrong one. Yet *he* feels right. I can feel the Boras pounding my mind with old mind tricks, so I push people away and fuck up my friendship with RV like I've done with others before. I don't want to do that this time, I really don't, and I can't find the truth through the Boras-infected filter obscuring love in my life.

Text him, call him, check he's okay, draw him a special picture, the Boras insists. *Why would he like you? Stupid girl, you must prove to him you're worthy, hassle him, show him,* the Boras continue to plague my thoughts with bad ideas.

I can't help but think though, if RV did like me in that way there would be signs, a natural progression or movement, and there aren't. Ultimately, I decipher, all the Boras does is assist me on my way to looking like a fool, unwanted once more – well not this time. I am breaking the Boras love pattern and will conquer it, even if it means a broken heart because RV and I will always be friends, but nothing more.

Open shield.

I faff around in the kitchen, opening the balcony doors feeling strangely special about myself as a Zeffo; the fact barely anyone knows this is empowering, and I'm growing to like who I am as a person.

"You lot," Felix yells to the four of them in the sitting room, "is the music playing loud in there?" he asks, twiddling and pressing buttons on the piped sound system until it is just right.

Ten minutes later Leo arrives. I let him in the front door and for kicks we shake hands in the empty hallway, sharing a look of pride for our secret. He places his hands on my upper arm as a secondary gesture and wanders through to the kitchen, yelling for Felix as though he's searching an ocean for him, his hands firmly back in his pockets. Leo doesn't seem to have had much luck with girls since being in Silversedge. I don't know why this would be – a bit of jock back home (according to Lizzie) but he has the heart of a lion and an ability to calm anyone down – and I guess it's down to Zeffo work, banishing his own families' curse and The J must have taken first place since his ex-girlfriend in Miami. I think Leo's onto something with this no girlfriend lark, and I decide in this random moment in Felix's hallway to develop my own gravity, with or without a boyfriend.

"Thought RV would be with you, man?" Felix asks Leo as I traipse back into the kitchen from the hallway.

"He texted me on my way here. He's still coming," Leo relays. "Being busy with study he said." Leo glances at me and we both translate our suspicions exactly.

He's not at study. He's across town.

Felix, Leo and I lean on the kitchen island munching a mixture of crisps and something dreadfully spicy which makes me gag.

"Are you sure your mum and dad are okay with all this?" I ask post gag.

"There's only a few more than they think. They're all decent people and besides, I'll kick everyone out well before they get home. You two can help me clean up," Felix says with a big fat silly grin. "Mate," he says to Leo, "the set of drawers in front of you. There's a string of lights in one of them, can you pass them over?"

"You think I'll be capable of cleaning by the end of the night?" Leo replies, messing about in the drawers. Eventually he yanks out a large, tied up bunch of LED lights and hands them to Felix across the island, but discussing the clean-up plan is forgotten as Yas appears in the doorway from the sitting room.

"Love Bea," she says to the three of us, holding up her open hand, "you should come and talk to her babe, tell her about your art and turning it into paid art. She's giving me business tips to use on my parents about being a stylist."

"Cheers, Yas. Means a lot you guys like her," Felix coos. "Why the business tips?" he continues. "Parents still giving you a hard time?"

Yas holds her glass out to no one in particular, indicating she's ready for a refill, and Felix dutifully grabs her wine bottle and lets pale pink liquid glug into her glass. This is the only green light Yas needs to launch into a lengthy road trip about the crisis over her choice of career and being told she has to study medicine. Leo taps my arm and flicks his head towards the sitting room and I follow him in, relieved not to be roped into Yas' conversation – again.

Close shield.

"Tell Bea I'll be there in a minute," Felix says to us both, "just sorting these out." Felix holds up the tangled blue lights, nodding and listening to Yas' speed talking.

"Felix's place is unreal; I say it every time I come over," Leo says, ogling the room as we try to remain unnoticed in a corner.

"Where is RV, really?" I ask, careful to speak below the volume of the music. Leo shakes his fingers through his hair and pulls one corner of his mouth up.

"I don't know, think we both know it ain't study class."

"I hope he's okay. Can't you see where he is?" I say with slight paranoia this falls into *pushy overbearing* territory. RV can look after himself, but what chance does he have against them lot? They won't have left it at a beating in the alley when they didn't get to finish it on their terms. "What if he goes back to them, Leo? Can't we intervene somehow?" I ask.

"Our powers are not for uninvited meddling," he says with a chuckle. "We can try and talk to him later, but we can't force him. It's rough but we can only be responsible for our own actions. It's all anyone can do; it'll be his choice what he does. Come on…" He ruffles my hair which annoys me – I hate people touching my head and tell him so as we manoeuvre to the sofas, not wanting to be anti-social and raise comments as to why we are whispering in a corner.

"Those two boring you with sport like they were with me earlier?" Leo asks Bea as we perch on the sofa next to her.

Lizzie throws pretzels at Leo in response, calling him a dick, and a round of sibling banter begins. I admire how nothing seems to rattle Leo – well, except Lizzie and Trans-Atlantic moves. As I sit and admire Leo's traits for a few moments longer; his calmness, his certainty, his passion for life purpose; I realise, for the first time in nearly a year, I'm thankful Nate and I split up. Now, new people, new ideas and a whole new bunch of circumstances can enter my life instead, and that is exciting.

"The game I played last week was bad. I seriously thought we were embarrassing history at one point," Nate rambles.

I want to tell Nate to give it a rest and – I think I speak for all of us on this – I'm done hearing about the bloody game. We're here to party, to enjoy the countdown of our last weeks at high school, not to continue dissecting a basketball game.

"Stop beating yourself up man and drink. Pick the game apart next time you're in training," Leo says.

"Bang on, man. Let's forget about it," says Nate.

We had forgotten about it, Nate – about two days ago.

"Here, have another," Leo says, passing him a bottle of beer from the stash Felix just carried in.

"Yeah, boys!" Felix says, raising his beer too. Yas has

followed Felix in and is standing between him and the sofas.

"We love you for this party, thank *youuuu*," Yas says, with an oversized hug draped around Felix's neck.

"Better slow down with the rosé, Yas. Still early *gurl!*" Lizzie says. "Where the hell is RV anyway? He should be here too."

Just then, the intercom buzzes.

"This'll be him, bet ya," Felix says, answering the extra-long buzz.

It was RV… It is RV… It's a stoned RV.

"Alright Gs, sorry I'm late. Can I put these in the fridge?" RV asks, holding his carrier bag full of beer cans like an orphaned child. "I've something for you as well." He opens the white carrier bag so Felix can peer in.

Please do not let it be more weed.

"My favourite whiskey! Mate! Where did ya get it?" Felix asks, pumped.

"Know someone who knows someone," RV replies, pulling his baseball cap down by its peak and ducking into the kitchen with Felix. Leo and I exchange looks and Lizzie screws her eyes up at us, pointing over Nate's head towards the kitchen – code for, 'we should go to RV' – but I wiggle my head at her as discreetly as I can. Nate doesn't even notice though, and my discretion proves utterly pointless as he's well on his way to being wasted. It's the wrong time to check in on RV I can feel it, and I'm listening to Vozareia's nudge instead of overriding it and diving right on into the kitchen, as I would have if the curse on me had its way.

"I'll talk to him later," I say to Leo and give Lizzie a thumbs up.

The intercom is beeping constantly as more and more people arrive, and I seem to have been assigned the job of placing the drinks in the fridge while Yas is taking coats and placing them in Felix's bedroom. The lights Felix hung around the sitting room earlier have lit the room cobalt, and as the sun sets, the friendship is strong and the vibe high, as is the alcohol fuelled laughter. It's a time we will never have again. Even Michael is belly laughing with Bea and Felix despite being the only sober one here; he's determined to make it to footy training in the morning. By default, Michael is the party's supervisor to help Felix out, making sure nothing kicks off and evicting any smokers outside.

My attention is drawn to RV out on the balcony rolling a joint after pear cider Penny, and her friend with the bad hair extensions, blanked him yet made a point of speaking to everyone else.

"Bitches…" Yas, Lizzie and I had yelled after them.

"Yeah, and what's up with your hair?!" Yas added even louder.

RV must be keeping a wide berth as he slouches down the comfy chair a million miles away from the party. I try to convince myself nothing more serious is going on and down my spritzer which brings on an unwelcome wave of queasiness, but I need courage, and a reason, to go up to RV and interrupt his palpable defence line. Taking another beer out to him is the only idea springing to mind.

Yas, sat with Andrew who waltzed in about an hour ago, is sitting on the sofa talking with Felix and Bea and have been since Andrew arrived. I'm undecided if I like him or not; he's a standard Silversedge posh boy. I shouldn't be disgruntled by this or by the evidence her and Andrew have hit it off with Felix and Bea, but it's all annoyingly 'Bea, Bea, Bea' from Yas who has unapologetically entered swaying kiss-arse mode. As I approach them, it feels like I'm creeping about on old floorboards. Why should I feel wary going to talk to my best friend? Yas is laughing hard at whatever Bea has blurted and hands her glass to Andrew to refill it again.

Guess you don't need another drink.

"You okay, Yas?" I shout over instead.

"Totally babe, sick party."

"Yeah, it is. I'll catch you later."

I decide not to gate crash their private soiree and retreat to the kitchen on my own to get RV a beer. I yank a bottle out of the fridge and fill my own glass half full of wine and decide that innocent Bea is tonight's capture for Yas' life fix.

"Do I warn Bea?" I ask Vozareia out loud. "Translate their energy fields to see what's going down, or do I stay out of it?" It isn't until I search the inside of the fridge door that I remember we are out of lemonade. "Fuck it. I'll drink the wine straight." I slam the door shut.

"Who are you talking to?" Nate asks, appearing from behind the fridge door, pulling it open again for another beer.

"Oh, no one, thinking out loud. Where's Lizzie?" I say, withering away from comment.

"She's taken Amy to the bathroom. Amy the amateur has been mixing drinks all night and is probably hurling right about now..." He trails off in amused disbelief as he leans over the kitchen island closer to me. "And if I remember rightly, so will you if you start drinking straight wine. You're already talking to yourself."

The feeling I sense behind his eyes is speaking to me more than his words are, and I'm not sure how to handle it.

"Pah," I joke, waving my arm up and down, which is looking slightly blurry, "it's only the one, I'll be fine."

"As long as you're okay. I came to check as I notice Queen of Arabia has ditched you most of the night for Bea."

"She hasn't ditched me; she's making Bea feel welcome. She doesn't know anyone here,' I lie.

"No mate. She's ditched you because new sparkly Bea has something Yas can use for herself," he says, jiggling his hands around. "I can see it from the other side of London, even if you can't. I've nothing against Bea, she seems great and whatever, but Yas – it's not fair to you, that's all."

"Which is why I'm staying clear of them. I'm not getting involved and acting all jealous. I've better things to do then let Yas make me feel bad. I need to take this beer to RV, if you don't mind," I say, brushing past him to leave, but he stops me.

"Before you go, can we talk?"

Nate takes the bottle of beer and my half glass of wine from my hands and places them on the island, pausing before inhaling a deep breath.

"I miss you, Seven."

Oh shit. I knew something was about to roll out of him, but I wasn't expecting to hear the words I had longed to hear. I can't help but think about the nights I laid awake hoping he would call or text when he didn't. Now, when I'm over him, he says it, or the beer says it.

I'm pretty sure it's the beer.

"Don't. This is not fair. You have Lizzie who's a good

friend, and I won't do anything to mess our friendship up – you're too late."

"Nothing is ever too late. I was an idiot, blocking you out. I'm not asking anything of you. I don't want to hurt Lizzie either. I just needed you to know."

He takes my hand, walking his smooth fingers down towards my wrist and hand. I'm frozen, transported to the Nate and Seven era – an iconic time. It always will be, and I think I will always hold that one ember for him that won't die out. I pull my arm back without releasing my fixed stare from him. I don't know whether I want to smack him or fall for him again.

"Nate, I'm sorry," I say, shaking my head. "You'll always be special to me and two months ago my answer would have been different… we're both sailing in different waters now. Let's leave it at that."

I need to exit before I catch Nate's feelings even more. I pick up my glass and RV's beer from the island, knocking over a bowl of crisps and a rogue drink at the same time.

"I'll clean it up," Nate slurs, like his heart fell in his boots.

He downs the rest of his beer as I walk out of the kitchen to go and find RV, leaving Nate looking somewhere between a lost boy and a broken man who let the beer say more than he had planned on.

"Right, Beer Pong everyone! Who's in?" Lewis yells as I wade through the sitting room to the balcony. The crowd is roaring, and Lewis lines up the red plastic cups on the table in preparation as Felix retrieves a ping pong ball hidden in a cabinet drawer.

"Hey, room for me out here?" I say, stepping out onto the balcony and taking a comfy seat at the round table. "Brought you another beer."

Chapter Twenty-Three
Only a Name

"It's getting claustrophobic in there," I say to RV, who nods his head in agreement.

"That's why I'm out here," he replies, offering me a turn on his joint lightly wedged between his thumb and index finger.

"No, no thanks. Can't cope with weed and wine," I say with a coy smile.

He smirks and lovingly calls me a lightweight, which I don't mind really, because I know I am. Never been one for throwing it down my neck, only to throw it back up the same neck later.

"Are you okay? You seem distant," I ask.

RV moves away from me, sinking back into the chair. He stays like this for all of five seconds before standing up. He slowly paces around the large balcony, blowing thick smoke into a bright beam glaring from the outside light. People inside, feet away on the other side of the glass doors, are rowdy and oblivious to us outside. Lewis lost at Beer Pong and downs a pint of beer to rounds of stamping feet and cheering. This side of the glass, out here on the balcony, is cooler and covered in a blanket of stars, but RV appears immune to its peace.

Penny and the tag-a-long bad hair extensions friend both appear at the open doors to come outside then turn around when they see RV, mumbling with hands over their mouth and noses how they thought he'd be the type to smoke weed. RV remains with his back turned and his arms resting on the railing. He breathes in the view out in front of him and blows another batch of smoke out into the night.

"If this is about them two, ignore them. They look at most people like they want to burn them to the floor," I tell him, but he doesn't answer, and I continue to watch the back of him, his arm lifting his joint up to his slightly parted lips is his only movement and I wonder what to say next.

"They don't let you forget what you were – or are. It's not just them, plenty of people do it," he says, leaning further forward onto the railing.

"They're bitches. I know you must get sick of it, but you, us lot, Mum and Richard know the truth – the real you – and truth will out, always."

RV finally peels himself away from the balcony railing and sits down in a chair opposite me. He places his joint in the terracotta dish and stares at his trainers, before sitting upright and looking me squarely in the eye.

"You can never leave, Seven. Never."

"What? Silversedge? I can never leave Silversedge?"

"No, you div," he says and laughs.

I've at least forced a smile from him before he drops his forehead into his hands, pinching his nose and temples with his fingers.

"My old life, gangs… look how hard I've tried to change and walk away from it, but it's impossible."

"It's not. You have walked away from it; you should be full of pride for yourself. I know they're back on the scene but—"

"Doesn't matter, any of it." RV cuts me off "I broke away from 27evens, risking everything, and still the fuckers find me." He passes the joint once more my way.

"Erm. No. It's still a no… What's happened, are they hassling you? I might be able to help or understand – I know more about mob culture than you might think."

"You're shitting me, right. You? You sit there with your pretty drink, pretty hair and pretty house like all the others who live around here and all of ya are conveniently blind. What could you possibly know about gangs and how we have to live?"

"Whoa, whoa, whoa. Don't attack me. I'm a friend trying to help." I scrape the wooden framed chair backwards and stand up ready to leave. I don't need this from him.

"I'm sorry, don't go," he says, lunging across the table to grab my hand. "You're the last person I have beef with."

"Don't speak to me like that. Some deserve it, but not me, and you'd be surprised at what I might know. It's a long story…" I reply, pausing before asking my real question. "Are you going back to 27evens?"

Right after I finish speaking, a stream of police sirens ring through the night air. Alerting me, not to the incident they are attending, but to pay attention to the moment.

"No. Sorta, but no." RV exhales a sigh the size of his puffa coat. "When Donnelly was bollocking me for saying what I did in assembly, I knew. I knew then it was 27evens, before all the alley shit."

"Richard said they've also been in Wavies. Leo was going to mention it to you later."

"Fuck. FUCK. Richard will be so pissed at me." He slams the table with his fist. "See what I mean? They always find you and the people important to you." He bores his torn eyes into me like his fate is pre-determined.

"I think Richard is more worried than pissed, like me."

RV is seldom this open or willing to speak deeply about things. Too much beer and weed can be the only reason, and maybe a touch of desperation. He didn't know about Wavies; it would have made no difference, 27evens got him anyway, via me.

"I don't want them causing trouble around here, and my mum and dad – goddamn it – they sacrificed everything for us to move here and live in that poxy flat." He drifts off into the inky sky and returns to me a minute later. He takes his baseball cap off and places it on the table.

"That's where I was earlier," he fesses up. "Talking with 'em."

"Please tell me you are not going back to them."

"They don't get me. They don't get why I want out… they want me to do one last job, then I'm free; they'll leave me alone for good. Chunk of good money in it for me too."

"You're not seriously considering this, are you?"

"It's hella money. I'd be set up. I can pay for extra tuition. I can help Mum and Dad with the rent, and I would be shot of 27evens. How can I not consider it?"

My stomach churns like a giant rusty cog in a machine. I take his point, but how can I let my friend go back to a life he doesn't want or deserve? A life most likely to land him back in trouble or dead. I don't see a grown, tough sixteen-year-old guy in front of me, I feel an abandoned, scared child staring back at me, searching for answers and a sense of belonging, and it breaks my heart.

"I've done this shit my whole life; I'll be fine."

"What's the job or what do you have to do?" I ask, terrified of the answer.

He gulps his beer, and I can tell he's weighing up if he can trust me enough to continue.

"Shooting some dude when he gets out of prison in a week," RV rattles off quietly, unable to hold my eyes. He runs his finger around the neck of the beer bottle and takes another swig. My face is locked on him.

"Murder!" I boom. RV shuffles in his seat, looking around frantically, telling me to hush, but I don't. "You can't get involved with this, jeez. I wasn't expecting that. I can't believe what I'm hearing."

RV leans in closer across the table, lowering his voice.

"I ain't pulling no trigger, Seven – I'm one of the youngest and I don't think they trust me with something like that, not now. They need me to assist in… other ways."

"You can't do this, what if you get caught? You've already got a record." My voice is rising again. The noise from inside is becoming louder as Beer Pong stakes get higher, but I've lost all interest in partying and drinking games.

"This is normal in our world." He heaves in the air again and picks his joint back up, stretching out in his chair.

"Who? When?" I ask.

"I can't answer that."

"Yes, you fucking can."

"Next Friday. Another G – mafia boss."

"Mafia?! And you think they will leave you alone after this? Are you insane! Trust me, you can't do this."

"What choice have I got? I tell the mandem no? They'll kill me as well," he yells back, as though he has the gall to be annoyed that I'm not supporting his decision to be part of a scene I know is way out of his depth, and probably out of 27evens' depth too. "I never wanted this, and I've told you too much. No one else knows, you have to promise to keep it that way."

I drink my wine like it's water. The sudden alarm I'm feeling is like an electric current between RV and myself, zapping me every other second. My breathing turns rapid and short.

"Are you okay?" RV asks. "Seven?" he says again, but I can barely hear him as his words fade out into the night.

The signs, images and messages I've received, the conversations with Mum are running like a movie on fast forward. *No way.*

No freaking way.

"No," I say as I stand up and lean towards him with my hands on the table, "I am not alright. The man, the one you are shooting, what's he called?"

"I can't tell you. What does it matter anyway?"

"It matters a whole lot to me. WHAT'S HIS NAME?"

"Alright, calm down! It's a fancy Italian name I can't pronounce… *er*… Vin, Vincey, some shit like that."

"Vincenzo?" I answer, monotone.

"Yeah, yeah that's it. How come you know the name?"

My diaphragm is stuck in my throat. I can't move. I can't

breathe as my hands feel around the tabletop for stability.

"You okay? What's up? Seven, you're freakin' me out."

My eyes crawl up the front of RV to meet his gaze. He reaches his arm across to touch my shoulder, but I knock it away, harder than intended and the force shocks him. His eyes stare at me, wide.

"You can't do this," I say with a strength of purpose I'm not accustomed to.

"I have to," he replies, his mind made up, his face searching my intensity.

Our conversation is interrupted by a knocking on the glass door. Felix is stood there with a cheeky smile, thumbing towards the bathroom behind him.

"Nate's having a whitie in the bathroom. It's fucking hilarious, but what do I do with him, bro?"

Apparently, Nate is laid on the bathroom floor hugging the base of the loo, his phone next to him on the floor with 999 highlighted ready to ring an ambulance as he thinks he's going to die.

"Nate doesn't smoke weed. RV, do something," I say, slapping RV's chest and the power accidentally hits it before my hand does, which RV clocks and his forehead scrunches up with confusion.

Must remember to be less obvious moving energy when around Bippers.

"How did you do that? he asks, rubbing the front of his chest and picking his hat back up as Felix waits for the guru to tell him what to do.

"Never mind that, what about Nate?" I say, changing the subject immediately.

"What's the fucking idiot done? Where's he got it from?" he asks Felix.

"Dunno." Felix shrugs. "But can you come and sort him out?"

We dash and dodge our way through the hoard of people and red plastic cups. Talking, laughter and music fills the penthouse, but it's all lost on me now.

Felix pushes the bathroom door open and true enough, there's Nate hugging the base of the loo muttering how bad he feels, questioning will he die and some other string of words I can't make sense of. Lizzie is sat on the heated tiled floor with him, stroking his hair and trying to talk him down, but he doesn't hear her at all – I'm not sure he even knows Lizzie is there. Nate clumsily lifts his hand, plopping it down on his phone screen to call 999. RV leans down, swipes the phone from him and hands it to Lizzie.

"Don't wanna do that. Is it just weed you've had?" RV asks, filling up a toothbrush mug with water from the sink and handing it to Lizzie who tries to get Nate to sip the water.

"*Yesh*," Nate groans.

"Where the fuck did you get it? If you want weed, ask me. Not some street corner wanker."

Nate doesn't respond other than waving his arm about and repeats how this is the end for him.

"It's the not the end, man. You need to sort your life out," RV says. "Let's get him up and outside." RV looks to Felix.

The two of them take a side each and haul Nate to his swaying floppy feet.

"No, no, put me back down. Where's my phone?"

"Shut up and walk. Lizzie, keep talking to him," RV instructs.

The five of us make it out into the hallway, Felix and RV practically drag Nate down the carpeted corridor, knocking a wall light to an awkward angle, when Leo appears. He's hurtling up the corridor with fists pumped aiming straight for us.

"Nate, you're an asshole. You crossed the line, man. Lizzie is my sister and Seven is a friend. Who do you think you are?"

We all stop at Leo's outburst, passing glances between each other. Leo's face is as hard as stone.

"What's going on?" Lizzie asks. "We need to get him outside, Leo, he's having a whitie."

"Good," Leo spits before he pushes Nate away from him, causing him to wobble and topple as Felix and RV steady him up.

"Go home, Leo. You're overreacting, and don't fucking push me either." Nate thrusts his arms forward, missing Leo by a mile, which riles Leo into more of a fury.

"Hey, let's get him outside, then we'll deal with your beef," RV says to Leo.

"What's happened?" I manage to ask as we pull Nate to the balcony. Leo stands like a warrior; I can translate his energy field and he's not messing. If the weed doesn't knock Nate out, Leo will. We wait for Nate to respond to him, but so far Nate's head is on the table and RV is dowsing it with water from the toothbrush mug. Eventually he sits up after coaxing words from Lizzie who's eyeballing her brother with hate, not love.

"What's got into you?" she asks Leo.

"It's him who needs air," Nate shouts back, pointing at Leo, ready to launch at him again. Leo pushes Nate back into the seat and he crumples with ease as RV cuts in between them both, holding Leo back with an extended arm.

"What's going on? You tell me, hey Seven?" Leo hurls. "Michael told me about your rendezvous in the kitchen. He saw you both."

"Michael saw shit, Leo. Nothing has gone on. We were talking," Nate spews. He attempts a pop at one more line before Lizzie warns him to shut up.

I feel bare and empty of words witnessing this, this carnage. My whole new life has slipped through my fingers like dry sand in the matter of an hour. RV slaps Nate's cheeks to keep the return of life coming.

"Not so hard, mate," Nate replies.

RV remains silent, focused on Nate as I scowl at Leo. "He's right, we were only talking," I say to him and turn to Lizzie who looks like I've just shot her dog. "Lizzie please, this is being made out wrong. Leo has it wrong, so does Michael." I scowl again at Leo, and I notice RV's distance return. Pressure builds in my eyes as the situation attempts to overwhelm me, but Lizzie just gets and up leaves with an expression as cold February.

"Okay. Is everyone done?" Felix asks, "I'll make this muppet a cup of tea, that always works." He back-slaps Nate, not pandering to the exploding male egos and the collapsing female one.

I think I could use that joint RV.

Chapter Twenty-Four
Black Coffee

The front door clicks shut and I lean against it, aghast at the evening I left behind at Felix's…

On the walk home, I was accompanied by a raven, rising and dipping in the air as though mimicking my erratic mind. I marched the pavements, past the grandiose row of multimillion-pound homes overlooking the entrance to the park and around the corner from home.

I can't comprehend what RV has told me. This conundrum must be the main part of my curse to break. The paradoxical messages and drawings have been leading me up to this, and it's all making sense now, as I resolved other parts of my family's curse – of my life – along the way. The man lying down is Palm, isolated in a prison cell. The building with the arched entrance is the prison he's in and the urgency refers to Palm's life and imminent release. Whether Palm is aware he's about to lose his life, on the brink of him getting it back, I have no idea. I don't think he does. That's why I'm involved: preventing a murder, facilitating the reunion of lost love between Mum and Palm and piecing back together a family who were denied the chance to be one, is another level I cannot fathom yet cannot fail on. I must not fall for the cursed whims of my old self – my Boras self. RV, as much as I adore him, thinks he's onto a win-win situation, and I can't exactly tell him he's operating from his own family's curse of the Boras, destined for a lose-lose situation – he'd think me barmy. Regardless, I can't help: according to the Book of Lights I couldn't assist even if I wanted to, I'd lose my Zeffo powers and with them my only hope of pulling this whole thing off.

The hallway is in darkness but the kitchen to the left and the sitting room to the right glow softly behind their glass doors. Mum must be still awake, knocking around upstairs.

"Mu—" I stop as she appears on the stairs all wispy. She gingerly takes each step down like she has finally surrendered to her own fight. She reaches into the pocket of her oversized dressing gown pocket and pulls out a folded piece of paper.

"I had a colleague who's an expert in art and symbolism examine Palm's picture," she says. "The triquetra is an ancient symbol, which has come to represent matters made up of three. In the case of the painting, he believes the triquetra refers to me, you and Palm. Our family of three… and his love, protection and honour."

I had researched the symbol after discovering the painting and Mum is telling me what already know. The triquetra is one of the oldest symbols, originally it represented the triple goddess – maiden-mother-crone – the three stages of a woman's life, and later the Holy Trinity. As the world modernised, its symbolism extended to include anything made up of three, and sometimes the three arcs are joined with a circle to emphasise unity, as Palm has done in his painting. Palm could have meant land-sky-sea, past-present-future, or life-death-rebirth as well, but I have a knowing

Mum and her colleague are correct on their interpretation.

She unfolds the note and hands it to me.

"More interestingly, my colleague also thinks it's been painted recently, perhaps within the last year. In the centre of the triquetra is a tiny drawing of this house, it took a while to figure that's what it was."

I hadn't noticed that.

"Then he found the note, hidden under one of the canvas edges glued down on the back," Mum says as I take the note from her and read it.

> *Meet me at the Roof Garden, the place of forgiveness, for this I will need.*

I turn over the note.

> *Call S.*

"I'm a good lawyer," she continues, "but this is beyond me. I can't figure it out. I can't speak about it to anyone, only you who seems to get all this. I don't know how you arrived at your suspicion of Palm being alive. I didn't understand it, so I dismissed it as fantasy, and I'm sorry." I hand her the note back, feeling smug but empathetic to her. "I think you're right," she says, "he is alive."

Hallelujah.

"How come this note is in English?" I ask.

"He uses both. I speak some Italian, but his English is far superior, less room for things to get lost in translation."

Of all the questions, the most irrelevant one is what I want to ask. I fiddle about pretending to adjust my top, all the while I'm placing my hand over the talisman for assistance in asking better questions, not ineffective questions, which provide pointless information. *I see you, Boras. I see your sly pollution in my mind attempting a heist on me so not to find bona fide information.*

"Who's S?"

"Sal. Salvatore. Big S. He answers to all of them," she says with a half-hearted smile.

"But who is he? Have you called him?"

"Not yet. He's Palm's underboss, like a deputy. Haven't spoken to him in years."

Trustworthy dude then. I cup her hands in mine.

Tell her, I hear my thoughts translate. *Move the needle.*

"Before you call him, which you will do, you need to know something…" I usher Mum and her fretting face into the sitting room and onto the sofa with Palm's picture and the note placed in between us, a weird yet factual representation of the current reality of my family. "Palm is in prison, Mum, due out next Friday. RV told me tonight because—"

Breathe.

Mum listens in disbelief as I regurgitate the earlier conversation with RV. She is livid, disappointed with him when both her and RV have invested so much time and faith in his reform. She moves onto rationalising my discovery by saying it could be one of many Vincenzo's, until I remind her that logic has yet to come up with anything of value in this shitshow of a situation.

"I think we both know the truth here," I say.

"Which prison?" she asks.

"I don't know, we were interrupted, and I haven't had chance to speak with him again, but we need to help RV, protect him too."

I am reminded of my drawing and tell Mum to wait whilst I bolt out of the sitting room.

"I don't understand why Palm has done this. Why the others let me believe this," Mum continues.

"Well, you're about to find out," I yell back, taking the stairs two at a time. I text RV, but he doesn't reply. On my knees, I yank the sticking drawer open under my bed and take out the drawing, placing it in front of me. I take another sheet of plain paper and a pencil from my desk and place it next to the drawing. Sitting cross legged, I call for quiet with one hand and place my fingers on my talisman with the other.

This might be a bit rushed, Vozareia.

"I need more information about the prison. Which prison is it? I need to tell Mum; she needs to know. Please give more information."

I sit and slowly I sense fizzy energy expand within me as the urge to draw compels my pencil. I sketch a fuller image of the building previously drawn: the archway has a huge brown door with castle-like metal gridding above, filling the arched space between the door and wall. A Union Jack is flying at full mast above the entrance point, and behind it there is a white circular structure in a gridded pattern, maybe a window? Old architecture? It's unclear, but above it is a clock face. The building extends both right and left with taller square turrets either side of the archway and at each end. All have dark brown arched windows, and all of it is deathly depressing.

Got it. Cheers.

"Regardless, we need to speak to Rio," Mum says as I walk back into the room.

"Wait. RV mentioned a few features of the prison," I lie and describe the drawing I made upstairs. "It sounded so depressing."

"All prisons are depressing, kind of the point," she replies. After a few moments, she leans forward thinking over the image I describe. "Oh, dear god. They put him in Wandsworth, that prison is…." She lowers her head, clearing her throat to change her words. "It's about an hour from here. All this time, and he's been an hour away from me? If this all turns out to be true, I am going to wring his neck myself."

It's a funny not funny moment which seems to lessen the sting when the doorknocker taps gently on the front door, like its apologising in advance for disturbing us.

"Don't answer it; pretend we are asleep," I say as we both look at the door, not moving.

"Stay there," she instructs.

"Who is it?" Mum asks through the closed door.

"It's Rio. Seven left early, just making sure she got home okay."

Mum throws the door open. "Like hell you are. Get in here. Now." She yells at full volume, flinging her arms all over and pacing the hallway as she lays into RV. "I know exactly why you are here," she fires, slamming the door shut. "Have you learnt nothing? You've got no idea what you are getting into, have you? None, and you stink of beer and weed too. Go in there and sit down," Mum orders, pointing to the space on the sofa next to me before she storms off into the kitchen. I think it's all she can do to stop herself from destroying RV on the spot.

RV's puffa jacket sounds like rustling taffeta in a silenced theatre as he walks awkwardly to the sofa. He perches on the edge, leaning on its arm like a nervous child.

"Shit, Seven. What have you done?" RV asks, his voice laden with betrayal.

"I had to tell her," I retort. "There is something you don't know. So, before you kick off, shut up and wait."

I get up from the sofa annoyed at RV's selfishness and go to Mum in the kitchen. She's propping herself on the fridge in the corner with her hand over her sobbing eyes, and I hold her until the tears stop.

"Mum," I say quietly so RV can't hear, "I know you're mad, worried and stressed, I am too, but if you carry on screeching at him, he's gonna clam up and go straight back to 27evens. He's as scared as we are."

Her breathing slows, and she wipes her face with the sleeve of her dressing gown. "How did we get to this and how do I have such a genius for a daughter?" A light smile appears on her face as she leans her head on mine. "Tell him I need five minutes. Don't say anything about Palm."

Not a minute too soon Mum springs across the hallway from the kitchen with a fresh face; she has a metal ball in the freezer that de-puffs and glows up skin. I sneak a go when she isn't in because it actually works.

I was stumped knowing what to talk about with RV and I ended up banging on about a new eyebrow pen I saw on Instagram to create high-def eyebrows at home. RV's face was not impressed, but I rambled on anyway to stop him leaving.

"I assume you'll have the munchies by now," Mum says, setting a tray on the coffee table.

"Err, yeah. I am a bit hungry. Thank-erm-you," RV says, shocked as I am. I didn't think Mum knew about stuff like this.

"Have these and the black coffee. We're all going to need coffee tonight," she says, handing him a mug from the tray of crisps and biscuits. "Rio, take your coat off and quit panicking. I'm angry and upset, but I'm on your side. It will make more sense to you shortly. You can stay here tonight; text your parents and let them know."

Mum keeps hesitating between sentences and waffling semi-irrelevant stories to RV about how I am a bohemian-type person, unlike herself (which I think is a compliment) and continues to talk about our similarities despite or surface-level differences.

"Seven and I are both the same," she tells RV awkwardly. "This is how it is between you and us too. It appears as though we are opposites in many ways, when in truth we are batting from similar ground."

The rustle of crisp packets and crunching of biscuits fills the room as RV troughs his way through his munchies; he's lost in Mum's waffle, poised for a rant about not returning to his old ways.

"Get to the point, Mum," I say, fearing we will be here till the morning light.

The sound of crunching crisps and biscuits continues to magnify the silence from the pause Mum takes, and I flick a slap on RV's arm for him to pay proper attention.

"What you don't know is, Seven's real father, and the love of my life, is also a gangster. A boss in the Mafia, to be precise. His name is Vincenzo Petralia, the same man we believe your gang is going to kill."

The rustling of crisps and the munching of biscuits abruptly stops. RV gawps at the pair of us like he's just been thrust from hot water into ice-cold water.

"For reasons I do not know yet, I was led to believe Palm – Vincenzo – was killed many years ago. It seems this has been a cover up. I need to confirm it is the same man, but I think we all know it is," Mum says.

"I wondered how you knew the name," RV says, turning to look at me, he's still holding an open bag of crisps and half a biscuit. "Damn, man. I thought I was in hell before, it's even worse now. You two? Involved with the Mafia? What the fuck." He shoves another crisp in his mouth, and another. "Palm, you say. Yeah, that's the dude's name; I can't remember that Vino one."

"What do you know about him?" Mum asks.

"Not much. Been inside a long time. Something to do with fraud and screwing over an artist causing him to lose his money, home, family. A life's work. His kids are messed up, one of 'em knows Kris from the mandem. Shitty of your man, to be fair."

I beg RV not to do this, to withhold judgement in the same way he wishes others would quit judging him. He crumples, trying to back away from us, uncomfortable and uncertain of how to handle women and the situation. Mum sits on the floor, nestling her hands in the space between RV and me on the sofa. She gazes up at us both, takes our hands in hers and comforts my tears and RV's anxiety.

"We need him, Rio," Mum finally says. "We deserve him back with us. Seven hasn't even met him! I get it, 27evens are nasty, but taking on the Mafia is stupidity. They are more refined and experienced than any street gang and more brutal, but they will help you. I can talk to them. If you go through with this, Seven and I – the whole world, actually – will lose two great men: you and Palm. You both deserve your lives. He's served his time, and so have you. What is done is done, and enough is enough.

"It all makes sense now, why the guys are here: it's to pick Palm up on Friday when he's released." Mum shakes her head at the insight.

RV swigs his coffee until he can bear our faces no longer.

"Alright," he says, thinking twice about placing his empty mug on the floor, scared of the cream carpet and Mum's face, he puts it back on the tray and presses his thumbs into the bridge of his nose. "I'm in a real shit position. You need to do what I ask, or no deal, because I…" he says, pointing with force to his chest, "do not want to end up dead."

Chapter Twenty-Five
Switching the Steering

The sun has been up warming Saturday morning for hours while Mum and I, and RV on the sofa, slept in beneath the weight of the night before. The stale air downstairs of old coffee and that weird boy smell is freeing up, becoming purer as Mum opens every window in the house. She leans forward across the island, her red glass beads tapping against it like a pendulum.

"We're all clear? I'll see you two back here in a couple of hours," she says.

Nate's group text for the MGs to meet at Wavies just before lunch is timely; RV and I can disappear to Wavies while Mum rings Salvatore 'Big S' Caruso.

'I don't know if I still have the right number,' Mum wailed earlier.

'I'm sure you can figure something out,' RV replied.

I rang Lizzie this morning, her voice on a downer as I re-explained the scene to her about Nate and me in the kitchen. I'm not yet sure if she fully believes me, I mean, would I have believed me if it was the other way around? We agree to see each other later on in Wavies, and I'm grateful Lizzie is of a broader mindset, willing to listen and chat calmly. Discussing my personal behaviour with another scrapes at my bones and makes me want to run from myself. My childhood taught me it was unsafe to do so and results in being unwanted. Despite all the Zeffo work I've done, I would still rather not have these conversations. I don't know how to communicate my feelings at times, preferring other's to magically understand me and everything to return back to normal as quickly as possible. The fear of intimacy, the fear of seeing into myself and the fear of myself: will it ever go away?

I can't be bothered to wash my hair, so I roughly clip it up at the back to create a messy, very messy, up do instead and move onto mascara and blush. RV just throws water on his face and runs a comb through his dark hair. He's ready in about five minutes and sits on my bed perplexed by my array of sprays, pots and trays of beauty and hair care products.

"You look fine. Come *onnnn*," he says, now standing in the doorway to my bedroom, banging his hand on the frame. I groan at my messy up-do, which does not resemble anything like the natural *I haven't tried* look I'd hoped for.

"You don't need all that stuff on ya face. Beats me why you girls go on about it so much," RV witters.

I throw a cushion at him, but he leans to the side, and it flies straight past him, out of the door and onto the landing. I twirl myself under a few good sprays of perfume; Mum says I shouldn't be able to smell my own perfume on myself, because it's too much if I can, but it doesn't last unless you do, and I've found this method of applying perfume works well. RV pretends to choke, coughing and spluttering as I squeeze past him in the doorway.

"Come on then," I say, poking him in the ribs mid cough. "I'm ready, unlike you who's messing around."

We head straight down the hill towards town but split up near the bottom of the hill; we want to turn up at Wavies separately to avoid being quizzed over why we arrived together when we live in opposite directions.

I sit down next to Leo and Yas at our table, Lizzie is friendly, but something is still off, and I want us to go back to how we were: enjoying our new friendship. Leo gives me a wink as much to say *it's not you* and I smile back. RV saunters in minutes later but slinks off into the corner with Richard, I assume to quell recent concerns. I'm half listening to all the hangover comparisons and re-runs of events last night, distracted by watching RV and Richard. Whatever RV says seems to have worked, because Richard slaps the back of RV's shoulder and watches him walk back to our table with a glint of pride in his eyes.

"Y'alright, man?" Leo asks as RV finally joins the rest of us.

"Yeah, all cool. Cheers, bro." RV nods at Leo in man talk and the group falls quiet as Nate calls for everyone's attention.

"Cheers for coming down, it's just to say sorry for being a dick last night. I was shitfaced and riled about the game. Didn't mean what I said, or to piss anyone off."

"We've all been there, mate… that damn lemonade, it's a beast," Felix says, easing the tension.

"Leo, I was out of line, man," Nate says, offering a handshake to Leo. "Seven, I'm sorry. I was a twat, I told Lizzie what I said, and she agrees I'm a twat as well," he says with

Lizzie sat next to him laughing and nodding her head.

A balloon of tension seems to have been popped for everyone, to be fair; tensity amongst us is unpleasant, and I particularly don't handle it well. The MGs reign once more as our friendship towers strong, and we all agree to let it float away with the rest of the water under that there ole bridge. And that includes my friendship with Lizzie, which means more to me than Nate's apologetic spiel. Yas, Lizzie and I plan to meet up tomorrow – barring any more random mafia madness. I don't think Nate is going to get away with this as unscathed as he appears to think he has.

***

Oh my god. There is a real-life mafia man in my house. He's standing in my kitchen talking to Mum, who is completely unphased by a real-life mafia man being in the house, they are reminiscing over days gone by, you know, like you do when the Mafia shows up.

His pinstripe suit and pristine brown shoes (finest Italian leather I assume), emit an attractive authority. Sunglasses are balanced on top of his dark, silver, but surprisingly thick hair, given his age. He must be in his fifties. RV looks like he's bricking it and hangs behind, half in the kitchen and half in the hallway, and part of me wants us all to sit by the fire and listen to Mr Mafia spin tales to my intrigued mind. *That is not normal, Seven, those hands will have murdered.* Regardless of my apprehension, I'm smiling sweetly at Sal, listening to Mum introduce me and RV to him.

"Seven, this is Salvatore, or Sal. He's Palm's colleague and part of your family," Mum says.

"Oh my… Seven! Palm's precious, precious bambino." He throws his arms up to the gods and jibbers on in Italian. He waltzes over to me and kisses the top of my head before admiring my face. I'm eyeballing Sal's hands as they hold my now squished pug looking face in them as he continues to rejoice in meeting me. After a few minutes of face admiring and hugging, Sal lets me go, releasing my features back to normal; Mum is grinning like she did the day I came home from school with a star of the day sticker.

"And you must be *Signor* Rio Vanns. *Piacere,*" Sal says.

"It means, pleased to meet you," Mum adds.

Sal holds out a solid hand to shake RV's, which is, ironically, already shaking on its own, a stark difference from tough 27evens boy. Sal is perfectly reassuring with RV; I suppose he has to be. RV has information to foil the murder of a Mafiosi boss. Sal wouldn't have known about it otherwise, so really, RV has no need to be bricking it, I decide – like all of a sudden I'm an experienced woman in these matters.

Sal insists we all sit to discuss this situation and holds his arm out in the direction of the sitting room.

"*Gabbee.* After you," Sal says.

Aw, that's sweet. I repeat it in my head: *Gabbee.* I wonder if Palm says it like that too; I pray I'm lucky enough to find out.

I'd prayed for years for a father, a family and true security. I'm not sure what it feels like to be safe – how do we know if we are? Who is the boss of dishing out rules and deciding whether I feel safe and happy or not anyway? I guess one lesson to learn is to let go of how I wanted all my dandelion wishes to work out, because what if the answer is totally different to what I thought it would be, and I miss something better whilst I wait for my version of it? I only have the past to go off, and that experience and knowledge, is but a mere slither of what life really has available to me.

We take our places on the sofa as Sal chooses to stand.

"*Gabbee* has told me of your recent discovery of Palm in Wandsworth and of your gang," Sal says, turning to RV.

"They are not my gang, sir. Well, they were, but I'm trying to leave," RV butts in.

"*Si, si*, I know," Sal replies, raising his hand to calm RV. "You are right to do so. Make no doubt, *signore*, we are switching the steering. Seven and *Gabbee*, I will talk to you two more – alone – later, to explain a few things that need not concern Rio. Tell me their plan Rio, all of it," Sal insists.

I can feel Mum revving with questions and demands for explanations, but Sal insists we stay and support RV while he unveils the details for Friday morning's plan. I feel conflicted over whether I want to know or not as I listen to the premeditated fate of Vincenzo Petralia.

"I'll be on a scooter," RV explains. "It belongs to one of the boys from 27evens. My instructions are to hang out at Wandsworth, near the prison entrance from eight in the morning, and wait for Palm to walk out when they release him. The boys estimated he'll have one or two sidekicks collecting him. No more than three.

"I'll have a radio mic set up and linked in my helmet, which will feed back to 27evens nearby. I follow Palm's car and report the route back; there's only a few ways out of Wandsworth Prison." RV pauses, looking upwards. He's finding this hard; it must be uncomfortable for him to tell this story to the people who love this marked man the most, and to a man who could break his neck with a finger.

"Let me guess, they plan to block us both ends and hijack our car?"

RV manages a sheepish nod and continues. "They know Palm will be weak, unfit and unguarded from being inside. With you lot in your car at gun point, one of the mandem will drive your car, backed by three 27evens cars to a place near Kris' crib, where the trigger will be pulled on Palm, probably after tormenting him for a while."

Mum is gasping. RV is shredded over his own words, and he soaks up the devastation of this one last job. I don't think he expected the impact of emotion, and he can't look my mum in the eye. Meanwhile, Sal doesn't flicker. His response is beyond weird as I can't comprehend being so chill after hearing all of that. Sal casually comments about how it's a plan of amateurs and it's similar to what he thought RV was going to say. *OMG, I'm so not up to speed with mob curriculum*; clearly, I have much more to learn than homework this weekend.

"How big is this gang, how many?" Sal asks.

"There are fifteen all together, with twelve on this job, including me."

"Forgive me, Rio, but I need to understand." Sal clears his throat and takes his sunglasses from his head to swing them in his hand. "Tell me, why would a person recruit sixteen-year olds to carry out a shooting of this level, no disrespect. How do your people know Palm? Who are they dealing with?"

RV's eyes are following the swinging sunglasses back and forth while he finds the courage to return to Sal's eyes. "We're not all sixteen, only me and Tommy are. Mick is nineteen. The rest are in their twenties and thirties. I grew up with them all, born into it, sir."

"*Sì*. That I understand. How your people came to be hired on the other hand… *errr*… not so much."

"Kris is the gang's boss. He dealt with it; I've not spoken to the art man," RV explains.

"Art man?" Sal replies, distinctly intrigued.

"Kris told us that Palm forced him – the art man – out of his art gallery and lost him all his savings. He said Palm then set fire to years' worth of the guy's artwork, caused him to lose his business, home, wife, all their money, and his children are in therapy because of it. He wants revenge. Says 27evens are the best. He's living in a dumpy council flat, sees his kids every now and then."

Sal is nodding; the story seems to be familiar to him. "The art man, do you know his name?"

RV hesitates as the last of his fears is squeezed out of him. "Peter Bloom. I don't know anything else, I swear."

"Peter Bloom. Well, well, well. The lowlife rears his vile head again. The man is bad news and his pity story is not quite correct, but no matter for now," Sal says, waving his sunglasses in front of his chest and pausing before he continues.

"He's hired your gang because they are foolish enough to fall for Bloom's money talk, not because they are the best. Bloom has no money, maybe a little, but not what he'll be boasting. They are doing it for *nootheen*, the fools!" Sal wanders around the sitting room, staring at the floor. He pulls out his mobile and excuses himself for a few minutes.

The rest of us stay in silence but keep looking at each other, hoping the other will break the awkward ice.

"Well done, RV, you've absolutely done the right thing. Very proud of you," Mum whispers over.

"Uh, you reckon? I feel like I'm dangling by my ankle off a fifty-foot building right now."

"What's he doing?" I whisper, looking past Mum and RV through glass doors.

"Changing the steering like he said, I presume. He'll be… Wait, he's coming back. Shush," Mum replies.

Sal swings back through the double glass doors. He takes a seat on the chair and turns to RV.

"Rio. You are a true man, and on behalf of everyone, we thank you. You will be repaid well, and you will remain safe from your gang, I promise."

"I don't want to be repaid, it's fine. Honestly. I don't want anything. I don't want to owe anything. I don't want any more involvement. I just want this sorted and these two to be okay," RV says, straight up.

"I know this. What I mean is, you can be at peace from the fear of your gang. You are a man, but still a boy. We will take care of this for you." RV is plagued with wondering how, and its repercussions – I can almost smell it on him – but he eventually agrees and hands over his trust to the impeccably well-dressed Italian man he barely knows.

"For the rest of the week, I want you to continue the game with your gang, act like you're doing this for them. Any changes or other information let me know, immediately. On Friday morning, you will do the same thing as they asked."

I'm confused, how is this preventing Palm from being shot? Can't they do something simple like change the release date? I'm sure Palm won't mind staying inside a couple more days if he knows it will save his life.

"But you will direct them to this place." Sal hands RV a piece of scrap paper with a small map penned on it. "We will have your back. You will be kept in sight at all times and there will be another one of our guys following you too.

I will take you on this route and to the destination this afternoon – practice run. Young Rocco and I are already here, originally to pick the old goat up on Friday, but the rest are flying in." Sal scans all of us to reassure us he's got this. I'm glad someone has because I feel neurotic.

"By the time we are through, 27*err…*" Sal says and flickers his hand around in the air, "…won't bother you again. Bloody rookies."

Chapter Twenty-Six
My Seven

I get a message from Lizzie in the private chat between me, her and Leo while painting my nails and, naturally, the distraction made me smudge my progress – typical.

Message from Lizzie

Hey, you two, do you want to go to the movies tonight?

I barge into the kitchen, and Mum and Sal are in deep discussion now that RV has gone home. I imagine they'll be nattering like this until Sal picks RV up later for the practice run.

"Mum. Leo and Lizzie have asked me to go to the cinema tonight. Can I go *pleaseee*?"

Gangsterdom has begun to dominate my thinking and body, to the point I feel choked by it, and I'm not moving forward past the drama of it. I just want it all to be over. For it to be next Friday with Palm safe. When I think of meeting him, I am transported to a different world, and I don't like to leave it or the euphoric feeling it gives me. I can't wait for him and Mum to be reunited, and to see RV free and happy with 27evens a distant memory. Sal and the rest of his crew have this in hand, and RV is on board. Missing a couple hours of

260

family talk with Mum and Sal won't be detrimental.

"It gives you two more time to talk in private," I bargain. *Please say yes.*

"Not tonight, and Sal has also offered to make dinner," Mum announces with her arms out wide.

"Leo? Lizzie?" Sal enquires.

"Seven's friends from Miami. They moved here last Christmas for a year," Mum answers.

"That's the thing, Lizzie thinks they might be going back in July now. She's upset, Leo's annoyed and July isn't far away," I ramble.

"Ah, I see. *Gabbeeeeee*," Sal says, turning to look at her. "What is more important than young friendship?"

"Exactly," I say. *I like this dude.*

Mum isn't convinced.

"We have plenty time," Sal adds, "I'll pick Rio up in half an hour, after, we have dinner. I'll cook quicker than my usual three-hour affair," Sal mocks. "Seven goes out and we can speak more. It's *perfetto, non?*"

"What about the letters?" Mum asks.

"What letters?" I counter ask.

Sal tells me Palm wrote two letters, one to me and one to Mum. Palm had instructed Sal to keep the letters secure until such time of his release. He has babysat these letters for years, and since he arrived in London the letters have been kept safe in Sal's hotel room at The Savoy. And now, they are in his car outside. I want to read mine this instant.

"There's no rush, Vincenzo will always be the hopeless romantic," Sal says. "Let Seven be," Sal says to Mum with his persuasive tone.

Mum disagrees there is no rush to hear what Palm has to say but admits space from each other is welcome.

"Go and enjoy yourself with your friends," Sal adds, and we agree to read our letters when I get back later this evening. "Have the cinema treat on me, I'll ring them and sort that out for you all," Sal offers.

My face drops, unsure of what is meant by he'll sort it out.

"It's the least I can do. This is okay, *si?*"

"NO," I say too fast and loud. "No, thank you. It's kind of you, but I don't' need you to do that... Leo is paying." I splutter on the spot.

"Good man," Sal replies, nodding with a downturned mouth in surprised approval.

Note to self: ask Mum when the correct time is to accept gifts from real life mafia men.

Sal disappears outside, leaving the front door wide open, and a gust of warm refreshing wind tumbles into the hallway, trickling into the kitchen. Moments later, Sal returns with two envelopes, one addressed to Gabby, and one addressed to me. The once crisp envelopes with our names written in black ink have become creased with time and have developed nicks on the edges. They have turned an off white and the names are faded, but I don't care and hold my letter tight to my chest.

I hope Palm has written nice things; the kind of words that make all this feel okay. What if it doesn't say those things? What if it says he doesn't want to meet me because it's all too painful and late... *Stop! Stop with the dark shit, Seven.*

It's boring; my dark talk is boring me, and I'm bored of hearing it.

Expect good shit only.

****

"That was cringe. I'm choosing next time," Leo says, laughing as the three of us walk out of the cinema halfway through the film.

We head to the bridge which crosses from Silversedge over the River Thames into the next town, and we lean over the wall at the middle point, watching the moored rowing boats lap against each other and the people drink coffee at the late-night riverside café below.

"The trailer was better," I say, laughing in agreement.

We trace our steps back to the Silversedge side, take the steps down to the café and mooch on past it, before heading onwards along the riverbank.

Lizzie heard her dad on the phone earlier to someone back home in Miami, and whilst she couldn't make sense of the conversation, it was leaning in the direction of leaving in the summer instead of Christmas.

"I want to go back, but not yet," Lizzie says, picking up a twig from the track and throwing it in the river.

"Thought you'd be up for it. Get back on the waves sooner," Leo says, throwing a twig into the river as well.

They're both torn between two places, with no control over which side of the pond they want to reside. Miami is home, with many aspects they prefer, but they have fallen for London and the friends they have made, although I sense Nate might not be in that category as much anymore. Having just settled, it seems uprooting is about to occur again. I pick up the conversation about Nate and me at the party, gushing explanations and apologies as I haven't been able to put down the feeling Lizzie has backed off from me and that Leo trusts me less.

"I'm annoyed with Nate. I see now, you were just being straight, given the position he put you in. Although I would have rather heard it from you," Lizzie says, smiling and throwing an arm around my shoulders.

"If he says anything else to me, I'll let you know," I say, smiling back up at her and holding her dangling hand over my shoulder.

Leo has calmed down about it and is back to his regular self, he says. "I was looking out for my sis. It's not a good idea you and Nate being together," he says to Lizzie.

Lizzie removes her arm and before they start bickering over who is running whose life, I return the conversation to Miami. "I don't want either of you to leave, but if it were me, I'd go. I'd love to get out of London: travel the world, live in the sun and own a yellow house," I yell over the snaking river, my arms stretched out to the gods.

"Your London is our Miami though. Go figure," Leo adds.

We saunter on as I fire questions at Leo about Zeffos and the Boras Curse; I'm convinced I've solved my quest, yet this overwhelming change within me and my family hasn't appeared. I can't say I feel free; I still don't have my family back together or my guy in my arms. Wise Leo thinks it's about to hit a crescendo, otherwise it all would be solved by now.

"Is this why you'll be going back to Miami early?" I ask

Leo, "Because your work with me is done or is about to be done?"

He shrugs his shoulders, and no one is certain about anything anymore.

"I've known you two the shortest amount of time out of everyone, and yet I feel closer to you both, understood by you both so much more than by the others… except maybe Felix," I say, looking at my feet as I walk and then up at their faces.

"Time means nothing," Lizzie says, "me and Leo said the same earlier actually… soul fam." She fist bumps me and then her brother and we walk in comfortable silence until I ask Leo about the text from Love Quotes, but he can't help me work out what it means without breaking the rules, although teasingly he says he has an idea what Vozareia is trying to tell me.

"It's a dumb rule, and it's not fair. Can't you give me a hint?" I say to Leo as he stops to skim pebbles across the surface of the river with the sun in his eyes.

"I do miss the sun of home, and the humidity that I did nothing but complain about when I lived there." Leo drifts off, still looking out over the water and for a few moments closes his eyes.

"Ask Lizzie," he says with his eyes remaining closed. "She's brilliant at translating metaphors, and she's a Remmie not a Zeffo, so no rule breaking." He opens his eyes and turns to us both, letting Lizzie and me walk on first and we give Leo a few minutes alone by the water's edge as though his reflection will hold his own hand. It's isolating work being a Zeffo.

"What did it say?" Lizzie asks.

"'You heard my call because I heard yours. Be equal in self

to the romance you ask of life, for they are already here. Are you?'" I reply.

Leo catches up with us as I repeat the passage for a third time. He's messing with us, saying he knows exactly what it means, as Lizzie repeats it and turns it over and over until we reach the café and climb the steps back up to the top of the bridge.

"It means," she says, stopping to speak aloud her discovery as noisy traffic flies past the three of us on the bridge, "you have to be the person you would be if you were already going out with your dream guy. You have to *be It* before you *see It*." She emphasizes the key words as I stand completely blank and muddled. "If you were already with the hypothetical guy of your dreams, let's say RV." Lizzie smirks, "How would you feel, act, speak?"

She's got me thinking.

"Life can only give you what you *deeply feel*. Energies match first before anything physical."

"You're as paradoxical and confusing as the quote," I say, linking both of their arms and pulling them on. "Some help you are," I add, joking as we all laugh our way across the bridge into Silversedge – but I think I'm beginning to understand what she means.

I would have happily walked for miles with Leo and Lizzie, the quote alone could spark hours of talking and unearth many revelations of the inner self, but I'm aware I need to get home, and I want to read my letter.

"Duty calls," I say as we spilt up. Leo and Lizzie understand my code wording, knowing I need Zeffo time as I have work to do. They catch the bus in the centre of

Silversedge to go home, whereas I can walk up the hill. "See you tomorrow, Lizzie." I wave as they disappear into the crowd of people shuffling down the pavement.

***

My Seven,

If this letter has found its way to you, then you know the truth as to who I am: Vincenzo Petralia, your proud father. I hope this does not lay heavy on your heart and shoulders. I bear the past for all of us. My work and lifestyle are risky and unconventional, and I do not expect you to approve or understand, just that you hear me out when the time is right.

Unfortunately, certain factors beyond my control went wrong and my death is being faked. This is to protect, firstly, you and your mum, and secondly, my confederates, my family, and my dear friends. In reality, I will be in prison. It is not the decision or life I want. I am broken, yes, but my love for you is not, and your protection and well-being is and always will be my priority.

I am so sorry, so hugely sorry for everything. Please know, my precious Seven, that you are very loved and wanted. I seal this envelope as my dear friend Salvatore stands here to take this letter for you and a letter I have written for your mum, before I am sent away for a while. Salvatore is trustworthy and can be relied upon. Your mum is the most powerful, loving, clever and angelic lady, and I will think of you both every second of every day, until comes such a time that you may grant me the honour of meeting you.

If Salvatore has delivered this letter to you, then that time is soon and my release imminent. I ask you and your mum to talk and consider this. Salvatore will do anything he can to help, and I pray your answer is yes.

I have much to rectify and many questions to answer,

but I stay hopeful we will all have the rest of our lives together.
    Forever loving,
    Vincenzo

Chapter Twenty-Seven
Next Sunday

"What I don't understand, Sal, is why Palm's picture was at Jamming Minds? It's only because Seven wandered in to look at Gusti's artwork that it was found?" Mum asks as Sal places down the pile of Sunday papers he bought on his way over onto the kitchen island.

He makes a face at the takeout espresso he's drinking as I hold out my hand, agreeing with Mum.

"Not like the Sicilians make," Sal remarks. "Coffee and cannoli: it's the best breakfast in the world."

"Sal?" Mum asks again, growing impatient.

Sal launches into the story behind the mystery of Palm's painting, but I'm adrift in thoughts over coffee, cannoli and Sicilian high sun. *I'm adding this to my ever-growing bucket list.* Given my family dynamics I reckon I can pull this one off sooner rather than later.

"That makes sense now," Mum says, turning to me for agreement to a question I didn't hear.

"Sorry, can you repeat that? I was thinking about cannoli," I reply.

Sal's face lights up, chuckling to himself he throws an arm around my shoulders and walks me to the kitchen window, the wooden shutters wide open.

"Most definitely Palm's daughter," he says, smiling and squarely looking me in the eyes, before turning his gaze to the window and looking out into the garden.

The picture, Sal explains, was drawn by Palm in Wandsworth last year and collected by him on a prison visit. The note was stuck under the folded canvas by Sal, who had kept the note Palm had written before he was sent down all those years ago: Palm had wanted to announce his breaking news to Mum and me in the gentlest sweetest way. The two estate agents who helped Mum purchase this house were, apparently, Palm's lower associates within his organisation he calls *The Family*, and I suspect, therefore, this is the reason why Mum received such a good deal. The associates were supposed to leave the painting in the house when we moved in, but they left it at Jamming Minds having mixed up the addresses and instructions – a costly mistake and misunderstanding.

"'Have you heard? Have you heard from her?' Palm would ask me at every visit or call I made," Sal says. "Every time I would have to shake my head and watch him shrink further away. It was heart breaking to see the old goat like that. The letters he wrote, I was to give to you both after your mum rang me."

"Heart breaking? HE'S heartbroken?" Mum spits out from formally being quiet as Sal re-tells the story. "What does he think I've been?" she yells.

Of course *now* Sal realises Mum never got the picture, or the note, and this is why she had never called him. Apparently the two associates are no longer working with *The Family*, and I don't feel like asking what happened to them.

"We always knew where you both were, keeping an eye on you." Sal smiles and tries to comfort Mum, who frankly looks like she is about to explode but is trying to contain herself in front of me.

"Even if I had the picture when we moved in here, there is still all the years before to consider, when you led me to believe he was dead."

"Palm will explain, but know it hurt him and all of us as much as it did you… You can still walk away; he would understand,' Sal says with sincerity pouring from his eyes.

Don't. Don't give up now.

"We are still gonna meet him though?' I ask Mum, concerned her anger won't let her agree to the meeting at 'their place', the garden of forgiveness, next Sunday.

Assuming we make it past Friday, after Palm is released next Sunday lunchtime, I will be at the Roof Garden in central London with Mum to meet Vincenzo. My stomach feels silly. I get to meet him. I get to see him for real. I've chosen to call him Vincenzo, too soon if ever for Dad – Palm is his nickname, a mafia-work name, but he is my father and I want this to work, for everyone.

"How can I walk away?" Mum says, looking at me and then Sal. Neither of us know what to say. Mum leans towards the island, grabs a paper from the pile and with an air of feeling beaten, vacates to the sitting room, closing the doors behind her.

I wonder if Sal knows of the Boras, or even if *The Family* know… Mafia work seems an obvious option for the Boras to inflict their curse on certain people and families, though perhaps too obvious. Despite their work being far from spirit building and legal, Sal doesn't appear conflicted or in pain like RV is about his gang life, indeed it is the humble opposite. I know because I am translating Sal's energy field right this minute. I talk to Sal for a while about the type of work they do and *The Family*, of which I am part of whether I like it or not, and he doesn't dismiss my questions and answers as though I am an equal, not a child. His wife left him because of the Mafia, and he's never loved again. Not too different from Palm and Mum. The Boras Curse haemorrhages through all. It dawns on me slowly the brutal work of the Mafia: from their perspective, all the bloody work they do is actually rooted in loyalty, respect, justice and fairness, and I dare say it's the same for crude street gangs like 27evens and RV. Aren't we all batting for the same in different misguided ways? Aren't we all seeking significance, validation, love and respect?

"What if RV backs out of the plan on Friday and stays on 27even's side? *They* are what he knows, *they* are his history?" I ask Sal, staring down at the island worktop, turning over a coaster in my fingers and suddenly feeling incredibly uncomfortable about the task ahead.

"He won't. Leave this to us and don't you worry about it," Sal says, walking over to the bin, pressing the pedal to open it and throwing his coffee cup in.

If I'm a Mystical Gangster, then in some ways I'm no better than they are – hell, I beat up people the other day. This isn't about which gangster is more powerful, it's about *more life to all.*

Message to Gusti and Leo

Emergency meeting. Today. Zeffo Room 3pm.

***

Lizzie is already at Wavies; she's sitting on a smaller table, staring out of the window and running her hand over her nails. She doesn't notice Yas or me when we trundle in until we scrape the chairs back, making her jump. Lizzie is troubled.

The three of us pass around small talk. First up on the menu, Yas is still rabbiting on about Bea and how Bea is helping her put together a persuasive plea that Yas can present to her parents, which would allow her to study fashion. My own best friend help and tear drying is long forgotten, not as valuable, it feels – but I do sincerely hope she can change her parent's minds. It will mess Yas up and her parents would rob the world of a talent if they don't.

Yas takes a break from talking and shoots off to the loo and Lizzie fires a quick question at me, "Are you okay?"

I tell her yes, although life his heating up in my house and being unable to talk about the specifics of it with her is hard. Lizzie flashes a sympathetic smile.

"You'll come out great from all this. You'll see," she says with a confidence, making me feel better instantly.

Moving back to Miami in July has been mentioned to both Lizzie and Leo last night. Their mum and dad have managed to gather and secure what they need for the paper more quickly than expected and it will be sewn up by June. The J is taking off rapidly and requires the Joseph's back in their base in Miami. I'm happy for The J; this is good news and likely will involve visits to London from time to time from the Josephs. Change all around seems imminent, but I'm not sure how I feel about losing them both. I've made many friends in Silversedge only for them to move away, it's that type of place, and I always found a way to cope with the etch my new missing friends made on me; but it's different with these two, and they don't know how they feel about it either now it's becoming real.

"It's made my decision easier with Nate though," Lizzie says, looking up at me from her empty glass.

Yas returns with three juices for us, which she grabbed on her way back from the loo. Richard's new Sunday helper, Miles, is working, so Richard can have a day off. Miles is okay, but not as fun as Richard and doesn't yet know all our little nuances. The type of information another knows only because they have spent time paying deep attention.

'Can't be here twenty-four seven,' Richard said last week to us all. 'Particularly when I've earned a second date for myself, and yes – before you ask, Felix – it's the same lady' he joked at the time, and the three of us recall it with heart.

"I hope Richard's date is going better than my dating life," Lizzie states.

"Oh no. What's happened?" Yas places her hand on Lizzie's, but Lizzie continues to stare into her glass, and I think I know what's coming.

"Leo spoke to me on Friday when he got home. We had a good chat about Nate," Lizzie says.

"Nate was wasted, and Michael got the wrong end of the pineapple. Seven didn't do anything," Yas says.

"I know, but Nate still has feelings for you." She glances towards me. "I know he does. Leo told me to dump him, and I deserve someone who is sure about me all of the time, not eighty percent of it. Nate denies it, but I can tell. Have done for a while. I can't go out with someone knowing this, and if we're going back home in July, well…"

Yas is gobsmacked at Lizzie's news. Me? Less so.

"I'm so sorry. I feel responsible," I say to Lizzie, who is obviously sad and hurting.

"I know nothing went on with you and Nate. It's not you at all," Lizzie says finally. "I really like you, and I'm glad we are friends." Lizzie's eyes begin to well and the tears are going to roll any second, so I faff around trying to find a tissue in my bag for her. A napkin will have to do because who under the age of thirty carries tissues?

"Friday was the cold water I needed," Lizzie adds. "Shouldn't have avoided my female intuition."

I knew exactly what she was meant. Yas on the other hand didn't have clue and her perfectly made-up face was sweetly comical as she tried to understand what we were talking about.

"Are you sure about this? Nate has been blown away by you since you got together," Yas asks.

There's no convincing Lizzie to try and make it work, and I support her in her choice to end things. I saw the truth in Nate's eyes when he was telling me, beer or no beer, and it's a shame Lizzie and Nate can't be when Nate and I are nothing but an old chapter in the school yearbook.

Yas and I rally round Lizzie for the next hour. Then, after ice creams at the park, we huddle on a wooden bench and watch the same families and nannies play the same ball games with their children.

"Please don't mention going back to Miami, I can't cope with that as well today. Everything is going to be different," Yas says, leaning on Lizzie's shoulder.

Lizzie is feeling better after off-loading to us and this

warms me. Friends are vintage, although I'm fully aware I have committed the number one best friend sin lately: preferring Lizzie over Yas. I admit this only to myself, of course; no one else needs to know.

Yas, in vain attempt to pick up the mood, ropes Lizzie into a little therapeutic window-shopping, but I make my excuses due to a family thing this afternoon and get ready to leave. As I'm leaving, Lizzie hits me on the shoulder.

"I know!" she says with her first genuinely happy smile all day, "Come to Miami for the summer! School will be long done by then. I'm serious. We have a spare room at home and Mom and Dad love you both." She smirks, elbowing me in the ribs. "Leo can do all the arty things in Miami with you, and I can get your ass' on surfboards. It will be awesome, what d'ya think?"

I think I feel a little jealously spring from Yas; Yas and her family, without fail, return to Dubai every summer for the holidays; but I also think this is a banging idea.

"Don't be daft, Lizzie. I'd be an embarrassment on a surfboard."

As we leave the park, Yas tells us we can't be in Miami without her, and part of me feels I shouldn't consider this idea unless Yas can come. Part of me feels it's only fantasy talk anyway, and I stop myself getting carried away with the idea.

Ten minutes later, I'm hiding in an overstocked newsagent in the Tube station as I know I won't bump into Lizzie and Yas here whilst I kill time. At 2.55pm, I set off for Jamming Minds, when I get a text.

Message from Lizzie

I'm serious Seven, think about it. L x

Chapter Twenty-Eight
Double Eye

I feel important walking through the archway into the Zeffo Room, and it doesn't get old; it's how I imagine A-listers must feel everywhere they go. I ask Gusti if he still gets a buzz from it as he releases the blinds of the small windows in the Zeffo Room, signifying our meeting is about to begin.

"Always," he replies.

Leo, sprawled out on one of the chairs at the table, patiently awaits to hear the reason I've dragged us all together at short notice. One round cup of the awful tea sits on the shelf next to two glasses of water; Gusti is out of juice and Leo agrees with me that the tea is rank. 'We need a more refined palate,' Gusti said to us.

Sat opposite Leo, I wait for Gusti who flutters back to his chair at the table, twisting his talisman bangle around on his wrist, and the thought of which talisman Leo has pops into my head, but I figure this is an inappropriate time to drift off into wonderment or ask him unimportant questions.

"I need help. I can't manage this on my own," I say to concerned faces as Leo shuffles himself upright.

They both listen intently as I explain the turn of events: the dilemma Vincenzo is in, the dilemma RV is in and the hit

I received yesterday from Vozareia that this current set up –
to save both Palm and RV and rid me and my family of the
Boras Curse – is off in some way.

Leo is in shock about RV, and it takes him a minute to
compute the complexity of this situation. Not only does the
situation suck, but I also feel like I've broken RV's trust,
again. Why is this all so difficult?

Gusti, not joining us in our heightened discussion, absorbs
all the information in silence, sitting in a mist of comforting
authority while bouncing a fingertip against his cheek.

"There are a lot of dodgy variables involved," Leo says
finally, leaning forward towards to me.

"I know! What if RV decides to back out and take
27even's side? He's still intimidated by them, it's a real
possibility. Although mafia are more powerful so maybe not,"
I say. Both Gusti and Leo nod quietly in agreement. "A whole
lot of people could end up dead or injured." I can feel myself
getting flustered under the stress of it all, and Gusti lowers his
flat, downturned hands over the table. I'm acutely aware of
how much uncontrolled rambling I'm doing, but I go again:
"How am I meant to deal with this? Mum is beside herself,
and I'm only sixteen! I should be worrying about how many
likes I get on Instagram not how to take down two groups of
gangsters."

Leo is chuckling at me, rubbing his brows and pinching
them together.

"What?" I say to him.

"You might only be sixteen, but you're a Zeffo," Leo says,
"I want to help you, but how can we G? It's against our code."
He turns to Gusti sat to his right.

"Did you ask Vozareia about this?" Gusti asks me.

"Of course I did!" I say, throwing my arms up in despair. "That's why I know this is all off and called this meeting."

Gusti reaches over to me and places his gentle amber skinned hand on mine. The familiar zing travels up my arm and it reminds me I'm more powerful than I currently think I am.

"You've placed your solutions, reliance and power in others, in Bippers. This is the problem," Gusti says.

"What other choice do I have? You, nor Leo, can help me work this out, but this is a real life and death situation… 'more life to all, less to none' remember? This is my chance to lift the Boras curse on me and my family for good."

Leo, still amused at my vomiting sentences, makes a suggestion that we all go to Wandsworth and fight both sets of gangsters, or do something to intervene the killing shot. "Gotta admit G, this falls into urgent – it needs bigger intervention. Me and Seven make a great team, we warded off 27evens the other day. If you come too—"

"No," Gusti interjects and shakes his head. "It's impractical, and there's a good chance we'll be seen in action." Gusti closes his eyes, holding his hand up to signal for no more interruptions as he waits for information.

Does Gusti have a more direct line? Can he speak more directly to Vozareia?

He's like the mystical version of Sal, an underboss to the Godfather. I must ask Gusti how he got to this level when all this is over.

"Vozareia and I agree this is urgent and requires more than what you can do alone." He rises from his seat and consults his copy of the Book of Lights, laid on the end of a shelf by his tea. He flicks back, and back further still, through pages and pages until he finds what he is looking for. He taps the open book with his hand then snaps it shut.

"A Zeffo Surge. That is what we need to do," he says.

Both Leo and I can't believe the choice of action, but Gusti's face is serious.

"What the fuck, G? They're dangerous, and I've never done it," Leo says.

"I haven't either. Obviously,' I add.

Gusti dismisses our concerns and opens the cupboard doors of the bureau, pulling out his tray of talismans and other enchantments and places them on the floor; he fishes about in the back of the cupboard as me and Leo look on opened mouthed. A minute later, he pulls out a flat object, the size of a hand, wrapped in a cover of purple velvet. Carefully he unwraps it to reveal a stunningly chilling jewel – the Hoci – given to each Zeffo in a ceremonial offering when they are invited to Dex status.

The Hoci is a solid triangle made of pure silver and is engraved with the Zeffo symbol, an exact replica of the Zeffo tabletop, with the gothic, black raven proudly bearing the same special turquoise stone for its eye in the centre.

"First, this." He raises the Hoci. "It is placed in the centre of the table, so the eye in the Hoci superimposes the eye on the table. It increases potency and power. Shan't do it now," he mocks, amused at his own joke. "I, as the Dex, then speak aloud a secret code, also highlighted on the Wall of Words to initiate the Zeffo Surge. We three then follow the surge ritual as you have learnt in training."

The Zeffo Surge ritual requires Gusti, Leo and me to stand each at a corner of the triangle embossed on the table with our arms stretched out and our palms flat, connecting each other. The Wall of Words will remain highlighted with the code and the ravens' eye will beam out its powerful glorious turquoise coloured light. A colour I've come to love so much. Together we will recite the Zeffo ode three times, followed by a brief sentence spoken by me indicating the situation, so the Zeffo Surge may take its route and work its power. The standard zing we feel in our connection increases 100-fold, and we will have three minutes to channel the force, timed by the highlighted Wall of Words – the letters darkening one by one as the light that once illuminated them will dim – to count down the intense time. It is this crucial time Zeffos can be thrown off guard with the force. If the power any Zeffo is channelling onto a situation is disrupted, the force U-turns away from the situation in question and into the Zeffo. Basically, it can fry us alive.

"Then, that's it. We wait," Gusti says.

Leo and I look at each other and back at Gusti. "That's it?" Leo repeats.

"We have to do a Smoke Out, for longer, afterwards. Otherwise, yeah, that's it."

"That's it?" I repeat next.

"Well, we need to tidy up," Gusti says.

"Not funny, G. What happens?" Leo asks.

"The surge works its magic through the easiest invisible route in order to change this situation for the better, and it will. Do not doubt this. How exactly, we can't know, not until it happens. Could be anything from a storm, a fight, to a change of mind."

I'm not sure I'm feeling any more secure about this. Sal and his posse might be a better option. I'd hoped Gusti had a grander more magical arrow in his almighty quiver of Dexical tricks.

Dexical is not a word, Seven.

"The outcome will happen within three days; you'll need to watch for it," Gusti says to me, jumping across to us like a cat. "It's Sunday, and we need this dealt with by turn of midnight on Thursday in time for Friday morning." He begins counting his fingers and whispering the days of the work. "Therefore, we need to do this tomorrow, after you two finish school."

Shit.

***

"You owe me one," Leo says, jovial as he is, as we go to hang up each of our phones after speaking from our bedrooms for an over hour about tomorrow. We mainly discussed how to craft my sentence into a laser precision one – now is not the time to add fluffy, careless words and stories that might send a Zeffo Surge to the wrong people and situation, or, you know, straight up kill me.

"Big time," I reply to him.

I'm so glad I have Leo.

***

I nurse the Sunday night feeling with Mum. She is telling me Palm and Gabby stories as we flip through a box of old photographs. It's a tatty red box I've seen a thousand times on the shelf in the dressing room; it was next to the box of hair accessories that I always have my hand in, but I was never compelled to look in it. All this time it had been there, a portfolio of my parents, so close, yet so far.

"You both look hot. I'm impressed."

"Seven!" Mum hits my head with a photo of them hanging out somewhere in Sicily. "But yeah, we do," she says, smiling at the memory.

"You're not so bad now either," I add, and another smack with the photo lands on my head. "Do you think Vincenzo will have changed much?" I ask.

Mum examines the bedroom air. "I don't know. He won't look his best. I imagine he'll be thinner, paler than his normal colouring. Prison, especially long stretches, has a habit of changing people. I can guarantee though, if Wandsworth hasn't completely stolen his character, he will turn up next Sunday dressed for the Oscars, and when Sal tells him you are coming too… no detail will be left untouched." She smiles and grabs her mug of tea from the bedside table.

The Roof Garden, Mum tells me, is situated on the roof terrace of an art gallery; one I didn't know of. It's tucked away behind one of London's square gardens, near Kings Cross Station. It was here Mum and Vincenzo knew they could be together without interruptions and lose themselves in each other for a while. He would often view the gallery exhibits on the lower floors with Mum trailing along behind, bored.

Sometimes Vincenzo would book the Roof Garden out so they could have lunch delivered and spend time with each other in solitude before Mum went back to the firm and he would hop over to Kings Cross or the airport.

Mum says it's not like a traditional garden, it's mainly

rocks and gravel, designed in such a way to look like islands in the water.

"A bit like me and Palm are, really," Mum says, drifting off into years gone by. "Islands in the water."

I tuck my head into her neck and hope to God that Vincenzo manages to get there for lunch next Sunday. I hope I'm there next Sunday too.

"By the way," Mum says, "Sal is driving you to school tomorrow."

"What? No."

"Thought you'd pleased at that," she says, cackling at her sarcasm. "He's dropping you off on the way to Heathrow airport to pick up the rest of them."

Chapter Twenty-Nine
Stay Wild

I'm typing like a mad woman this morning.

Z Group Chat

Message to Leo and Seven

Good morning! Be sure to eat, keep calm and be merry today. I'll see you around 3.30pm. All is well. G

I can hear the door knocker banging repeatedly downstairs. I ignore it to let Mum answer and type back like a ninja.

I'll try, just want it over with. We'll be ok right?

Message to Gusti and Seven

Sure thing G. I'm quite excited about it weirdly

The banging on the door continues and becomes louder, slower and deeper.

Message to Leo and Seven

By 5.30pm you'll be both on your way home, we'll be fine ☺. Leo… a Dex in the making I see!

I begin to text back how I think Leo would make a top Dex but the door— *for pity's sake, Mum must have already left for work.*

Mad my conversation is being interrupted, I heave up the sash window and lean out of my bedroom window, which looks directly down onto the shallow, wide step at the front door. Sal is stood in a pale pink shirt, looking left and right, checking his watch. He lifts his arm to pull the hefty brass knocker again.

"Hey, up here," I yell down, waving to stop him banging any more.

"*Buongiorno*," he yells up all spritely. "Ready?"

We drive along the main road in the hum of luxury, the ride as smooth as a love song, in the black car shining like the blade of a knife – the same car not too long ago I thought carried two men out to kill Mum and I; turns out I was wrong on that one as the other guy, it transpired, was Rocco. The leather seat holds me so perfectly I wish my ride were longer, and all the buttons and dials on the dashboard make it look like Sal is piloting an aircraft.

"You know, my friend Yas is well jealous. She had to catch the bus on her own this morning," I say.

"Ah. *Si si.* For now, it's safer I drive you, but tomorrow I can pick your friend up too?" Sal offers.

"Cool." I was going to ask why it's safer but it's obvious really. I'm the daughter of a Godfather-type who's earmarked to be gunned down on Friday, and getting the bus is a pain in the rear anyway, so, no complaints from my corner.

"You can drop me just here," I say, motioning to the side street coming up on the left, a good distance away from the main entrance. Sal ignores my request and rolls on past the side street, joining the road where swarms of students are walking on both sides of the pavements. To my dismay, he pulls to a stop in front of a group of Year 13s.

Oh no. Danny is there.

"*Non.* I drop you at the gates," he says, grinning at me like he knows he is embarrassing me. He cranes his neck around the view in front, to the side and behind, checking it all out.

OMG. What Year 11 gets dropped off at the gates.

I place my elbow on the door frame with my hand gently on my forehead.

And there's Felix, brilliant.

"I pick you up at three, here," Sal says, as I grasp the handle to click open the door.

"No, no, it's totally fine. Me and Leo are…" *Think, think!* "…are studying at the library after school."

He searches my face, leans over to flick the glove box open and slides out a scrap of paper before handing it to me. On it are two numbers written in pencil, one identified as S, and one as R.

"These are mine and Rocco's numbers. Put them in your phone. Call when you are ready to be picked up. Call any time you need us. *Si?*"

"*Si,*" I reply with a pouty face, gesticulating with my hand in the air in homage to the Italian way.

"Needs practice," Sal replies.

I swing myself out of the car as Felix strides down the pavement towards me. He's holding his arms out wide, eyeing up the car, glancing at me and checking out the wheels – generally being a goof.

"What do we have here then?" he asks.

I stuff the scrap of paper in my blazer pocket and link Felix's arm, telling him to shut up as I salute Sal goodbye.

Felix catches Sal in the windscreen and pays him the same respect.

"Give up you idiot," I say, pulling his hand back down with giggles. "He," I continue, "is real life mafia, so I'd watch your antics."

He stares at me speechless, a slight wash of panic on his face turns his cheeks a shade rosier.

"I'll tell you about it on the way, come on," I say, pulling him onwards.

I give Felix only the bare bones of my story: Palm, my gangster mafia dad, is alive – not dead – and currently in prison, Sal is here to pick him up on Friday and I'm meeting him on Sunday. This was by far enough information to enthral Felix for the next ten minutes before we join Yas in form room for the start of the school day. I can't tell Felix *everything*.

We all listen to Mr Tammus calling out the register, all except Felix as he's holding onto his chair and jumping it forward to tuck himself under the desk. Mr Tammus pauses the register call, waiting for Felix to finish.

"Sorry, sorry. Here sir," Felix says to Mr Tammus who groans and throws an eye roll at Felix. Mr Tammus continues not acknowledging Felix or rising to his comedy value any further.

As the room falls back into the usual drill of calling out the register, it dawns on me that the only people who do know *everything* are Leo and Gusti. With Lizzie a close third. Out of all the people and friendships I know and have, these are not the people I expected to form rapid and deep relationships with. Everyone else, from the MGs to Mum, has a tailored, edited version of the current story of me, and yet I wonder how far away from the truth of being a non-magical human I am, anyway? Doesn't everyone offer edited versions of themselves and their life to each other to suit? Or am I seeking my own permission to justify white lies, half stories and secrecy?

I make a mental note to journal all this in the Book of Lights and to explore this concept further.

At lunchtime, the boys decide to head out to the field to play a version of American Football with a rugby ball. RV is firm in his belief the sport of rugby is a better game, and a more manly game in comparison, and now finds himself in a mock-up lesson of American Football led by Leo to prove him wrong.

Felix reckons he already knows how to play, having watched countless American TV shows, and runs confidently backwards to face Leo, RV and Nate as they leave the café. "Twenty-two, blues twenty-two. H-u-P-P!"

Leo laughs at the idiocy of his mate, shaking his head, and spins the rugby ball in his hands as they near the door.

"What was that?! Gonna whip your ass, man," Leo replies.

Yas, Lizzie and I watch the ego pack disappear outside. "How old are they?" Yas asks, "Five?"

Lizzie, her food eaten but not enjoyed, pushes her tray back and folds her arms on the table, gazing out of the window.

"You okay?" I ask.

She sighs, nodding her head slowly, which transforms into a shake instead.

"No, not really guys. Gonna tell Nate tonight it's over."

Yas leans on Lizzie's shoulder, rubbing her arm, and I pass Lizzie my small bag of sweets I just opened. She accepts my gesture with a cute half smile and takes an jelly egg. I think she is doing the right thing, for both of them. Lizzie deserves a boyfriend who is more together like she is, a guy who makes her a priority whilst still being his own person. Nate, as RV said, needs to sort his life out, and I don't think he can do that when he's dating to mask his lost-in-life feelings. His mixed-up emotions are getting him by the cojones, and the external pretence of the basketball star with a hot girlfriend is failing him. Lizzie letting him go allows Nate to find himself, figure out who is and what he wants.

"I feel bad about it. How do you think he'll take it?" Lizzie asks me.

"I don't know, he'll be upset for a while I'd imagine. But it's not really about him, it's about you Lizzie, and not accepting less than how you want your life to be or deserve. Don't feel guilty for that," I say, feeling surprised at the wisdom I have learnt but also adamant about it too. Too many girls, I included in my assessment, put their self-worth in others, or take a guy's negative reaction as a sign they are wrong to stick to their gut, personal standards and expectations.

We all make a pact, in the middle of the bustling café, to forever make decisions in our lives based on what we truly want: to have the faith it's possible, to know we are worth it and to not let the words of others who don't know our visions tell us otherwise.

"Just tell him the truth, babe. Be compassionate, but don't lie or make shit up to sugar coat it to him," Yas says.

Lizzie rustles about in the half empty sweet packet, because what better way to seal our deal of staying wild to our lives than with a cola bottle, a ring and a fried egg?

Because that's the truth of life, isn't it? To know your own heart, and to dare to be whatever it beats to you. It's that simple and that complicated. Yet somehow your heart knows your magnetic north. The heart, the soul, the real self – they speak through *deep desire*. And so, the only question there ever is, the only real truth there ever can be, is: what is it you so deeply desire?

Stay wild to it, my girl.

Chapter Thirty
Casting

By the time me and Leo arrive at Jamming Minds, Gusti is prepped and smartly dressed with an extra, larger talisman bangle on his other wrist, and a ring bearing the Zeffo symbol on his right thumb. The blinds are down, juice is on the shelf and the turquoise speckled candles are lit, flickering like fairies all around the room. The Hoci, wrapped in its purple velvet covering, sits alone on the bureau, waiting. I gander at the gothic archway as I repeat my key sentence to be used.

With guidance from Leo and Gusti last night, I have carefully prepared my words to direct this surge. Ready to be twisted and formed into a coherent substance that Vozareia can grab onto; to us it sounds like talking, but to Vozareia it is precise vibration activating future untold events. 'It's like I'm a magic wand,' I said to Leo earlier.

"Ready," Gusti says, tapping me on the shoulder. I smile back, and Leo, stood by the shelf silently surveying the room, takes a gulp of juice and moves with ease to the table. We shake hands, the zing tingling and transforming our mini moment into a hug.

I consider spewing a thank you speech and hope this all goes well, a *we can do it wit-woo* type of pep talk, but at this point it seems tacky and made of the stuff which dooms the great.

Gusti unwraps the Hoci and places it in the centre of the table, superimposing the eyes, and we take our places at each point of the embossed triangle on the table. Gusti at the V, the head of the table, signals for us all to join our palms. We stand in a connected circle around the triangle and the show begins.

The blue eye glows and shoots a powerful beam of light directly in front of its gaze, before fanning out to encompass the three of us in its glare. I can feel the floor rumbling beneath my feet.

"*Acta Non Verba,*" Gusti firmly instructs.

The Wall of Words fires up, and the letters equating to *Acta Non Verba* dance like children across the wall. We watch the spectacle for a few seconds before we, in tandem, repeat our ode three times:

> *"Our mystery is just a sky,*
> *we need no gas, we run on fly,*
> *with Vozareia, House and Energy,*
> *unite us with the eye."*

The force is building; I can feel it all around me; the rumbling below deepens, my feet no longer distinguishable from the ground beneath – it's like they've melted into the shaking floorboards.

Gusti curls his fingertips around mine and gives them a little squeeze before releasing them to indicate it's my moment; the Wall of Words still dances patiently with the letters of *Acta Non Verba.*

I dither, I can't find the courage to speak, fearful of the outcome. I was always useless in the spotlight. What if we all die, fried to a crisp and found by police a month later accused of being a dodgy weird cult?

Gusti curls his fingertips around mine again, squeezing them harder. A subtle hint to hurry up. It's now or never. I think of Mum, of Palm, of RV, of me and all the life I – we – can have, if I dare.

Fuck it.

"I cast the true reality of Seven Madison to be. Rectify impossible strife and those with mutual love to stay with me. Let it roll."

The blue light grows brighter, making me and Leo squint. Gusti stands tall and unmoved as he demands *Acta Non Verba* again.

Then it hits.

The force of a hurricane envelopes the Zeffo Room, and it rocks me, Leo and Gusti back and forth like pendulums. We stay connected by our hands and feet, now feeling welded to the rumbling floor, and focus with intent on the Wall of Words waiting for the letters to disappear one by one. My hair ripples and tickles as darker waves of blue energy swirl deeply through the beam circling around us, and I feel something deeply weird in my stomach, like being so excited that you feel you might vomit.

It's going through us!

I can see the phenomena happening on Gusti and Leo but return my concentration to the wall quickly.

Keep the focus. Concentrate, Seven. This is so hard!

My breathing begins to race as I fight to remain upright;

Leo is doing the same which is comforting, and together we stare at the wall finally giving into the power all around and through us. Every second feels like an hour until I feel almost numb, dissolved into the space around me. No longer a separate entity from the force but part of it.

One by one the letters disappear from the wall, and when the final *A* pings out, at the end of the third minute, the force begins to settle like a mist lowering and clouds parting. The blue beam retreats into its focal point of the eye, and out.

I want to do a jig I'm so happy we did it, but I daren't move. Swaying blackness begins to fill my vision. I'm heavier than lead and more delicate than silk. I crumple downwards to the ground, and darkness pervades.

***

"What time is it, is it still today?" I say, but it's barely a whisper and no one hears me.

I lie on the floor, my opening eyes fixated above; I never noticed the Zeffo Symbol painted on the ceiling directly above the table before. It looks pretty…

I nearly drift off into sleep again but make myself wake up, forcing my droopy lids to stay open by rubbing them slightly too hard. I can faintly sense a distant phone buzzing. Must be mine or Leo's. Our bags have to be left outside the archway and phones should be switched off, but I tend to leave mine on silent as I don't like to be cut off from the world. I know it will be mine ringing as Leo obeys this rule better than I do.

Sal!

I move an arm, then a leg, then two arms, then two legs.

All feels normal, present and correct, and I proceed to check the rest of me. I roll onto my side, touching my face and hair. My talisman is still there.

"Leo, Leo," I call. He's flat out on the floor. "Are you okay? Wake up."

I look around the room and see there's only us two here. The Hoci has gone, the candles aren't here. *Where's Gusti?* I crawl on my hands and knees across the floor to Leo, tapping his arm and body.

"Gusti," I yell. "Where are you?"

The room feels like early morning, nothing undisturbed and the world not yet awake.

"Leo, please wake up," I beg. "Gusti is gone."

"Gusti!" I yell, louder.

I'm all alone. What have I done?

Chapter Thirty-One
Shaking Shells

My phone is buzzing again, and I can hear footsteps coming up the spiral staircase. Whether I'm hearing it normally or supernaturally I can't tell, either way, my heart is pounding. I'm shaking Leo by his arm and then by his shoulders in desperation. As the footsteps grow nearer, I'm transported back to old memories of hiding from violent hands and a foul mouth, and I feel once again the desperate churning in my stomach and the desperate cry in my mind that turns over the only thought it can formulate: what do I do next? The curse is still here, and it makes me quiver and whimper like the scared young girl I've always known myself to be.

"How many times do I have to tell you? Turn your phone off. Not onto silent."

I snap my head around to the direction of the voice. "Gusti! Thank God!"

I have never felt so relieved to see him. I rise awkwardly to my feet and stumble across to the archway. Gusti is stood across the other side of the threshold, holding two glasses of fresh juice and a big smile. He's changed into his more natural attire of a white shirt and dark blue jeans and wears only one talisman: his standard bangle.

"I thought you'd gone, or left us, or been sucked up into Vozareia's beam of light," I say.

He laughs, larking about with me, but then tones it down as he notices my sheer panic. He hands me a glass filled with my favourite juice and apologises. He had woken first, bored of waiting for me and Leo, so he tidied up and went to his flat to refill the glasses.

"You did well," he said with all seriousness, "you've both been out for an hour. I closed down the Smoke Out about ten minutes ago, although sleepy head there is taking his time." He nods over at Leo.

The small, scared girl memory fades away, much like the wide beam narrowed to a single line and then down to a point before disappearing completely…

I can take it from here. I got us.

"You said Smoke Outs after a surge can take hours; you had a terrible time when you did it last. How come you're so perky so quick?" I ask as Gusti steps in, and we walk over to Leo and look down on the sleeping blonde American.

"Last time was a larger ritual with more Zeffos involved, and it was my first one. As a Dex, it's harder on us than you guys as we have more power and space to hold."

I don't remember anything after the blackness, I'm glad Gusti was on the case sorting all this out. Left to me, or sleeping beauty, the Smoke Out wouldn't have happened at all and recovery would have taken until at least tomorrow.

"I'll send him a fun message via telepathy," Gusti says, "that'll shake his shells awake."

Shake his shells?

I want to laugh but clearly this is normal talk for Gusti.

Instead, I go over to my bag and retrieve my phone. I scroll through a million notifications, mainly all from Sal enquiring where I am, and do I not need picking up yet. There's another from RV and a few new Instagram followers.

"Is he round yet?" I yell to Gusti, "I really need to go, people are wondering where I am."

"Sure am," Leo says, dazed and doddery, leaning on the archway.

"Lizzie said you can sleep through anything. She's right."

"Not Gusti's telepathy it seems," he replies.

We listen to Gusti wrap up the most bizarre hour and a half of my life, which was nothing more than to remember to document it all in the Book of Lights and rest well tonight. No partying or working out as we can relapse, and for me specifically to watch for the alteration Vozareia will deliver and act on it.

"How will I know what it is, what to do?"

"For once, can you stop questioning yourself. Surely you must trust the Zeffo in you by now," Leo says, agitated and keen to leave as well.

"He did shake your shells, didn't he?" I snigger.

"What?"

"Never mind, let's go."

Leo and I are gnarly with each other; as good friends as we've become, we need space to be away from Zeffo world and do something normal like watch TV or even do some homework (at a pinch). So, we leave each other outside Wavies, and I call Sal, cringing when he answers and launches into Italian dramatics. I wave to Richard through the window as I try to explain to Sal I can't answer the phone in the library and that I forgot to call him because I can be a muppet sometimes.

"Where are you now?" he asks.

"I'm at Wavies."

"Wait there, on my way."

He hangs up before I have a chance to object. I want to stroll home, blow the webs from me and reboot, but there's no arguing with Sal. I shouldn't diss it, this is family, care and love. Despite how much I've wanted it, I'm not used to this, and I guess it's easier to push back on it than let it in.

Richard raps on the window, pointing at a take-out cup he's holding.

"Want one?" he asks, which I managed to make out through lip reading.

"No thanks, but cheers!" I reply, which I think he understood as he returned to his counter with his back turned to me to serve a new customer. My light-hearted response turns south of the river when Richard leans down under his counter to locate a take-out holder and bag, and I see the customer is Asher. The guy from the alley. Asher meets my eyes with similar surprise and stares harder than a scorpion, pretending to shoot me from a gun formed by his heavily tattooed and gold ringed fingers. The evil smile he flashes turns my stomach, and in a split second I dart past the window, out of sight, keeping myself flat against the wall of the building next door. I scan the area to check for others, but it's all a normal Monday evening with no one paying mind to anyone. I rush around the corner towards the main road of the high street and see Sal rounding it in the chunky wheels.

I flag him down frantically and jump in.
  "What has happened?" he asks.
  "Drive," I say, "just drive."

Chapter Thirty-Two
Dear Diary

I flip the sun visor down, slink low in the hugging seat and bluff my way through my sketchy mood. Sal is persistent with asking what is wrong and why the urgency as we stop and start our way up the hill. Half of his attention is on me, the other half on the road as rush hour traffic stacks up.

"Leo and I had a fall out. I just want to eat and have a bath," I say, looking out the window at every person on the pavements with paranoia.

"That I understand. Food, and going to the water, fixes *ever-re-thing*," he says.

Finally, Sal leaves me in peace for the rest of the journey home and concentrates on the road properly as I busy myself sending RV a text, telling him I'll be ringing in ten minutes, and the three moving bubbles start waving at me immediately.

> *Message from RV*
>
> You OK? Can't be much longer than that as going out.

I know his extra study class is done for today, and he isn't meeting any of the MGs, so perhaps he already knows Asher is here? Of course, I think, placing my phone back on my lap, RV will know Asher is back again! Why wouldn't he? He's playing along with them, for now. It's more than likely it's 27evens who he is meeting.

Sal follows me into the house but stops in the hallway holding the front door ajar. Mum came home from work early, so I find out. Whilst this is a strange time for her, I can tell she is enjoying Sal been around, and it makes me feel happy to see her breathe out and relax. Her ice blue eyes are gleaming more, not that she can see it yet, but I can. Sal and Mum have been chatting this last hour, so I'm encased in a cloud of coffee aroma when I walk into the kitchen.

"Back safe and sound," Sal says to Mum from the hallway, leaning to look into the kitchen to make eye contact with her, even though he still has his sunglasses on and car keys in hands.

I dump my bag on the floor, grunt 'hi' to Mum and flick the kettle on for a cup of tea. Tea, ring RV, food and bath I think to myself, watching the kettle gurgle.

"Hope Rio enjoys his evening. See you later!" Mum says.

I swing around from watching the kettle to face them both. "What evening?"

Sal is going to collect Rio, apparently. He and Rocco are going to entertain Rio at The Savoy for a couple of hours, with dinner and a slice of the finer life.

"How come we don't get to go The Savoy as well?" I ask, including Mum in the question.

"Ah, you will, my dear child," Sal replies. "We have things to discuss with Rio and there is no danger of him running into his gang at The Savoy. Plus, the boy deserves some of the good life for a couple hours."

"Has something else happened?" I continue to pry, unable to shake Asher off.

"It's nothing to worry over. Only details to ensure a slick morning on Friday."

"Nothing to worry about. Nothing to worry about?!" I am yelling at a real-life mafia man, and you know what? I don't care. "Are you kidding? How can you say that? Have you any idea how Mum and I feel? Any at all? We've been pushed from naught to a hundred and back to zero again. And…"

Mum whooshes over to sooth my rage and prevent more overdue, overly emotional ranting and, to my surprise, Sal closes the door and does the same.

"I get it. I do," he says, taking my hands in his, "I know this is tense, especially when it has been dropped on you from a height. You are both stellar women and brave and you, Seven – wow – are an incredible young lady who has her father's talent and spirit. I saw it the moment I saw you. This is why I have taken control of this situation, so you and your mum don't have to."

Sal is still holding my hands, and mum is hugging my head, stroking my hair. I feel like a volcano about to erupt and excuse myself for a minute to go upstairs.

From the safety of my bedroom, I text RV instead of calling him. I can't ring him to weigh him down further, with my Asher incident and how he scares me, when he's is about to have the time of his life. Sal is right, RV does deserve this, and I don't want to ruin his glam night. I've already jumped to wrongful thoughts this evening and decide to ask Leo about it when I ring him later to see if he is okay.

> *Message to RV*
> Heard about The Savoy, how jealous am I! I'll talk
> to you later. X

Message to Seven

Cheers. I'll ring when I'm back.

Message to RV

It's fine, I'll see you tomorrow. enjoy it! Don't forget to take your puffa coat off … and clean your trainers! X

Message to Seven

Already have. Ha. Have a hairbrush with me too, in my pocket.

He sends me a mirror selfie; he's wearing dark jeans, a checked shirt with clean trainers and newly styled hair, and I wish he could see the size of my smile.

I stare at the picture and save it to my camera roll.

Message to RV

I'm impressed, and you look handsome. x

Message to Seven

Good, bit nervous actually. Speak later x

"Is that better?" Mum asks as I slope back into the kitchen. Sal is lingering about, waiting to check all is good before he leaves to collect RV. I nod a *yes but not really* smile. What more can I say to them? Sal kisses us both goodbye with a peck on each cheek and swoops from the kitchen into the hallway to the front door but pauses before opening it.

"What we must do is make sure Palm returns with me to The Savoy on Friday, so the old goat may lavish himself in fancy shower products, fine food and clothes," Sal says, laughing lovingly at their extravagant Italian ways. "I can't wait to see his face when I tell him you both have agreed to see him on Sunday. Keep your eyes on Sunday, not the stress.

I'll take care of Friday morning."

Mum's doing that thing with her cheek again.

"It's going to be fine, you see? But first, let's get through the week," he says and then leaves for his boy soiree at The Savoy.

***

I steam myself like a lobster in the bath until I'm all red and feeling faint. Wrapping myself in shea butter and my dressing gown, I sit down at my desk to write the details of the surge in the Book of Lights, and about meeting Asher afterwards. Unexpectedly, I hear Vozareia speak a sentence to me: *'Their fear is your fear. Don't be fooled.'*

I note it down and continue writing more pages of what appears to me to be complete drivel. As I read it all back to myself, I begin to understand the sentence is referring to 27evens. My Book of Lights is becoming a piece of art, and I'm proud of what I'm creating. I decide to also document the next few days in it, like I used to do in my Dear Diary days when I was twelve. I giggle at the embarrassing journals I kept – which I tore into tiny pieces and binned but now wish I had kept them – wondering if they were, in fact, filled with slithers of wisdom rather than the stupid thoughts of a turbulent Seven Madison as I used to think they were.

Leo is doing the same with his Book of Lights when I call to check in with him, although his Book of Lights is filled with far more information and supernatural insights than mine as he's been a Zeffo for nearly a year.

"What talisman do you have?" I ask.

"Tattoo, at the bottom of my spine."

"No way, how? You're only sixteen?"

"Laws are different in Miami. Gusti did it when he was living there temporarily; he knows my aunt and she is a friend of Ni Luh's."

We talk about how small the world actually is and how big the Zeffo skies are. Lizzie is moping in her bedroom, feeling bad over the breakup with Nate; it didn't go all that smoothly, but do they ever? I speak to her though, after Leo, and she is faring better than Leo had dramatised; she just needs a friend to listen, not a brother to solve it.

***

Tuesday
Failed a geography test, so have extra homework, brill.
Nate pulled a sick day.
Must remember to ask Mum to get more hairspray, the one in the black and gold can, not the 90p stuff she thinks is no different.
Went to Felix's after homework; he's writing his own play and smashed a glass coffee table in his sitting room when he ran into it on his penny board. We swept up glass for an hour.
RV wants to live at The Savoy.
Sat in stillness and dialled into Vozareia… I drew a picture of our house, with 27 written on the door??? Do I need to prepare for round two?

Wednesday
RV is a pro at keeping up appearances, my stomach is constantly gurgling and bloated – drink peppermint tea YouTube said.
Nate isn't talking to Lizzie and is blunt with everyone else, lunchtime was shit.
Yas is meeting Bea tonight.

OMG – arrived home after school, Vincenzo is being released tomorrow not Friday! Mum said an admin error had been made, I know it was Vozareia delivering its magic. Surely, it's over now? He's avoided the whole thing, without even knowing!

Thursday
Sal wants to keep up the pretence release day is still Friday, so he and the others can deal with 27evens and free RV.
Lizzie, Leo and I spoke about going to Miami in the summer. I really want to go.
More importantly, Vincenzo is at The Savoy, briefed on the way about events <3
Mum is deliriously happy – good time to ask about Miami maybe?? (
I am deliriously happy too, until I remember about RV. (
Drink more peppermint tea, it's nearly Sunday.

Friday
Did not go as planned…

Chapter Thirty-Three
Knock-knock

At morning break, I read the text RV sent forty minutes ago. I hadn't wanted to go to school, but Mum said she was going to work and there is no reason for me not to go to school either. 'Leave them lot to it. We have to continue as normal as possible,' she said.

Sal, or one of them had called RV in sick at school. Me and Leo are the only ones who know he isn't, but when I read his message, the game I thought would be over, isn't. Miraculously, 27evens never showed up, leaving RV stood up at the location where they were supposed to meet, near Wandsworth Prison, early this morning. 'Grapevine travels fast' RV said in his message, 'they'll know he was released yesterday. You could have told me.'

Sat on the grass at the far end of the field, the boys are elsewhere as Nate is still licking his wounds and didn't want to hang out with us. I wander away from Yas and Lizzie and pace a slow circle a few metres from them as I hold my phone close to my mouth and send a voice note to RV:

> "I'm really sorry. I wanted to tell you, but I
> couldn't. Sal wants to help you, that's why we all
> had to pretend it was still happening today. Are you

okay? Where are you? Why didn't 27evens tell
you?"

Voice note to Seven

"I'm at the Savoy. Discussing a different plan with
Sal, Rocco and… your dad. 27evens know I want
out; they smell a rat. Gotta go, meet up after
school? Your dad is cool by the way. Think you'll
like him."

He spoke quietly and with an echo – he must be sat in the
bathroom of the hotel room. Hearing those last words stops
me pacing another circle and my breathing stutters inwards;
this man, Vincenzo Petralia, is really real. He's flesh and bone
as well as name, and RV is with him right now; he can see
him and talk to him.

I asked Mum why she hasn't spoken to Vincenzo after he
was released. She said she didn't want their first conversation,
a difficult one at that, to be on the phone. She said it's
awkward and clumsy and needs to be in person.

The bell rings out for end of morning break, and Yas
and Lizzie begin heading over to make their way back into
the main school building. Sneaking a glance at them, I
reckon I can send a quick text back to RV before they both
reach me.

Message to RV

Tell him I said hello.

No. Can't say that. Delete.

The sentence evaporates as I hold the back button and try
again.

Message to RV

Tell him I'm looking forward to Sunday.

That's shit. Delete. Delete. Delete.

I get what Mum means now.

***

My stomach rumbles as I read the instructions on the back of the ready meal packet Mum left out for me for dinner, and I stab the film with a fork several times and throw it in the microwave. The rest of the school day dragged like the grey skies, and a different associate of Sal's picked me up at a school as he is otherwise engaged. I'm still dropped off and collected outside the school gates, but I've given up asking not to be and have become lazily accepting of it in a short space of time. The chap wasn't all that talkative, so I succumbed to embarrassment.

I've heard nothing since from RV, and I want to know what's going on.

I play the voicemail left on my phone by Mum on loudspeaker as I take a carton of orange juice from the fridge and fill a glass. Her message is made up of the same instructions on how to cook the Spaghetti Bolognese twirling around in the microwave, and that she'll be home late.

> "Going for a facial and getting my nails done after I finish at the office"

I smile at her juvenile cuteness and suck up the tongue burning dinner sat at the island alone.

Not a bad idea, might put on a face mask tonight and file my nails.

I'm taken away from my pampering thoughts by the knowing someone is approaching the front door; I'm getting better and better at translating energy from a distance, even with obstructions like walls and doors, and although I can't 'see' supernaturally like Leo, knowing and feeling are just as useful. I slide off the leather bar stool and tip toe out of the kitchen to the front door and place an eye over the peep hole. No one is stood there that I can see, but I know a person, intent on coming here, is around. I open the door yelling the loudest 'hello' I can in order to cause a scene in case it's a set up. It worked: passers-by all turn in startlement. I turn to the left to check out the street and jump a mile backwards with a squeaky scream when I see RV stood there. I automatically place my hand on my chest and breathe a release sigh.

"It's you. Come in, come in." I wave him in with my arm whilst clocking the remainder of the street, and he looks at me baffled, stepping into the hallway.

"You alright, you look freaked out?" he says.

"Fine," I say, closing the door and signalling to RV to follow me into the kitchen. "What's happened? Nobody has told me anything?" I ask him.

I clear my meal for one away and stick the kettle on to make RV's coffee with milk and two sugars.

"Hungry?" I ask. "There's another delicious Spaghetti Bolognese, yours if you want it?"

He laughs briefly at me but allows his eyes to linger on, and I don't reject them. Instead, I hold his eyes with a softness I haven't felt before.

"Nah. I'm stuffed. They've been feeding me all day, proper fancy stuff," he replies, snapping himself out of it, running his hand over his hair and fanning his arms out with a long stretch.

Judging by the crisp white t-shirt and blacker than black jeans he's wearing, I'm assuming they've also taken him shopping.

"You look good," I say, returning to coffee making.

After it was obvious 27evens were a no show this morning, Sal had gathered the men and RV back into two cars and drove straight to The Savoy, keeping RV out of 27evens' radar. There, they gathered to make a new plan with the Godfather himself, Vincenzo.

"I used to think Kris and the rest of 27evens were *all that*, but those guys – your lot – are something else," RV tells me, his eyes wide, suggestive of how impressed he is – in awe, maybe – and it's clear how interesting this all is to him.

"Don't be getting any ideas about joining them," I say, half joking, handing him his cup of disgustingly strong coffee.

"It's a thank you, as Sal said. Nothing else. Anyway, I'm too young, British and have no Italian father, so I can't join."

I raise my eyebrows at his comment and how he knows the score.

"Kidding," he replies.

He assures me he's not becoming swept up in the high-end mafia life; he wants to be free of 27evens, and at this point, the mafia guys are his only option. But despite his fear he's humbled with gratitude for them. RV knows 27evens will come after him for sure, especially now they've twigged something else is going on; they wouldn't have stood RV up if they didn't. I was going to bring up Asher at the expense of it making RV feel more guilt and sparking his frustration, so I decide against it. He can't do anything about it now.

Their newly adapted plan involves an early morning call

tomorrow to Kris, by Sal and a few others. RV will remain at The Savoy with Vincenzo and the rest, until the warning is delivered, and Kris agrees to let RV go with no part of 27evens to return to his life again. I have a feeling Kris will accept the offer.

"Why don't they go now?"

"Subtlety, Seven. Element of surprise and sophistication."

Of course, how dumb of me to ask.

"I just came around to say hi and let you know what's happening. Sal will be here in twenty minutes to check up on you and pick me up; he's taking me back to my castle for tonight," RV says, strutting around the island like a god. I giggle at him; it's warming to see him more confident and happier.

I dive in, wanting to know more about Vincenzo, who has been asking RV a tonne of questions about me too.

"I told him all your embarrassing stories and what an awful person you are," RV says, knocking my arm.

I hit him back, but I feel funny, and maybe a bit jealous, that RV is getting to know Vincenzo first. I ask what he looks like, how tall he is and if he's nice, and then I stop. I don't want to know. I don't want my expectations or experience tainted by another's opinion, and RV will see him differently to me. Vincenzo will be different with RV than he will be with Mum and me, and so we choose not to talk about this crazy situation for the rest of the time until Sal arrives.

We sit opposite each other at the island, rolling a tangerine back and forth between us as we chat about TV shows – no surprise we watch opposite ones – and MG drama: Nate and Lizzie mainly.

"Not gonna lie, he's a mate but he's being fucking annoying lately. Maybe it's just me," he says, getting up and shrugging his shoulders.

RV checks the time on his phone. Sal will be here in less than ten minutes. I get up off the bar stool chair as well and observe Silversedge's hill through the shutters on the window and see the early rush hour traffic is building up outside; it's Friday, rush hour starts around three to be honest some weeks, which might buy me a little more time. My pamper evening doesn't feel as enticing as it did earlier. I could see if Yas is up for Wavies later on, but I don't want to do that either. I watch for Sal's car and think about the love quote and Lizzie's analysis. I try to fill the kitchen with my personal love, thoughts and energy and it's pulling me towards him, and I turn away from the window to face him.

"Wish you didn't have to go," I blurt out, "it's been great hanging out, just the two of us."

He agrees and steps over to me as I lean on the worktop counter by the sink, more for support than anything else. I think Leo and Lizzie are right, he does feel the same way too. He stands in front of me, placing a hand on the sink to the side of me and the energy in the narrow space between us is so potent I lose all ability to speak, only managing a small smile instead. I don't know what is coming over me, I really don't, but I trace a finger down the side of his cheek, not letting his eyes go for a second. He takes my finger and webs his fingers through mine, holding my hand, and my stomach flips flops into next week.

I think he's going to kiss me! I hope I do this right.

My arm and hand are quivering slightly with nerves, and

I feel like an idiot until I realise RV's is doing the same. I didn't think he would be nervous, why would he be nervous?

He leans in further, closing the gap. We brush lips to the side, and it feels like soft electric wafted across me. We look at one another like it's the first time we've ever seen each other, and I'm lost. I lean forward into him, our lips barely a hair width from connecting, and we move into slow kissing… until that damn door knocker pounds, throwing us both out of a place we have never been too before.

Fucking fuck!

"Sal. I don't believe it," I whisper, unsure whether to laugh or be mad.

RV rubs his hand across his face with a scoff. "Great timing," he says to me, "it's like he knew."

Chapter Thirty-Four
Through the Window

I wander around the house bored, staring in the fridge for the tenth time and pulling out random grapes to munch on before traipsing back upstairs to wander some more. It'll be over another hour before Mum is home. I might watch the film RV was telling me about, I think, and press the remote to turn on my TV. RV messaged me earlier on Snap, and it started an emotional fire when I saw his name on the notification. He's chilling in the hotel room by himself; the guys have all gone out to a restaurant for dinner, but RV didn't want to go. He said he was still full from lunch, but I suspect it was because it was his way out of having to handle uncomfortable posh shenanigans he doesn't know how to. I don't blame him. Dinner with mafia dudes in a boring restaurant, or Savoy hotel room to yourself for a couple of hours? I know what I would choose.

He texts me to say, 'Check me out', adding a video of the swag room with an empty room-service plate on the bed and its trolley parked by the table and chairs.

Seven is typing

That's sick. How are you? x

RV is typing

Ok, considering… bout earlier.

I feel my belly start to drop. Oh please don't blow me off, I think, or say it was a heat of the moment thing.

> *Seven is typing*
>
> I understand if it was a mistake, it's an intense time.
>
> *RV is typing*
>
> Mistake? Hell no. I thought… didn't think I was your type really x
>
> *Seven is typing*
>
> I was hoping you would make a move ☺ Why not my type?
>
> *RV is typing*
>
> ☺ ☺ … I'm hardly a Silversedge boy.
>
> *Seven is typing*
>
> Well, you are my type, and I'm off to watch the film you say is outstanding, but I think will be shit x.

We sign off saying we'll talk later, and I can't stop smiling to myself, I swear I skipped to the bathroom, but I can feel his hesitation about who my family are, and I sense the current situation messing with him. Whether going on a date with me is a good idea or not is yet to be seen.

I fling the bathroom door back open and decide I will call Lizzie, so excited and dizzy to tell her about my evening, it wasn't until I was halfway across the bedroom floor I realise I've walked into Mum's bedroom instead of mine.

Dozy cow.

Her room is plush and tidy as always, even in the twilight as the sun is beginning to set, it still feels beautiful, not empty and dull. Her box with her and Vincenzo's keepsakes in, has moved from the dressing table to her bedside table – which is painfully cute – and her clothes for Sunday are laid out on her bed, ready.

I hear a noise, people, a group talking outside, friends on the way home from the pub most likely, but the knowing has returned. With only a few more seconds spent in the room and I know their intention is to come here. I turn towards the window which looks out onto the main road in front of the house; the curtains are still open, hanging heavily in draped masses at either side. I get down on the floor, crawl on my belly and stand to the side of one of the curtains, peeking out from behind the weighty material onto the street below.

Shit, it's them: 27evens.

I let the curtain fall back and think for a beat, trying to control my breathing. I signal for silence, touch my talisman to feel safe and, holding my hand out behind the curtain, I move a wave of strong energy to a wheelie bin across the street. It sends it crashing, making enough of a racket to enable me to open the sash window an inch without them noticing.

"Fucking hell, who knocked that over," one says, joking, snorting a gross snort and spitting it out.

That's disgusting.

"This is it; she lives here," another says.

"Do ya reckon this a bit much?" a meeker voice pipes in.

"RV is a fucking snake, not surprised he loves a bitch like her."

"Yeah," another agrees, "if he wants out, he can have it."

A bitch like me? It shouldn't hurt, but it does.

"It's payback," the two say together.

I feel heated panic sweep my face: they're coming for me, not RV – me.

I stay motionless while I try and recall the plan I made when I drew the picture with '27' on the door. I knew something like this was coming, and now it's here I'm anxious, but…

"Open shield," I say silently, causing my heart rate to drop a little, and I whisper, slowly.

"One: Open shield, done that. Two: Ring Sal. Three: Their fear is my fear, remember this. Four: Keep them here but outside until back up arrives."

I crawl on my belly back out of Mum's room and charge across the landing into my bedroom. "Ring Sal," I yell at my phone on my bed, "ring Sal!"

"Calling, Sal," it replies.

I scoop my phone up as it begins ringing, and Sal answers immediately as I move to my windows, tugging frantically at my curtains to draw them closed.

"You need to come. They're here," I say.

"Who? Seven, are you okay? What is z'matter?" Sal says.

I assume they are all still at the restaurant, as the clanking of cutlery and chattering in the background stops as soon as Sal replied. I repeat what I've just witnessed and fess up that me and RV kinda like each other – which wasn't planned but not a time to be cagey – and how Mum isn't here but will be soon. Before I've finished, he's babbling to the others in Italian and there's a chaos of talking, chairs scraping and plates being moved about.

"Seven is on her own. Put the wine down Rocco and get the car," Sal adds with a fierce tone clarifying the severity of the situation to me.

It sounds like they are all beginning to move out, and then

I hear him, demanding he comes to… Vincenzo. I know it was him. The energy of his voice matched the energy I felt all those weeks ago, and I zone out of what Sal is saying to me.

"Did you get that? Are you still there?"

"Sorry Sal," I say, returning to the matter in hand. "Can you say that again?"

"Stay away from all windows and doors. Get as far away as possible from them. Luckily, we're at a place only ten minutes away, won't be long."

"You're not coming, Palm, go back to the hotel. You're no good to us on this one," I hear Sal instruct as he hangs up.

Hearing Vincenzo's voice makes it all the more real and close. It all feels like a TV show and I have to pinch myself pink occasionally to remind me it's not. At least they're not eating out in central like I thought, it would have taken them ages to drive across town.

I sit on the floor hugging my knees. The pale grey carpet, freshly hoovered and smooth, invites me to stay there, but I soon move to standing. I re-clip my hair up and, feeling tidier, I rush out of my bedroom, across the landing and return to crawling on my belly through Mum's bedroom. All the while, I try to remember the tactic Gusti showed me this week: I'd asked him, following the '27' drawing on my door, should a situation arise where I don't want to drain myself – having no time for lengthy Smoke Outs or day long sleeps – or a Zeffo be discovered by a Bipper, what options I have to use.

I reach the window and stand behind the side of the curtain, locating their positions; they're spread about, not doing much, and one is holding a large can, half in his hand, half tucked up his jacket sleeve.

"Bastards are going to graffiti the house," I say.

I switch to watching another, Asher, as he slides his hand inside his jacket pocket and pats it, and I return to being flat against the wall next to the curtain, breathing harder than I want to.

My breathing stops sharply as I hear Vozareia again: *'Their fear is your fear.'*

This needs to be over. I'm not frightened of myself anymore, and I need to lift the curse for good. Standing in front of the window, in full view should they look up, I hold my arms forward and shape my hands in a triangle so my eyes look centrally through it and firmly, out loud, repeat our ode:

> *"Our mystery is just a sky,*
> *we need no gas, we run on fly,*
> *with Vozareia, House and Energy,*
> *unite us with the eye."*

They must be able to hear me speaking the ode through the open window as a couple of them gaze upwards, noticing me as I reach the end of the verse, and they alert the others. A round of raucous laughter brews throughout the group, but too late – I've sent the energy, encasing them in a triangular boundary of Zeffo energy. It will hold them, but only for five minutes without using more of my resources. Suddenly, the tables are turned as I watch them with heavy laughter escaping my lungs; they attempt to walk towards my house, but none of them can pass the invisible boundary, and they are utterly flabbergasted and angry.

This is actually hilarious.

By the time the boundary begins lifting, Sal and four others are casually walking down the pavement, dressed in smart trousers, creaseless shirts and long woollen coats, towards to 27evens, who are trying to leave 'this fucking freak and freaky town', and I continue watching in wrongful but genuine glee.

Sal and his four pals grab and secure a 27evens member each in one swift, impressive move and frog march them to the park, one arm behind their backs.

I watch until they disappear out of sight, knowing that will be the last time me and RV, and this town, will see any of them.

I stay by the window, viewing everything and nothing. It's over. The night sky is beginning to close in but to me it feels brighter and safer than ever, I raise the sash window higher and stick my hand out. The breeze winding around my hand and fingers reminds me of RV's hand earlier, and I smile at the thought of him living it up at the Savoy while I have been altering the course of my life, my family's lives, for good. I don't like the way 27evens operate, but I do understand fear, and I'm sure that my fear is the same as theirs, only expressed differently. I hope they are not dead, but I do hope they have met their match and stay away. I hope more they find their own way to break their curses, because every human deserves that.

The door downstairs clicks open and booms shut. I close the window and scamper out of Mum's room and downstairs to meet her.

"Look at my nails!" She's holding her hand out twizzling it around. "Aren't they stunning. I feel like a new woman.

How's your evening been darling?"

"Interesting," I say, "I think Sal might be here shortly. I'll let him tell you. Your nails look fabulous."

Chapter Thirty-Five
The End is the Beginning

Even on Sundays, students at the neighbouring university hoard around this small patch of London, all darting around with book laden bags or strolling with friends between buildings into the central square garden to the side of the gallery.

I look up to the top of the enormous gallery building, hoping for a crafty glimpse of what is waiting for us up on its roof terrace, but the sun is blinding, and Mum is eager to go.

The marble rich lobby is cooler and darker than it is outside in the afternoon sun. A sign by the information desk states the Roof Garden is currently closed to visitors and the gallery apologises for this inconvenience. Mum approaches the wooden desk and the receptionist signals to a man in a slate blue suit standing next to a pillar at the end of the desk. A closer view allows me to see his badge: Horace, Security Guard.

Mum points me towards the doors over to the left that lead into the main gallery rooms. She indicates for me to go through them, and the heavy door sweeps the ground as it closes behind us.

The exhibit rooms are vast with piercing illumination, yet

they hold the intense quietness of a library. Single pictures and pieces of artwork are displayed like the prizes they are, and an odd few people wander around and pause for a while to view each one.

"It's closed for us," Mum whispers as she whisks through the rooms to a marble cream stairwell on the opposite side to the entrance. I keep glancing back at the art that is calling to me from the walls, like a dog that is being pulled away from a smell he simply must sniff. "You've plenty of time to look at those later," she tells me, and I reluctantly look away.

Mum halts at the bottom of the four flights of stairs. "You look stunning, darling, absolutely stunning. Are you ready? Are you sure? We can leave at any point."

"It's fine. I'm nervous, but I want to go. You look beautiful too. I love your hair."

Our shoes slide in unison on each of the marble steps, echoing around the lonely stairwell as we climb. My eyes are kept entertained by photographs of different global cultures gracing the walls, until, before I know it, we are on the top floor. Sunlight beams through small square windows, all in a line on the left-hand side of the corridor, one after another until they reach the short and narrow double doors leading out into the roof terrace garden.

I see what Mum means about it being more rocks and gravel than flowers and grass, and normally I would analyse this art form more thoroughly, but not today.

"It's him. It's really him," Mum says, her hand frozen on the silver door handle. Across the other side of the Roof Garden, a tall man in a suit is looking out at the view of London. His back is facing the door, from which we – well,

Mum – still hasn't moved from as we stare at him through the glass panels on the door. He's donning a cream Panama hat with tell-tale short, dark hair visible underneath, not a grey or silver colour I thought his hair would be.

There is a table of prepared picnic food and drinks next to him with two bouquets of flowers, one in deep reds with greenery and the other in soft pastel colours. Both bouquets decorate a stark white tablecloth that is flapping happily in the circling wind.

I place my hand on top of Mum's and together we unclick the handle. The noise alerts Vincenzo and he reacts immediately. He swings around to see us, and his energy oozes both eagerness and love, and it gingerly pulls us towards him. I can feel connection immediately, even without any words and explanations, and I wonder if he feels it as well.

Vincenzo removes his hat and places it next to the flowers before taking a few steps forward. His hair is thick, and his shirt is as bright as the tablecloth. His dark green checked suit is striking with an orange handkerchief poking out of the pocket. A gold lapel pin matches the gold pocket watch on his waistcoat and the cufflinks on his shirt. The pocket watch I drew…

I love it. I love all of it. No one I know dresses like this.

He's a handsome man who appears to be hypnotised by us as we come to a standstill in front of him.

I stare at his face and smile; I have no clue what to say. I'm floored by the spellbound magic in the air yet scared of the unknown. All of this, just for us, I think, taking in the sight.

I was expecting the same Italian dramatics of Sal, but Vincenzo can't find his words. He starts and stutters, stops and starts. He seems bewildered by foreign emotions.

"You came," he eventually says in a deep voice and Italian accent, "you both came, I was so frightened you wouldn't."

Mum reaches for a triangle sandwich from the table to our right.

She is seriously not going to start throwing food, is she? Oh, no way, I think this is exactly what she's going to do.

She lifts up her arm, ready to lob the salmon filled sandwich at him. "I want to hate you. I want to throw this at you and hate you, Vincenzo," Mum yells so loud her voice bounces off the walls.

"Throw it at me. All of it. Throw all of it," Vincenzo replies, "I deserve it, but please don't hate me. I could not bear the hate of the two people I adore the most."

"ADORE! You have finally lost it, Palm. ADORE. You don't understand what adore means!" She continues to yell, sending two birds flying away that were perched on the edge of the wall.

I softly guide Mum's arm back down and remove the offending sandwich from her hand. "Don't, Mum," I say, "remember what Sal said, hear him out. Besides, that's an incredible suit."

They both allow a small smile to shine on their faces.

"I want to hate you, turn around and never see you again. Hell knows I know how to do that. Have you even the slightest idea the nightmare I have been through, and now Seven? Hey?" Mum continues firing off and tears stream easily. "But I can't hate you. Goddamn it. I can't."

Vincenzo stands his ground with the power of a jet and stretches his arm out to Mum, but she is in distress and remains hesitant to take it.

"Mum, it's okay. It's okay," I say, and she collapses into his arms, sobbing and thumping his chest until the kisses he continually plants on her head diffuses her rage and all the years of hurt. I should feel misplaced, standing here watching, and I should be pissed off at him myself, but I don't and I'm not. I want answers, but the authenticity of these two people and this entire situation cannot be denied. I feel honoured to observe these two meeting again. It's the love story of the year and it feels like home, and that is enough for me to believe whatever he has to say.

He breaks the hold on Mum and turns to look at me.

"Seven," he says. Both of them move apart just enough to create a space for me to make this trio of love united. "My beautiful girl. My word, look at you. Look at you both. I have missed you so much."

I feel small but ten miles deep, the journey to this giving me a depth most grown adults don't have. I feel protected by this man; he's a man I don't know, yet I feel I've known him forever – is that normal, I wonder? He's holding the three of us as though he is sticking us together with glue, and the black hole inside me which has sabotaged me my whole life disintegrates, and I know the Boras Curse has finally gone. I feel a veil being lifted, revealing the real me who was there all along, and from this moment my story, and my family's story, will change. It's as Gusti and Leo said it would be.

Vincenzo babbles more about how proud he is, how much he loves us and how he can explain and that he will do anything that may ease the pain and torment we have endured.

"I am here now, you are both safe and this time, I will not let you go," he says.

I can see through a gap of our entangled arms towards the door that Horace has appeared. He's turning visitors away who have ignored the sign and dwindled into our space. Horace peers across the window and our eyes meet for a second. He gives me a double thumbs up, smiling as he proudly moves more people back down the stairs.

"Is he one of your lot too?" I ask, trying to indicate towards Horace.

"Kind of, he's an old friend," Vincenzo answers, as he pulls the seats out for us to sit. He hands the red bouquet to Mum and the pastel one to me.

"Do you like?' he asks me, "I wasn't sure if you would like flowers or if it was too… naff."

"They are perfect," I say, smelling them and instantly overcoming a cascade of past traumas. "I love flowers, anything botanical actually." I snivel. "No one has given me my own flowers before. It means everything."

There isn't a dry eye in the house, even Horace is touched as he zips over to remove empty plates and re-arrange the table back to its original beauty.

"So then. Let's hear it?" Mum demands. "Whatever you have to say, you say in front of Seven. It's because of Seven we are all sat here."

"I want to know too. No frills. Just tell us," I add.

He nods with a slow grace, places his elbows on the table and his chin in his hands and composes himself as we become privy to the world he cut us from.

"Bloom. The man your friend mentioned, many years ago

he was, *errr*, a client of mine, and a well-known artist at the time. We protected him and his gallery in Italy. He returned to London to open a second gallery at a building I own in Silversedge – it's rented by Jamming Minds, I believe you know the one. The chap only rents the building from me, no extras by the way."

I'm relieved to hear Gusti isn't paying protection money; he's a good guy, busy in his own world and helping Zeffos, nor does he need the hands and weapons of gangsters… not that the Mafia know this.

"We already had business here in London, your mum was here too," he says to me, "so our services to Bloom continued."

"Why do I know this man's name? I've heard it before," Mum cuts in.

"You have. Stay with me," Vincenzo replies, laying his hand on hers.

"Bloom and my… organisation, all entered into a deal with big fish in London. Pieces of art for large sums of money, that sort of thing. Admittedly some were not ours to sell.

The deal went south, we both lost lots of money and integrity, and Bloom lost his life's work. He blamed me. Without money and his art, Bloom quickly fell into a dark place, determined to take me with him. He would have recovered, had he not been intent on doing me in, trying to get me to pay him back what he lost and raise his profile again.

"It was also known in certain circles that Bloom was a lady's man. One affair too many sent his wife filing for divorce. The ex-wife came out of it well, and Bloom was publicly humiliated in what became a high-end case and a media frenzy. All led by the talented and brilliant… Gabby

Madison." He turns to her, love falling out from his smile, still with his hand on hers.

Mum is horrified. I can hear pennies dropping all over the place. "That's where I know the name. It was so long ago I'd forgotten. I did a bloody good job on that case though."

"Oh, you did honey, you did."

I am, once again, gripped by story time with my family. Then, Vincenzo continues. "Not only did Bloom owe half of London, he lost everything and then some to his ex-wife, thanks to darling Gabby here – and rightly so, he's a jerk. His children turned to despise him and for this part of his demise, he blames you, Gabby." He turns from Mum to look at me.

"Your mum has not ever been involved with our side, to be clear. Bloom's ex-wife chose your mum to represent her because of her reputation." Vincenzo leans back in his chair, taking in a refuel of air and popping in a caveat that the information he is revealing must remain in our circle of three.

"When Bloom discovered we were together, Gabby, he was throwing nasty accusations all about town and spread the word that everything was premeditated. He wanted us both to pay, or die, all this carry on. I had far better things to do with my time and more decent people to be with than him, but he wouldn't let up.

"I suggested we separated, Gabby – which I did not want – but the fool was dangerously angry. My first concern was you. If Bloom could see he broke us, he would back off.

"Unbeknown to you, Gabby, I had the guys constantly checking on you, and I was on the verge of dealing with your vile husband, that I cannot even call a man, and coming to rescue you both – you must have been a few years old by this point, Seven, but someone ratted me out to Bloom that I was back in town. Understand this man was crazy, and in short, his plan was to kidnap both of you and hold you for ransom. A sure way, Bloom thought, to get his own back and his money."

What? I could have been kidnapped? The reality of this lifestyle is hard.

"I hope you see my dilemma more clearly. Your friend, RV, was correct in that, yes, I did set Bloom's stuff on fire – a warning he'd pushed it too far, a message for him to let it go. It all got out of hand. You two are my universe, I would never let anything happen to you two, they'd have to take me first. I admitted arson, fraud and a few other things, and the police were ecstatic!" He laughs, although I don't know how.

"The law had wanted to get me for years and they threw the book at me as hard as they could, but I didn't expect such a long stretch. I went inside while my death was faked to take the fuel out of Bloom. If I was dead then I had the karma I deserved, the cretin would crawl back to the pond he emerged from." He leans forward, cupping and joining all our hands. "I had to be dead across the board, and I couldn't let you see me in a place like that. Sal made an agreement with Bloom that he would leave you two alone. I would come back for you both when my time was done, and Bloom, long gone."

"So, you were going to come back for us?" I ask, ready to bawl again, but I try that weird biting the cheek thing that Mum does instead.

"You couldn't have stopped me. I did this for us. Please believe me. I want to be with you both every day, if you can find enough forgiveness to have me in your lives?"

It seems ridiculous to me how a silly grudge can turn into deadly personal vendetta. So much wasted time.

"I beg," Vincenzo says. "Can we start over? I'll stay in London for as long as you need me. I'll move here, whatever you wish." Vincenzo closes his outpour of truth with the multimillion-dollar question.

I turn to Mum and grab her hand. I'm pumping her hand with mine to show my approval, I hope she gets that is code for yes.

This story will take time for me to process because, well, wow in general, but living a life with Vincenzo is not going to be normal. Even with the Boras Curse gone, the Mafia is his life, the same as law is Mum's life. Then again, living with a violent alcoholic isn't normal either, but I survived and became a better person for it.

"Hang on," Mum interrupts. "Why did Bloom rope in 27evens to shoot you when you were released? He thought you were dead?"

"Someone Bloom knew was in Wandsworth last year and snitched to him. No one else would touch Bloom. That… something-evens lot…" he says with uncertainty, and he flicks his hand around trying to recall the rest, "they were his only option and took Bloom at his word. They foolishly thought they could take on the likes of us. They were wrong. They're wounded, but they'll live. Rio is a good kid, I like him," he says and winks at me. I dip my head to avoid the eye contact. I think Sal told him we like each other and it's embarrassing.

Horace scuttles by politely and tells Vincenzo they need to re-open the terrace to the public as management are becoming ruffled. A staggering two hours has passed with family mysteries being explained and rambling to Vincenzo about my life over years lost and my art display at school.

"Would you like to see it?"

"I would love nothing more than to see it and meet your friends," he says, struck to his heart by my asking.

In my enthusiasm, I had told Vincenzo about the MGs and my loathing of conformity at school. I think he likes he can see himself in me.

"Actually," I say as we manoeuvre away from the table. "Maybe you could meet Leo and his twin sister Lizzie next weekend?"

"I would be honoured, my Seven," he replies, cracking and allowing big bear tears to escape down his face.

Mum juts in, placing her arms around us both.

"Ahem. Slow down you two. It's all going to take time. We need to get to know each other, the logistics need addressing and—"

"*Si. Si.* Of course, anything," he cuts in eagerly, responding to Mum's downer but willing to comply with whatever she asks. "Does this mean..." he trails off, waiting for Mum to finish the sentence.

"Yes. It does mean that. Let's give us a shot," Mum says.

"Really, REALLY?" Vincenzo roars. He lifts us both high off the ground, spinning the three of us around as we scream like spinning fireworks.

"Take us home, Vincenzo," Mum says, when our spinning draws to an end. "Take us home."

Their arms enclose around each other's waists, and their eyes meet with fierce intensity. I know what's coming next, and they lean in and kiss – a lot – and I have to look away.

"Too much guys, too much. Save it for later," I say, holding my hand out to block the view. "Oh, by the way," I add, still turning away with my hand up and my eyes half shut, "I need to speak to you about Miami, Lizzie and Leo… guys? Can you hear me? Guys?"

Chapter Thirty-Six
Strategy is Dead

Two weeks have rolled by, and my world is different not being ruled by the Boras Curse; life is lighter and happier. I'm confident and comfortable being all I've wanted to be, and I get to keep this forever. My family is free forever. I'm a Zeffo for life, whatever this may bring my way and I hope to see a time when the Boras Curse is eradicated by the power of the Zeffos.

"Your joy is brightening the town, and you and your family have all they wish for," Gusti says and we hug each other in pride and relief, "but remember to continually use your powers for your good. You will be called upon to assist other Zeffos, sometimes in other places, and together the Zeffos will grow until we win the war against the Boras."

"Thank you, seriously. I don't know what would have happened to me if you hadn't appeared in my life… I'm ready always, Dex," I say, smiling.

"You're the one who called out to me… and I'm a proud Dex," he says, as he opens the tinkling door of the tattoo shop. I step out onto the cobbled street, feeling like my entire body is smiling. The Jamming Minds sign is swinging despite no wind, people are both meandering and rushing through another day in Silversedge and I wonder how many others are soon to find out they too are the chosen ones and are Zeffos.

Vincenzo is still staying at The Savoy; the staff have grown to know me, and it's so much fun. It's all, 'Good morning, Miss Seven' or, 'nice to see you again, Miss Seven' and, 'we have your favourite milkshake, Miss Seven'. The attention snowballs as I morph into a new lifestyle.

The three of us have met a lot: we've eaten together, watched television and walked the streets of London. Mum has taken some time off work – shocker – whilst her and Vincenzo figure life out. Love looks good on her, and they are together most of the time. I don't know how all this will pan out, and I don't think they do either.

RV, after the 27evens incident, went ballistic in the hotel room. A few plates were lost that night, and it took numerous conversations with Vincenzo and Sal to calm him down and stop him in spiralling into a tunnel of guilt. I'm pleased they could help, understand and offer wisdom to a situation few truly could.

He asked Vincenzo if he could take me out, refusing to kiss me or date until he did.

'It's not the 1950s,' I said, though secretly enjoying the traditionalism.

'They're not the type of men I want to piss off,' he replied. He also told me he'd liked me for months and thought he was punching well above his weight, especially with Nate being around. I told him that was ridiculous, and he said: 'Whatever happened, I'm not fucking it up now.'

For the rest of that most sweet afternoon we laid on the gravel at our thinking spot, the ravens all around, watching the river and the cherry blossoms losing their flowers. We held each other tight like a perfect fit, but no kissing, which was a strain growing in heat. By all accounts Vincenzo was extremely touched when RV asked him, and RV has ravished me in kisses and attention from that point on. We haven't told the MGs about us, except Lizzie – I can't not tell Lizzie – and besides, her advice keeps me in check, but the rest of them can wait. This time is for RV and me, and it feels like a powerful love.

Tonight, we say goodbye to Sal as he returns to Sicily tomorrow, back to work and back to his own home. With the Boras Curse lifted on our family, his wife came back to him, and they are taking another run at it, and the colour and delight of life has found him again.

Back home from seeing Gusti, Sal and Vincenzo have taken over the cooking for a farewell dinner, and I'm starving. I don't understand why it takes them so long to cook a meal. They've been preparing, cooking and messing around for two hours. Two hours!

Vincenzo opens the fridge, sipping wine and pulling out more peppers and tomatoes. He finds a ready-made Spaghetti Bolognese lodged at the back and mutters something in Italian before throwing it in the bin, which I find funny – Mum doesn't.

RV has been allowed to attend our special family dinner and keeps his most gentlemanly behaviour on tap within the camaraderie of a lively kitchen, and I want to squish him, but I'm careful to be respectful also to this fledging romance in unusual circumstances.

As dinner ends, and RV is leaving to go home, I stand at

the end of the island, ready to walk out with him and steal a kiss on the doorstep, but Sal and Vincenzo waltz into the hallway ahead of me, waiting for him.

For god's sake.

RV raises his eyebrows with a smile as he hugs me and gives me a peck on the cheek, and the boys all gather by the front door. Pretending to collect dirty dishes at the door end of the island, I watch with half an eye through the glass door as a note is passed to RV from Sal and Vincenzo. There's low talking and more hugs, a Ciao, and then RV is gone.

I dash around the other side of the island with a random spoon as they stroll back into the kitchen.

"He's a good kid, that boy," Sal says.

Vincenzo twirls Mum towards him and holds her in front of him as she continues to fret about dishes. They're all pissed, except me and RV.

"I've told him any trouble, he's to call us," Vincenzo adds, twirling Mum again.

Must be what the note was about.

"You've given him the hard word, haven't you?" I ask them.

"Of course," they both say together, beaming cheeky grins.

It's sad when the car comes to pick Sal up to take him to the airport hotel. I've liked having him around; he continued to drive me to school and rang periodically to check I was okay. One time I sent him on an emergency trip for eyeliner as I was meeting RV and had lost mine. It was hilarious; he came back with half of the makeup counter because he couldn't understand what black eyeliner was.

"I shall miss you a lot," I say, hugging Sal goodbye in the hallway.

"You will see me again soon," he says, "and come to Sicily, anytime." I cast a pleading look to Mum to say, *yes, let's – it sounds like fun.*

***

Proudness inflates me when I see Vincenzo standing by the school gates waiting for me, so I can show him my art display at the main reception. He's dressed in smart trousers, a waistcoat and a striped shirt. It's stupid, a small thing, for it to mean so much, but I've never had that before – a dad waiting to pick me up at school. It feels different to a mother, somehow.

The MGs are tagging behind, all nosey for a peek at him. He's met RV (obviously), Felix, Leo and Lizzie already – Vincenzo had walked me down to Wavies at the weekend and we all collided outside. He refused to leave, and he sat at our table charming the pants off everyone, including Richard. Nobody seemed bothered that a parent was sat with us.

Me, Leo and Lizzie have concocted a plan for Miami, which we wanted to bring up, seeing as he's in such an amenable mood, but seeing as Lizzie has already arranged a meeting of the parents about it, we'll unleash our begging then.

"It makes so much sense now!" Yas bats my arm. "You're half Italian! Your dark looks, your art fascination, all the talking you do with your arms flailing about all over the place..." Yas laughs and pauses to do a terrible and almost offensive enactment. "I'm happy for you, babe. You look... rested."

Yas leaves to catch up with the others and I walk Vincenzo to the main reception to show him my artwork. He bids good afternoon to teachers and students alike as they pass him, and I tug him along as quickly as possible. *He'll be coming to class next.*

"We have the Petralia connection for sure," he says, fixated by the tiny exhibit and pacing a peacock strut in front of it. "Your art is incredible, and I have no doubt you will have your own exhibits in galleries," he says.

It's one of the most rewarding validations to get in life, a genuine one, and one from a parent, especially for me.

Danny and a bunch of Year 13s wander towards us down the corridor to head out the doors, and Danny looks over inquisitive.

"This is my daughter's work," Vincenzo rolls off in a deep Italian way and an extravagant arm.

"Right, that's it. We're going," I say, and I drag him off, back into the familiar black luxury car to go home.

I see a can of pop in the compartment of the door and ask if I can have it, and apparently, he'd bought it for me thinking I might need a drink on the way home. I swig at the can and take my chance to prep him for my Miami for the summer speech. Lizzie and Leo have asked their parents, who have said yes, to see if it's okay with my parents, and are now looking forward to the dinner to discuss it.

"They all know the art scene out there, I'll be back in time for school, and it would give you and Mum time together, without me hassling you both," I say as he beeps at various car drivers.

"A case put forth like only the daughter of a lawyer could."

He smiles. "We'll see what your mother says when we get back."

Miami Bound Group Chat.

New message from Lizzie

Did Vincenzo like your display, are you ok? X

Seven is typing

I'm good. He loved it; he's telling everyone, including Years 13s. I didn't know where to look. How are you? x

Lizzie is typing

Cute. Not feeling bad anymore over Nate. I'm so pleased for you, oh powerful gangster!

Seven is typing

Glad you feel better. Love we are friends.

Lizzie is typing

Me too.

Leo is typing

This is meant for Miami stuff, not girlish talk.

Lizzie is typing

Go away Leo.

Leo is typing

Not gonna happen Lizzie. How did you get on asking about coming to Miami for the summer?

Seven is typing

Mum isn't up for it. Says we need family time, but Vincenzo is trying to talk her round. He's ok with it, thinks it's a good idea.

Leo is typing

> We'll change your Mom's mind with Zeffo pressure
> at dinner tomorrow ;)
>
> *Seven is typing*
>
> If Vincenzo can't do it, no one can. Night xx

***

All the parents are downstairs; Mum is helping Antonia set the table while Bradley talks with Vincenzo. It was all boring, so Leo, Lizzie and I are in Lizzie's bedroom.

Pictures of surfers, the ocean and earth are pinned on the cream walls. A vision board hangs on the wall directly in front of her bed with cut out pictures of first placed surfers, cuttings of newspaper columns with the journalist's name marked out and replaced with hers, stylish clothes and a photograph of a couple making out in (I presume) a Miami bar.

"Is this you?' I ask, pointing at the photograph.

"Might be." She smirks and giggles.

"Will you get to see him, when you go back?"

"We're going to meet up," she says, hugging a cushion with her chin on it.

"Are you and Ben back on?" Leo asks.

"We're talking… I'm actually looking forward to going now," she says. "Nothing to do with Ben. It's time to go home, that's all." She cuts Leo off before he starts going on.

Leo loses interest and splats down a copy of The J on the bed for me to read; it's like an old paper meets glossy rock concert brochure, and it's full of writing, drawings, references to musicians, photography – all compiled by young people. It's refreshing to read and plain fantastic.

I begin reading a short article Lizzie has written about

young surfers and plastic in the ocean that Leo featured a few months ago, and it's surprisingly interesting.

"I love this, Leo. It's special."

"It is," they both say as Lizzie untangles her long legs from the bed and places The J back on her desk, just as the bellow from downstairs sounds for dinner.

"We were just saying what a lovely home you have," Mum says to Leo and Lizzie as we sit at the table with them.

Lizzie and Leo both thank her while Antonia comments about how it's taken time to adapt to an indoor lifestyle, and houses with separate rooms rather than all open plan.

"See Mum, how can you deny me a summer of open plan and outdoor living? It's healthy for me."

"I agree," Vincenzo adds with a sly wink to me.

Mum flusters and begins outlining a regimented plan she has for the three us over the next few months to bond as a family, and to finalise where we will all live.

I giggle to myself as Vincenzo is being lovingly respectful to her idea but clearly doesn't agree. The Joseph's understand, they say.

"Absolutely, family first," Bradley says, taking a glug of his red wine. "But, Seven is more than welcome to join us. It will be a pleasure to have her," he says, and Antonia nods in agreement.

Leo, Lizzie and I all stare at Mum with the best hurt faces we can pull off. She is not being fair, I won't have this chance again, and my new family has already bonded; I would have thought she would have liked the time on her own with her beau.

"Look at their faces, *Gabbee*," Vincenzo says with extra drawl.

"Also," Leo says, "seeing as you owe me one…" He looks mockingly at me, smiling with big eyes.

"Why do you owe him?" Vincenzo jumps in.

"Oh, he did some schoolwork for me, it's not important," I waffle, slurping juice and kicking Leo hard in the knee.

"If Seven can come to Miami, we can run a main feature on her in The J, with a new Miami painting from you? Free, of course. It would be our first feature of the new Miami/London merge?"

"OMG this would be everything! Leo, Bradley, really? Mum! Please?"

"It's a few weeks, *Gabbee*. We broke our daughter's heart once, we said we wouldn't do that again."

Get. In.

Way to go, Vincenzo: Mum is buckling. We all stare her down, Bradley and Antonia included.

Mum pushes her finished plate and fiddles with her glass of wine.

"I suppose I'm being a little selfish. We've only just all found each again," Mum says with an edge of emotion, which the Joseph's sympathise with.

"You know, honey," Vincenzo adds, taking her hand and smoothing her hair from her face, "sometimes you have to follow the energy, not the strategy."

Slam-dunk, we have a winner.

"You'll phone me every day?" she asks.

Every day?

"Yes absolutely," I respond, prematurely hopeful.

Mum eventually gives in and agrees, and I run around the table ushering thank yous and cuddles all over them both as

Leo and Lizzie throw their arms up. Bradley shakes Vincenzo's hand, promising they will take care of me.

"Oh, I know you will," he replies firmly, and I glare lovingly at him to stop the subtle intimidation as I re-join Leo and Lizzie.

"Although… Seven is pretty good at taking care of herself too – a force to be reckoned with," Leo says to Vincenzo. I prod Leo in the back, hard. "Miami will be interesting for us in many ways," Leo adds with a wink to me.

Thank you for reading.

If you enjoyed Stay Wild, love Seven and her friends or think you might be a Zeffo too, sign up to Annaliese's newsletter **and receive a free and exclusive copy of the Book of Lights**

In her monthly newsletters, as well as a free and exclusive copy of the Book of Lights, the magical text used by the Zeffos in Stay Wild, you will be the first to know about **Stay Wild Book Two!** Receive content not available anywhere else, author and personal life news, behind the scenes information, meet up's and much more.

Visit here to sign up – Annaliesemorgan.com/newsletter

If you would like to leave a review it is much appreciated! It helps others discover Stay Wild and Annaliese loves to hear from you.

Write:
Black Daisy Press
Annaliese Morgan
49 Greek Street
Soho
London
W1D 4EG

E-Mail:
hello@annaliesemorgan.com

Follow:

annaliese.morgan

annaliesehmorgan

annaliesemorgan.com

www.ingramcontent.com/pod-product-compliance
Lightning Source LLC
Chambersburg PA
CBHW011147190726
48288CB00010B/3217